WIDOW MAKER

A Novel

QUINN KAYSER-COCHRAN

For Col. Joseph R. Clearfield, USMC,
for leading

and

Darcy L. Garretson,
for reading

PART ONE

CRUCIBLE

ONE

I hate stakeouts. Hate everything about 'em. The boredom, discomfort, and routine futility could drive anyone mad and me, I've too much on my mind to spend hours alone this way. Too much by half.

The drive out here took four hours. A little after nine a.m., I parked my autocar inside a ruined stone building above the crossroads. Piled tumbleweeds over the hood and windscreen for cover, propped a rifle against the door, and settled in to wait.

And wait.

First rule of surveillance: never take your eyes off the target—easy enough here because the target never showed. Going over my notes, at 12:07, a buckboard bringing up hay from the valley's southern meadows rolled through. Forty minutes later, an ore wagon went the other direction, southbound behind twenty mules. At 3:22, the Nye-Lincoln auto-stage turned onto the Pahranagat Road toward Hancock Summit but since our informant said the target would ride horseback from Alamo to the old camp at Logan, I didn't follow. That's it. Eight hours, three vehicles, total, and none relevant to my investigation. At least no one saw me.

I hate stakeouts.

Hate lots of things lately. How sullen I've been. How anxious, unsettled, and mean. Hate loneliness, too, yet I don't much care for company. Hard to know whether silence is what I want or fear the most. Depends on the hour, I guess.

I grab a bottle from the passenger seat, pull the stopper, and take a drink. Mail-order whiskey from Hayner's Distilling Co., Springfield, Ohio, shipped right to my mailbox in Delamar. Isn't my favorite brand but it's cheap and it's easy to get. I know I shouldn't drink on stakeout but this whole affair's been a waste of time and I can't see how it matters. Isn't as though getting back to camp will be difficult. Out on these rutted roads through the sagebrush, automobiles behave about the way horses do: just give the thing its nose and it'll practically drive itself home. I'm counting on this, in fact.

Watching the sun slide behind the mountains, I take a longer pull off the bottle and wince. Empty. Throw it against the wall. Shatters. Whole day's been a waste. Whole year. Wasted time, wasted effort. Can't even remember why I took this assignment. Should've given it to one of my deputies but I wanted to leave town for an afternoon, just so I could catch my breath.

Foolish of me, seeing how everyone in Delamar is a target.

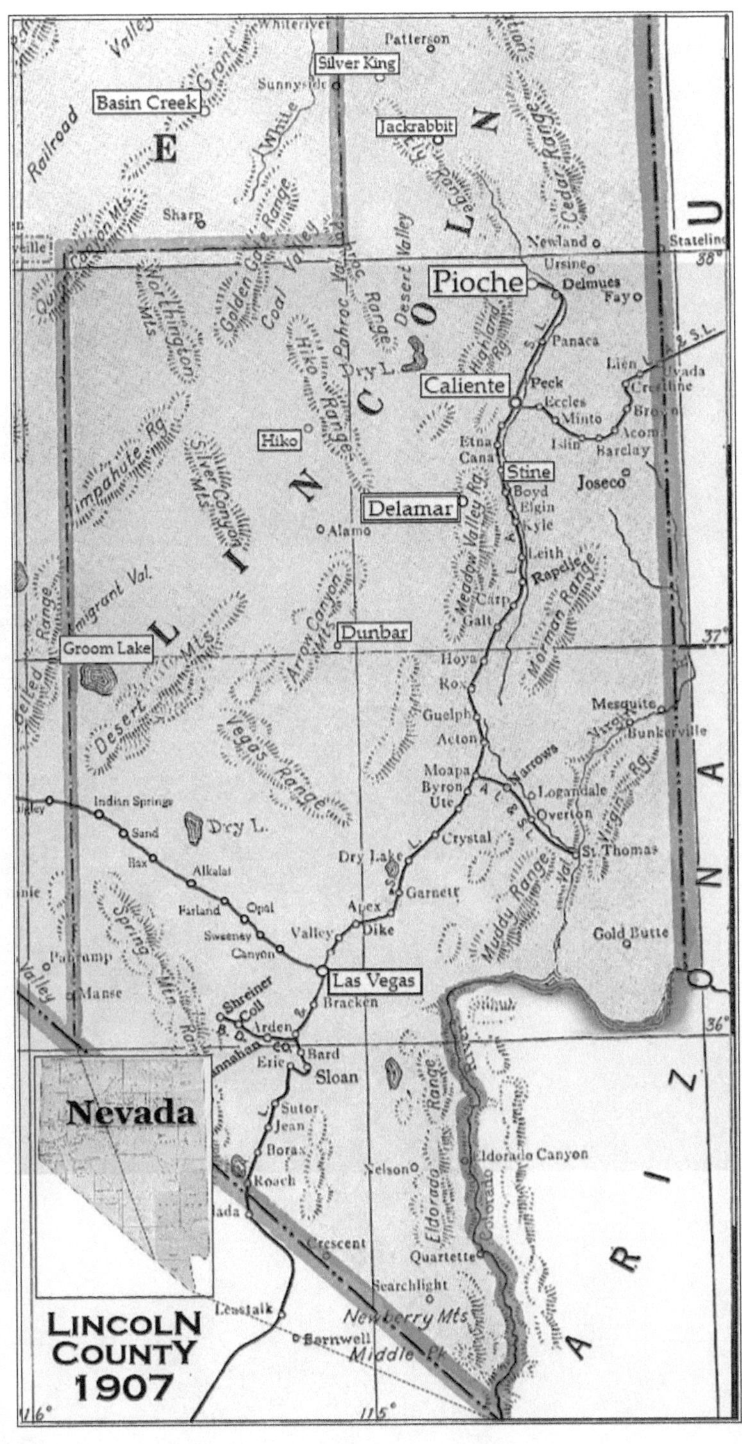
Whiteriver
Patterson
Silver King
Sunnyside
Basin Creek
Jackrabbit
Railroad
Grant
White
Range
Sharp
E
Newland
Stateline
38°
Ursine
Pioche
Delmues
Fay
Panaca
Lien
Uvada
Crestline
Caliente
Peck
Eccles
Brown
Minto
Acom
Etna
Islin
Barclay
Cana
Hiko
Stine
Delamar
Boyd
Joseco
Elgin
Kyle
Alamo
Leith
Rapelle
Carp
Galt
Dunbar
Hoya
37°
Rox
Mesquite
Guelph
Virgin
Bunkerville
Acton
Moapa
Narrows
Byron
Logandale
Ute
Overton
Indian Springs
Dry L.
Crystal
St. Thomas
Sand
Bax
Dry Lake
Alkalai
Garnett
Farland
Opal
Apex
Sweeney
Valley
Dike
Gold Butte
Canyon
Pahrump
Las Vegas
Manse
Shreiner
Bracken
Coll
Arden
B.
Bard
Eric
Sloan
Nevada
Sutor
Jean
Borax
Nelson
Eldorado Canyon
Roach
ada
Crescent
Quartette
Searchlight
Leastalk
LINCOLN
COUNTY
1907
Newberry Mts
Barnwell
Middle Pk.
116°
115°
36°
LINCOLN
U
A
N
A
R
I
Z
O
N
A
Quinn Canyon Mts
Worthington Mts
Golden Gate Range
Coal Valley
Pahroc Range
Desert Valley
Dry L.
Hiko Range
Highland Rg.
Cedar Range
Pahute Rg.
Silver Canyon Mts
Meadow Valley Rg.
L. V. & T.
Mormon Range
migrant Val.
Groom Lake
Desert Mts
Arrow Canyon Mts
Vegas Range
Muddy Range
St. Virgin Rg.
Spring Mtn Rg.
Eldorado Range
Colorado River

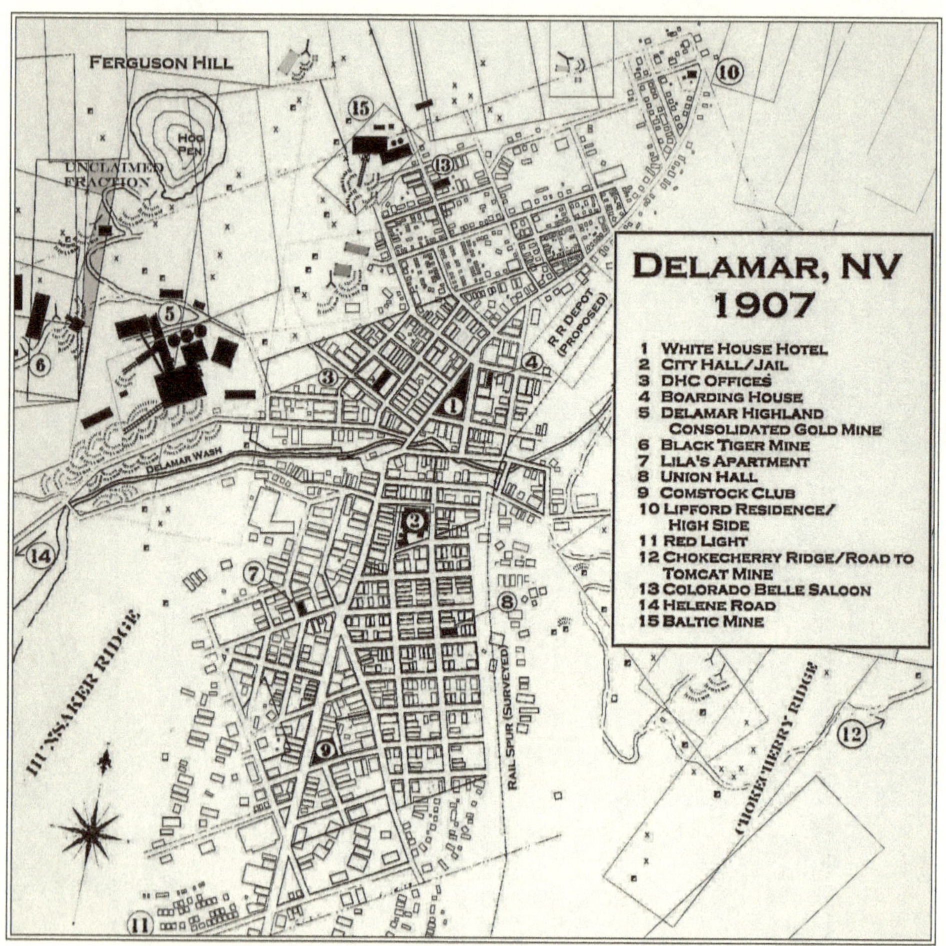

FERGUSON HILL
HOG PEN
UNCLAIMED FRACTION
DELAMAR WASH
HUNSAKER RIDGE
CHOKECHERRY RIDGE
R R DEPOT (PROPOSED)
RAIL SPUR (SURVEYED)
DELAMAR, NV
1907
1 WHITE HOUSE HOTEL
2 CITY HALL/JAIL
3 DHC OFFICES
4 BOARDING HOUSE
5 DELAMAR HIGHLAND
   CONSOLIDATED GOLD MINE
6 BLACK TIGER MINE
7 LILA'S APARTMENT
8 UNION HALL
9 COMSTOCK CLUB
10 LIPFORD RESIDENCE/
   HIGH SIDE
11 RED LIGHT
12 CHOKECHERRY RIDGE/ROAD TO
   TOMCAT MINE
13 COLORADO BELLE SALOON
14 HELENE ROAD
15 BALTIC MINE

Eastern Nevada Mine Owners' Association
Delamar, Nevada

Surveillance Form A – Team: 1

Date: November 15, 1907
Importance: HIGH – Black Book
Objective: Apprehend & return for interrogation.
Armed, probable.
Target: Boudreaux, Francis A.; aka Boudrow, Frank
Target Affiliations (if known): IWW. WFM: Wallace, Idaho & Tonopah, Nev. Locals
Location: Hiko Jct., Lincoln County, Nevada
Duration: 9:15 a.m. – sunset (approx. 4:30)
Target photo available? No
Is Target otherwise known to Operative(s)? No

Surveillance Team: 1. Operative 1-72
2.
3.
4.

Concealed Location(s) Available to Operative(s)? ~~No~~ Yes

Target Activities or None
Observation(s)

SUMMARY: Target did not appear as informant predicted.

Record Expenses &
Attach Receipts Gasoline only, attached
(NOTE: Expenses w/o receipts will NOT be reimbursed)

Report and One (1) Copy are REQUIRED Within Twenty-Four (24) Hours of Cessation.

TWO

Around midnight someone pounds on my door and in a fit of panic, I fall
out of bed. These past few months, anything can set me off so whoever's out
there is lucky my revolver isn't where it belongs. If it were, trust me, the son of
a bitch would be scrambling to plug leaks instead of trying to knock my door
off its hinges.

Only fell asleep a few minutes ago and my boots and overcoat were all the
clothes I shed before collapsing facedown on the mattress. Shoulder rig's still
cinched, though I can't find my revolver. While this frightens me, it's probably
just as well. Things we think we need, props we reach for in moments of crisis,
often cause more problems than they solve.

Bam-bam-bam!

The room lurches into focus and I pick myself off the floor. Head aches and
my heart races. Dry mouth and cold hands, too. Jesus, I can't keep doing this
to myself. I lose several more seconds groping for the gun, eventually finding
it wedged between a bottle and a photograph on the nightstand. Ain't that the
damnedest thing? For the life of me, I can't remember how it got there and
this makes me nervous. Of all people, you'd think I'd have learned to keep up
my guard.

Bam-bam-bam! The pounding continues, or is it kicking? My neighbors
shout and complain about the noise but whoever's there pays them no mind.
Jackass won't lay off even for a second, which tells me either he's in serious
trouble or else he's looking for it. Leaning against a wall, I study the shadow

beneath the door. Only one? Others must be waiting on the stairs. That's how we handle these jobs, with one agent face-to-face and backup just out of sight. As well as anyone, I know how things work around here. Kneeling to steady myself, I raise my Colt New Service, a heavy .45 I've carried since the Philippines. Careful to keep my finger outside the guard, I hold it close and squint to make sure a round is seated.

"Knock it off or I'll shoot!"

The pounding stops and the shadow moves away from the door.

Two, three seconds of silence. Then, "Come on, Sunday, open up."

My head clears a little. Maybe they aren't here to take me down. Maybe.

"Come on," he shouts again, "it's me."

It's muffled but I'd recognize that voice anywhere: Big Curt Broe, a fellow operative for the Association and Team Two's captain. Not the last person I want to see but nearly. I stand, holster the revolver, and unlatch the deadbolt.

"Jesus, Curt. Time is it?"

"Twelve-forty."

My heart won't stop hammering. "Couldn't wait 'til sunup?"

"Need you up at the shop."

"Another bum take the company's rocks?"

"Bigger." He glances toward the staircase. "Hell, *way* bigger. I'll explain in the car."

He looks nervous, which is unusual. Normally, Curt's the cockiest bastard I know.

Down the hallway, my fellow boarders peek cautiously from behind their doors. Fine work, Broe; appreciate your restraint. I study his plug-ugly features: mashed-up, thrice-broken nose, high forehead, and crooked jaw.

"This an emergency?"

He glares at my neighbors—Finn carpenters, Hungarian muckers, and two hop-heads with smoke-blackened fingers—before turning back to me. He rolls a cigarette, lights it, and drops his match on the dirty planks. Crushes the ember with his boot heel. "Grab your hat—I'll explain in the car."

"Not a chance," I say. "I only got back a few minutes ago."

"So what?"

"*So what?*" I pull the door a few inches closer and shake my head carefully. "So, I followed *your* report out to Hiko this morning and didn't see *anything.* Boudreaux never showed, hell, *nobody* showed, so take your emergency—"

"C'mon, be serious."

"I *am* serious." I wipe my mouth with my hand. "Go get Bob Thompson or Warren Jim; they need the hours and I need sleep."

"Nah, son. This crop ain't regular—this is big casino."

"Ah, go drift." All this posturing makes me tired.

"General work," he whispers, "but the politics are touchy, understand?"

Can't say as I do.

Outside, the wind moans like a ghost. Glancing down the hallway, Curt scowls and lets his coat fall open. Catching sight of his sidearm, my hard-luck neighbors scuttle back inside their drafty rooms and lock their doors. Pleased with himself, he grins.

"You'll want a heavy coat. This storm has half the desert on the move." He drags on the cigarette until its end glows red.

Again, I shake my head. What do I care about roughing up another grass-level organizer? Work one over and the union sends five more to take his place. Hell, they're why we have job security. World's brimful of little men too stupid to recognize when someone bigger has 'em strapped. I've *seen* what happens when people take stands against the fellows who really run things; the result is never pretty and it's always the same. Always. Just thinking about it makes my head hurt.

"You handle it," I say. I push on the door but Curt stops it with his hand.

"Wouldn't mind if I did." With the cigarette dangling from his mouth, he fixes me with another nasty grin. "Know a fellow named Joe McCuskey?"

McCuskey. *Joe McCuskey.*

My jaw hangs slack and my tongue goes numb.

"Hear what I just said?"

"Hold…hold up…"

"Yeah, you heard," Curt says. He coughs once, a hollow boom that aggravates the pain in my skull.

Son of a bitch did this on purpose. Ran me ragged before handing me a ticking bomb. Can't think, *can't think.* Come on, stupid, figure this out.

"No fooling—*the* Joe McCuskey?" I say. "Where?"

"Just before nine, we arrested him over in Caliente. Quick and quiet so nobody saw nothing." More coughing; spits on the floor. "Your boy, Stu, and the twins drove him up to the Tomcat just before this storm cut loose."

"Bullshit. You're bullshitting me, right?"

Now Curt looks as confused as I feel. He drops the last of his cigarette on the floor and grinds it out with his boot.

"Fuck's wrong with you, Sunday?" He spits again.

"*The* Joe McCuskey?"

"Christ, you're a mess. Maybe you ain't up for this…"

Is Curt serious? Dear God, I think he *is*. For an instant, I itch like mad for that bottle on the nightstand but now even thirst can't compete with the rage welling inside me. The room spins, so dark and formless I might as well be down at the bottom of a mineshaft. Mere feet away, Curt's face and the tattered wallpaper behind him are blurred beyond recognition. My mind disowns every sense except a sour taste in my mouth, because hatred's flavor is the strongest thing there is. Swallow enough and it poisons your thoughts, your speech, and eventually your deeds. Wrath supplants reason and you become the animal every law since Moses was meant to keep you from becoming. Look, Big Curt doesn't know ten percent of what stands between McCuskey and me—I try to keep *some* things to myself—but chins wag and I drink too much so maybe he's heard something. Probably has. Why else would he be here on the coldest night of the year, grinning at me this way, except that he knows he'll get a reaction? And why not send a subordinate? Something's bent.

One deep breath and my vision resolves. I tell myself that Curt's news doesn't mean anything more than another long night on the job. Hell, everyone west of Omaha knows Joe McCuskey's a bagman, a dynamiter, and a killer: all valid reasons to take an interest in his sudden appearance. Still, I can't show all my cards; silence is a raised drawbridge.

At last, I realize Curt is speaking, "…like you seen the Devil. Maybe this one's too heavy for you."

So much for covering my tracks.

Big Curt steps backward. Standing below a bare light bulb, the shadow beneath his hat devours his features. Faceless and looming, he is such a vision that all I can do is blink and hope I haven't already gone to Hell.

He scrapes his boot on a warped floorboard. "I'll go get Bob."

"Just give me a minute." The fog in my head starts to lift.

"Dammit, we don't have a minute. You coming or not?"

"Hold up." I don't like that he's trying to rush me out the door. "What's your play here, Curt?"

He shrugs. "Just work."

I wouldn't buy that with someone else's money. "Why would Joe come here? He knows better."

"Why not ask him, yourself?" Curt scratches his cheek and glances at the ceiling. "Think I know what motivates these assholes?"

"You were any good at your job, you might."

"Oh, yeah?" Curt's eyes blaze. "How about some gratitude for bringing you in instead of taking all the credit, myself?"

"How about you tell me what happened?"

His eyes narrow. "Been after this one a while, haven't you?"

"Me and everyone else, so what?"

"Yeah, but that business with your girl—"

"I swear to Christ, Curt, shut the hell up and tell me what happened."

He coughs into a handkerchief, frowns at the result, and shoves the cloth back into his pocket. "Okay, look, Roy knows this operator who showed him a telegram from Denver saying McCuskey was waiting over in Caliente—"

"Waiting for what?"

"Didn't say, so I sent Thompson, Sweeney, and Yukon to smoke him out and by damn, they hit the jackpot. Caught him sleeping in that little hotel by the hot springs there. Storm's pulled down the telephone wires, though, so they couldn't call it in, see? That's why I'm so late getting here."

I ought to be *thrilled* by this news. Ought to. Clearly, Curt expects as much and it's the reaction I wish I had, but it isn't. Revenge is tricky that way. Getting what you want doesn't always go according to plan, especially when it's eluded your grasp for a long, long time. Given the wretched history between McCuskey and me, for years I've told myself if only I could wrap my hands around his throat, I might be happy again. Might scatter the clouds hanging over my head. It's a notion I've clung to, anyway, despite the nagging sense that my problems run deeper than occasional run-ins with a bad actor.

"Why didn't you tell me sooner?"

"Tell you what?"

"About the telegram?"

He yawns. "You left camp."

"Son of a bitch, Curt, you knew where I was—you're the one who told me about Boudreaux!"

"So what? We all take dead reports." He looks around as if someone might be listening. "Listen, amigo, *I* wanted to sweat McCuskey myself but Charlie showed up on a high horse and made us wait. Said it was your case so I backed off."

I ignore most of what he says. "Charlie's at the shop?"

Curt yawns. "Roy fetched him. You're welcome."

This is good news. Charlie Witherill is my right hand and about the only person in Delamar I'd trust with my life. Saying this, I also mean that I don't trust Big Curt, not with my life nor anything else. And while I'm glad to hear Charlie's minding the store, I still can't shake the sense that something isn't on the level. Is this all a coincidence? Or for once, just exactly what Curt says it is? Everywhere I turn, I see trouble.

"Always looking for angles, ain't ya?" His breath is a potent mix of tinned oysters and cigarettes and the smell jolts me from my catalepsy.

"It's called thinking. Give it a try sometime."

"Yeah, yeah. You coming or no?"

Irrationally, I wonder whether he's reading my thoughts. Hell, we've worked together long enough I suppose in some ways he *can.*

"Go start the car," I say. "I'll be down in three."

A sudden blast of wind shakes every plank, rafter, and windowpane in the boardinghouse. The whole structure creaks and groans—awful sounds from Dante's Second Circle. Eyes wide, Curt throws his back against a wall, clearly afraid the building might fall to pieces. Seeing his expression, I can't help but laugh.

"Relax, we get those all the time." I clap a hand on his shoulder. "Good work tonight. Real good. Sorry I'm so tired—I'll come around."

"Course, you will," he says, shaking off my hand. Again, he's wearing that ugly, misshapen grin of his.

Voices down the corridor but Curt's coughing again so I can't tell what they're saying.

"Boss know?"

"He's sleeping."

"Sheriff?"

Curt shakes his head. "Kept this one quiet."

"Weren't so quiet a minute ago."

He wipes his mouth again. "Answer your goddamn door."

Glancing at his boots, I notice streaks of orange mud on the toes. "Been up on Ferguson?"

"Hog Pen, sure. Someone cut the phone line between security and Two-Fifty twice this past week. Highgraders trying to smuggle around a bulkhead, I'll bet. Sat in the dark with a shotgun but couldn't see nothing on account of this snow.

Then this other thing blew up and since I have the heaviest car, Witherill asked me to come get you." Curt takes out his makings and rolls another cigarette.

"He's following procedure."

"Yeah, yeah, you and your procedures. Just hurry, huh? Word gets out, we'll have a riot on our hands. Union lawyer'll rouse Judge Brown and then it's habeas corpus and all that bullshit." He tucks the cigarette between his lips and lights it.

"I'll be down in three."

"Course, you will." Turning toward the staircase, his expression tells me he doesn't trust me any more than I trust him.

I shut the door.

∾

No need to look outside for proof the weather's gone dirty. Frigid air gusts between the wallboards and crumbs of snow march across the floor like bleached ants. I *do* need light, though, and since every bulb in the White House Hotel is always on, all that's necessary is to raise the blinds. Set across the alley from my boardinghouse, its glare is stupendous. Even this weather can't stanch it. Point of pride for the owners, I guess (it's rumored my boss gets a ten-percent cut of revenues; last October, one of the managing partners objected to this arrangement but no one's seen him since). Earlier this year, a Denver newsman wrote that so long as the White House's lights are burning, Delamar is on the make and in a general way, I suppose it's true. Beneath the casino's gilt ceiling, more Champagne is spilled nightly than most joints sell in a week and the roulette wheel never stops spinning—signs most people take to mean the district is booming. Plungers, whores, and every kind of sport keep the place hopping, and desert rats and outlanders alike always know where to start their sprees. Me, my fun-money's spoken for, so come payday, I sleep on a couch in the Association's offices. No one within blocks of the White House sleeps on payday, jack. No one. Nothing's dimmed those lights. Not foreign wars, accidents in the mines, nor the President's assassination—not even the bank-panic a few months back when three-quarters of their rooms sat empty. *Nothing.* Turning them off would be an admission that the main chance has moved on and no one here is ready to face a calamity like that. Everyone who sees this beacon, this lightship on a sagebrush sea—even those who never had a shot—tells themselves their break is coming next.

It's been my job lately to tell them that it isn't.

With the blinds raised, I can see quite well, thanks: everything except my face in the mirror. Lost in shadow, my reflection is nothing but a corona of light on my collar, ears, and hair, although that's just as well. I no longer recognize the man staring back at me.

I break through a skin of ice in the washbasin and splash water on my face. Still bleary-eyed, I grab a bottle of Richland Rye from beside the basin, pull the stopper, and drink until I have to gasp for breath. Guess that's better.

Despite the wind, from down on the street I hear a Pierce-Arrow's horn. So much for keeping things quiet. Even so, thank God Curt brought a car. Gives us a little protection from the weather. Very little, though, so I take my canvas mackinaw and woolen scarf from their hooks near the woodstove. They're still frozen and it takes a moment before my body heat softens them so they'll bend.

In the mirror, the lights in one of the hotel's rooms go dark. Those two empty sockets stare at me, searching for what's left of my soul, and I have to look away. When they go back on, I glimpse a beautiful woman closing the drapes to protect her customer's identity, but before I can turn for a better look, her image dissolves in the light.

Yeah, the White House is the brightest star in a dark corner of the world, beckoning to anyone with the capacity to dream. God knows I want a different life, too, but tonight there's work to be done and I can't think like that. Can't think at all. Curt honks the horn again so I lock my door, head downstairs, and step into darkness.

THREE

Funny thing about these desert snowstorms: rarely does anything accumulate. On the highest peaks, sure, but down in the basins or on west-facing slopes like the one Delamar occupies, often nothing stays. It can storm for hours on end but the stuff just blows away. God knows where it all goes.

Tonight, it's coming down sideways. Thankfully, Curt's put chains on the tires so our drive up to the Tomcat is largely uneventful. Shouting over the wind, we talk about work and nothing else. Nothing friendly and nothing too important, and since neither of us can keep our half of the windscreen clear, he leans over the door just so he can guess where the road lies. Nearly as bad, so much glare comes back from the fast-falling snow that before long he simply shuts off the headlamps and runs dark. Even so, Curt is nothing if not confident and we continue at a pace that seems excessive in view of conditions. Road uphill is narrow but not especially steep and good thing, too, given how it turns back on itself five or six times below the summit of Chokecherry Ridge. Down the ridge's back, though, Christ, the track's a rocky mess and it's a wonder my teeth aren't chipped. At last, Curt throttles back until we are barely crawling between the cedars.

Typical for this corner of the district, the Tomcat Mine is a shirttail outfit. Its dumps are small. A six-man crew, around five-hundred feet of workings, and three buildings clustered near the main incline's mouth. Fifty yards to the south, a concrete magazine for storing explosives hunkers in the woods. I know this because I carry one of the keys that opens its heavy steel door. To date, I don't think the property has produced more than a few carloads of shipping ore. Could be the Association keeps it going so those of us in security have someplace to put in scutwork without drawing attention. Or maybe it's a blue-sky concern, operating just so our boss's agents can curb stock in San Francisco and New York. Again, I don't know.

Curt says something but he has a frog in his throat. Wasn't paying attention so I ask him to repeat himself.

"The Palmetto, bub; Doug McFarlane's property."

"What about it?"

"Full-fucking-boil."

"That right? I'm done playing the markets."

"Seriously?" Curt clears his throat, spits over the door, and wipes his mouth with his sleeve. "Shifter there told me they struck a new ledge—said you could see native gold running through it—but they weren't gonna announce nothin' for three days so last week I bought a thousand shares at twenty-five cents. Closed this afternoon at four and three-fucking-quarters and I sold it all right before the bell. How 'bout that?"

"It's something." Ten bucks says at least half of his story's a lie.

"Minus commission, I'll clear about $4,100."

"Great. Good for you." Pull a flask from my jacket and take a slug. Lord, I could use a chunk of change like that.

The car's rear wheels spin and spit rocks as we climb a rough stretch. I grab a strut to keep from bouncing out the door and a shotgun lying across the backseat clatters to the floor.

Soon as the car reaches firmer ground, Curt coughs and spits out the window. "Really don't play the markets no more?"

"Nope." Not since March, anyway—the whole system's rigged.

Last February, I was a blue sky millionaire, too—rich beyond my wildest imaginings. Lasted about a week before the floor collapsed. Me, I'd been reading about bigwigs Charles Schwab, Bernard Baruch, and George Wingfield scalping the markets and son of a bitch if I didn't catch Greenwater fever at the eleventh hour. What a sucker. Put two-hundred down and bought $2,000 worth of shares on margin. Over two week's time, I watched these soar to $31,327. Then I went out on an overnight job and came back to find I owned a trunkful of paper worth about thirty dollars, whereas the sachems had all skated away with millions. Since then, I've worked off-book to pay what I owe the broker, collecting debts and such, but I'm still short about $600 so I've been living like a bum. I'll bet five-thousand people all across this state could tell you how they've been taken in similar fashion. Nevada has more former millionaires than New York and Boston have real ones. And despite this smashup—hell, *because* of it—I can't help looking for the next big play. That's how it is here. Everyone's afflicted, everyone's trying to get rich overnight. Something new ever comes along, mark my words, this time I'll get out faster than I got in. I just need another break.

"Who knows?" Curt coughs and wipes his mouth. "Might still have room to run."

"Not interested," I lie.

"Suit yourself." He spits out the window again.

Glancing sideways, even as he's straining to see through the swirling darkness, I can tell he's wearing that ugly grin of his. Bastard.

∞

For weeks, I've been obsessed with a single case. Late last summer, I caught an assayer named Pete Kastning fencing highgrade: exceptionally rich pieces of ore smuggled out of the mines and sold on the black market. Gave him a choice: go to jail or help the Association build a conspiracy case against the miners' local, and for months, everything was hunky dory. Then in October, someone shot him in the back and burned his shop, all in broad daylight, too, so of course no one saw anything.

See, the Western Federation of Miners believes its members have the right to highgrade because working underground is hazardous. But then shouldn't the butcher's boy who cuts himself get to take home the best steaks? If you're wondering why anyone gives a damn about bits of rock trickling away inside hats, lunch pails, and false-bottom pockets, it's because even by conservative estimates, one out of every seven pounds of bonanza-grade ore here is stolen this way. No small calculus in a fourteen-million-dollar district.

This Kastning business is why I drove out to Hiko yesterday. An informant told Curt a roustabout named Francis Boudreaux was headed for a lumber camp up on Mount Irish, looking to sell his pistol, but I never saw him. By the time I set a stakeout, Boudreaux was long gone, presuming he'd ever gone that way in the first place. Like I said, the trip was for biscuits; only thing good about it was that I made it back to Delamar before this storm hit.

For weeks, I haven't let much else inside my head. Not the markets, nor Julia or my family, and certainly not Joe McCuskey, yet now that *he's* here, even Francis Boudreaux has taken a back seat.

Joe McCuskey, god*damn.*

My hands clench into sweaty fists. I've dreamed of this day for a long, long time.

໑

Rounding a bend, the Tomcat's plant comes into view. The buildings all have corrugated tin sides and green malthoid roofs. Reddish light spills from an enameled fixture above the stairs and steam billows from a stack above the compressor house. Parked outside the office is a buckboard, a Rainier, and a brand new Ford Model S, all covered with enough snow to suggest they've been here awhile. Bundled against the cold, someone's on the top step cradling a shotgun: Jerry Rosen, by appearance. Behind him, frost occludes the windows, which is just as well. Best no one sees what happens up here.

I pull my coat tight around my chin and step down from the car. Have to shout over the wind, "You coming?"

Curt coughs into his gloved hand. "Going back to the Hog Pen. Good luck in there." As the car swings around, it passes through light spilling from the shops and I catch one last glimpse of him, still grinning at me.

Rotten son of a bitch.

No matter. More important things on my plate now than some heel's strange ways. Even before Curt and his autocar vanish, I've nodded to Jerry and climbed halfway up the stairs to the office.

"Fine lines on that Pierce. How'd she handle this snow?" Jerry says.

"Well enough."

Jerry's half-mad for automobiles and I know he'd love to talk about Curt's, but I brush past without saying more.

"Good talking to you, too," he says.

FOUR

Stepping inside, I nearly collide with Stuart Fisher.

"Taking the mules back before this gets any worse," he says.

"Good idea." I nod. "Get anything out of McCuskey?"

"Not a damn thing. Man's a handful."

"Oh, I'll deal with him. So long, Fish."

"'Night, Shep."

I shake off my hat and set it on an empty chair. My frozen hands ache and since no one thought to put coffee on, I linger beside a red-hot woodstove. My thoughts race: precedents, outcomes, contingencies, and I'm grateful for this opportunity to plan. First and foremost, I need to stay calm. Can't lash out, can't overreact because despite the ugliness of my job, I have a reputation to protect. Blowing your stack is a sign of weakness, a liability for others to exploit. Beyond that, I need names. See if I can learn who ordered the run against Pete Kastning. McCuskey will know. Hell, he might even be involved. The Western Federation of Miners is a hand-to-mouth outfit and doesn't compartmentalize projects the way they ought to, which means at any given moment, too many among 'em know more than they should. Corner one and you're liable to learn about interrelated events three or four states away. And finally, there's no avoiding the fact that I have a score to settle. A big one. I take the flask from my coat and drain it.

Through an open door into the next room, I see him: Joseph J. McCuskey. Chief among the Federation's heavy hitters, in and out of the jug for dozens of crimes. Suspected in a mine owner's shotgun-murder in Telluride. Bombings in Colorado and Utah. Brought to trial for second-degree murder in Montana and acquitted, true, except that six weeks later, the judge who let him off was caught taking bribes from the WFM. McCuskey's a viper, through and through. Someone the Association's board wants dead. Not deported, *dead*. They're all terrified he'll come for them someday and not without cause.

While I can't see Joe's face, I judge he looks the way I remember him: dark hair and stocky build, though the beard's new. Seems he takes care of himself. Isn't starving, anyhow; no one near the top of an organization, even of anarchists, ever starves. Shorter than I remember, maybe five-foot-seven, but it's hard to tell since he's tied to a chair.

"You won't…" he pants, "won't get away with this." His shoulders heave and he's dripping with sweat.

"Course, we will," Roy Garland says.

"I haven't *done* anything."

"Then why'd you run?"

"It's a free country. Ain't I got a right to be left alone?"

"Stupid question. Boys, ain't that stupid?"

Roy yawns, something he does when he's stressed. Nervous tic, I guess. Like others who spent time in the Yukon, Roy's wearing his usual green, woolen sweater. Real heavy, too. Must be a uniform they wear to help identify others of their fraternity: suspenders over green sweaters, corduroy pants tucked into tall boots, and wide-brimmed hats.

Joe spits on the floor which earns him a slap on the face and blistered ears for failing to respect Association property. When he does it again, Roy lunges and Charlie Witherill has to pull him back. Nothing in this exchange surprises me. For as long as I've known him, McCuskey's rubbed people the wrong way and Roy-boy's default is to overreact.

Defiant as ever, Joe leans as far forward as the ropes permit. "You'll get yours," he snaps, "every one of you."

Under different circumstances, I could admire Joe's cotton, but tonight I'm more of Roy's mind than Charlie's.

"Go on and yap, jack," Roy sneers. "Won't live to see tomorrow."

"You cowards," Joe seethes. "Revolution comes, you'll be the first ones hung. Labor can't be stopped, not by hoods and class-traitors like you."

Roy takes a step toward the chair but Charlie bars his way.

"Ignore him," Witherill growls, but Joe won't stop needling Roy.

"Tell me, *jack,* what's the going rate for trampling the Constitution? More than Jack Lipford spends on horses? On cigars? Hell, I doubt it. You're disposable, every one of you—ledger entries is all, or are you too stupid to see it?"

Again, Roy lunges toward the chair but Charlie catches him by the collar and drags him through the door and into the hallway.

"Damn it, I *said* don't talk to him," Charlie seethes. "Not even for sport, understand?" Seeing me in the doorway, he exhales. "Hey, pard, I thought Stu was in here."

"Morning, Charlie. Roy," I say, keeping my voice low. "Stuart took the mules back to camp. Listen, inside and out, you gotta keep track of all and sundry, understand? We're all tired, but don't get sloppy."

Charlie nods. "Sorry, Shep. That one's driving me to distraction."

Not sure whether he means Roy or Joe. "He does that to everyone. Any names? Anything useful?"

"Only bluster."

"Don't know what we're waiting for." Roy yawns again and runs his fingers through his lank, blond hair like he's trying to keep the crazy inside his head from leaking out.

In the other room, Joe continues to rage, "Think Black Hand gives a damn about any of you? Think you're covered? Like hell, you are! He's gonna cut you loose just as soon as someone talks and you can bet your ass someone will. That Lutz fellow at the hotel—he saw what you did."

Roy leans around me and sneers. "Lutz gave me the key to your room, stupid." This spills the wind from McCuskey's sails and Roy shoots Charlie and me a look to say, *"How do you like that?"*

Joe tries to turn but the chair's too heavy and the ropes are too tight. "You can't keep me here. I have rights, goddamnit! What do you *want?"*

"So many questions," I say and he startles at the sound of my voice.

"Sunday?" he says but stops trying to turn.

In the silence that follows, other sounds are revealed: a wall-clock's ticking; the wind moaning across a stovepipe; and Jerry Rosen's boots crunching snow on the steps outside.

"Told you," Roy gloats; "told you there was fun in store. Wobbly son of a bitch, who's full of himself now?"

I dig my fingers into Roy's shoulder. This makes him angry, but the hell I care. Roy is on Curt Broe's team and I'm under no obligation to keep him happy.

Staring at the back of Joe's head, I am acutely aware of the revolver beneath my jacket. It's cold and heavy, like it wants to be picked up; like it'll pull me through the floor if I don't. Locking my knees, I stand still and straight, hoping the feeling will pass, though it never really does.

I clear my throat. "Where you been, Joe?"

McCuskey's voice shakes, "This is a mistake. You can't…can't do this."

"Sure can. About time someone held you to—"

Before I can finish, Nicholas Reed practically falls through a side-door, startling everyone in the room. He's lucky he isn't shot. Snow follows him in at such an angle that it spatters the opposite wall and gives us all a dusting.

"All c-c-clear," Nick says through chattering teeth. "F-f-fence line's clear." Struggling to close the door, he glances at his twin brother, Isaac, in the far corner.

Stepping away from the wall, Roy waves his hands. "Stop," he snaps, "boy, *stop!* Back outside and wipe your boots, hear?"

"Goddammit, Yukon, do you mind?" Now, forgive my starch but I can't say I share Roy's sudden concern for housekeeping.

Roy shrugs and holds up his hands. "Boss don't want us tracking filth in here, is all. Y'all want another two-hour lecture on the subject, then never mind me."

As preposterous as it sounds, he has a point. Management can be irrational about the little things so I grit my teeth and motion for Nick to head back outside and scrape his soles. Ridiculous.

Stepping around the chair, Joe's pale blue eyes are wild with fear. I think so, anyway; my old comrade won't look at me square. I lean forward and lower my voice, "Don't draw this out—you know how it ends."

"Come on," Joe pleads, "this is crazy! You're still sore about Edgemont, right?"

"'Til the day I die. Surprised?"

"Ah, hell, I know." His voice quakes, "I'm sorry, Shep—sorry for everything. You gotta believe me! For pity's sake, I'm *sorry!*"

Me, too. Sorry we ever met.

Joe won't stop pleading, "It was an accident, Shep, an accident! We didn't know she'd be there!"

"Yeah? Well, she was."

Then Joe mutters something even I can't hear but it doesn't matter. Not even slightly. Nothing he says will ever change my mind.

In Edgemont, the wind blew all the time. Perched on a mountainside overlooking the Owhyee, the camp and its mines took the full brunt of everything that barreled down from Oregon and Idaho. Rain fell sideways and snow lay twenty feet deep but there was gold there and that was reason enough to stick it out.

On the camp's fringe stood the Buena Vista, a frame-tent saloon propped up against the wind by stout logs, and Lord, what a place. No matter how cold the weather outside, inside the woodstove was always hot and the laughter raucous. Along one side was a rough pine bar. On the other, an upright piano that must've fallen from a transcontinental train before someone hitched mules to it, dragged it uphill, and set it there without thought for its condition. Every night, by guttering oil lamps and wreathed in a haze of tobacco smoke, some itinerant professor would try and fail to coax music out of this hilarious wreck. No matter: someone always bought him a drink and thanked him for the laugh. Dealers had card-games going at the tables in the back. Customers slipped and slid their way through the door, carrying in snow that melted all over the place, but no one cared. Men in steaming coats leaned against the bar waiting for a tender to recharge their glasses, carelessly pitching coins into an overflowing cigar box. Yeah, the Buena Vista was the genuine article, a rare flower that blooms only in mining camps where something's doing, and believe you me, things were doing in Edgemont. Best of all, no one there cared that I'd spent my first eight weeks in camp trying to drown myself in rye.

Except one night, I didn't.

That evening, the Elks, Red Men, and Odd Fellows conspired to throw a dance for the whole camp and on a lark (and because the Buena Vista had closed for the event), I played along. As fate would have it, that's how I met Julia Mari Wells, the love of my life, my sun and moon, my everything. Brilliant, patient, and kind—she was the acme of perfection. She walked right through my defenses and saw more good in me than I believed possible and for this sin, she paid with her life. Every minute with her was better than the last but since even an angel can't break the Devil's habits, before long I was back at the Buena Vista. A couple weeks later, I was introduced to a man standing behind me. Dark hair and stocky build, this fellow, with pale blue eyes. Turns out, we already knew each other. Too well, honestly. From the moment I recognized him, it'd taken everything I had not to kill the son of a bitch.

Charlie throws a switch and a string of bare bulbs flickers to life. Roy Garland drags Joe, still tied to the chair, down the short, tin-covered walkway between the mine office and the assay and sets him before a banked furnace.

Joe chokes back a sob, "Oh, Jesus, don't burn me!"

"I like how you think," Roy smirks.

Charlie and I talk across a workbench crowded with mortars and pestles; bone-ash cupels; flasks filled with mercury, chemicals, and acids: nitric, sulfuric, and hydrofluoric, among others. Slagging hammers, tongs, and bulky asbestos gloves hang from pegs along the walls. Gray dust covers everything.

Curious, Charlie glances at Roy. "What'd he say?"

Roy shakes his head. "Not a goddamned thing." He tips the chair backward until both it and Joe are lying on the floor. "Where's the drain?"

"You set him on top of it," Charlie says. "See how the floor slopes?"

"Come on," Joe pleads, "what's this? What are you doing?"

No one pays him any attention.

"This work, Mr. Sunday?" Isaac Reed holds up a thin, steel stirring rod. "Supply closet's locked, go figure."

"Sure, that'll do." I send his brother to fill a bucket with water from a fire barrel.

Charlie offers me a flask from his coat pocket and I throw back a shot. Then I kneel near Joe's head and we stare at each other, our faces upside-down to one another.

"What do you know about Peter Kastning?" I say.

"Nothing! Come on, Shep, we were friends, you and me!"

Hate to admit it but he isn't wrong. After our rocky re-acquaintance there in Edgemont, for a while again we were sociable, but that was ages ago. Tonight, even the mention of those bonds fills me with rage and I bring down my fist like a hammer on the bridge of his nose.

"Forget what you did?" I snarl. "I haven't."

Gasping for air, eyes watering, there's no way he can answer. Doesn't matter. Didn't want one, anyway.

"You were in the Philippines," I continue; "you've seen the cure."

He lets out a moan.

"Want to head this off? Then give me a name."

"Whose?" he groans, coughing to clear blood from his throat. "Whose name do you want?"

"Who shot Pete Kastning?"

"Don't know."

Stiff backhand. "Who shot Pete Kastning?"

"I'm telling you, *I don't know!*"

"Boudreaux? Steve Adams? Come clean, jack: Kastning's death has the Western Federation's boot-prints all over it. And what brings you here? Someone local make a call or did the Denver heavies send you? Don't tell me no one talks down at Union Hall."

"Not about things we haven't done. Jesus, Shep, what do you want?"

I slap his face, hard enough that blood from his broken nose sprays the floor.

"T-t-take me to the sheriff," he sputters, "I'll spill everything."

"You're out of luck. This is beyond the pale."

Words pour out of him in a torrent, "I'm sorry about *everything*, Shep. Lawaan, Dobbins, Covington, *everything!* Christ, I'm so sorry! I swear I wish things were different; wish I'd never gone to Edgemont. I was stupid, trying to pull stunts like that, *stupid!*"

I squeeze my hand into a fist and Joe flinches. Moments later—three? thirty?—I realize I haven't moved. Can't think for all the noise in my head but over in the corner, I see Roy muttering to Isaac Reed.

"Please, Shep," Joe whispers, "you gotta forgive me."

"Not tonight." I backhand him again, splitting his lip. "Not tonight."

How many grudges can one man bear? Where's the limit? I don't know, but it feels like I'm staggering toward the answer. Preachers say that anger is weakness—that angry men fall on their own swords, and while anger is a blade with no handle, what kind of fool would go emptyhanded in a place like this? Part of me wants to go down from this mountain and never look back but hell, I wouldn't know where to go or what to do. Can't take back things I've said or undo what I've done so for now, I've no plans except to carry on like this until the day I die. Doesn't matter that I hate it, I can't stop. Don't know how. Julia nearly set me straight. Nearly. Heaven knows she tried but now she's gone and since that's McCuskey's fault, I swear to God I will *never* forgive him.

"Whose name?" he groans. "Whose name do you want?"

"I'll know once I hear it."

"Wait—"

"No."

"Can't think like this—"

"Five seconds."

"Wait—"

"Three."

"Damn it, Shep," Joe whispers. "You know I can't give you names—"

I punch his solar plexus as hard as I can. Eyes bulging, he thrashes the way you'd expect, the way everyone does when they lose their wind, and I lean away in case he vomits. Seconds pass before he can breathe again.

"Want to reconsider?" I hiss.

No words yet: only gasps and groans.

"Lawaan's old news," I say, and Edgemont, too: none of that matters now. Pard, this right here, this is *work,* nothing more. Just tell me who killed Peter Kastning, okay? That's all I'm after."

He tries to speak but can't. His eyes are screwed shut and he breathes in little sips.

"Come on." I slap his face again, just hard enough to reel him in. "Speak."

At last, he manages a few words between gasps, "Shep, if…I…give you…a hundred names, won't none of 'em…bring Julia back…so go…go fuck yourself."

Across the room, Roy hoots softly. Maybe he wonders whether I'll haul off and beat Joe to death. That's what his boss, Curt Broe, would do, but that isn't my cut. I'm grateful, in fact, because Joe's just given me a pretext to draw this out. By sticking out his neck this way, no one here can object if I lay it on, and goddamn, that's just what I mean to do.

"Suit yourself." I set my knees on the floor so they bracket Joe's head. "Isaac, hold his feet. Joe, you gonna open your mouth or do you want help?"

Tears stream from his closed eyes and while his lips tremble, his mouth stays shut.

"Crackers, then. Nick, push down on his chin; Roy, pull on his nose, no, *harder."*

Joe is sweaty and quarrelsome but there's nothing he can do. Soon as his lips part, Charlie jams the stirring rod between Joe's teeth and presses on the ends so he can't close his mouth. Blood trickles down his cheek.

"That good?" Charlie says.

Nothing good about it but here we are. "Sure. Nick, hand me that cloth and go fill one of those pails."

The kid obliges, handing me a shop rag filthy with rock-dust.

Grasping the edges, I hold it loosely over Joe's face and lean forward to whisper in his ear, "Last chance, comrade: who killed Pete Kastning?

A gust of wind rattles the windowpanes. Charlie locks eyes with me and I nod.

"Start talking, Joe, or I'm gonna take the starch out of you."

Spit rattles in Joe's throat. He might be frightened, angry, and suffocating but he still won't speak. Already, he's struggling to breathe.

"Tap your fingers and I'll stop, understand?"

He understands—I *know* he does—but for pity's sake, he squeezes his fingers into white-knuckled fists and I hate him anew. Hate him for thinking he can hold out. No one holds out; it isn't possible.

"Suit yourself." Pressing down with the towel, I gesture for Nick to tip the pail and start pouring.

Seconds pass, eighteen, nineteen, twenty, before Joe's body convulses from head-to-toe. As he fights to breathe, his hands curl into quivering claws; he pulls against the ropes until they cut into his arms. Doesn't matter. The water keeps coming and the towel clings to his nose and mouth, sealing them shut. At this moment, Joe's brain is convinced he's drowning.

Charlie and Roy have seen the cure before so they know what to expect. The Reed brothers, though, they're just boys, real greenhorns, and Joe, increasingly desperate for air, thrashes so violently he knocks Isaac against a stack of cast iron roasting plates.

"Nick!" Issac howls, clutching his head. Blood seeps between his fingers.

"Yukon!" I shout, "Grab the chair!"

Roy obliges and pins Joe's legs.

"Nick, keep pouring!" I snap. Struggling to hold the cloth tight to Joe's face, the veins in my forearms bulge. "Feel that, Joe? That's death, brother, crawling down your throat."

Wide-eyed, Nick Reed shoots me a look I can't read. "Son of a bitch, Mr. Sunday, where'd you learn this?"

"Samar, kid," I hiss, "bloody Samar."

"Where's that?"

"Visayas, eastern Philippines. Don't ever go there."

The pail's empty so I lift the rag, but I tell Charlie to keep the steel rod where it is. Over my shoulder, I gesture to Nick. "Go find a bandage for Issac and look outside. Tell me if Jerry sees anything."

Nick scouts around for a less-filthy cloth and hands it to Isaac before starting down the hall. Straining to see outside, the boy cups his hands and presses his face against a glass pane set into the door. He knocks and evidently receives a reply because he turns to announce that we're still alone.

Down on the floor, Joe coughs and tries to speak but I won't let him. Not yet. "Everyone, back on station."

Again, I clamp the rag over Joe's face and order Nick to resume pouring.

"Mr. Sunday?" Nick ventures, "he wants—"

"Start pouring or you're next!"

I hear Roy suck air through his teeth. Wrong thing to say but I'm not thinking clearly. Not by a long shot.

Nick complies but now his hands are shaking. Counting to myself, this time I only reach twelve before Joe starts thrashing. Nick looks at me, expecting me to call it off, but I order him to continue until the pail is empty, maybe thirty seconds in all. Only then do I pull the rag and motion for Charlie to lift the steel rod.

Desperate to clear muddy water from his throat and sinuses, Joe retches and coughs; water and bile splash across the concrete. Panicked, he shakes his head back and forth and I wonder what I'll do if he doesn't stop. I've seen it before: some targets clock out forever and then there's nothing you can do.

The water cure really is a pitiful sight and while I can't say I'm used to it, neither does it cause my eyes to water or heart to race the way it once did. In the Philippines, Macabebe scouts showed us the old Spanish water cure: insert a funnel into the prisoner's mouth and force-fill them with water until their insides stretch. Then punch or jump on the subject's stomach to produce simultaneous sensations of drowning and being torn up inside but since the victim always vomits and occasionally dies, we Americans developed the saturated-cloth method as an alternative. Cleaner, faster, and generally safer: proof of our genius for benevolent efficiency.

I stare into Joe's red, watery eyes. For a moment, I consider walking away; taking my coat and high-tailing it into the woods but fifty bucks says Roy would put a bullet in my back if I tried. Hell, who am I kidding? I bought this ticket years ago and no one steps off without the conductor's say-so.

I grab Joe's shirt collar and give him a shake. "No one's coming, bub. None of your people even know you're here so unless you want me to pencil another dance on your card, you'd better open up, understand?"

Since he can't speak yet, McCuskey nods and taps his hands frantically against the chair.

"Samuel Morse, himself," Roy hoots and I swear if he was closer I'd punch him.

The workroom is terrifically overheated, a fever dream of sweat and fear, and I'd like to step outside for some air except that if I show weakness now, it'll get back to Curt or even Jack Lipford, making my precarious situation even worse. Glancing around the room, the others look shell-shocked and miserable. Only Roy looks happy but that's because he's even sicker upstairs than me.

I stand and give Joe time to collect himself. What's more, I have a moment now to rationalize what I've just done. As though that were possible

Maybe Charlie senses the storm in my head because he leans around my shoulder and hands me his flask. "Take it," he says. "I'll get something back in camp."

I'm sure he will. Pouring it on only way to blot out these nights, numbing ourselves just so we can stomach the sounds of our own voices. Cracks in the dam, though, and I hate to imagine the flood once it breaks.

I take a long pull, feeling the familiar burn at the back of my throat. How many drinks is that? Probably a dozen these past eight hours. But since Balangiga? Since Samar? God only knows. Much of what I've seen these past few years has been through the bottom of a glass.

I glance at Joe. His eyes are closed and he flinches at every sound as the others turn and shuffle back down the hallway toward the office. Son of a bitch, he caved too soon. If he'd fought harder, I could claim I was only following orders. Didn't though. He broke quickly. Funny, with some fellows, all it takes is the threat of abuse and they'll tell you everything they know, while others hang in longer than you'd expect. Toughest case I ever saw was a thirteen-year-old boy on Samar who hardly made a sound, even after an hour of the cure. In the end, I believe Captain Porter ordered him led outside the village and shot. But not Joe. He shattered like a teacup. I figure everything that's happened tonight will be used against me. Knew it before I got into Curt's autocar but even that foresight couldn't keep me from plunging ahead. Couldn't reel me in. No matter; I can take a punch. Always have.

I wipe my hands and reach for a pencil and pad of paper. "Okay, Joe, enough with the games: who shot Pete Kastning?"

Before tonight, if anyone doubted that Jack Lipford's Association and the WFM were at war, henceforth no one would. My boss, a man who owns and operates this corner of Nevada, has cried havoc and let slip his dogs without considering where it all might lead.

Me, I have a pretty good idea.

FILIPINOS KILL
48 AMERICANS

Company of Infantry Almost Wiped Out in Samar.

Natives in Superior Numbers Surprised
the Troops While at Breakfast—
Gen Hughes Organizing Large
Force to Go in Pursuit.

ONLY 24 MEN SURVIVE

The Survivors, 11 of Them Wounded,
Escape from Insurgents.

———

MANILA, Sept. 29.—A disastrous fight between United States troops and insurgents occurred yesterday in the Island of Samar, near Balangiga. A large body of insurgents attacked Company C, Ninth Infantry, only twenty-four members of the company escaping. All the others are reported to have been killed. The company were at breakfast when attacked, and made a determined resistance, but the overwhelming numbers of the insurgents compelled them to retreat.

Of the survivors, all of whom have arrived at Basey, eleven are wounded. According to the latest returns the strength of the company was seventy-two. The survivors include Capt. Thomas W. Connell, First Lieut. Edward A. Bumpus, and Dr. R. S. Griswold, Surgeon.

Captin Edwin V. Bookmiller of the Ninth Infantry reports that Gen. Hughes is assembling a force to attack the insurgents. The insurgents captured all the stores and ammunition of the company and all the rifles except twelve.

———

FIVE

Mornings on the desert are a wonder. The Milky Way's slow, steady fade, until all but the last few stars are gone. Like a lover disrobing, the land reveals itself slowly, one curve, one feature at a time. White stones like tumbled bones and black trees in silhouette. From darkness, the sky runs from deep-sea green to blue and gold until the sun sets fire to the horizon. In every direction, mountaintops redden and shadows give way. Of course, the temperature hardly budges—that comes later, after the rocks have soaked up a little sunlight—but all at once, everything feels better, as if the mere *promise* of warmth was as potent as the real McCoy. And all this while, the world holds its breath, waiting, waiting. The silence in these moments is profound—as much a physical sensation as the weight of a heavy quilt. No wind, no insects, no birdsong: only the sounds of my own breathing, my pulse, and a high-pitched whine that I take to be the workings of my nervous system.

Alas, on this particular morning, very few of these things hold true. For now, all I can hear is the coughing and sputtering of a 1904 Welch Model 4-0, straining to bear my passenger and me up a short, steep grade. Gotta be careful, as I tend to ride the clutch and grind gears while downshifting—mortal sins in the Welch, which is notorious for shaking its rear assembly to pieces on these rough roads—but so far, this trip's gone well. Well enough, anyhow. At one washout, I had to shovel down an embankment to enter and pile sagebrush under the wheels to exit. At another, cattle have torn up the soil so that if we'd come along any later in the day, the car would've sunk up to its axles in mud.

With a full head of steam, though, the Welch skated across this partially-frozen dirt, digging in for just one sickening moment before purchasing firmer ground. All these things and a flat tire, too.

Thrills like these notwithstanding (and provided you bundle up), winter is still the best season for travel in the Great Basin. No springtime mud, none of summer's choking dust. Sure, the wind can be brutal but that's true year-round. Generally speaking, Nevada takes it on the chin from any system that makes it over California's High Sierra. Not this morning though. Other than a milky haze on the far horizon, the sky is clear and the air is still.

Like many mountain roads in this state, this one follows a dry stream—the streambed *is* the road—and the wheels shatter pockets of cat-ice as we climb. Twisting and turning, the car's headlamps pick out sagebrush, cedars, and junipers; even scrubby pines near the Naquinta Range's summit. From here, the road angles west and the low Jumbled Hills fall away on our left. The sun is rising swiftly now, putting the shadows filling Groom Dry Lake to flight. Hardly any snow out here, far less than what fell on Delamar six hours ago, yet it's bitterly cold. Sometimes, frigid air settles into these closed desert basins, dropping the temperature thirty degrees or more below whatever it is up in the surrounding mountains.

Atop one rise I stop, put the Welch in neutral, and set the hand-brake. A small mining camp lies just north of here and while I believe it's deserted, I want to be sure. Taking up binoculars, I lean across the hood for several minutes to study a cluster of ramshackle buildings. Condensation from my breath keeps fogging the lenses, but everything uphill is quiet. No smoke rises from the stovepipes. No lights in the windows, no dogs or chickens in the yards. Sure enough, the camp's a ghost. Nevada's interior is full of little settlements like this, intermittently active according to the smelter trusts' appetites, bustling one year and deserted the next. Luckily for me, this is an off year.

◎

A few miles on, I stop to refill the tank from one of six, four-gallon tins tied to the running boards. Soon as I'm finished, I lean across the rear door and pull back a tarp to check on my passenger. Bound and gagged on the vehicle's floor, Joe McCuskey is sunk in shadow and nearly unrecognizable. Left eye swollen shut, caked blood on his gray face.

"Still there?"

I watch until his chest heaves and his breath steams in a spill of light. Damn it. Would that he'd have done me a favor and died already but that's Joe for you, stubborn to a fault.

I turn to look for a route between spatterings of greasewood on the valley floor. Not much farther, I reckon, except there's no road out here—this is wilderness. I re-tie the empty gas-tin to the left running board and check to see that everything is where it belongs. Can't afford to lose anything because here in the Black Belt, especially, the likelihood of needing something relates directly to whether you have it with you. If so, chances are you won't need it but if not, your problems will multiply like rabbits. Based on this theory, I'm carrying enough spare parts to rebuild the Welch from scratch: two axles; a drive shaft and gear assembly; spare tires and tubes; a small parcel of oilcloth to patch holes in the cover; enough bailing wire to run a fence around the entire state; grease and oil by the quart; tools; a full camping setup; and enough food and water for days. All this plus an extra pair of boots. Hard experience has taught me that even with meticulous preparation, it's not uncommon to end up afoot in rural Nevada.

Honestly, considering the extra work it takes to drive out here, it's a wonder anyone bothers. While the mileage may be better than you'd get with a wagon team, you're guaranteed a trunk-load of headaches that even five years back no one could've imagined. Thinking this, I smirk, remembering how often my father said essentially the same thing about wagons and mules.

"Hell, I should've just walked," he'd curse, usually after an animal threw a shoe or a leaf-spring broke. "Spared myself this nonsense."

One summer, it rained every day for weeks and we stuck *hard* crossing Plymouth Creek. Quicksand up to the axles. The animal screamed and fought and I wasn't much help, over-mindful that recently a neighbor of ours had been kicked to imbecility by a mule. It took hours to pull all four free before Dad decided he'd had enough and walked five miles to the Lora place for help. Eleven years old, I sat beneath a cottonwood, oilskin raincoat over my head and a single-barrel shotgun balanced across my knees. Rain fell while the mules cropped grass and I waited, waited, waited for Dad to return, all the while secretly hoping he wouldn't. Wished he'd stumble and crack his skull so we could bask in the sympathy reserved for widows and orphans. Maybe get a step-father who didn't drink so much.

No such luck. He came trudging back, red-eyed and nasty as ever. Despite Mr. Lora's help, plus his four hired men and all their picks and shovels, *and* a six-mule team, our rig stayed stuck until nightfall. Should've known better but after a few hours' digging, I asked Dad why we didn't just abandon the wagon and get a new one. Rather than backhand me, tell me I was stupid, or that my mother had spoiled me, for once he just grinned and shook his head.

"Sooner abandon the ranch, kid; without a wagon, I'd never get away."

"Away from what?" is what I wanted to ask but didn't. Didn't dare.

Instead, I took those words as gospel and ever since, no matter how secure my situation, I make sure I have a way out. This philosophy hasn't made me many friends, I know, but more than once it's saved my hide. And while I might've embraced what my father said in a way he never intended, it's strange to think how he couldn't get away from *anything*. Like he never even saw it coming.

∾

As the crow flies, the western shore of Groom Dry Lake is only five miles away—but I'm taking a longer course around its edge. Some desert rats will shortcut across dry lakebeds but not me. Not in winter, anyway. Too risky, counting on frozen alkali mud to support a buckboard or a 1,500-pound autocar. Sometimes after heavy snows, or even a little rain, these ghost-lakes will suddenly refill and although the pool is rarely more than inches deep, only drunks and idiots will venture out into it. A week or two later and all that water evaporates. Thick salt-crusts form and anything stuck is gonna stay there forever.

Stuck or buried, that is; here's the reason I've driven all this way in advance of another winter storm. Some fifty feet from shore, due east of Oak Spring Butte, four bodies lie entombed beneath the lakebed's crusted surface. One of these is my handiwork. Curt Broe and our former boss, Sam Rice, planted the others; somewhat ironic, as many believe Rice himself is buried in one of the mine dumps on Ferguson Hill. Most figure his demise was union-sponsored, while others point to the Association. No surprise since no one can agree on which side ol' Sam worked. If lessees re-work Delamar's dumps someday, then maybe we'll know.

Seven hours behind the wheel and I'm exhausted. Could be why I shout, "Hey, Joe, you ever tangle with a fellow named Sam Rice? Couple years ago, he was the Association's chief of security. Ex-cop. Slick hair and brushy mustache. Always wore a red vest beneath his coat. From Kansas City or St. Louis. Missouri, certainly. Met him on my second day in Delamar and he disappeared about three weeks later. One of your jobs? You or Steve Adams, maybe?"

Joe doesn't answer.

Coasting downhill, I concentrate on steering.

Bored, though, so before long I'm yapping again, "Figure Lipford's old man caught him pulling stunts. That, or the Union put him down. Kick the seat if you know anything, Joe; I'd love to put that mystery to rest. Even take off the gag if you'll talk."

Joe neither kicks nor makes a sound so I continue as before, blinking away tears as the bright light and stinging wind assault my eyes. I have goggles to block the wind, sure, but they're a borrowed pair and the strap's too tight. I can wear them for only about twenty minutes at a time before I have to take them off and carry on with my eyes exposed.

Fifteen more minutes pass in relative silence.

For a long time, a herd of feral horses watches our approach. Now, antelope normally run before you can get anywhere near them, but not wild horses. Most times you can drive up close before they'll budge. Hard to say whether they're merely curious or in the throes of some primal memory of a time when their ancestors lived alongside ours. At the last minute they spook and retreat to a safe distance, tossing their heads as they go. I do love Nevada's wild horses.

Tired, bored, and lonely, so I resume shouting, "Hey, Joe, guess who I saw in Las Vegas last May? Charlie Marak, how about that? Changing trains, headed for Los Angeles. Stepped off to buy a newspaper and we nearly collided. Small world, huh? Said his arm still hurts. Poor bastard. Guess the ligaments weren't properly reattached. Goddamn, I wish I'd never set foot in the Philippines. Ever think that? Think you'd be better off if you hadn't gone there?"

I tap the brakes and steer around an enormous boulder. Funny things, these giants, miles from outcropped bedrock. Geologists say when it rains on the desert, hardpan holds only so much water before 'sheet-torrents' form. Inches deep but miles wide, these flows are powerful enough to tumble rocks across debris fans skirting the mountains.

Once the Welch is safely past this erratic, I re-sight Oak Spring Butte and continue dead-reckoning my way around the lakeshore.

"Can't recall," I resume, "what Marak said he does. Farming? Something to do with fruit trees, I think, but I might have that wrong. Early for my memory to go but we've taken some knocks on our heads, haven't we? Forgetting might be a blessing."

Not everything, though. Like a ghastly picture show, awful sights from our posting on the Philippine island of Samar wash over me, a 'sheet-torrent' miles wide and deep as hell. Images of friends and acquaintances. Of death and reprisals. Deaths by the score. Don't want these things in my head but there they are.

I reach into my vest pocket for a flask, pull the stopper with my teeth, and drain it. Drinking hurts, too, but it's a bracing kind of pain. Only problem is, before long, everything it soothes away comes roaring back. Always.

"Poor Pat," I mutter. "Christ, him and Covington, both. You could've done something, Joe. Anything. Warning shots, thrown rocks, anything at all but you *didn't.* You coward, you turned your back on 'em and then lied about it."

In frustration, I shake the last drops from the flask onto my tongue.

"Same way you abandoned me, except I got lucky and stuck, yeah? Couldn't write me off. Pat and John, though, son of a bitch, you just stood there and let those animals—"

To my complete astonishment, Joe kicks the back of my seat. The image of Dobbins and Covington's bodies in a red Philippine river fades so I stop the car, wipe my eyes, and step out.

૭৲

The Philippine War wasn't a fair fight. The natives had bolos—a type of machete—axes, and bamboo spears; we had Krags, Gatling guns, and heavy artillery. Near the coasts, Navy gunboats supported us, too. Up north on Luzon, their national troops had Mausers: fine, German-made rifles they'd taken from the Spanish, but not the Samaraños: bolos, axes, and spears, solamente. Here and there, a gingal or antique flintlock, too, but those were rare. Even so, these primitive weapons were all they'd needed.

Six years on and sights and sounds from the Philippines still haunt my dreams. Some are pleasant. Most aren't. If I learned one thing there, it is *never* to underestimate an adversary and that *everyone* is a potential adversary. Anyone will fight if pressed: male or female, highborn or low, dark-skinned or light, and all are capable of staggering cruelty. No matter how well you think you know someone, there's more there than meets the eye. Much more. Masks can hide treachery and lies come wrapped in kindness, so you'd best not forget that sometimes it's friends who inflict the deepest cuts.

૭৲

As soon as the gag is out of Joe's mouth, he shouts, "Help! Anyone! *Murder!* Somebody, *help!*"

I step behind the car to relieve myself. He can yell all he likes; what do I care? No one else is within sixty, seventy miles of here.

My bladder emptied, I check the oil and the tires while Joe screams himself hoarse. I close the hood and latch it. "Bet it hurts to yell, knowing what the cure must've done to your throat."

"Go to hell," he rasps but he can't get me to rise that easily.

I lean across the rear passenger door, grab him by his hair.

"Sit up, you son of a bitch, up!"

Back at the Tomcat, the boys trussed Joe so well it takes no great effort to raise him to a seated position.

He blinks as if emerging from a cave and takes a cautious look around. Groom Lake Valley is thirty miles wide and fifty miles long. Nothing out here but sand, salt, and sky. For a moment, this vast and awful emptiness appalls even me, and I'm leaving soon. God knows the agoraphobic gut-punch it lands on Joe.

"Think anyone heard?" I snarl.

Soon as I let him go, he moans and slumps to the floorboard. "Get on with it," he whispers. "Have some decency and do whatever it is you're gonna do."

"'Decency?' *Decency.* You're funny, Joe—that's a good one."

The wind gusts cold and hard, a forlorn sigh through the Welch's struts. Clouds on the horizon now, evidence of a storm building in the west. Better get moving or else I'll still be out here when it hits.

"Water?" I offer, but when I glance at my hand—the one I used to pull Joe's hair—I notice blood on it. Stepping away, I wipe my fingers on a rock. Figuring a Shoshone prospector could pass this way and see my handprint, I roll the stone with my foot to hide the evidence. Highly unlikely but like I said, it's unwise leaving things to chance out here. I scrub my hand with sand until it's tolerably clean.

Joe hasn't answered so I lean over the door and splash his face; even hold the canteen to his lips for a bit. He flinches at first but soon he opens his mouth and laps up every drop that hits his black and swollen tongue, dissolved blood and mud notwithstanding. Closing his eye, he coughs, spits on the floorboard, and settles back across the transmission tunnel.

"Thanks," he says and coughs again. "Thank you."

"You're welcome."

For a moment, we're comrades again, hacking our way through a jungle overgrown with bamboo and vines. Scared kids, unsure of what we're looking for or what we'll do if it finds us.

Then an image of Pat Dobbins returns and I have to close my eyes.

Within the hour, we reach the end of a low ridge sheltering the lakebed's northwestern shore. The Welch chugs to a stop near five gigantic boulders. Like the fingertips of a buried giant's hand, these rocks rise thirty feet above the salt flat: the Hand of God, Sam Rice called it. Back then, I'd rolled my eyes, although perhaps the old boy was onto something. These days, he'd know better than I would where God's been poking His fingers.

I untie a pick and shovel from the car's back and start digging.

Two hours later, the hole's finished and I toss my tools aside. Given the viscosity of the clay beneath the salt, I'm guessing I have around four hours until this pit refills and seals itself shut. Plenty of time.

Five feet from the pit, Joe's lying on his back, his hands and ankles tightly bound. He's staring at the sky but since his face is swollen, he doesn't—or maybe can't—blink. Lying on the pit's other side, I fold my fingers above my chest and tilt my head so that I, too, can stare at the sky. Strange but for the first time in a long while, I don't feel quite so lonely.

The desert this afternoon, my God, what a show. Four o'clock, nearly sundown this time of year, and the sun's glare has softened. High overhead, bright clouds with dark undersides tear themselves to pieces, coalescing one moment and separating the next. Bright as searchlights, sunbeams pour through the spaces in-between, sweep the valley floor, and withdraw.

"This is a good place," Joe whispers. He coughs, turns his head, and spits in the dirt beside his ear. "Peaceful."

I bite my tongue. The less I say, the better.

"Can't always gather my thoughts. Ever feel that way?"

More silence.

"Like things in your head never come out the way you mean 'em?"

I'm all talked out, but my loneliness gets the best of me. "Sure."

Red and tan hills surround the lakebed. Black shadows crawl down Oak Spring Butte's eastern face.

"Ever since I was little," he continues, "couldn't help the things I did—things I knew were wrong."

I shrug. "I wasn't like this."

"Balangiga?" Joe coughs miserably.

"That's the crossroad, sure."

"It's why we're here, ain't it?" He coughs again. "We took the same trail, right? Maybe not exactly, but better than most, you understand what's in my head."

I exhale heavily. "Don't count on it. I have my own problems."

"Hell, yeah, you do."

I laugh in spite of myself.

The wind gusts and the clouds roil.

"Never took you for a heavy, Shep. How'd you end up with the Association?"

I glance at my pocket watch. "Only ones hiring."

Joe grunts. "Worked that side of the ledger, too, but things the owners wanted done, the things I saw…they turned me, see?"

I don't so I keep my mouth shut.

"Early on, remember those Flips we penned in Manila?"

"Kinda," I say, though this is something I remember vividly. As fighting in the northern islands tapered off, we rounded up hundreds of prisoners: insurrectos, mostly, but more than a few hacendados and uncooperative officials went into the cages, too. All corralled like cattle, without enough water and no shade anywhere. Every evening, we carried away those who'd died during the day. All those bodies, swollen and reeking in the heat, it was horrible. Demoralizing.

Joe coughs once. "Saw the same damn thing in Victor, Colorado, late in '04—"

"Son of a bitch, I *knew* you'd gone to Colorado. Knew it! How in the hell did we never run into each other?"

"I didn't stick around." Joe sighs. "Heard you were there so I split."

"I'll be damned."

A cloud races across the sun.

"Drifted up from Florence," he continues, "but the mines weren't hiring so I took a job in security. Security, *shit*. Deputized us, called us 'peacekeepers,' but that was for cover. Hamlin and the other owners sent us in at night to roust union-types from their beds and run 'em out of town. Emptied the town of Altman, completely. Busted up their co-op store. Took our prisoners—regular, tax-paying citizens, except they belonged to the WFM or didn't oppose it, any-how—up to a bullpen east of the mines. Hell, you know the district: Victor sits at ten-thousand feet on the side of a mountain. Some of those fellows couldn't stand the exposure; died out in the open. Guardsmen made us carry 'em out to the cemetery and I swear it was like I was back in Manila. Same dirty job, except this time it was Americans I was burying. Burying *us*, Shep. Throwing dirt on those bodies—it *changed* me. Figured we'd all end up dead unless the owners were stopped."

"Yeah? Where'd that get you?" I say, not for spite but because I don't care to consider what he's said.

Sometimes I wonder whether I've chosen correctly but then I hear Federation recruiters in the saloons, shouting about outlawing private property, five-hour workdays, and a million other fine and fancy things, yet these same fellows will put out each other's eyes over work songs and which armbands to wear to their May Day parades. Yeah, if harmony's the goal, then I don't see the WFM or the IWW as the means to that end. Besides, I know what they're up against and it frankly terrifies me. Firebrands like Joe are fooling themselves.

"Pard, the owners hold all the reins. Congress, the courts—all of 'em."

"I know they do," he says between coughs, "but someone's gotta kick."

Well, not me. No good comes from stepping in front of a train.

Wind screams across the playa and a dust cloud dances between us like a ghost. Wouldn't be surprised to learn this place really is haunted.

Joe turns his head and stares at me with his one good eye. "Gonna kill me, Shep?"

I take my time before answering, "Orders."

He grunts and strains against his restraints. "We were friends, remember?"

"I remember." I exhale slowly. "Wish I didn't."

He turns away. Settles onto his back and exhales heavily.

I am so tired of this. Tired of everything. Delamar. Joe. Me. I glance at my hands, cracked and dry from digging in the salt. "You knew I was here, didn't you?"

He coughs and spits again. "Yeah, I heard."

"Why come here, then?"

"Orders."

"Was the job in Caliente?"

"Delamar. I was only waiting in Caliente for the assignment."

"Jack Lipford?"

"Don't know—your boys collared me before I found out."

Something here isn't right. If Big Curt was up on Ferguson and the telephone lines were down, how would he know to come get me? Everyone involved was up at the Tomcat. I try to remember what Curt said about that telegram Roy Garland intercepted. Roy isn't known for careful detective work so either it was an unprecedented stroke of luck or something's hiding in the shadows. What am I missing?

Suddenly, light and heat pour through a hole in the clouds—a fire in the sky like nothing I've ever seen. I raise a hand to shield my eyes but all Joe can do is close his. A minute later, this breach seals itself shut and we're cast back into shadow. All that sunshine must've done something to my head, though, because now I can't remember what we were just talking about. I try to recall the last thing Joe said. Something about the owners, maybe, but after a few minutes, I give up and hope it wasn't anything crucial. Too many knocks on the head.

Joe's eye closes and before long I figure he's fallen asleep. The wind rises and falls, raising little skiffs of salt that catch on my clothes and hair. Stretched out on the playa, Joe looks as though he's covered with frost.

For another twenty minutes, I sit and think about people and possibilities, puzzling over what to do next. Is he really worth all this trouble? Dead? Alive? I don't know. No, that isn't true: I gotta cut him loose. Guaranteed to cause hellacious trouble down the road but at least I'll be able to live with myself. But how to do it? And where? Can't take him back to Delamar. Do I make a run for Tonopah, or Las Vegas? Vegas is my best option, yet in every possible way this plan is foolish. Dangerously so.

Temperature's dropping again so I stand, dust my clothes, and return to the Welch. Jesus, I'm exhausted. Irritable, too. Walking past, I kick Joe's ribs, jolting him from sleep. "You had me fooled," I shout. "Back in Edgemont, you told me Klaas and Mumby got their stories wrong. Told me I shouldn't believe my own eyes." I lean over the front passenger door and pick up my revolver.

"I was nineteen," Joe says. "Six months off the farm and scared out of my mind."

"Hell, who wasn't? They told us everything was under control; told us we didn't need to worry and look what happened! The mess tent; Pat and John by the river; the beach at Lawaan. What did you tell them, Joe? What did you tell Marak and the others?"

"Told 'em you were dead." Joe sighs.

"You were looking right at me!"

"Dying, I figured. Didn't think you'd make it and gu-gus were everywhere."

I've half a mind to take up the shovel and beat him with it. "Figured you'd save yourself and that was enough, right?"

"No one was saved," he whispers and I get what he means—we all left pieces in Balangiga.

I kneel and he turns to look at me. He sees the revolver; I haven't tried to hide it.

"I froze," he says. "The action on my Krag jammed and maybe I could've worked it loose, I don't know—"

"You even try?"

"I *panicked,* Shep. Arnold and Cliff ran up and started shooting but I was out of my mind. I know I screwed up—knew it even then."

"In Edgemont, I forgave and forgot and how'd you repay me? You lied again! Lied right to my face and now Julia's dead. You're a snake, Joe, and I hate snakes."

He rolls onto his side, trying to catch my eye. "I regret everything, Shep, honest to God."

"Shut up."

"Dobbins and Covington; you and Julia; all the others."

"Julia," my voice shakes, "didn't deserve what happened."

"You know I didn't pull the trigger, right?"

"Doesn't matter." Wanting to steady myself, I press my left hand against the earth. Breath hisses in-between my teeth. "That business at the Lucky Girl—that's all on you. All of it. Fifty times, a hundred, I told you to knock it off but goddamnit, you wouldn't listen."

Now I'm spun up again, right back where I started. I still have options—absolutely, I do—so why does it feel like I don't? Why does it feel like I'm the one with cuffs on my wrists? I stare at my revolver and consider throwing it into the pit. Jesus, I want to leave Delamar behind but I can't see how.

The sun is halfway behind the mountains. Another wind-gust screams across the lakebed, scouring our faces with sand; I clamp a hand over my hat and lean to keep from falling. A tumbleweed bounds between us and catches on the Welch's left front wheel.

"Gonna kill me?" Joe shouts.

I stand.

"What do you get?" he pleads. "Five-hundred? A thousand? Won't solve anything."

"We'll see."

I drop the gun, grab Joe's shoulders, and drag him toward the hole. He struggles but there's nothing he can do—one shove with my boot and down he goes. Eyes wild, he writhes and coughs, trying to roll onto his back. Bits of salt and mud pepper his face and chest.

"Shep, *please!*" he gasps. "Not like this!"

I pick up the Colt.

"Shep, *wait!* At least let me gather my thoughts."

I glance around the lakebed's edge for any sign of the other graves. They're here somewhere but the playa's surface is as flat and featureless as a marble slab.

"Shep, I'm begging you," he whispers. *"Please."*

I lower the revolver. My heart tries to pound its way through my ribs.

Glancing around the valley, I see nothing to suggest anyone's near. Hell, nothing lives out here. Nothing but salt flats, barren mountains, and for at least a little while longer, Joe McCuskey and me. Groom Lake is its own universe: a dead-end bound by the sky. No laws here except those I choose to obey, yet despite everything that's happened, I don't want Joe's death on my conscience. I don't. A little contrition is all I'm after. One honest apology and I'll take my chances and cut him loose. I want him to say he's sorry—to believe I can get beyond this. Beyond this miserable life.

The sun is sinking fast and shadows are racing toward us. High above, the clouds pinwheel as before, conjoining and pulling apart, bonding and breaking away. *The courses of the seasons, and of the sun and moon, are followed without any strife among them.* Where did I read that? China? Probably, but I can't remember what it means. I think I'm going crazy.

Lying at the bottom of the pit, Joe mutters to himself. When I step up to the edge, he goes quiet and turns to look at me. So dark in the pit I can barely see him: just his bloodstained shirt and the whites of his one good eye.

"Say you're sorry and we'll talk. Tell me how sorry you are."

"'Sorry?'"

"Say it." I kick a lump of salt into the pit. "Last chance."

He laughs—phlegmy sounds like a fish gasping for air.

"Hell, sure." He turns his head and spits. "Fine idea, because I really *am* sorry; sorry I'm so careless. So goddamn weak. Could've put an end to this years ago, see? Twice in Edgemont I had you in my sights; thought about putting you out of your misery. Hell, even once in Cripple Creek, but I didn't…I didn't. Ain't that something? Pathetic."

"Shut up. For once in your life, just shut your mouth."

The sun disappears behind the mountains.

"Pard, there's no point now. See, I *knew* Julia was there. I *watched* her go inside. Wasn't part of the plan but I didn't really care, neither. Heard she was in that hospital for what, three, four hours before she bled out—did I get that right? Shame, too, such a pretty thing she was."

He's grinning at me now. Leering.

I raise the Colt and empty it—six shots in rapid succession. The report echoes off the rocks, rolling away across the salt flats. Two crows in a Joshua tree startle and take flight. Flapping and croaking, they skim the lakebed's surface before rising the gathering wind. Before long they disappear, swallowed by an endless desert and the deepening gloom.

Once again, I'm on my own.

SIX

"Jesus, kid, you look like hell."

Odd salutation but since this is my employer speaking, I say that I'm fine, thanks.

From behind an enormous oak desk, Jack Lipford—Prince Jack when he's out of earshot—gestures toward a heavy, high-backed leather chair. I sit. The receptionist brings in two cups of coffee, sets them on the desk, and leaves. In the mirror behind him, gilt letters painted on the door behind me reverse again to read "Jackson M. Lipford, President, Eastern Nevada Mine Owners' Association" and in smaller print below, "Delamar-Highland Consolidated Gold Mining & Milling Co."

Lipford sets a fountain pen on a green blotter pad and glances out the window. "Heard you were ambushed outside the Greenback. Three men, four?"

"Two picketers blocking a door."

"That how you got cut?" He waves at his head like he's trying to cool off.

I'd forgotten the stitches above my right ear, or, to be honest, I've done a bang-up job drinking them into the background. I run my fingers along a short pucker in my scalp: still crusted with dried blood, it parallels two older, longer scars.

"Told 'em to clear out and one hit me with a scrap of wood. Serbs don't grow up playing baseball, though, so none of 'em swings worth a damn."

"One does."

I shake my head slowly. "Stick broke and too bad for him."

Lipford raises an eyebrow. "Anything else I should know?" He takes a sip of coffee and frowns at the cup.

"Might've broken one fellow's arm. Charlie Witherill helped me bundle both of 'em onto the 1:10 to Los Angeles; cuffed both to a radiator. Railroad bull said they'd sit as far as Kelso before they were released."

"Their names will go in the black book." He checks his watch. "And I'm glad you weren't seriously hurt," he hastens to add.

"Thanks."

"Glad, because there's something we need to discuss."

That can't be good.

"But…hold that thought," he says, leaning toward the door. "Dolores," he bellows, "bring me the sugar and shut the door as you leave."

Dolores—the wife of one of Lipford's mine managers, I believe, and plain as pancakes—carries in a delicate bone china sugar bowl. She sets it on the edge of the boss's desk and backs toward the door. She glances at me as she edges past but her expression says nothing. Come to think of it, I don't recall her ever saying more to me than, 'Mr. Lipford will see you now.'

"You *know* I don't take coffee without sugar," Lipford scolds, but Dolores retreats and closes the door without saying a word.

Good for Dolores.

Pulling a bottle of rye from his desk, the boss fills two glasses (plus another splash in his coffee—this, in addition to the sugar). He hands me one and we drain them.

"Hell, that's better," he continues. "Listen, kid, I told you I'm going to make changes…" His voice tapers off. He moves an inkwell and blotter around on his desk. Lines up a stack of papers just so. "Everything's changing, see?"

Things *have* changed, but damned if I know why. Lately, some chill has settled over our relationship, yet from my vantage, I've done everything he's asked of me and more.

He clears his throat. "Your role here, it's time—"

Someone knocks at the door. Robert Freese, one of several ambitious ass-kissers Lipford keeps on a short leash, leans inside.

"Goddamnit, Bob, *what?*"

"You wanted that letter to Wynn Scott posted this morning. Only six minutes until Archie leaves for the post office."

Irritated, Lipford still waves him in. "You don't mind, do you, Shep?"

I tell him I don't so while Lipford dictates, Freese takes up pen and paper and writes, "Dear Mr. Scott, your letter regarding the Silver Lake claims was an unpleasant surprise. I am unwilling to add to this letter any provision in the way of option. I do not make bargains one-sided and will not do so here. I do not bind myself when the other side does not bind himself. When he is ready to take the property firm—'Bob, underline that'—and put up a payment on account, if within a reasonable time, and if satisfactory to me—'Underline that, too'—I would sign a contract and allow the proper time for examining the title, &c., &c."

Looking over the rim of my cup, I study Prince Jack's face as he speaks: full lips, a pugilist's nose, and heavily lidded brown eyes. He isn't tall but he's broad-shouldered; an all-conference wrestler back East, I've heard. It occurs to me that although I've worked with him nearly every day for the past two years, I can't say I know him much better than the day we met.

Lipford turns to stare out the window. Heavy snowflakes spatter the glass. He takes a sip of coffee and continues, "I think it worthwhile to say that the property might be disposed of in one of two ways, i.e., a deed executed by the Big South Mining Co. under its seal or by transfer of company stock. I mention this because a purchaser might prefer to have a good organization already in place. Big South is incorporated under the Laws of the State of Wyoming. Stock is full paid and no debt. Capital five-hundred thousand shares of $2.00 each; 200,000 of these are in trust, readily available, and might be used to represent other property which might be purchased and turned in—'add *by conveyance* in parentheses'—to the company. If you will forego the idea of a one-sided deal, then perhaps we can do business. Very Truly Yours, and we're done."

Lipford signs his name and hands the letter back to Freese. As the young clerk exits, Lipford turns back to me.

"Like I was saying, I appreciate everything you've done here. Losses are down and that's due in no small way to your…talents."

"Thanks," I say, although I don't feel especially thankful.

"Drinking's under control?"

I say that it is.

He studies me a moment longer, glancing between my eyes and my hand. Maybe he's looking to see whether the cup I'm holding shakes but while my head aches and my feet are cold, my hands are rock-solid: no tell there.

He glances at a wall clock and frowns. "Shoot, I have an important meeting in a few minutes and you'll just have to excuse me. We'll wrap this up over lunch, okay? Ninety minutes, any place you want."

"North Star's fine."

"The North Star," he scoffs, "should be condemned. Gee, how about the Comstock? Ever been?"

I say I have, although I haven't.

"Best spread in town, right?"

"Right."

Damn it, snow's falling again and the Comstock Social Club is a half-mile away.

"I'd give you a ride but this other thing…"

"Understood."

"Good. Great. See you at the Comstock in ninety, kid."

I *hate* that he calls me kid; he can't be more than four or five years my senior.

We stand and shake hands. Lipford exits through the front door while I fetch my coat and hat from the rack.

Lila Hannigan, the lovely young stenographer I've been seeing these past three months, isn't at her desk today—Dolores says she went home feeling poorly—so I take a seat on a leather sofa in the waiting area. Funny, Lila seemed fine last night. Then again, she did seem agitated hearing I was stopping by headquarters today. Been like that for weeks now that I think about it, but who knows? Routines go out the window when the weather's like this.

Seated in the reception area, I leaf through a copy of the *Mining and Scientific Press*. Good to keep up with industry trends but within minutes, my eyes glaze over and I can't stop yawning. Tired today. I've read the same sentence three times in a row. Need to take better care of myself.

Forty-five minutes later, Dolores rouses me from my nap. Still groggy, I head down to the street and start walking.

SEVEN

People like me—miners, tradesmen, and security—aren't welcome at the Comstock Social Club, yet without our work, it wouldn't even exist. In Cripple Creek, one thing that kept hostility between labor and capital in check—until the rupture of 1904, anyway—was that men from all classes belonged to the same lodges and fraternal organizations. Awkward, roughing up your lodge's Grand Pooh-Bah, yeah? But Delamar isn't like that: this camp is distinctly stratified and the Comstock is Exhibit A. Mine promoters and stockbrokers occupy the first floor; meeting rooms and a private restaurant, the second and third. Red granite façade; silver-leaf on the pressed-tin ceiling; patterned silk wallpaper; leather and satin-covered furniture, and its members are just as ostentatious. I despise the place but since this meeting is Lipford's call, there I go, trudging downhill through shin-deep snow.

Hell of a day for walking, too. At Malapai and Pinyon, a Studebaker fishtails around the corner and nearly clips me, and just past Bedbug Row, an ore wagon jumps a rut and splashes my trouser-fronts. By the time I've crossed town, I am cold, soaked, and my pocket flask is empty.

Stepping indoors, mud and slush spatter the floor. Frowning, a lord-mayor rises from behind his polished mahogany desk to take my shabby coat and hat. He holds these abominations at arm's length and directs me up a wide set of marble stairs to the dining room, where I'm told Lipford is waiting.

I pause on the landing to warm my hands over a pot-bellied stove and stare out the window. Below town, Cedar Wash snakes far out into Delamar Valley.

Beyond this are the Pahrocs: barren mountains where nothing grows and no one goes. Close on the right are the camp's crown jewels: the Highland Con's big five-story mill; the crater-like Hog Pen Shoot, where a block-caving system has punched through to the surface; and the Black Tiger Mine. Surrounding these are other, variously productive properties. This is the district's compact core. Old desert rats, who cling to quaint notions about mines producing pay-rock, say that anyone without claims on Ferguson Hill just isn't in it, whereas stock-jobbers and wildcatters genuinely do not care where their dirt's located—not so long as it's legal to foist shares upon suckers with more money than sense. Lately, this latter type dominates Nevada—in my opinion, anyway—but those who know better say they perform a vital service, ginning up interest in our camps, and therefore must be tolerated. Perhaps this is true. I'm no financier, certainly, and I'll admit there's much in this world beyond my understanding.

Atop the stairs, a second prig intercepts me and points toward a corner booth where I spy the back of Jack Lipford's head. For a long moment I stand at the prince's elbow, feeling like a fool, waiting for him to acknowledge me. "Mr. Lipford," I say and he gestures for me to take a seat, not bothering to look up from the note he's writing.

The view from here is even better: not just of Ferguson Hill, with its forest of headframes and snow- covered dumps, but beyond the Pahrocs to Mount Irish and the Black Belt's cinder-strewn ranges. If the weather was better, apt I could see Bald Mountain, more than 50 miles distant and almost halfway to Tonopah. As it is, pewter clouds race across the summit of Ferguson Hill and in less time than it takes Lipford to finish writing, the weather turns and the view disappears. Snowflakes pelt the glass.

"How about this weather?" he says, startling me.

"Sorry, what?"

"A full-blue blizzard this early in the season. Roads closed, freighters stranded at Stine. Ore bins are full yet I can't ship more than a few tons per day."

I notice a smear of lipstick on his collar—that and his hair's plastered to his forehead. Important meeting, my ass. I'd say something except maybe these things will forewarn the next woman who gets too close.

"Once the short line's in place," he continues, "shipping costs will plunge. "Never again will I pay full-freight for a half-empty wagon. Competition's the ticket, right?"

"That's right." '*Competition*,' says a man who does everything he can to kill it.

He coughs into his hand. "If only the governor would quit stalling and approve my goddamn charter…" Takes a sip of whiskey. "Ah, enough of that. How's business, Shep?"

"Busy."

"So I hear."

I lay a one-page report on the table and he leans forward so only he can read it.

∽

Eastern Nevada Mine Owners' Association
Delamar, Nevada

Surveillance Form A – Team: 1

NON-FILE DOCUMENT

Date: November 17, 1907

Importance: HIGH – BLACK BOOK. **PRESIDENT ONLY**

Objective: Apprehend, interrogate, remand to custody outside district.   Armed, probable.

Target: McCuskey, Joseph J., aka Murray, Joe; John Murphy; J.J. Murphy, et al.

Target Affiliations (if known):   IWW. WFM HQ: Denver, Colo.; Various districts, Nev., Mont., Idaho, Utah

Location: Various, Western Rest Home

Duration: 24 hours

Target photo available? File

Is Target otherwise known to Operative(s)? Yes

Surveillance Team: 1. 1-72
                       2. 1-32
                       3. 1-17
                       4. 2-60, et al.

Concealed Location(s) Available to Operative(s)?   N/A

Target Activities or Observation(s)   Team Two apprehended target in Caliente; 1 & 2 interrog.; 1-72 final transport & relocation

SUMMARY: All objectives met

<u>Record Expenses &</u>
<u>Attach Receipts</u>   <u>Gasoline, provisions – submitted separately</u>
(NOTE: Expenses w/o receipts will <u>NOT</u> be reimbursed)

~~Report and One (1) Copy are REQUIRED Within Twenty-Four~~
~~(24) Hours of Cessation.~~

NON-FILE DOCUMENT—DESTROY

❧

Prince Jack glances warily around the room, folds the paper, and tucks it into the same pocket. "It's done?"

"Yes."

Won't tell him I seriously considered letting McCuskey go, and I really don't like that he kept my report. He should've torn it into pieces and dropped them into a cup of coffee or something. My name isn't on it but in my line of work, anything on paper is a liability.

"I don't want to look up agents' numbers; just tell me who was there."

"From One, Charlie Witherill, Jerry Rosen, Stu Fisher, Bob Thompson, the Reed twins, and me. From Two, it was Curt and Roy Garland. Scott Sweeney provided backup over in Caliente, too."

Lipford frowns. "Why was Garland there? Son of a bitch can't keep his mouth shut."

"I agree; you'll want to ask Curt."

At Lipford's direction, a moat of empty tables separates our booth from the rest of the dining room. From beyond this perimeter, the camp's bankers, brokers, and strivers all strain to hear what Prince Jack wants with a coyote like me but for the weather against the windows, nothing reaches their ears.

"I'll speak with him," Lipford says. He reaches inside his coat. "Here, this is for you, kid. Curt tells me you did the hard work."

Why? Why is Curt talking about my projects?

The boss takes a fat envelope from his vest pocket and slides it across the table. I take the packet and discretely transfer it to a pocket inside my coat, pleasantly surprised by its heft. Curt's meddling is temporarily forgotten.

"Some extra, too," he says. "We'll cover what-for in a minute."

"Thank you, Mr. Lipford."

"Did McCuskey give you any names…" he says before coughing so hard he can't finish his sentence. Wet and percussive, too; he can't catch his breath between jags.

"You okay, Mr. Lipford?" Jesus, don't tell me he's been dusted?

"I'm fine," he snarls but he can't stop coughing.

To my astonishment, this fit continues for at least twenty seconds. Sure, the miners and chute pullers here all succumb—millhands and teamsters, too—but who ever heard of an owner with silicosis? More than any other camp in Nevada, Delamar is feared for its dust, see? Day and night, sharp quartzite particles fill the air—powdered glass, essentially, and all because there isn't enough water here to wet-process the ore from its mines. Instead, dry Griffin mills pulverize rocks to release the gold inside and spew choking clouds of dust as a byproduct. Summers are the worst. Grit covers every surface—even food— and laundry never comes clean, yet this is *nothing* compared to the human toll. Annual turnover in the district's mines is about eighty percent as hundreds of broken men limp back to Pueblo, Spokane, or St. George to die slow, painful deaths. Even so, until the wage cuts this autumn, for the past five years, High-Con has paid $4.25 per day, no questions asked, so no job goes unfilled for long.

I wait until his fit subsides and try again. "I doubt the WFM had anything to do with Pete Kastning's murder. Pete had money troubles—"

"Of *course* the Federation's involved," Lipford wheezes but I continue.

"—everywhere he went. One fellow McCuskey named is still in the district but I have an idea where he's hiding. Expect we'll have him in custody by nightfall. Another one left town last week, whereabouts unknown, and the third is already in jail in Pioche."

"So, was McCuskey here for me?"

"Don't know; we snared him before he received orders."

"Andy Maguire send for him?"

"Again, I don't know. Joe said his orders came by telegram, but only Curt and Roy have seen it."

"And what about this Boudreaux fellow Curt keeps mentioning?"

"Complete mystery. Not even sure he exists."

Lipford nods but says nothing.

I glance around to make sure no one's listening. "Mr. Lipford, this thing with McCuskey is *huge*. The Pinkertons, Thiels, and state police everywhere have been after him for years. We don't keep this quiet, it could blow everything to bits."

"I know." He stares at me like he's getting ready to say something except just then a waiter arrives in full penguin: white shirt and bowtie; black jacket, vest, and pants; and a long, white waist apron.

"Good afternoon, Mr. Lipford," he says. "Drinks, only, or will you be dining with us today?"

"We'll see." Lipford wipes his mouth with a linen handkerchief. "Anything good today?"

The waiter gestures toward a piece of green slate by the door. Propped up on a brass easel, the flat light coming through the venetian blinds makes it impossible to read.

"We have beefsteaks, chops, chicken à la king, sweetbreads in a sherry-cream sauce, grilled fresh Lahontan trout, prime rib, and oysters Rockefeller. Entrees come with a Bibb lettuce salad, mashed potatoes with gravy, green peas, and bread with sage-butter. For dessert, we have apple and mince pies and ice creams. I can take your orders or return in a moment if you'd prefer."

"What do you recommend?"

"Sir, the trout is fresh and superbly prepared."

"Nah," Lipford says, "the rib. Big cut, very rare, and tell the chef I mean that: sear it and plate it. And I'll make it worth your while if you can rustle up some asparagus; I'm sick of potatoes."

"Sir, I'll see what I can do."

"And apple pie à la mode for dessert."

"To drink? We have teas, lemonade—"

"Christ, man, do you see my wife here? Champagne to celebrate and whiskey for business. Shepard, what'll you have?"

"The trout and black coffee."

Lipford looks at me like I just set something rotten on the table between us. "Why?"

"Why, what?"

"Get what you want."

"I did."

"Sir, the trout *is* exeptional," says the waiter but Lipford waves him off.

"Don't feign modesty, kid. Big steak? Two-dozen oysters? Both? Get what you *want*."

"The fish and coffee." I nod at the waiter who looks to Lipford for confirmation before departing toward the kitchen. Not wanting to sound ungrateful,

I force a smile. "Long shift later and rich food and drink make me drowsy. I appreciate the gesture, Mr. Lipford, but I can't."

Lipford nods. "This is a 'thank-you' for everything you've done but I understand. You have your passions under control—good for you."

Despite these words, the boss-man's expression suggests that he does *not* understand why someone in my shoes would turn down favors. By refusing to wallow alongside him, I've raised another red flag. Back at my wickiup, there's nothing but canned beans and stale bread—the poorest bachelor's fare imaginable—and the thought of steak and oysters makes my stomach growl, but I won't let him pull me in. I won't. Work is work and I've taken sides but I'm not like him. Never have been, never will be.

Lipford shakes his head. "Most fellows here are looking for their next handout."

My nod fails to placate him.

"Ingrates. Kid, you ever work a bonanza-camp before?"

"Edgemont and Cripple Creek. Fairview and Manhattan were booming, too."

"So you know what I mean?"

"Sure. Yes."

Our salads arrive. Lipford drowns his in dressing.

"And it's bad here, right?" he persists.

I shrug. "In some ways."

All across the West, the labor situation has been unsettled for decades: the Coeur d'Alenes, Butte, Telluride, and Cripple Creek—pretty much anywhere you look. Rank exploitation; strikes and picket lines; riots and assassinations, too. This year, it's Goldfield's turn, and now maybe Delamar's, as well.

"How could it possibly be worse?" Lipford shakes his head. "Highest wages in the state and I'm repaid with highgrading and sabotage."

Another waiter arrives with a bottle of Champagne and makes an annoying show of filling our glasses.

"Goddamn *socialists,*" Lipford spits. He gulps his Champagne, pours himself a second, and drains it faster than the first. "Won't stop highgrading—*stealing*—yet every day they come to me with new demands."

I nod, wondering where this is going.

He turns to stare out the window but clouds have descended and there's nothing to see. "Since 1905, do you know how much they've stolen from me? Archie ran the numbers and it's $640,000 and change—do you know what I could've done with that money? How much *more* I might've accomplished? These bastards—what did *they* spend it on? Booze and whores?"

Food and rent, I figure.

"The audacity!" he rages. "After all I've done for this camp, not one in a hundred knows his place!"

The headwaiter delivers my coffee and I use the cup to push my glass of Champagne toward the center of the table.

Still steaming, Lipford stares at the bite on his fork. "I *hate* these people, Shep. Hate 'em all. Every time I think about the situation here, it's all I can do not to open a window and shoot the first man I see."

Is he serious? Warm despite the weather, French Champagne, salads on fine English china; situation looks mighty fine to me. Still, every man cherishes his delusions and there's no profit in pointing them out.

"I hear that the WFM—" I say but he cuts me short.

"I'm done negotiating," he snarls, pounding the table so the knives and forks bounce. "They can all go to hell!"

"—is searching everywhere for McCuskey. We need to be thoughtful about our reaction."

"Yeah, 'thoughtful.'" The boss stabs a bit of cucumber but as he's lifting it to his mouth, he pauses and shoots me a funny look. "Are we square, you and me?"

"Sorry, what?" I've been sucker-punched before, sure, but none have surprised me as much as this one.

He rests his fork and the impaled cucumber on the edge of his plate. "Don't know, kid. I get the sense your heart isn't in the game anymore."

"What do you mean? Of course I'm invested."

Seems this fails to reassure him because that pinched look stays on his face. "Heard rumors we aren't on the same page, you and me."

He stares at me and I stare back, but damned if I can tell what he wants so I turn up my palms and raise my eyebrows.

"Mr. Lipford, my loyalty to you, to the Association…Not once…" I don't even know how to finish. Who started this? Big Curt? Jerry Rosen?

He stares for a moment before shaking his head. "Ah, forget it. Forget I said anything. So much chatter these days. Not so long ago, I could sort through all the bullshit but now it comes so fast I can hardly keep up. You've been a good soldier, Shep. My father certainly thought the world of you so I hope you won't take anything I say personally."

I say I understand though it sounds like something personal is right around the corner.

He takes up his fork and finishes his bite. "My father was a pioneer. No handouts back then, no unions, no workingmen's committees. Man started with nothing—*nothing*. Took risks, fought like hell, and turned High-Con into a monster." He downs a shot of whiskey. "More than once, he held off bankers and outsiders who tried to take it from him, which means this company and this town are his legacy, understand?" Then he pitches his voice so low I can barely hear what he's saying, "I won't let these animals take it from me. I *won't*. Peace and prosperity is all I want but these socialists, these *anarchists,* they hate those things. Hate success and they hate ambition, too, so now there's no other way. We've crossed the Rubicon and now there's no turning back."

Again, I don't think anything about Delamar is exceptional but its confirmation he wants, not counsel, so I nod.

"Try to tell me how to run *my* business," he seethes. "The wage cuts last month aren't popular—I *understand*—but what choice do I have? Markets haven't recovered from the panic and Ferguson's geology is no fault of mine. WFM won't look beyond its own interests, though; won't acknowledge my investors' demands. Doesn't understand the *game,* right?"

"Right."

"The Wobblies, the Bolsheviks, they're spoiling for a brawl, so I'm gonna give 'em one."

Now I get it: he wants 'em wound up so he can drop the hammer. I've seen this play before: in Cripple Creek, a military commander bankrolled by mine owners arrested the local judges so he could ignore their writs. A rented mob threatened to hang an impartial sheriff unless he resigned. Yeah, I've seen mine owners and their statehouse cronies go toe-to-toe with the WFM, so I get what he's after. That fire's been smoldering almost from the day this camp was founded. Only thing now is to add a little gasoline: hire provocateurs to infiltrate the union, deputize a few dozen lowlifes who don't mind mixing it up. Easiest thing in the world; I could steer that ship in my sleep.

I take a sip of coffee—the good stuff I don't get at home—and lock eyes with the boss. "So, you need a pretext? Something so urgent that Honest John has no choice but to call for federal troops?"

Workingmen form Governor Sparks' base so convincing him to act against them would be a tall order. Then again, this is an era of shameless self-dealing and it rarely takes long to dig up something shady. Last summer, the governor's adversaries made ugly noises about kickback schemes involving railroads and water developers in the Quinn River Valley. Now those same people—Lipford and U.S. Senator John Christy among 'em—have bankrolled a special election in March to decide whether Sparks should be recalled. If the governor can be prodded to intervene in Delamar's labor dispute, his base might object but at least the state's powerful business bloc would abandon that embarrassing recall. A Silver-Democrat who strays into Populist territory, Sparks rarely works with Lipford and Christy on *anything* so it seems they found a chink in his armor. They usually do.

"I knew you'd get it." Lipford downs another shot of whiskey and forces a smile. "Knew it. Damn, I hate to sideline such a valuable asset but here we are."

Here comes my scolding: I can see it in the way he's looking at me. "Something the matter, Mr. Lipford?"

He nods. "Yeah, Shep, there is."

I stare at him over the rim of my cup.

"Before we address that, look inside that envelope I gave you. No one's watching, kid. Open it."

I take the envelope from my coat pocket and lift the flap. Crackers, there's at least eighteen, nineteen hundred dollars inside. That's more than my entire annual salary—a good bit more.

"Mr. Lipford—" I start but he cuts me off.

"Twenty-two hundred and fifty: a bonus for all you've done here plus some extra to cushion your move."

I stuff the envelope back inside my coat. "'Move?'"

"I'm reassigning you away from Delamar. You've been here over a year now; people are starting to recognize you and I think you're distracted, too. This plan I have for smashing the union, I want someone who can give it their full attention."

Distracted? Full attention?

"Mr. Lipford, have I done something wrong?"

"Nothing. I appreciate all your help."

I furrow my brow. "Do I have a say?"

"Not this time, kid."

"My books are clean."

"I know."

I glance out the window. Snow's falling harder now. "How long do I have?"

"Weather permitting, I'll leave Saturday for meetings in Ely and return a week from then. I'll send word about your new assignment and I'd appreciate it if you took advantage of that time before I return."

I stare into my coffee cup: no answers there.

"I'm not firing you, Shep. This is just…temporary. I have interests in Rhyolite, Lida, and Blair. And you'll still be salaried. Nothing changes except for the scenery."

"Who'll run this union thing? Jerry Rosen? Bob Freese?"

Lipford takes his time chewing. "Curt Broe, and if he stumbles—"

"Of course he will."

"—you'll be the first to know."

"Curt, though?" I say. "You're making a huge mistake."

"I disagree."

I can't believe this. Big Curt is demonstrably stupid, possibly the dumbest man I've ever met. More than once, Lipford has said so, himself, and now he wants to hand this dope a complicated, potentially dangerous campaign? Curt's a hatchet man, not a strategist.

To anyone who doesn't understand how Lipford operates, all this may sound like an amicable parting, but it isn't. He's basically given me two choices: take a payoff and leave, or stick around and suffer the consequences. Most people he finds inconvenient aren't given options so I ought to be smart about this and go.

Ought to be.

Won't make an ugly show here. Not yet.

"I'll wrap up my cases," I say, sounding too eager by half. Like I said, they always find a way to put their hooks in and once they do, there's no getting away.

"Good." He nods. "Don't think I don't appreciate your service, kid. I don't want any hostility between us—neither of us needs that."

The waiter delivers our entrees. Another makes a show of refilling the boss's Champagne. Our business concluded, Lipford steers the conversation toward harmless nonsense: his stable of racehorses, his autocars, and social stirrings on the coast: hogwash I normally take pains to avoid. This time, I feign interest and nod along, savoring every mouthful of what turns out to be the best meal I will enjoy for a long, long time.

ᕀ

Walking to Lila's, the streets are nearly deserted. It's only 2:30 in the afternoon but the sky is so dark that everyone's gone inside and turned on lights. Snow's falling hard now, stinging my face as the storm's full weight descends.

Taking shelter inside a doorway at the corner of Ruby and Main, something inside me twists itself into a knot, a cancer with only one possible cure. Hell no, I won't leave Delamar; not until I figure out what's going on. Maybe not even then. Better men than Jack Lipford have trained their sights on me; I'll be damned if he's the one who takes me down.

Ain't that something? American workers are like hammers and hay—assets to be catalogued, used up, and then discarded according to the numbers in a rich man's ledger. My thoughts are as violent as the weather. Son of a bitch, I've bled for this company. Done things for which I'll never be forgiven, and this is the thanks I get? Ungrateful bastard. Wedge a stick of dynamite in the tailpipe of his Garford. See what he thinks of my service on his way through the windscreen.

∾

For a week, everything goes unnaturally quiet. No follow-up from Prince Jack, gone to Ely along with Bob Freese; the Association's accountant, Archie Owen; Lila Hannigan to transcribe and notarize everything; and for security, Bob Thompson. No one tells me to pack my bags or who to see in Rhyolite. Payroll has a check waiting for me. Stranger still, it appears no one's told Big Curt he's been promoted, but why?

For one last week, I go about my business. My eyes are wide-open and my head's on a swivel but the days unspool as they have for the past eighteen months. Pretty much, anyway. With Lila away, I revisit several of my old haunts. Put in a shift at Dennehy's: a ratty ten-seater down by the freight yards. One long evening at the Palladium, too, drinking and snoozing my way through an embarrassing coon show, two musical acts, and a psychic medium. One afternoon, I blow twelve bonus-dollars at the Midland: no small feat when every drink in the joint goes for two bits. Took all the next day to sleep that one off.

EIGHT

On a sidewalk outside the White House Hotel, I run into picketers from the United Association of Hotel and Restaurant Employees No. 21 carrying signs enumerating their union's grievances with management. With their collars turned up, none of these dispirited shades confront me as I pass. Even as revelers spill through the casino's doors, laughing too loudly and jostling the strikers, nothing happens. Swallowed by darkness, the drunks' forced hilarity quickly fades and the strikers resume their weary circuit.

I hustle northeast on Rhyolite Avenue toward Mazuma, a hard-luck neighborhood named after the road that slices it in two. No lofty aspirations here. No fine homes, no picket fences; only malthoid shacks, tin-sided squares, and dead Chinese elm trees. Hookshops, pawnbrokers, and penny-beer saloons line the side-streets. Squatters camp on its fringes. At the head of Mazuma, the Baltic Mine rears up like a battleship and only a complex system of cribs and trestles keep its dumps from spilling into the right-of-way.

A man walking the other direction starts coughing and can't stop: silicosis, clearly. Poor bastard. Stooped and miserable, he looks about sixty years old, although he's probably no more than thirty-five or forty. Folks don't call Delamar the Widowmaker for nothing.

Cold tonight but I need a walk. Need to clear my head because I can't get over being fired. Where's the setup? It wasn't over money. Unlike several of my counterparts, he knows I never stole a dime from the Association and hell, bookkeepers in the office all say High-Con is ready to declare another 5-cent dividend. Can't be my work, either. Only five days ago, Charlie and I busted *another* sham assay for processing stolen highgrade and three weeks before that, we uncovered two millhands' clever scheme to skim highgrade from bins inside the mill. Yet even before our meeting last week, Lipford was taking pains to avoid me. Told a buddy the next town over that the atmosphere at headquarters had gone sour but even so, I never thought I'd be one-upped by goddamned Curt Broe.

Keep your eyes open, Sunday. There's a bullseye on your back.

I continue toward the Colorado Belle Saloon, a smallish jink compared to the palaces downtown, but its booze is cheaper and its tables fair. Walk into a place like the White House, jack, and in no time flat, your two-hundred-dollar stake becomes a three-hundred-dollar marker. Happened to me once and it'll never happen again. I hate the anxiety debt creates so I try—*try*—to keep my books clean. Don't get me wrong: I've wasted plenty at the Belle, too, but at least there I get something in return.

Elbowing my way toward the bar, I wait for Helen Molloy to come around. She owns the place and most nights, you'll find her rustling drinks, sweeping up sawdust, and doing every other job necessary to keep a roomful of thirsty brutes happy. I think she's dazzling: dark hair, fine figure, and best of all, a rootless drunk like me. Earlier this year, we courted some but it didn't take. Wasn't because we didn't like each other; bad luck and bad timing is all. Around here, even good things fall apart.

Coastal folk are often surprised to see a woman running a joint like the Belle, but Nevada and much of the interior West are pretty wide open. Not Utah so much, but out here I've seen women running freight, prospecting remote areas, and that quack doctor, Frances Williams, never stops talking about how she was among the first dozen people on the ground in Goldfield. In Helen's case, not only does this camp accept her as a fair proprietor but we're also sympathetic as to how she washed up here in the first place. A few years back, her father made a small strike at Battle Mountain, cashed out, and came here to open the Belle. Wouldn't you know, the poor bastard suffered a heart attack and died on his second night behind the bar. A week later, his youngest daughter arrived from Trinidad, Colorado, to bury her father and re-open his saloon. Dear Helen, welcome to Delamar: our water's dry and the sun is cold.

Catching sight of me, she does a double-take before setting up a shot of whiskey. "Why are you here?"

Tossing back the drink, I enjoy the burn. "Want me to leave?"

"Yes. Maybe."

"Understood." I set a coin on the bar"

"No, wait." She wraps a bar towel around her fist and looks past me, toward the door. "You can't just…" She sighs and glances at the ceiling. "Shep, why do you keep doing this?"

"Doing what?"

"What do you want from me?"

"A drink." I ignore the nasty looks around me.

"You can drink anywhere; you often do."

I hook my boot under the brass rail to steady myself. "Prefer your place."

"When it suits you, you mean."

"Always come back, don't I?"

"Shouldn't let you." She turns to throw my coin into a tin pail on the back bar.

The patron on my left starts coughing, leaning with both hands against the counter. Everyone moves away from him, reacting as if he's contagious. Of course we all know he isn't; he's merely paying the price for a couple years' respectable wages.

"Helen—" I say but she cuts me off.

"It's getting worse out there."

I feign ignorance. "The weather?"

"The Association," she whispers. "I *hate* how you earn your money." She narrows her green eyes and leans across the bar until our foreheads are almost touching. "How many have you run out of camp this week?"

"Don't know what you mean."

"What, too many to count?"

The fellow on my left can't stop coughing so his friends help him toward the door.

"People are starving," she hisses, "families are *starving!* Lipford's class has millions stashed in Newport and San Francisco but what about these people? Where can they go?"

"Christ, is this Union Hall? Did I take a wrong turn?"

"You sure did," she says but her eyes soften. "Want another?"

I tap the glass. "And one after that. Look, the kid-glove crew can't mine anything themselves. Association brings in fresh blood every month—"

"Scabs," Helen growls, keeping her voice low.

"—which means these groundhogs never realize how much water's in your whiskey."

Helen shakes her head. "God knows why I put up with you."

"Because I never do you wrong."

"Do you hear yourself?" she scoffs. "Still playing house with the flimsy blond, aren't you?"

"I don't know." I glance around the bar. "Can't tell if she's serious."

"Well, no sympathy here."

"Helen," says the drunk beside me, "this fellow bothering you?"

"Mind your business, jack." I don't even bother looking at him.

Helen motions for me not to overreact. "No, Rick, he isn't."

"Helen, honey," the drunk continues, elbowing his drowsy companion, "you say 'yes', I'll marry you tonight. Bascom here was a minister back in Ohio; only take a minute."

"Shucks, Rick—," she forces a grim smile; "—not tonight." Pouring a beer for someone farther down the bar, she shoots me a look. "You're playing house and see what I get?"

Before I can speak, she steps away to look after someone else. Damn. I guess we missed our shot, her and me, but like gamblers who can't leave a bad table, whenever either of us feels low, we fall back on old habits. Isn't healthy, isn't fair, but neither of us can be bothered to change.

I watch her work the counter, white shirt-sleeves rolled up to her elbows. God, she's lovely. Savvy, too. I hear she's made several shrewd plays down at the exchange. Wish things had worked out between us; everything about her is right. Almost everything. Her temper's as fickle as the weather, but so what? I'm no one to point fingers.

I finish my drink and wince. Leaning against the counter, I try to follow scattered reflections in my empty glass. Hundreds of thoughts keep me awake at night: avenues closed by time and circumstance; how decisions I made have stranded me here; and how there's nowhere to go where I won't find trouble. Helen does what she can but lately I've been falling too fast to take her hand. And why would I? Only pull her down, too.

Prince Jack. Curt Broe. Roy Garland. Lila Hannigan. Why do I protect this wretched place? These wretched people? Tired of these thoughts, for the next several minutes I stand there, letting the noise wash over me. Feels good to be ignored in a noisy bar, you know?

A few minutes later, Helen returns. "I'm going home at one."

"I'm on until two."

"I'll wait up; key's in its usual place. Anything else from the bar?"

"A beer while I wait."

"Wait for what?"

"Warren Jim."

Helen glances nervously toward the entrance. "He can't drink in here, you know."

"Yeah, but tell me why? Handles his liquor better than I do." I gesture toward the drunks beside me. "Better than Rick and the Reverend Bascom here."

"Take it to the county commission, Shep; I don't write the laws and I don't need trouble." She steps away.

I take a long drink and stare at the floor. Never understood why people have it out for the Indians. Base prejudice, I guess. Warren's Northern Paiute, solid as a church, and someone I trust over Big Curt or Roy Garland, among others. A few years back when I tried prospecting, I'd bump into Washos and Shoshone all over the hills and never had a problem. Just the opposite, in fact. Still, these people are barred from all but the most basic interactions in camp and apart from Warren, few linger within town limits. Instead, you'll see them walking along roads, driving mules loaded with firewood down from the hills, or dropping off bags of charcoal in a mine yard before quickly slipping back into the desert, as quiet as shadows at noon.

Lost in thought, I'm startled to find a man standing beside me, gesturing toward the door. "Your name Sundown?"

"Close enough."

"Some Injun outside is asking for you."

I leave twice what I owe, nod to Helen, and turn toward the exit.

Pig-eyed and wobbly, the stranger persists, "Mister, maybe no one's told you but Chinamen and Injuns ain't welcome in Delamar."

I turn to face him and he takes a step backward.

"Say that again?"

Chairs scrape the floor and conversation stills.

From behind the bar, Helen shouts, "No fighting in here! Outside! Take it *outside!*"

Fuck you ignorant pricks; I'll take on every one of you right here.

Even though no one moves, I feel them close ranks around me, the same way those of us in the army might've stuck up for some slobbering-drunk infantryman the locals had cornered in a waterfront bar. Never mind that back at barracks we might've hated him, too. No matter what, he was one of ours and damned if anyone else was gonna rough him up.

Despite this buildup, nothing happens. Stumbling, eyes glazed, the drunk raises his hands in surrender.

"Shucks, gov'nor, no trouble," he says. "Forget I said anything."

Seeing their comrade is in no shape to uphold his end of the bargain, the others spit on the floor and return to their cards. No one will look me in the eye as I leave to go find Warren.

◌◌

Around four a.m., scourged by the wind, I make my way from Helen's apartment back to the boardinghouse. Tumbleweeds and trash race down the streets. Now my eyes hurt and I just want to sleep but Helen isn't the only habit I can't shake; I'm fastidious about paperwork, too. Yeah, technically, I've been sacked but I *did* tell Lipford the transition would be smooth and since I don't know what else to do, I guess I'll keep working.

◌◌

Eastern Nevada Mine Owners' Association
Delamar, Nevada

Surveillance Form A - Team: One

Date: November 27, 1907

Importance: LOW - ROUTINE ACTION

Objective: Mail intercept: parcel from WFM HQ Denver
to A. McGuire, WFM Local Delamar Pres.

Target: Postal Box 77

Target Affiliations (if known): N/A

Location: Delamar, Lincoln County, Nevada

Duration: 1:20 a.m. - 1:30 a.m.

Target photo available? N/A

Is Target otherwise known to Operative(s)? N/A

Surveillance Team: 1. 1-72
2. 1-32
3.
4.

Concealed Location(s) Available to Operative(s)? N/A

Target Activities or Parcel obtained from mailboxes
Observation(s) at Mitchell's Supply Co.

SUMMARY: Correspondence (3)- will assess and report;
Bank Drafts (2)- $50 and $225 (attached).

Record Expenses &
Attach Receipts None
(NOTE: Expenses w/o receipts will NOT be reimbursed)

**Report and One (1) Copy are REQUIRED Within Twenty-Four
(24) Hours of Cessation.**

Locking the door, I prop a chair under the doorknob, set a small locksmith's kit on the bedside table, and tuck the Colt beneath my pillow. Don't think there's much to worry about this morning but I see the value in precaution.

My head aches. Hands smell like Helen's body. I take a long pull on a bottle and kick off my boots. Light from the White House pours through my window and I have to wrap a towel around my head so I can sleep. Soon as I'm out, though, I'm back in the jungle on Samar. Crashing through underbrush, chased by shadows within shadows. Slashing vines and leaves with their bolos, they're shouting, shouting as they close in around me. Like I said, it wasn't a fair fight.

NINE

Five days since Prince Jack and his entourage left for Ely and still nothing about my reassignment. Don't think it's too soon to worry.

"Read the Lode this morning?" Charlie Witherill says, dispersing steam above a coffee cup held to his lip.

Charlie and I meet every Tuesday at a tiny breakfast counter shoehorned between the Great West Bank & Trust and a men's clothing store. I tell him I've done nothing this morning other than dress and march my sorry, slightly-hungover carcass downtown.

He lets out a grim little laugh. "Western Federation's liable to burn Boyd Layton's press if he don't lighten up."

"You and I might get the assignment if he does."

Charlie and I have known each other for years. He was a reservist, called up to fight in Cuba, but we didn't meet until after the war in Colorado. He's shorter than I am but far better looking and he has that certain charm; most women simply adore him.

He pushes the paper my way and taps his finger on a front-page editorial. "Read."

I skim the headline and shake my head. "So what?"

"Last paragraph."

Let there be no question where this paper—indeed, where every right-minded member of this community—stands. No fair-minded man can mis-take good for evil in this struggle between the district's commercial pillars and the socialist mob howling at its gates. Who can fail to hear their cries for class war, revolution, and murder? For the sake of our families, our property, and our churches, we cannot concede even one inch to these dynamiters. And yet, it is not too much to insist that the brave souls manning the ramparts hold themselves to a higher standard of conduct than our adversaries, whether in commerce, politics, or their personal affairs. Those White, Christian principles upon which this great nation rests are the surest bulwark against such depravity as these Euro-anarchists and their perfidious shock troops mean to unleash, and unworthy is he who flouts them. The law-abiding citizens of this district deserve better.

⌒

I set the paper down. "So what? Old wine, new bottle."

"He's talking about Lipford."

"How do you figure?"

"Bonny Prince Jack ain't even subtle anymore. Shirt-collar crowd is terrified he'll cause a scandal and spook the markets."

"Son, *everything* spooks the markets so apart from Boyd Layton and Mrs. Lipford, who cares if he has love affairs with every shop-girl from here to Bozeman?"

Charlie sips his coffee and and shoots me a funny look.

"What?"

He sets his cup on the counter and wraps his hands around it. "Big Curt was shorthanded last night—"

"Short on smarts, you mean."

"—so he asked me for help. Staked me on Eureka Street across from Lila's. Wanted me to follow Calvin Stance; see if he made any stops between Union Hall and his home. Well, I lost Cal in the crowd but there on the curb was the one and only green Garford in all Nevada."

"So what? Curt probably took it out."

"You know Lipford won't let *anyone* else drive it."

"Jerry Rosen, then. You know how he is about cars; wouldn't put it past him to have a little fun while the boss is away."

Frowning, Charlie exhales heavily and sets his elbows on the counter. "That girl has you so twisted."

Charlie's wrong, though: I get what he means but prefer to believe he's wrong. In a camp where eighty-five percent of the population is male, I'm aware that Lila has plenty of options but even in my worst nightmares, I never thought Lipford was on the menu. Son of a bitch ruins everything.

Charlie claps a hand on my shoulder. "Listen—"

"No, *you* listen: Curt's just trying to cause trouble. Lila, Bob Thompson, and Freese all went to Ely with the prince; they're gone until Thursday afternoon." I wince; even that sounds bad.

Charlie shakes his head. "Don't know about Bob or junior Freese, but Lila and Prince Jack pulled in yesterday."

"Bullshit."

"Told Curt about the Garford and he said Lipford telephoned from Caliente to come sneak him and the girl back into town."

"Curt's lying."

"Sorry, pal, I know you're crazy about her."

Crazy, hell, I'd been thinking about asking her to marry me. To move away from Delamar to Los Angeles, maybe, or somewhere a fellow might still make a living without having to swallow his pride or shelve his conscience every goddamn minute of every goddamn day. Now that notion's as dead as Caesar and I've been laid out in my corner. Ah, hell, who knows? Maybe things aren't as bad as Charlie says. We're broken people, Lila and me; we do okay together.

"You never liked her, Charlie. You sure—"

"Yeah, I'm sure." He takes a long sip of coffee.

Hearing Curt's name sets off all kinds of alarms. He's been cropping up in strange places lately. "Something here is bent."

"You're looking for a Chinese angle, pard, but I'm telling you—"

"Hold up. Curt practically shoves you into Lipford's autocar: that didn't seem suspicious you? Like something he might've staged?"

"Sure, it did, but for once Big Stupid wasn't blowing smoke." Charlie stares into his coffee, looking as uncomfortable as I've ever seen him. "I know how you think so I went up to Lila's for a look."

My heart races. "And?"

"Forget it, Shep."

I grit my teeth. "What did you see?"

"Pard, don't torture yourself."

"What did you see, Charlie?"

He turns the other way, though I can see his reflection in the dusty window.

"Through the keyhole." He exhales heavily. "Both of 'em were on that big green couch, 'cept she wasn't wearing nothing."

I brace myself against the counter, staring at my funhouse reflection in a nickel-plated samovar.

"Wasn't the first time, either."

"Shut up," I say, though he doesn't.

"That big snowstorm last week?"

"I said *shut up.*"

"Middle of the day, he went down to her place."

Son of a bitch, right before our meeting at the Comstock Club—right before he fired me. Afraid I'll punch something—possibly even Charlie—I wrap both hands around my coffee cup, instead. "Thanks a lot. Could've lied, you know."

He looks away. "Thought you might be tired of 'em."

Is this what dying feels like? This weightless spiral? And Prince Jack, the backstabber: cutting me loose so he can make time with Lila? I'll kill him. So help me God, I'm gonna kill Jack Lipford.

And Lila, Lila, what about Lila? She's hurt and embarrassed me, sure, but who am I to complain? Damndest thing is, I already knew we'd jumped the track. Things have felt hollow for months, like we were into each other for security instead of love, and now it's clear we never had that, either.

I should've known. She lives too well for someone without an inheritance and she's always traveling, or so she says. Reno one week, San Francisco the next. Of course I'd ignored all this because I was in love. Thought so, anyhow. For months, I ignored my No. 1 rule: never trust anyone. I trusted Lila and now look at me.

I open and close my hands into fists, imagining how it's gonna feel to break Prince Jack's jaw. How I'm gonna knock him down and stomp his ribcage until his lungs collapse. Drown him in his own blood.

A counterman sets plates of eggs, bacon, and toast in front of us but my appetite's gone.

"Nope." I drop a coin on the zinc surface. "Take it away."

The poor fellow, an Englishman with a neat mustache, striped vest, and dish clout tucked under his belt, looks confused. "Is something the matter, sir?"

"Yeah, something's the matter. Take this away before I crack it over your limey skull." I shove the plate across the counter, a little too aggressively because it falls and shatters, spattering the counterman's trouser-fronts.

"Sir!" he objects, too startled for anger, and for some reason this infuriates me even more.

If he came at me with a knife I'd know what to do but we just stand in our corners, chests heaving like punched-out prizefighters. Hefting a meat cleaver, a burly cook leans out to investigate. I dare him to step forward but he merely tells the counterman to summon a constable.

Charlie pushes me toward the door. "We'll go," he says and by way of apology, throws a gold quarter-eagle onto the counter. "Some for the plate, too."

Outside, I start walking toward Lila's but stop even before I've reached the bank's western wall. Despite bright sunshine, it's freezing today. Leaning against a granite pillar, I feel the cold seep through the thin fabric of my coat. My head swims. I want to shout myself hoarse but what would be the point? Maybe I wasn't really in love, I don't know. What Lila and I had never felt right and huge the way it did with Julia. With Helen. I loved Lila for what she might've been rather than for what she is. Cut so many corners, so desperate to outrun loneliness that I took for granted what was never really there.

"Hell of a show back there," Charlie says.

"I shrug. "Sorry—off my game."

"Understood—tough news for anyone to swallow. So what now, Shep?"

"Find somewhere else for our breakfasts. Sure liked that place."

"Yeah, yeah. Stay away from headquarters, hear?" He hands me my hat, which I'd forgotten in the restaurant. "I'm serious."

"How am I gonna pull that off?"

"I'll think of something. Pard, look, this whole year's been a grind. Few days ago, a fellow told me Wells Fargo is hiring payroll guards over in Humboldt County. Pay's about the same and you wouldn't have any of this other…nonsense weighing you down. Want me to give him your name, too?"

"Yeah, I'd better start looking. Big changes coming."

Charlie eyes me warily. "What have you heard?"

I glance up and down the block, even scanning windows in the surrounding buildings.

"Lipford cut me loose. Says he's reassigning me to look after his interests over in Esmerelda County, but that's just talk."

Facing the bank's big glass window, Charlie lets out a low whistle.

"It gets worse: Curt's gonna replace me here."

"Oh, goddamn." Charlie taps the bank's cornerstone with his boot. "May as well hit the road tonight."

"Sorry, pard. This is all my fault."

"Nah," Charlie says. "Prince Jack wanted Lila and you got in his way."

"He won't act right and guess why? You and me, jack. He does what he does because we back his play."

"Well, not any more. What's your plan?"

"Back away until I can come back heavy. Gonna do it carefully, though. Disengage slowly—can't tip my hand."

"I'll cover you for a couple days. Start getting my things together, too."

"Appreciate it."

I cast about the avenue for a sign, some token of Divine ordination, but there's nothing to see: a great, teeming nothing. Delivery wagons and men on horseback shout and make way for a noisy auto-stage from Pioche. Three ladies in heavy coats and opera boots stop to watch the commotion. Traders throng the sidewalk outside the Stock Exchange, barking orders with an Old Testament fervor. Everyone's hustling, scrambling for more than their share.

"I'd better go," I say but quickly shake my head. "Meeting Billy Meeks at ten-thirty. Can't let that slide."

"What do you care now?"

"Just something I want to wrap up."

Charlie grunts. "Keep away from the office, hear?"

"I will." We shake hands. "You'll write that fellow over in Humboldt?"

"Yeah, I'll let you know what he says. Meet you in Alamo this coming Wednesday; hit the trail from there. Watch your back, Shep."

"Front and sides, too. So long, Charlie."

We part company as the High-Con's ten o'clock whistle blows. Blasting time down in the mines; time for the ground to shake and the dust to fly. At the corner of Portis and Main, something tells me to look back and I see Charlie hurrying west, his collar turned up against the wind. Watching him go, I'm struck by a feeling I might never see him again. I look away and shake my head but the premonition lingers. Nothing I can do now except go about my business and hope I'm wrong.

∽

My meeting with Billy Meeks is brief. Billy's a miner and our spy: someone I managed to recruit from the WFM's local. Hell, they think so much of him down at Union Hall that six months ago their rank-and-file elected him secretary. For months, he's been our best source of information about the union's inner workings and I won't let anyone else handle him. I slide a thin envelope across the table and he tucks it into a pocket.

"Thanks. Goes to my wife and kids back in Iowa."

"You're a good man, Billy."

"Not hardly," he says, looking sheepish. He says he hasn't any news except that Union Hall is in an uproar over Joe McCuskey's disappearance. "Makes me nervous, Shep; everyone's sure Black Hand Jack's pulled a stunt." He coughs twice and wipes his mouth with his sleeve.

"I hear you. Any idea why McCuskey would be here in the first place? Fellow's bad news."

"Honestly, no. We were as surprised as anyone."

"Someone from the board contact him? By telegram, maybe?"

"If so, they were quiet about it."

Yeah, I'll bet. Billy's proven himself trustworthy but I keep most of what I know to myself. Safer for everyone that way.

"Association isn't involved, Bill; not this time. One of our operatives made McCuskey at the depot in Caliente but he disappeared right after. Don't know if he struck for Salt Lake, Las Vegas, or somewhere in-between. Believe you me, I'm curious to know where he's gone."

Twice, Billy glances out the window. "Andy has the rifle club drilling every other day and timber crews are gonna start patrolling at night."

Timber crews. That's one of those Colorado-isms that crops up all over Nevada: evidence that a fair percentage of the miners run out of Cripple Creek in '04 came here.

"Yeah? What does Andy expect they'll find?"

"Joe McCuskey. The man's a bastard but he's *our* bastard. Now someone's gone and made him a martyr."

"Do what you can to keep things calm, okay?"

"Folks are really agitated, Shep."

Odd, I notice his hands are shaking. Normally, Billy's as slick as glass.

"Me, I'd guess an inconvenient girl came around or a debt came due so McCuskey went underground."

"Swear—" Billy doubles over coughing and presses his face into the crook of his arm. He spends a minute like this and when he looks up, his eyes are watery. "Swear you ain't involved?"

"Yeah, I swear." This is odd, too; don't recall him questioning me before.

He glances at his sleeve, speckled with bright red droplets. "Never mind me; I'm dying and my head ain't right. Every day, I feel it stealing over me. Yesterday, I almost blacked out climbing a ladder to the stopes above Three-Hundred Level."

"Sorry, Billy; Delamar's a hard place."

He runs a hand through his red hair. "My lungs are shot; Dark Angel's gonna take me soon."

I don't know what to say. Miners lead hard lives—some of the hardest men I know earn their wages in the tunnels—and every district has its share of accidents but Delamar is altogether something else. This camp is a Moloch, a meatgrinder that cuts down men in the prime of their lives. Take Billy: here only eleven months and already silicosis has him gasping for air and anticipating death. Poor fellow can't be thirty, thirty-five, yet he looks nearer to fifty. He came to us from the union's conservative side; from the majority who just want to put their heads down and work. Hours, wages, and breaks are their concerns; not like the anarchist Wobblies, calling for the death of capitalism and the confiscation of private property. Man just wanted to take care of his family and now look at him.

"How are your wife and kids set?"

"Poorly. Once I'm gone, the Workingmen's Benefit Association will send $500 from an insurance pool but that's all."

"I'll talk to Lipford; see if he'll throw in something more." The gesture's sincere but hollow. For one, I've been "reassigned," and moreover, we both understand that Prince Jack believes all success is entirely self-made, and that charity subverts this natural order. 'Retards the competitive impulse', I've heard him say.

"Course you will," Billy says.

I study his face, wondering what I'm missing. Has Curt been leaning on him behind my back? Things here are so tangled I know I can't see everything, just hints and intimations, shadows in the corners. Walking the streets, I hear people whispering and their heads turn as I pass. Maybe they think I'm the Dark Angel and who knows? Maybe I am.

Billy looks away and I notice beads of sweat at his temples.

"Anything more?" I say, anxious to wrap things up.

"Hell, I clean forgot. A millhand up from Searchlight told us there's a fellow stranded down at Dunbar Station—gave the correct handshake and all—waiting for someone to bring him money for a railroad ticket."

"Hot damn. Boudreaux, you think?"

"Maybe."

I take out my notepad and pencil. "When was this?"

"Millhand transferred his membership at last night's meeting. Ain't been in town but a day, which puts him in Dunbar, what? Monday?"

"Millhand describe this other fellow?"

"No but he ain't local, that's for sure."

"From Denver?"

"Could be; headquarters don't always tell us what they're planning. In any case, the millhand says this fellow told him he found big trouble in Delamar so he's hot to quit this country. Take it for what it's worth, Shep. Soundest thing I've heard in weeks."

I put away my notebook. "I'll go have a look."

Billy coughs again but this time it's a minor jag. He stands and shakes my hand. "Keep your eyes peeled, Shep. Bound to get ugly soon."

"Got that right. Thanks for your help, pard. I'll talk to Lipford about your situation next time I see him."

"Appreciate it," he says. He shakes my hand again and steps outside into bright cold.

Me, I head over to the post office to mail a check to my family's home. Back to my room for a handful of items and then it's time to hit the road.

♋

I take a motorcycle out on the freight road that follows Cedar Wash southwest to Dunbar, a shipping point for mines on the Pahranagat Valley's far western side. My bike is a Reading Standard Model A: one cylinder; no clutch; battery and coil ignition. Traded a .38 pistol for it at Manhattan over in Nye County. On a board track or even a macadamized road, I'm told she'll reach sixty miles per hour but here on the dusty, rocky tracks crisscrossing Delamar Valley, I'm lucky to attain a quarter of that.

It's a little past noon when I leave, bundled against the cold, and nearly dark by the time I reach Dunbar Station. The entire town-site consists of six buildings, the largest of which combines a hotel, saloon, small store, honky-tonk dance hall, and five-seat eating joint. Two codgers are seated on a bench out front, smoking pipes.

"Heard you coming a mile away," one says, pointing at the motorbike.

"That right?"

"No good, these godforsaken things," he continues but I'm in no mood for conversation.

Catching my reflection in a window, I see my clothes are caked with dust and a gray 'raccoon's mask' encircles my eyes. I'm a sight, certainly, but I ignore the old boys' stares and head straight for the bar.

"Well, howdy," another old fellow says, "What brings you to Dunbar?"

Good question, friend. A few days ago, my boss fired me, yet here I am, still working a case. Of course, I tell him none of this and shrug.

"Anything you need?" he continues and I tell him whiskey always helps.

A calico cat threads its way between my feet and meows.

"Means she likes you," he says and for some reason, this makes me laugh.

I ask him if he has any rooms available and he says that for fifty cents a night he does. He sets a glass on the bar, pours two fingers' worth of bourbon, and slides it toward me.

"Planned to meet someone here but maybe he hasn't arrived yet. Any other guests?"

The old fellow stares out the window. A bare cottonwood stands in silhouette against the pale horizon. "You're my first customer this week. Mines in this part of the county have closed and I'm about to shut 'er down, too."

"No one's come through?"

"None have stayed."

Gee, thanks, Billy. Thanks for nothing.

I consider returning to Delamar immediately, darkness be damned, but I'm way too tired. Might as well go to my room and start on paperwork. Washout or no, there's no escaping notes, forms, and reports. Without a steady diet of paperwork, the Association would wither and die.

〜

Eastern Nevada Mine Owners' Association
Delamar, Nevada

Surveillance Form A - Team: ___1___

Date: December 7, 1907

Importance: HIGH - BLACK BOOK

Objective: Apprehend & return to Delamar for
                    interrogation. Armed, probable.

Target: Boudreaux, Francis A.; aka Boudrow, Frank

Target Affiliations (if known):   WFM: Wallace, Idaho
                                      & Tonopah, Nev. Locals

Location: Dunbar Station, Lincoln County, Nevada

Duration: 4:50 p.m. - TBD

Target photo available? No

Is Target otherwise known to Operative(s)? No

⁓

Know what? To hell with this. Lipford fired me; he can fill out his own god-damn reports.

I light a match and watch the paper burn, dropping the ashes into a washbasin.

⁓

Returning to the bar, I buy two fifths of rye and ask the old man to send a meal to my room. Beans, cold bacon, hard cheese, and bread are all he has but no matter. I'm not hungry except I figure if I'm going to drink, I'd better have something in my stomach to sop it up.

Between the bottles and me, I don't remember much else. I'm in bed by eight o'clock but for a long time can't fall asleep. For a good half-hour, I stare at the revolver on the pillow beside me, its barrel pointed squarely at my head. Right there, just inches away. Isn't the first time I've had these thoughts but things aren't so heavy tonight and same as before, it's fatigue that keeps me going; feels like it'd take more effort to raise the gun than it will to wake up tomorrow.

As a hall clock chimes midnight, I doze in and out of wakeful dreams. Crows skimming the surface of Groom Lake; Lila and Lipford entangled; but mostly about the Philippines. Some of these are pleasant enough: Intramuros, the old, walled section of Manila—perhaps the prettiest city I've ever seen—and emerald-green seas stretching toward horizons lined with peach-colored clouds. The rest are awful, though, and my God, I can't stop shaking. Over and again, I see Pedro Avila, a Samareño I thought I knew, burst into the mess hall and slash Sergeant Martin, nearly severing his head from his body.

By the time I finally pass out cold, the sheets are sweat-soaked and cold. Honestly, if not for a leaky woodstove in the corner, I believe I'd have frozen to death.

❧

Setting out in the pre-dawn darkness, I strain to see by the Standard's carbide headlamp. The going is slow, but once the sun rises my time improves and I strike Cedar Wash a little after noon. Stopping to refill the tank, I study Delamar's layout and the place looks as ragged as I've ever seen it. From below, it resembles an ice block left out in the sun: the core's still solid but its edges are crumbling. Is the boom really over? If so, you can bet everyone who missed their shot is gonna rush to renew their socialist bona fides.

With a presidential election on the horizon, this is a front-page concern: what'll happen if the Socialists carry Nevada? Despite our state's size, we have a small electorate and merely a dozen—hell, even one red precinct could tip the outcome. Rest assured, this thought keeps every member of the Comstock Club awake with the night-sweats. On days when I'm feeling perverse, I think I'd *like* to see the Socialists take over, just to see what happens. Honestly, between the federal government and the courts, I fail to see how anything would be different. Every proposal would be ruled unconstitutional or litigated to a standstill. Sure, their speeches would roll with thunder but as soon as the budget came up for a vote, all the graft and self-dealing that keeps Lipford and his fellow Republicans in beans would continue, only with different constituents. Mark my word, within a year of Election Day, more than ten miles from Carson City limits you'd be hard-pressed to tell any difference. Fact is, no matter what high-minded pledges get made in Nevada's churches and social halls, everyone here is in it for the money. Everyone.

❦

Warmer today and no clouds. Pawing through a saddlebag behind the Standard's seat, my hand falls across the second bottle I bought from the old bartender last night. Too bad it's almost empty but since the saloons and dance halls along Mazuma Road are only minutes away, there's no need to mope. A moment later, I send the empty spinning far out over the wash. No sound of breaking glass so it must've struck sand. Nice to imagine my own soft landing, though that's nothing more than a traveler's daydream.

From the look of things, some ruckus is building downtown. Marchers are pouring out of Union Hall (and the saloons surrounding it), shouting and carrying red banners up Main Street, so I take the lower road into town. Don't feel like dealing with a rabble and besides, I have other things on my mind.

❦

Every morning, J. Miller's Bakery sends its loaves out before six a.m. and for the rest of the day, the staircase leading to the apartments above smells of fresh bread. It's fainter today, though. Could be J. Miller closed up shop and joined the exodus to Goldfield.

Reaching the second floor, I tiptoe down the hallway and rap lightly on a door at its far end. Inside, the floorboards—ones I've failed to silence with nails and pegs—squeak. A chain rattles and the door opens a few inches.

"I told you, *not today*—" Seeing me through the gap, Lila's eyes widen. "Shepard!" she exclaims. She glances between a clock and the street-facing windows, clearly nervous. "What a surprise!"

"I'll bet. Glad to see me?"

"Goodness, yes! I only got back a few hours ago—"

"Trip cut short?"

She opens the door and I step inside. Her apartment smells of perfume: perfume and fresh bread. God, it smells good in here.

"Oh, I had to, Shep; I was bored the whole time. Bored senseless! They only needed me to record one little half-hour meeting and then I spent the rest of my time reading in my hotel room. Imagine my disappointment when I heard you weren't here."

"Business down south."

"Well, I'm thrilled you're back." She stands on her tiptoes to kiss me.

I let things ride until we're both out of breath.

"Missed you," she says. "Can you stay a little while? I'll bet you're working later but I think I can spare an hour. How does that sound?"

"Hard to say." I look into her eyes before shaking my head and turning away. She's so beautiful she makes my heart ache and I'm tired of my heart aching.

Pulling a patterned-silk dressing gown over her pajamas, she reaches out to embrace me but I brush past her into the sitting room.

"Darling, what's the matter?"

"Why him, Button?" I turn to face her—too quickly, perhaps, because she flinches. "Why *him?*"

"Shep, what…who do you mean? I don't—"

"Knock it off. You've been here for days. Lipford, too."

Lipford.

Just saying his name makes me want to puke. Five bucks says he wasn't even interested in Lila until he found out she and I were together. That's how he works. Son of a bitch grifts everything. Scrapes a hundred yards of public road so he can charge tolls for twenty miles; replaces functional valves at the waterworks and doubles rates. Cheats his business "partners" on technicalities. Bullies everyone with attorneys and when that doesn't work, sends in curs like Curt Broe and me. He wants what others have and now he's taken the only thing I had that was worth anything.

I step away from her. "Why him, Button?"

She won't even look at me. "I…I never meant to hurt you, Shep. Never. He kept pushing; he wouldn't take no for an answer."

"That's what he does." That's what every rich person does. Once they've obtained all they can legally, ethically, they break rules. They turn to power and cruelty, because an appetite for these things, once whetted, is insatiable.

Her face reddens and while I expect her to cry, she doesn't. Instead, she closes her eyes and holds a fist to her forehead. Her heart must be pounding, though, because I see a vein along her throat fluttering madly.

"Please don't be angry," she says, "You don't know the position I'm in."

"No, I heard about your positions."

"Oh, go to hell, Shep! That's low, even for you." Wide open now, her eyes flash with anger. "Which one of your hooligans was it? Charlie? Curt Broe?"

"Broe's an idiot." Glancing out the window, I see a crowd of men surging up Main. Even from half a block away and one flight up, I can hear the anger in their voices.

"Charlie, then?"

"Charlie confirmed what I already knew."

She turns and walks away. "That is *so* unfair."

"Is it?" I glance out the window. "I'd better go."

"Oh, please don't."

"Why? Won't he be along soon?"

"I don't…I don't know. I don't want to see him again. Will you let me think for a moment?"

Hell, take all the time you want. Won't change anything.

Lila goes to the kitchen to make coffee, perhaps as an overture kindly meant though just as likely out of habit. God knows my sweet Southern belle goes out of her way to make her guests feel welcome. A little too far, lately.

I glance around her bedroom: nightgown draped over a tall, oval mirror; a box of Dr. Rose's French Arsenic Complexion Wafers on one nightstand, and Dr. Hammond's Nerve and Brain Pills on the other; a new, thirty-five-dollar Edison phonograph and a stack of hard-molded records. Brushes, combs, hair ornaments, and jewelry by the fistful. One embroidered pillow on the rocking chair is askew. So unlike her, leaving something out of place, I'll bet *he* left it that way.

While the water heats, she returns to stand behind me. Says something then but for the commotion outside, I can't hear it.

"What was that?"

"Whatever you think of me, I still have feelings for you."

"Okay."

She reaches out and rests her hand on my forearm but I pull away, unwilling to let her touch me.

"Can you ever forgive me?"

"I don't know. I never cared about the others—you know that—but this is different."

"Oh, what have I done?" she whispers. "How do I fix this?"

"What's left to fix?" I step around her toward the door. "Don't worry about it."

This time, tears do spill and she retreats to the kitchen to steady herself. Even now, I fight the urge to go to her, to take her into my arms and tell her that no matter how bad things seem, everything will turn out right. Problem is, things *won't*. Between her tears, my rage, and that mob down on Main Street, it looks as if nothing in Delamar will ever be right again. For ten minutes, I stare at the floor while Lila sobs in the other room.

Down on the street, a car arrives. The familiar rumble of its idling engine cuts through the rising noise from the other block. I move toward the window for a look.

Of course.

Jack Lipford's green Garford autocar is at the curb; the prince himself is halfway out of the driver's seat with one foot on the street. He looks up at the window while I look down at him and even from thirty feet away, I can see his eyes widen and his lip curl. Lila can't see me from the kitchen so I reach inside my jacket, take my revolver from its holster, and press it flat against the windowpane.

Crossed the Rubicon, he said. Hell, yes, we have. Let's see where it gets us.

In the kitchen, the teakettle screams.

Lipford glances back over his shoulder and my eyes follow this movement. A group of miners is milling around the block's end: spillover from the procession on Main. They're just standing in the intersection, shouting and waving red flags, and I can't tell whether they've spotted Lipford and his distinctive autocar. If everything were normal, I'd hurry downstairs to make sure no one hassled the boss but now that nothing's normal, I stay right where I am, deliberately provoking a man who treats Lincoln County like he owns it.

From somewhere down the street comes the sound of breaking glass. Can't see what's happened but I'd guess someone put a rock through a big plate-glass window at the Chadwick Hotel or the offices of Whitelock & Hull, both Association-friendly, which makes them potential targets. Two constables knock a man to the ground and drag him into an alley. Despite some pushing and shoving from the mob, no one follows. Damned if I know what this means.

Lipford's stares up at me again but this time, his expression is blank—his 'business face', I've heard him call it. Without further ado, he turns, retakes his seat, and closes the door. The car eases away from the curb and at the next intersection, turns left, uphill toward High Side.

I close the curtains. All at once, the weight of everything comes crashing down on my shoulders and forces me onto the edge of Lila's bed. Heavy and weightless all at once. Hollow. Don't want to drop the revolver so with shaking hands, I take a towel from the washstand, wrap the revolver, and set this bundle on the floor an inch or two inside the dust ruffle.

Behind me, I hear Lila's footsteps and the rattle of coffee cups on a lacquered tray.

"Shepard?"

"Yeah, Button, I'm here."

She sets the tray on a small table between two wingback chairs. "Can you ever forgive me? If not now, then someday?"

I stare through the sheer curtains, watching those men with their red banners make their way along the street. "Probably." I'm a wreck, myself, and this business with Price Jack is only partly her fault.

"Will you stay with me? Please?"

"Don't know if that's such a good idea, Lila."

"If it takes a hundred years, I'll make it up to you."

"Let me think about it," I say but already I'm thinking about tomorrow. "He won't let this stand, you know. We'd better leave Delamar tonight."

"If that's what it takes," she whispers. "You'll…protect me?"

I exhale slowly. "I'll protect you."

"No matter what?"

"No matter what."

"Then I don't care what else happens."

That's sweet, but perilously naïve. Lila doesn't care because she didn't see what just happened. Me, I know what I've set in motion so I *do* care. How has it come to this? I should go. I step away from the window and see her standing at the foot of her bed. How lovely and vulnerable she is. Wish I hadn't because now it's too late and I'm lost and in no shape to resist.

"Stay with me?" Lila whispers. "Please?" She wraps her arms around my waist.

Between the wildfire I just lit and the smell of her perfume, I think I'm going crazy. Everything's spinning faster and faster and now I've no delusions that I can do anything except hold on for dear life.

"Yeah, I'll stay."

TEN

Walking back to the boardinghouse, I figure I'd better get some heavy insurance. Real heavy.

Turning, I follow some men making their way toward that mob occupying Main Street. From the back of the pack, I single out one I'm certain won't recognize me and tap him on the shoulder.

"Hey, pal, what's the stir?"

Hostile and confused, he stops and stares. "You haven't heard?"

"Buddy, I got here the day before yesterday."

He continues to stare at me and I worry maybe he's seen me before, or perhaps we've had a run-in. His pals, already half a block ahead, turn and shout for him to catch up.

"Western Federation's marching on the courthouse," he says.

"Why?"

"We're demanding that Marshal Finch arrest Black Hand Jack and anyone else who works for the Association." He turns to spit on the street. "Someone found a dumping ground with ten bodies—all miners."

"Here in town?"

"Dry lakebed way out in the Black Belt."

"Ten, you say?" He's spun-up and exaggerating; that number's way too high.

"That's the word. We don't get answers soon, we're gonna burn Delamar to the ground."

"Jesus, what kind of place is this?" No need to fake a reaction; my pulse races and my face grows hot.

Anxious to rejoin his friends, he points down the canyon, toward the setting sun. "Mister, you don't want to know. If I were you, I'd get the hell out of here."

Best advice I've heard in years.

❧

Hastening uptown, I realize here Lipford has the pretext he's been working toward all along. Things get hot enough, federal troops will come in to restore order and they'll turn every member of the WFM clean out of town. That's what happened in Cripple Creek, certainly. One day, unions ran the place—you couldn't do *anything* without their say-so—and the next, they were gone. Hard to issue demands with a bayonet against your spine. The Colorado National Guard arrested judges, county commissioners, and civil servants of every kind right along with the striking miners. Threw hundreds into cattle cars and shipped 'em to the Kansas state line; others never made it that far. The place was remade practically overnight, with the militants all replaced by docile foreigners. Same thing's happening over in Goldfield now, one-hundred and fifty miles west of here.

Damn it. Wish I'd asked that fellow more questions but how could I? Five bodies or ten, and if it's the latter, who planted the others? For months, I've heard dark rumors that don't square with what I know: midnight beatings, kidnappings, disappearances. Maybe it wasn't just chatter.

I feel sick thinking I've been outplayed by Curt Broe. With Sam Rice out of the picture, Curt's the only other person who knows where Joe McCuskey and the others are buried. Groom Lake is just one of several gigantic playas in southern Nevada and the Black Belt is justifiably fearsome—no one would look out there unless someone drew 'em a map. Suddenly, that notion about needing insurance becomes an obsession, so I lope across Hewett and head for Malapai.

❧

Finding my keys still work, I breathe a sigh of relief. Hurrying upstairs to the Association's offices, I leave the lights off. It'll be dark soon and I don't want to attract attention. Besides, I know exactly what I'm looking for and where to find it.

I open one oak filing cabinet among the dozens lining the walls of Lipford's office, remove three folders marked RE: WFM—CONFIDENTIAL, and set these atop the boss's desk. Leafing through the contents, I see every report Curt and I submitted over the past two years, the first one dating *to the day* Jack Lipford took over his father's interests. Dossiers on the local's officers and intercepted letters between them and the national office in Denver, too.

Next up, the wall safe. Lila may not realize it but a month ago, she inadvertently disclosed the combination—Lipford's wife's birthday—so although the light is failing, if I squint, I can still see numbers on the dial. Seconds later, the tumblers align and the door opens. Inside are tidy stacks of paper and coin—$3,000 dollars in all; prodigal specimens of gold ore—jewelry rock, it's called, so loaded with metal it's mostly yellow; and four gold ingots weighing twenty troy ounces, apiece. All these things, I leave; whatever else I might be, an aimless clip ain't one. Instead, I thumb through batches of folders, stopping at one in particular. It's a slim sheaf of papers: only three pages attached to a carefully folded map. A note stapled to the corner reads "Standard Trust Fraction, survey and notes."

Holy God.

My heart pounds. I take a deep breath and stare at the title, incredulous to find this time-bomb here in the Association's offices, aghast that it hasn't been destroyed or stashed somewhere far, far away.

Christ again, I sold my soul for these papers.

I turn and set this sheaf atop the others on the desk, pausing once to glance over my shoulder and make sure my eyes aren't playing tricks on me.

Farther in, I find letters from Senator John Christy to Jack Lipford detailing plans and schemes that even to my un-political mind look like grounds for expulsion or even prosecution. High crimes and misdemeanors, indeed.

At the back of the safe is a another small bundle of correspondence, sorted by date and tied with string. I'm about to return these letters to the safe when I spy the sender's name on the latest one: Miss Lila M. Hannigan. Posted late last month, too. How do you like that? I scan its contents and wince. In it, she thanks Prince Jack for a ruby bracelet and a swell weekend in Reno. I sniff the paper; it smells faintly of her perfume. Jesus, why did I fall for her? Of all women, why her? Because you never learned normal, bub, that's why—broken looks for broken.

Within this bundle are more notes from Lila, plus others from women all over the state and beyond. Classic 'old mule, young mare' stuff. One girl from Berkeley, California, is named Maude, only nineteen years old, and perfumes her letters, too. Fetching. Still others are from some of Red Light's better-known residents, including "Frenchy," "Jitters," and, to my immense delight, a girl working under the name "Fancy Pants." Need to look her up some time and see what's so fancy.

Lila's letters excepted, this jackpot thrills me. Mrs. Jack Lipford may find these documents thrilling, too, but those fireworks are for another day. I close the safe, stack all I've collected, and place it inside a large envelope. Set this fat parcel on an armchair by the door. Before leaving, I step behind Dolores' desk and roll a sheet of paper into her new Underwood typewriting machine. I've watched her use it and figure it can't be too difficult to operate, though I soon discover I'm wrong. After several botched attempts, I return to Lipford's desk, take a clean sheet of letterhead, and hand-write:

COME GET YOUR PAPERS

That'll do. I gather my spoils, tuck the envelope into a knapsack, and slip away like a thief in the night. Not even sure I locked the door behind me.

ELEVEN

It's dark by the time I reach the boardinghouse, yet as always, the White House's lights have blasted a hole in the darkness so bright even a blind man could find his way around. The streets are eerily quiet. God knows where that frenzied crowd from earlier in the day has gone; at least nothing was dynamited or set on fire.

Stumbling upstairs, I sniff my shirtsleeves and realize they still smell faintly of Lila's perfume. No counter-notes of freshly baked bread here: this place reeks of old sweat, stale coffee, and rock-dust. Two steps from the top, I glance down the hallway, see the door to my room is ajar, and freeze. Sounds that normally filter through the boardinghouse cease like crickets silenced by passing footsteps. I catch a whiff of cigarette smoke. Big Curt's here.

You are so careless, Sunday.

Behind a door, the floorboards creak. Reaching into my jacket for my revolver, cold, creeping panic takes hold as I remember where I left it. The knife I carry sometimes is buried in a drawer in in my room; I am unarmed now and it doesn't take a genius to realize how many mistakes I've made. Can't run. No doubt at least one shotgun is covering the door; more likely, two. Hell, with the window behind me and the hall lights on, I'll bet I make a splendid target.

"Steady," I hear someone murmur.

Are they down on the first floor? They must not know how sound travels in this shoddy sieve of a building. I don't recognize the voice. Are they Thiels or union men? Did Curt sell me out to the WFM or is this an Association job?

Does it matter? I press my back against the wall and try to control my breathing. A door rasps, this time from somewhere on the second floor. Ears straining, I hear another board creak, loading slowly as someone gathers their weight on it. A man in one of the far rooms coughs.

Then silence.

I reach inside my jacket and unclasp my shoulder holster. Bend my knees and crouch, partly to decrease my profile through the window but also so I'm ready for whatever comes. A buckle on the holster clinks; the tiniest of sounds and while I'm probably the only one who hears it, it's awfully loud in the dead air on the stairs. Realizing I'm holding my breath, I force myself to exhale.

A door at the top of the stairs bursts open. A man with a shotgun barges through, turns ninety degrees toward the window, and fires. Must've thought he'd find me several steps higher, because although the slug demolishes lath and plaster inches from my face, I am unhit. Singed, deaf, and covered with dust, but unhit. I leap over the last three steps and before he can work the pump-action, I lash out with my holster and smash a bare bulb in the fixture over his head. With a pop and a shower of glass, the hallway goes dark. He cycles another cartridge but I grab the barrel with my right hand and shove. The gun discharges, blowing a hole in the floorboards. I slip on broken glass, but falling shoulder-first into the wall helps me regain my balance. Haven't let go of the barrel, either, and since a cord runs through the gun's stock and around my attacker's neck, he can't straighten his back. With one hand on the pump, he jerks his whole body backward and we slam into the opposite wall. My roundhouse elbow grazes his chin but the backswing finds his jaw and he staggers. The gun slips from his hand, swaying between us like a pendulum. Even as he tries to control it, he punches with his left hand, striking a glancing blow on my chest. Gripping the holster-belt's ends, I square off, left hand high. He throws a wobbly right-handed punch that I block with the belt held taut and vertical. Slam my left fist down on his forearm and land a counterpunch below his eye with my right. Recoiling, he tries again to grab the shotgun except now his arm won't cooperate. I throw the belt over his head and lunge forward, behind his right foot so we are back-to-back. Pulling hard on the ends, they cross over my shoulder and cinch tightly around his neck. He reaches back to grab my sleeve but when I fold at the waist, even this handhold can't save him. With a hard pull, he flips over my back, crashes through the banister, and falls headfirst into the stairwell. Don't know if his neck was broken before he fell but given how he lands, there's no question after.

"Back!" someone shouts. "Everyone, back!"

Blood's running from a cut on my cheek; did the slug graze me or did one of his punches connect? Hearing Curt's voice outside, I throw myself on the floor. Another shotgun blast shatters the window and ceiling above the place I was standing. Cutting my hands on shards of glass, I scramble across the darkened hallway toward my room and dive headfirst through the door.

Funny how people react to danger. Strong men and women can shut down, and in other cases, weak ones surprise even themselves. Me, I've faced mortal hazards before and figure if I'm gonna die, it won't be because I wouldn't fight. Ever since Samar, I've been hyper-vigilant—it doesn't take much to set me off. Most times, this leaves me anxious and depressed but tonight, I'm grateful I've stayed on alert for so long. Picking pieces of glass from my hands, I won't say I'm thrilled, exactly, but I sure feel vindicated and for God's sake, I'm alive.

Alive but trapped.

First thought is to go downstairs for the dead man's shotgun but it's too risky to pass in front of that hole where the window used to be. They've sacked my room and the knife is gone. Pocket-watch, also. Books strewn everywhere. Bet they found my cash-bonus, too; no point in loitering.

More voices outside. Voices and footfalls, though it seems no one's in a hurry to come upstairs and try again. Hell, I wouldn't be surprised if they tried to burn me out, the other boarders be damned. I sniff the air for gasoline even as I crouch in the hallway.

While every lot in Delamar slopes, the ground beneath my neighborhood is especially steep. Here and there, one building's second floor is level with another's foundation, or is separated by mere feet from the hillside behind. This means if everyone's still out front, I might be able to slip away through a rear window.

The building goes go dark: they've thrown the breaker. The other boarders howl in protest but none dares to leave their room. Through the window, I see carbon arc-torches playing across the boardinghouse's front, their beams opaque with smoke and dust. Guess they expect me to come barreling through the front door, blasting away like the Dalton Gang did in Coffeyville, Kansas. Idiots. That's how Big Curt would handle a situation like this, which tells me he's the one who planned this run. His stupid fingerprints are all over it.

All over, because it turns out no one's watching the building's rear. All that's required is to slip inside a vacant room at the hallway's far end, open a window, and jump seven feet to the ground. Getting loose is just that easy. Out on Endacott Street, a crowd has gathered behind the torchbearers. I can even see figures watching the action from their rooms in the White House. Hate to disappoint but as far as I'm concerned, the show's over. I dust off my clothes, clamber up a rock wall, and tightrope-walk my way between buildings over to Wingfield Street. Charlie Witherill stays in a rented house near the Colorado Belle and given my situation, that seems as good a place to go as any.

TWELVE

Honest accounting is a big thing with me. Take Charlie, for example: a rifleman in the Second Wisconsin, he saw only small action in Puerto Rico. A half-hour firefight with an entrenched enemy across the Coamo River and he cannot say with certainty whether he 'killed his man.' No embellishments, no bragging.

Curt Broe, on the other hand, apparently ended Spanish control of Cuba all by himself. Carried Teddy Roosevelt on his back to the summit of San Juan Hill and took fifty prisoners with nothing but a buck-knife—all this as a provost guard. Insufferable son of a bitch. Once, he cautioned me not to "…throw the baby out with the dishwater." These facts notwithstanding, as I hasten along Delamar's darkened streets, can't think of anyone I'd rather see. Finish this business once and for all.

My guard's up still but now that the immediate crisis has passed, I feel hollow, weak, and tired. Like to throw back six shots of rye and sleep for twelve hours. Can't though; no way I'll let them catch me sleeping after what they tried to pull. That's how we caught one highgrader at the Hog Pen last year, don't you know? Exchanged shots above the old Ferguson townsite. Followed him into the hills east of town only to catch the bugger napping under a tree beside an abandoned prospect. Damned if I'm going into Lipford's black book like that.

The wind is howling tonight and streetlamps are swinging on their posts. The door of an abandoned house blows open so suddenly that a pane of glass in its window shatters, startling the hell out of me. Startles me so badly that I stop to consider going back to Lila's to retrieve my revolver.

Lila, Lila, what about Lila? Is she in danger, too? Possibly, but having found her letters in Lipford's safe, I'm back to thinking she's no one I can trust. Pretty face, pretty lies. Hell, I don't know. Doesn't feel right, leaving her to deal with Curt and his stooges but after a moment's deliberation, I decide she'll be fine. Either that or I no longer care. And anyway, Lipford won't hurt her—he wants her for his own.

Again, the abandoned house's door crashes against a wall. More glass falls onto the front steps. Torn calico curtains flap through its broken windows. Pieces of clothing, dust-stained and tattered, still wave on a line strung between one eave and a dead Joshua tree. I know I ought to hurry on but I stay and watch that swinging door. Uphill toward Charlie's, downhill toward Lila's. After a while, I decide to count to five and go whichever way it points.

Based on no better guide than this, I continue uphill. A hundred feet farther, I'm still not sure that door steered me correctly. I'd prefer to have my revolver back but surely someone's watching her place. Therefore, Charlie's bunk is the safer destination. Probably. And besides, Union Hall is downtown, too, so unless it becomes necessary, tonight I won't go within a mile of the place.

The saloon district along Mazuma Road isn't exactly hopping but a few people are out walking the planks. I stand my collar, ostensibly to block the wind but moreover so I can cover as much of my face as possible. The Colorado Belle is ahead, its lights reflecting off enameled tin signs for Mathis Beer and Richland Rye. Small crowd on the boards and off to one side, a man in a long coat and hat. Appears he's watching the entire street. I'm sure he sees me; nothing to do but keep walking and hope I don't stand out. A moment later, I glance across the road and see he's no longer there. Can't tell whether he's gone inside or somewhere else but I'm not gonna make a show of searching him out. Just hurry. I shudder from the cold and walk faster. Five blocks. Four blocks. Three…

Once I reach Charlie's, I'll be re-armed. I know where he hides a spare key, and that he keeps two shotguns, a rifle, and an old Smith & Wesson .38 revolver in a locker under the floorboards. Preoccupied with planning my run against Big Curt, I'm caught flat-footed when a man steps out from behind a wall.

"Hold up, Shep—it's me."

I recognize the voice but don't know how to react. Reaching for my revolver, I remember again where I left it. "You here for me, Warren?"

"Not like that. Don't go to Charlie's, pard; they took him at sundown."

"Took him where?"

"Killed him, Shep, same way they were gonna kill you. Roy Garland broke in and waited 'til Charlie came home; shot him as he walked through the door. Packed up his guns and papers. Someone's still there in case you come around."

Oh, my God, Charlie, I'm so sorry.

This news hits me like a landslide. Charlie Witherill was the one fellow in Delamar I felt I could trust, no matter what. I had no better friend. Warren's a close second—I don't want to sound ungrateful—but tonight, I'm unsure even where he stands. Damn it all to hell. Goddamn every one of 'em: Lipford, Broe, and every other rat in this wretched sewer.

I struggle to keep my voice level. "How do you know?"

"Curt called an emergency meeting. Roy was bragging about it; threw Charlie's bloody hat and pocket watch on the table. Now Fisher and Thompson are missing, too."

"For God's sake," I mutter as my chest tightens. Practically my whole team's been wiped out. Best figure out where Warren and I stand, pronto. "Are we okay, you and me?"

"I'd never switch sides, Shep."

"Good. Thanks, pard. So, what's your angle here?"

"Same as yours. Big Curt don't like me but he's shorthanded so he sent me out in case you turned up at the Belle. Wouldn't tell me what was the matter, wouldn't deputize me like the others but I figured it out. Got out of there as fast as I could."

"'Others?'"

"Circuit-court judge came down from Pioche and swore in a bunch of outsiders at headquarters. Come on, pard, let's get off the street before someone spots us."

To my white ears, Warren speaks in a monotone but here with the whole world collapsing, I find this reassuring. He isn't thrown off by turmoil the way Roy, Curt, or I would be. I'd better calm down and think. If there's anything the Philippines should've taught me, it's that any situation is survivable, even when the signs say otherwise. That, and to pay attention—something I haven't done enough of lately.

"So, where will you go?"

"Yerington Colony," he says, "before they kill me, too."

Indian lands on the other side of Nevada, close to the California line and not far from my family's ranch in Esmerelda County. Of course, Warren should have no trouble getting away. He knows the desert's quirks as well as anyone:

knows to dig for wood and climb for water, and his people are out there still, living in places where only the most desperate or deluded white prospectors dare to venture.

He takes off his hat and runs his fingers through his straight, black hair. "Better come, too. There's nothing left here."

"Need my revolver." I gesture toward the White House's sullen glare. Even on Delamar's darkest nights, you can always get your bearings on the White House.

"I have an old Winchester you can take," Warren says. "Too risky, going back downtown."

"Made it here, didn't I?"

"Yeah, but lean on your luck too hard, it'll turn."

He's right but what can I do? "Can't help it," I say; "sentimental attachment." I press my sleeve against the cut on my cheek.

Cutting across lots and keeping to the shadows, we aim for a thin line of trees high on the northwestern shoulder of Ferguson Hill. From there, I figure Warren will continue over the saddle into Helene Wash while I re-enter town from High Side—the neighborhood where all the stockbrokers and mine managers own nicer homes. Clouds cover the moon and the night goes pitch-dark. Stumbling across the hillside, we catch our clothes on thorny scrub. The rocks underfoot are so loaded with silica they clink like china plates.

I expect Warren has more to say, except he doesn't. Here's something I appreciate about him: he doesn't talk just to fill silence. Everyone knows that saying about the Devil making work for idle hands but honestly, even more devilry comes from a yapping mouth. What is it about Americans that we're so deathly afraid of silence? Too scared to hold our tongues? Maybe we're so hollowed out by our struggles to make it big, so afraid of falling behind that if we sit still for even one second, we'll realize what we're chasing is someone else's dream. Prince Jack has a stable of racehorses and a 2,000-acre game ranch south of Minden, and I don't want 'em. Don't want his artworks, his collection of antique firearms, or his wine cellar, either, yet for eighteen months now, everything I've done has been so that he can accumulate more of what he already has in abundance. I'm ashamed even thinking about it.

☙

Ferguson Hill steepens near its summit. Below us is the Hog Pen Shoot, an enormous crater where blasting inside the mountain has broken through the surface. Stepping carefully now, we give it a wide berth, because the hanging wall up here is forever sloughing off into the pit. Must be hell on the miners inside, dodging rocks that management can't be bothered to stabilize. Costs too much, they figure; more than hiring replacement workers, anyway.

Farther down, the lights of Delamar sprawl across both sides of the canyon, with the White House Hotel set like a yellow diamond at the center. Damn it all if I don't still kinda like this place. It's as wide-open a settlement as you'll find—for white folks, anyhow. Warren can't usually get a fair shake; the Chinese fish-and-vegetable peddlers all live in ramshackle dugouts punched into the side of a wash below camp; and its few colored families all live at a remove, but there's work here and at day's end, unless you hold a union card and the Association doesn't like you, folks are free to live however they want. At least, they were when the mines were roaring.

At last, we reach a scraggly line of cedars too high on a steep slope and too misshapen to log. Here's the virtue in ugliness: sometimes it's the only reason people will leave something alone. Beyond these trees is the ridgeline between Delamar and Helene Canyons. A few steps more and we'll start downhill into the latter.

"Going over?" I say.

"Yeah. Wanna cross the White River before Saturday."

Bone dry on the surface, the White River runs underground north from Hiko before emerging in a series of marshes just over the Nye County line. It's nothing I'd aim for but better than most, Warren knows his way across Nevada.

"So long, pard," I say. "Things are gonna turn 'round here."

Warren shakes my hand. "Come west, Shep, and I'll help you however I can. Your family was good to mine when they lived in Pine Grove."

"Thanks, Warren. I might be hot on your heels."

"Anyone follows me, I'll make sure it isn't you before I shoot."

"Much appreciated."

We laugh, shake hands, and head in opposite directions.

THIRTEEN

Slipping back into town is relatively easy. At one point, I crouch behind a rock wall as two autos and a half-dozen men on horses thunder past, downhill toward Cedar Wash. I recognize Jerry Rosen behind the wheel of one automobile and young Nick Reed in the second. Nick has a shotgun balanced over his shoulder, too, but neither he nor anyone else in his party sees me. This is my only close call. Save for barking dogs, the streets of High Side are deserted and the shades are all drawn tight. Something's up but where can I go for information?

Between my revolver and the cash hidden in my room, the gun is more important. It's at Lila's, though, which is several blocks farther downtown. My boardinghouse, on the other hand, is one street over and apparently unguarded. Maybe they figure since they haven't caught me yet, I must've slipped out of town; hence, no one sees a need to post guards. This lapse sweeps away any lingering doubt that Big Stupid is the brains behind this whole enterprise.

Upstairs and down, the lights are still off and with the big window gone, more wind whistles through the corridors than usual. Someone's made a half-hearted attempt to sweep up the broken glass but evidently surrendered after just a pass or two. Uglier still, the staircase's lowest step is broken and bloody drag-marks lead toward the front door. I feel a twinge of conscience though it passes once I see an empty shell-casing on the third step.

Fuck him, anyhow; Curt and all his lackeys, too.

Behind closed doors, I hear hushed voices. Even so, no one dares to look out as I pass.

My room is a wreck. Clothes and books are strewn across the floor. The mattress is torn open and tufts of cheap woolen batting cover everything. Only things left untouched are Julia's photo on the nightstand and a quarter-bottle of whiskey. I kiss the photo and slip it into a pocket in my coat. For a long moment, I stare at the bottle, imagining all the good a drink would do me. Then, for reasons I'll never understand, I pull the stopper and empty it over the bedsprings.

Damn it, why did I do that?

As quietly as possible, I tip the bedframe onto its side against the wall; it rustles the blinds but doesn't part them. While I ought to worry whether someone in the White House notices this little disturbance, I figure if Curt can't grasp the need to post my building, it's unlikely someone's observing it from a distance. Pawing through the debris, I locate a knothole near the wall, stick my finger inside, and pull. Ordinarily, it takes effort to pry open this compartment but this time, the board slides easily. Perhaps all the commotion earlier caused the building to shift, or maybe for once the winter wind has done me a favor. Who knows? Either way, this hiding space is untouched and so is my cash.

To say I'm pleased would be a gross understatement. This is a bona fide victory: something I'd normally celebrate with whiskey but having just made that impossible, I content myself with tucking the envelope into the same pocket as Julia's photo.

Outside, the hallway is dark and deserted. Debating whether to head downstairs or exit as before, I opt for the latter. That way leads to Lila's apartment and although the streets seem deserted, I figure it's best to keep out of sight.

Behind the building, I discover another tragedy: someone cut the Reading Standard's spokes. No garage at the boardinghouse so I keep the motorbike padlocked to a metal handrail along the back stairs. Damn it, I *loved* that bike. Loved it. I'm guessing this is Jerry Rosen's handiwork. He usually carries wire cutters in his toolkit and as an act, it suggests the kind of forethought Curt lacks.

Looks like I'm walking.

ᑲᕋ

From inside an empty garage near Lila's apartment, I spot the first sentry I've seen since my uptown encounter with Warren Jim. What's worse, he's carrying a rifle. I study the avenue, looking for something I can use to create a distraction. Would that I had blasting caps or some gasoline and matches. Even rocks through a window, except now there are *two* men: the first plus another who comes hustling up Eureka, and this one's carrying a shotgun. Splendid: my troubles just increased by an order of magnitude. Nothing to do now but wait.

For five minutes, I keep to the shadows and watch, pressing a handkerchief against that weeping cut on my cheek. Several men come and go. Some even pass within feet of the open garage, so close I can hear them talking, coughing, and in one case, smell what he ate for dinner. I recognize Scott Sweeney and Issac Reed but the rest are strangers. Appears Lipford's imported monkey-wrenchers from another district—Tonopah or Searchlight, maybe. Since May, the Goldfield Mine Owners Association has been dealing with union troubles of its own so I imagine there it's all hands on deck; too bad for me, since I'm on solid terms with their rank-and-file. Don't like their boss, Clarence Sage, but the cadre are okay. Fellow veterans, mostly.

A quarter-mile uphill, a three-bell signal rings out from the Baltic Mine's hoist house. The sound carries clearly over this part of town. I listen for a response. Three more bells, signaling the hoist engineer that men from the four-to-midnight shift have shut off their drills, made their way to the cages, and are ready to return to the surface.

Pulling crews from the big mines is no small chore. Men working on various levels assemble at stations along the shaft and wait to be hoisted to the surface, eight to ten at a time. Some properties interconnect and during emergencies, men can make their way into other mines and ascend using their cages, but normal operations require miners to exit through their company's change room. There, officials watch as they strip off their digging clothes, looking for evidence of highgrading. The miners' union says it's humiliating, having to undress in front of suspicious eyes, but the Association estimates it's reduced ore theft by more than eighty percent. I've worked shifts as a watchman in the change rooms and let me tell you, the embarrassment and resentment are mutual.

Minutes later, another three-bell signal sounds and an idea begins to form.

⁓

Outside the Baltic's surface plant, I wait in the shadows until the hoist engineer takes his dinner break. Soon as he leaves, I slip inside the control room, pilfer hand tools from a bin, and look around for the telephone. Easy enough: it's attached to a post near the hoistman's seat. One of these newer Western Electric stick phones with a separate mouthpiece, receiver, and subscriber set. Back in July, an accident in one of his mines caused a rash of bad press so Lipford installed these things in the control room of every High-Con property, with dedicated circuits, no less, so stockbrokers looking to bend the markets can't eavesdrop.

I lift the mouthpiece from the switch hook and wait thirty seconds until an operator takes up the line.

"Baltic Mine to Delamar exchange. Number, please?" The woman sounds tired and a little surprised someone's asking her to route a call at this hour. Glancing at the clock, I see it's five minutes after midnight.

"5-671. San Pedro yard-office, Caliente."

"Please wait," the operator says and I hear her fumble with the ringing cord.

Frank Croft is the yardmaster in Caliente and a friend of mine. He works nights, checking trains on the San Pedro, Los Angeles & Salt Lake yards for loose couplings, stowaways, and the like. If he's in his office, my plan might work but if he's out on the yard, I guess I'll head back downtown and try something else.

All I can do is sit and wait; connecting a call usually takes between five and ten minutes. To kill time, I pass a screwdriver back and forth between my hands, nervously watching the door. I've cooked up a story in case someone enters but hope I won't need it.

Six minutes later, the operator's voice comes through the receiver. "Sorry, sir, but no one's answering. There's no charge for this call."

"Thanks," I say although I don't mean it. "I'll try again later." I drop the mouthpiece onto the switch hook, toss the screwdriver onto a workbench, and head for the door.

From atop the Baltic's waste-rock dump, I have a bird's-eye view of downtown. Everything looks peaceful. Probably a quarter of the valley's nine-thousand souls are in the bars and casinos, while the rest are at home, doing whatever people do on a cold winter's night: sleeping, drinking, screwing, and in Delamar's case, coughing their lungs out. Always with the coughing.

I don't like my chances down on Eureka Street. Without a weapon, I've no hope of overpowering those sentries outside Lila's building. Glancing back at the hoist house, I see the engineer still hasn't returned from his trip to the outhouse. That isn't good.

With no better option, I follow cart-rails back across the yard and re-enter the hoist house. Funny, the switchboard operator doesn't seem surprised to hear my voice again. She goes to work quickly, rattling cords against the plug board and humming quietly to herself. This night is slipping away. The wall clock says twelve-seventeen when she tells me the call's gone through, the cost is one dollar, and she'll be dropping off the line.

Frank's voice comes through the receiver loud and clear, "Caliente yard-office, Croft speaking."

"Hey, Frank, it's Shepard. This is out of the blue and I can't get specific, but I'm in serious trouble up here. Remember last time we spoke, I mentioned my situation? Work and all?"

"Sure do, pal. How you holding up?"

"Not so hot. Things went bad here tonight but if I can gin up a diversion, I can gather what I need and get a running start. Any chance you can re-route this call for me?"

I can ask him to do this because the railroad maintains a small, proprietary switch right in their Caliente offices. Couldn't ask the Delamar operator for help because I don't know her, whereas Frank is a friend, a fellow veteran, and someone I've helped more than once. With him, I'm not at all nervous about calling in a favor.

"Damned sorry to hear it, buddy. Give me the number, I'll patch a call together."

"Thanks. And stay on the line, would you? In case anyone asks, tell them I'm calling from somewhere else."

"Anywhere in particular?"

"Pioche is far enough."

"You got it. Lucky you caught me, Shep; I was about to head out on the yard."

"Appreciate your help, Frank. Number's 3-222."

The line goes quiet while he wrangles patch cords. The clock reads twelve-twenty. Picking up the screwdriver again, I remove the subscriber set's cover. Since the line is still connected, I'm risking an electrical shock. The screwdriver has a hard-rubber handle, though, and I'm careful not to touch the capacitor or induction coils. I whistle my way through most of Billy Murray's *Meet Me in St. Louis, Louis* before a burst of noise signifies something's happened.

Coughing. Then Prince Jack's voice comes over the line, phlegmy and tired. "Jack Lipford speaking. Who's this?" He coughs twice.

"Shepard Sunday, chief of security. We have a situation downtown."

Frank clears his throat. "I'll drop off the line."

"No, wait," Lipford says, "stay there."

In the silence that follows, I'm afraid the connection's been lost. At last, Lipford speaks, "I thought we had a deal, kid. Where'd you go?"

"Not far. Careful next time you step outside."

"Don't you threaten me." His tone is no longer civil. "Why don't you head up to the mine so we can settle accounts?"

"Because your accounting's crooked. Tell Curt and the others to stand down."

His breath hisses loudly in my ear. "No one's standing down until you turn yourself in."

"You don't want me around. Besides, I have business in Carson City. See if John Sparks knows what to do with some things I found."

"What things? What are you talking about?"

No one's been to the office; he doesn't know I have the Standard Trust survey and his letters.

"Nothing," I say. "Forget it."

Silence then, though not as long as last time.

"I *will* find you," he says at last.

"Don't bother. I'm coming back for Lila—"

"Like hell," he snaps.

"—and then we're leaving."

"You don't have a say, kid. Lila's mine and Delamar, too! My family built this goddamned town and what are you? A nobody, Sunday—a bughouse drunk who doesn't know when to quit."

"Aren't you curious why Lila asked me to stay this afternoon?"

"I don't *care*—"

"She knows what you are—everyone does. You aren't fooling anyone, jack."

"Oh, I'll deal with her, and I swear to God, when Curt finds you—"

"Yeah, he won't. Look, why don't we let Mrs. Lipford decide what to do? See what the old gray mare thinks of all this?"

"You *ever* speak about my wife that way—"

"She know about the others? She's gonna—"

"Goddamn you," Lipford barks. "Operator? *Operator!*"

Frank comes back on the line, "Pioche exchange."

"Where is he?"

"I'm sorry, mister, I'm not sure I under—"

"Quiet," Lipford snaps, "or I'll have you fired for incompetence. Where did this call originate?"

"Oh, right. Sorry, sir," Frank says. "The calling party is here in Pioche, sir; the Price Hotel."

Lipford draws a huge breath and afterward his voice is calmer. "Look, kid, return whatever you took and I won't press charges—"

"First, tell Curt and the others to stand down."

"What's the matter, Sunday? Scared?"

"Fuck you, jack."

"You just signed your death warrant." Lipford coughs and clears his throat. "Operator! Raise the sheriff's office. Don't stop until someone answers; I don't care what it costs."

I hang up and yank on the the cord until the copper pairs inside are exposed. With the screwdriver, I sever one pair before threading the cord back inside the receiver.

There's a sound at the door as the engineer returns, clutching part of a sorry-looking sandwich. Grabbing a heavy iron spanner, he crosses the room in hurry. "Stop!" he shouts, brandishing the wrench like a battle-axe, "what are you doing?"

"Easy, pal." I step behind the bench. "I work for Delamar Telephone. Boss sent me here because your line's dead; returns a null signal."

"Get away from those controls. You shouldn't be in here."

I dust off my sleeves and set my pilfered tools in neat rows atop the workbench. "The hell I shouldn't—that phone ain't this company's property."

Now, the beautiful thing about Delamar's high turnover is that hardly any miners ever know who I am. This hoistman, for example, is someone I've never seen. Accordingly, I can be whoever I need to get what I want. It's backfired only once, when someone recognized me out of context, but that was over something minor and I've had plenty of practice since then.

"No one's allowed in here without an engineer present." He still sounds irked but slightly less hostile. "Company rules." He glances over the collar's edge, where steel cables drop hundreds of feet into darkness.

"Security told me you'd be on-station. Said you'd be here at 12:30 so that's *exactly* when I came in." I suppress a laugh. Behind him on the wall is a large sign with red letters: DON'T TALK TO THE LIFT OPERATOR.

"I was on break." He sets the spanner down and jams his hands into his pants pockets. "Just go before someone sees you."

"The phone." I point at its exposed innards. "I'm shutting it off until a wireman comes on-shift tomorrow morning."

"Funny, it worked earlier." He steps around the bench and picks up the receiver. Listens, toggles the switch hook a couple of times, and shoots me a funny look. "What do you think happened?"

"Looked inside it but didn't see anything wrong. Wind might've wrenched an insulator; shorted out somewhere." I unscrew a wire coupler so the line running into the subscriber set falls out. "Careful, it's live. Have any rubber tape? I left home without a full kit."

He pokes through bins chock full of fittings and oddments, finally discovering some vulcanized canvas tape. He throws me the roll and I separate and secure the exposed wires.

"That's it?"

"All for now."

He glances around uncomfortably. "Look, do me a favor and don't say *nothin'* to security about me not being on station, okay? I got problems enough."

"Sure, bud; we've all got problems."

"Take this?" He holds out a few dollars in coin.

This paltry sum probably represents his entire day's wages and while I'm tempted, I wave him off. In fact, I feel badly for this fellow, wondering why he'd stay at a lousy job that requires greasing palms to keep from running afoul of management. Then I remember who I've been working for these past few years and it all makes sense. Except for those at the very top, this whole town is a shell game.

"Let's call it square." I say. "My boss would give me hell if he knew I broke your rules coming in here alone."

He holds out his hand and we shake. I scoop up "my" tools from the bench, toss them into the knapsack containing Lipford's papers, and duck outside. A line of miners is waiting there in the dark, ready to board the cages and head underground.

Time to go back downtown.

FOURTEEN

Returning to the open garage, those two sentries are still outside Lila's. Nothing's changed. I'm about to hightail it after Warren Jim when an autocar rounds the corner and stops in front of the apartment.

"Shoe Polish, let's go," the driver says. "Sunday called Lipford from Pioche. Cooper and Davis are already on their way there."

"What about me?" says the other man.

"Wait here. Tony and the locals will pick you up in thirty minutes."

Means I have to wait, too, except it occurs to me that because some of those love-letters I found in the safe are hers, asking Lila to mail them is a nonstarter. With time to kill, I'd better head the other direction and leave my parcel with Helen. I'm grateful I wore my newer boots when I set out this morning; the old ones would've fallen apart with all the miles I've put in since.

The clock atop City Hall reads 1:05 as I start up Mazuma Road. A crowd mans the boards outside the Townsend Club—eavesdropping, I hear the pot at one table has grown to more than $950 and a capacity-crowd has gathered to watch—but the Colorado Belle's entrance is unobstructed.

Helen's joint isn't entirely dead but she isn't having a banner night, either. The mood inside is sour, sullen. I take an obscure place on the rail and wait for her to come around. Seeing me, her eyes widen and her jaw clenches. "Get out."

"Helen, I promise—"

"I swear, Shep, sometimes I wish we'd never met."

I shake my head. "Whatever you've heard, I didn't do it. Curt Broe set me up."

Leaning against the bar with both hands, the hard light goes out of her eyes. "Do you mean it? Promise me, Shep."

"Helen, I promise. Charlie's dead and Thompson and Fisher are missing, Warren had to leave town and no one here will stand with me—"

"I will," she says, so quietly I can barely hear. "God help me but I will."

"Thank you. Hate dragging you in but there's no one else I can turn to. Will you mail something for me?"

"What is it?"

"Just papers but they're hot as hell; they'll be a danger to you as long as you have 'em. Address is Sunday Ranch, Sweetwater Station, Esmerelda County."

She repeats the address and I reach out with Lipford's bundled papers and a two-dollar gold piece for postage, except for something in her expression, at the last second I pull them back.

"Shep?" She rests her hand on my forearm. "What's wrong?"

I can't do this to her. I lean across the bar and give her a quick kiss on the cheek.

A look crosses her face that I can't decipher. "It's no trouble," she says. "I want to help."

"You don't want this kind of trouble."

She leans in closer. "I'm calling your raise, Shep: what's going on? I heard gunshots—"

"Tell you everything as soon as I can."

In the mirror over her shoulder, I see two men push their way inside and scan players' faces around the card tables.

"Out back," she says and I wholeheartedly agree.

I kiss her again and duck through a door leading to the outhouses along the saloon's back wall. Turning right, I scale a wooden fence and jump inside a narrow, enclosed breezeway between the Colorado Belle and the pawn shop next door. Moments later, those two men—with a dozen more entrained—storm outside for a look around. Cursing me, Prince Jack, and anyone else they can think of, they march up and down the alley until one says, "Damn. I thought that was him but maybe not."

Slowly, the mob filters back inside.

Inching sideways between the buildings, I peer through a gap in the fence fronting Mazuma. More of that crowd from the Townsend Club peels away and crosses the street in a hurry.

"Pat saw him go inside," someone shouts which seems to agitate everyone there.

Then one of the fellows from the alley steps onto the sidewalk and announces that there's been a false alarm. Some grumble and swear and a few go so far as to glance inside the Belle.

Maybe I'm not as anonymous as I thought. I wait until things calm down and the entire mob migrates back across the street to catch the rest of the game. Thank God, drunks are easily distracted.

Returning to the alley, I climb back over the fence, check for movement in the shadows, and thread my way between buildings until I am several blocks farther south.

∾

The White House Hotel is the only place I can post something at this hour. Nowhere in Delamar is more conspicuous but for that reason I hope no one's watching it. If Big Curt is still behind the wheel, I doubt anyone really knows what's happening, anyway.

I try to recall the hotel's layout. The lobby, bar, and casino, of course, plus a long, narrow restaurant. The service entrance in the alley between my boardinghouse and the hotel's back wall? That'll do. I know better than to enter through the main doors.

Line cooks and kitchen porters glance at me as I duck between their work stations but they're too busy to pay me any attention. Smells good in here, reminding me that I'm famished. I swipe two biscuits and an apple and slip these into my coat pocket. Turning left, I follow a corridor around the dining room, which allows me to avoid pushing between the crowded tables. Need to step aside for busboys carrying trays of dirty dishes but none look at me any longer than it takes to see their way past. So far, so good.

The corridor branches toward the lobby, opening beside a birdcage elevator. I look through its round window and scan the chairs and couches for familiar faces. No one I recognize. Ornate wallpaper, crystal chandeliers, and lots of brass: the White House really is a beautiful place. Heard the imported carpet alone cost $10,000.

Crossing the lobby, I avoid eye contact even as I try to keep everyone else in view. Far as I can tell, no one pays me any attention—not even the working girls near the front doors. Only a clerk behind the desk observes my approach, perhaps wondering why someone out for the night would wear such shabby clothes.

"Can I help you?"

"Need to mail a parcel. One parcel twice, actually." Christ, it's bright in here.

"I'm not sure I follow."

"Need to mail something to our regional office for processing before they forward it to headquarters."

"Ah, yes. C-O-D, I presume?"

"No, I'll pay." I hand him the bundle containing everything I took from Prince Jack's safe. He slides these things into a large envelope and sets this parcel atop a small scale. If he notices the cuts and scrapes on my hands and face, he has a hotelier's good sense not to say anything.

"A little over twelve ounces," he says. He consults a chart and frowns. "Even with the rate reduction last October, I'm afraid it's still going to be expensive."

"This doesn't get mailed, I don't get paid."

"Are you a guest of the hotel? If so, I can post this on the house."

"Not this trip." I glance around. "Swell place, though."

"Thank you; we think so."

He hands me another envelope which I address to my cousin, Luke Wainwright, in Boise. Luke's forwarded mail for me before so he'll know what to do. I take the first envelope containing Lipford's papers, address it to my family's ranch in Esmerelda County, and stuff it inside the second. The clerk re-weighs the combined envelopes and presents me with a bill for ninety-two cents. The mails aren't foolproof. My team and I intercept letters all the time but I'm hoping a nondescript post to someone not obviously associated with me won't attract attention. We'll see.

Crossing the lobby again, I'm within reach of the service door when a fellow seated in a wingback chair lowers his newspaper.

"Jerry Rosen?" he says, pretending he's still reading.

I stop in my tracks, trying to look like this was expected. Jerry and I *do* resemble one another; this isn't the first time a stranger's got us mixed. This one's close enough I could punch him, too, but since he doesn't move, I try to look unbothered. Hell of a chore, too, considering my heart's practically jumping out of my chest.

"Who's asking?" I say.

Glancing at him, he isn't someone I recognize. Lean, angular face. Thinning black hair, dark eyes, and a mustache. His clothes are decent but not flashy. Let's put it this way: I hadn't noticed him until he spoke.

"Anthony Cicero, Thiel Detective Agency. I'm early."

From somewhere beyond the casino's ornately carved entryway come the sounds of wild cheering and laughter. Good Lord, they're going crazy. Someone must've hit it big at roulette. Everyone else in the lobby looks that way; this Cicero fellow and I are the only ones not following the uproar.

"I'm early, too," I say. I glance at a gigantic grandfather clock against the lobby's far wall: two-twenty a.m. "Still in the middle of something, in fact. Sorry to keep you waiting."

"No trouble." He nods and takes a cup of coffee from the table beside his chair. "I'm on the clock."

"Ordinary routine, right?"

"That's right."

"Crew's upstairs?"

"Waiting for the call."

So many things I'd like to ask: how many men? Who's in charge? What's the plan? I can't, of course. Moreover, I need to get going before the real Jerry Rosen arrives. That'd be ugly.

"Twenty, twenty-five minutes," I say. "Time enough to grab a sandwich if you want."

"Think I'll do that." He stands and cracks his knuckles.

He's my height, maybe a little heavier. From the shape of his coat, I can tell he's carrying a heater on his belt. No expression on his face, though; he just stares. Should I offer my hand and send him on his way? Or start walking? Hope he didn't observe me mailing that packet; if our roles were reversed, you can bet I'd have a cash-conversation with that clerk behind the desk. At least I'm not sweating. Seems my time in the tropics reset my internal thermostat so that only serious exertion or the hottest weather makes me perspire.

"If I'm not back here on schedule, I'll send someone else."

"Understood." Cicero yawns.

Someone leans through the archway and announces to the room at large that for the next half-hour, Champagne is on the house. This triggers a mass exodus from the lobby. Taking my cue, I nod to the Thiel agent and start toward the service door. Reflected in its window, thankfully I see him walking away, trailing that stampede toward the casino.

Inside the service corridor, I let down my guard and gasp for breath. I've cut things too close. Should've left town with Warren. Better leave now; Lila will manage. My revolver, though: I *need* my revolver.

Tonight, I'm a gambler on a streak. Time and again, I've beaten a house with unfair odds and I'll admit it feels great. Foolhardy, too, but so what? Like that big winner at the roulette wheel, I should collect my winnings and walk away but now I'm in deep and I can't. Can't. Even so, no one's luck lasts forever and I'm painfully aware how far I've pushed mine. Time to get my revolver and run like hell.

FIFTEEN

From the White House's back entrance, I skulk down alleys toward Lila's apartment. The streets are practically deserted but discretion being the better part of valor, I approach from the back. Upstairs and down, its hallways are silent and the building feels as deserted as the streets outside.

A peek through the keyhole shows one electric light burning in the apartment but who knows whether she's in there? Don't have a key so I jimmy the lock with a screwdriver I took from the Baltic and turn the knob. The door creaks open on its brass hinges but not so loudly I fear discovery.

Turns out, all my sneaking around is for nothing. Wrapped in a pink robe, Lila is seated at the far end of that big green velvet couch.

"Shep," she breathes, "it's late."

She doesn't seem surprised that I've just broken into her place; merely a little sad, if anything. Her hoarsened voice and red-rimmed eyes tell me she's been crying. Presuming I'm the reason why, all at once I am ashamed, moved, and baffled.

"You okay?" I say and step across the threshold. "Jesus, Button, you haven't packed anything—"

"I'm fine," she blurts, although everything about her says otherwise. She doesn't stand, doesn't smile, doesn't move. Merely sits there on that damned couch with her back straight and her hands set primly atop her knees.

Her eyes flicker slightly to her right and from over in the kitchen, I smell cigarettes and hear Big Curt Broe's heavy, nasal breathing. With the open door between us, I can't see him but I can hear him. It's possible he'll shoot as soon as I step around the door, but I can't run now and see no other way to buy time and get my revolver, currently wrapped in a towel under the bed's far side. That gun is the whole reason I came back—well, it and Lila, too—and damned if I'll leave now without both.

"Hello, Curt," I say and shut the door behind me.

He's seated on a wooden chair in front of the washbasin, a coffee cup full of butts atop the counter beside his elbow. A sawed-off shotgun rests on his thigh, its muzzle pointed directly at me.

"Hands up, Sunday. Slowly…slow down. Lose the overcoat. Drop it on the couch there."

Given Curt's tendency to shoot first and forget to ask questions later, I'm careful to do as he says.

He grins and shakes his head. "Son of a bitch, I *knew* you hadn't left town; Jerry Rosen owes me twenty bucks." With the shotgun trained on me, he stands and throws a wall switch, turning the lights off and on. "I *knew* it."

"Luckiest pig in the sty."

Curt glowers so hard his eyes bulge but before he can speak, he starts to cough. Huge, wracking gusts turn his face dark red and spittle flies from the corners of his mouth. I take a step forward but even in his convulsed state, he raises the shotgun and waves me back.

"Don't—," he wheezes "don't move." Cough, cough, *cough*. "Try that again, I'll air you out."

"Shame about your lungs, detective."

He coughs again, spits up something, and deposits it in the cup with the cigarette butts. "Fuck off."

Again, he throws the wall switch three or four times.

"Need backup?" I say.

"Shut up," Curt snaps. He throws the switch again before massaging his temples.

"Shepard, I'm sorry—" Lila says but Curt barks at her, too.

"Nothing from you, sugar; I've had enough of your hysterics." He settles heavily onto the chair.

"Leave her alone."

"Shut up, Sunday. You think you're smarter than me and hell, maybe you are but guess what? I nailed you cold this time: how's that for detective work? Figured out your angle and now I'm gonna collect my bonus and head for the coast; enjoy the sunshine for a while. Don't even have to take out the trash this time. Lipford's brought in heavies to take you apart, piece by goddammed piece."

Slowly, I take off my jacket and lay it across the couch's arm.

Curt responds by leveling the shotgun and following my every move. He grins. "Don't have your revolver, do you?"

I hope to God he hasn't found it, though my fears diminish once I see him gesture at the empty holster beneath my arm. "You got lucky is all."

"Figured *you* out, didn't I?" he says and his nasty grin disappears.

"For once." I pivot slowly on my toes before straightening my feet, moving four inches closer to the kitchen in the process.

"Hell, won't need to do it twice." Curt grimaces and spits into the cup. "If Lipford didn't want you alive, I'd put a hole through your guts right now."

"Know why he wants me alive?"

"So he can watch me kill you," Curt snarls.

"So he can decide whether he's covered out at Groom Lake, stupid. Wants to know if you screwed up like usual and whether he needs to bring in *more* heavies to fix this mess you've made."

"He knows he's covered," Curt says but a shadow of doubt flickers across his face.

"You are dumb, aren't you? *Ten* bodies doesn't square with his accounts. He has to reckon his exposure."

"No, he don't."

"You freelanced and tried to pin it on me, didn't you? Yeah, I figured out your angle: how's *that* for detective work?"

"Ah, shut up," Curt says miserably.

He glances out the rear window, squinting to penetrate the darkness. While his head's turned, I take another half-step forward. He turns back, glances between Lila and me, and flicks the wall switch again.

"Your plans always fall apart."

Curt shoots me a cold look. "You talk a lot, Shep, and no one's gonna be happier than me when they rip your tongue out."

"It'll wag before they do. Lipford's gonna hear how you shake down High-Con miners. How you keep half the highgrade you recover and fence it yourself. Is that what happened to Pete Kastning? You two have a falling out? Don't think you're getting away clean, dummy."

"Pshaw." He waves a freshly lit cigarette at Lila. "Boss don't trust you no more. Not since you dirtied up his plaything here."

"Leave her out of this."

"Nah." Curt drags on the cigarette and blows smoke in Lila's direction. "Boss is done with her so maybe I'll have some fun, myself, before I put her on the next train south."

This time, Lila snaps, "Don't touch me, pig."

Curt exhales a plume of smoke and flashes another nasty grin. "Don't worry, gorgeous; I'm gentler than you imagine."

Switching the shotgun from his right hand to his left, he drops his cigarette. As his eyes follow it, I grab the table's edge and heave, knocking the shotgun from his hand. Despite this break, Big Curt is still a brute—maybe six-foot four and two-hundred eighty pounds—and he barely flinches. Kicks over a chair to keep me from closing. I manage to punch his jaw but there's no juice in it and the son of a bitch hardly moves.

Still seated, he plants a palm on my chest and shoves, sending me crashing against the stove. As he leans down to grab the gun, I kick him in the throat; his hand is inches from the weapon when he realizes he can't breathe. I bring my right elbow down between his shoulder blades, right on his spine, and he topples forward. Big problem though: he's on top of the gun now and when I try to grab it, he swats me with one of his giant paws. This time, I *do* tumble sideways over the upturned table.

Lila's screaming. I'm scrambling and swearing for all I'm worth, and Curt is bug-eyed and sputtering like a leaky boiler. Struggling for control of the shotgun, Curt and I elbow each other simultaneously in the face. He has one hand on the gun's stock; mine's on the barrel. He elbows me again—not a knockout shot but hard enough. Eyes watering, I can barely see. Only thing now is instinct; my reflexes don't deliver, I'll die right here. Gasping as he closes, I block his punch with my right elbow and knee him in the ribs. The shotgun tumbles from his hand and he doubles over, clutching his side. I snatch the gun, grab his hair, and yank him forward.

Shouting in the hallway, louder by the second. At the edge of my vision, the door bursts open but that's a problem for later. Swinging the gun like a hammer, I bring it down on the base of Curt's skull and he collapses. Doubled up on the floor, he coughs until he vomits.

My chest heaves. Blood's flowing from a reopened scar on my scalp and holding onto the washstand is the only thing that keeps me from sliding to the floor.

Lila's gone silent, though. Turning her direction, I see Roy Garland with his arm wrapped around her neck and a revolver pressed against her head. Another man—one I don't recognize—stands beside him.

Roy yawns. "Drop the stick, Sunday."

"Go to hell, Yukon."

He pushes his knee forward so Lila slumps harder against his arm. "Say that again and see what happens."

Lila winces as he presses the revolver harder against her temple. Glancing at the stranger, I see he's holding a sidearm, too.

To my right, Curt is on his side, motionless. One kick to the temple would finish him forever but I can't. Shotgun's barrels are loaded, too, but again, with Lila in harm's way, there's nothing I can do.

"Lila," I say, locking eyes with Roy.

"Shepard, please don't," she says.

I don't know what she means but I do know that despite all that's happened, I can't have her settling my debts. Not at this price. Am I weak? Roy and Curt would say so. Lipford, too. Knowing what's coming, I have my own doubts but it's a decision I can live with, however briefly. I set the shotgun on the floor and lean against the washbasin.

Roy maintains his cinch around Lila's neck but the stranger holsters his gun and moves toward me. "Turn around," he says, "hands behind your back."

I do as I'm told; no point in drawing this out. He clamps a pair of cuffs on my wrists, jerks me by the elbow, and shoves me onto the green velvet couch. Minus the cuffs, Roy does essentially the same thing with Lila.

The stranger takes a step backward and resumes talking, "Shepard Adam Sunday, on authority of the Lincoln County Courts, you are under arrest for ten counts of murder in the first degree." He rattles off a list of names before concluding with, "…theft, destruction of property, and inciting unrest. As soon as transportation is available, you will be delivered to Pioche for trial. If you attempt to escape, you will be shot. Do you understand everything I said?"

"Better than most."

"Good. Won't be long."

He and Roy move into the kitchen to pick both Curt and his firearm off the floor. Bleeding from his nose and a cut above his left eyebrow, Curt looks dazed but not so badly he can't glare at me and spit.

"Lila," I whisper.

Seated beside me, her head in her hands, she's crying so hard she can't answer. "Button, nod if you can hear me."

"I'm so sorry, Shep," she whispers. "You shouldn't have—"

"No, listen." I keep my eyes on the trio in the kitchen. "My revolver's under your bed, wrapped in a towel. Whatever else happens, don't let them find it."

She lifts her head from her palms and turns slightly toward me. "Want me to get it?"

"No, keep it hidden."

"You two," the stranger says from across the room, "no talking."

He, Curt, and Roy all watch us a moment before resuming their low conversation.

I shift my arms behind my back, stick a finger inside my left pants pocket, and hook my keys. Only three on the ring, they hardly make a sound when I drop them on the couch.

"Lila, sweetie," I whisper, nudging the keys across the space between us. "Put these with my gun."

Thank my lucky stars, Lila's savvy enough to take the ring and discretely transfer it to a dish on the end table beneath her elbow.

"Shep, I'm so sorry," she whispers again. "I never meant for any of this to happen."

"Just protect yourself."

"Sunday!" Curt roars, "shut the hell up!" He limps across the room and lashes out with a backhand. I roll my head enough to avoid a burst eardrum but the blow has me seeing stars. "Son of a bitch, a hole in the ground's too good for you."

"You're the authority," I say.

He takes another swipe at my head but only clips me. "Union's all out of hitch just now. Might get careless on the drive to Pioche and let 'em lynch you." He glares at Lila. And you, Sugar, you have until six to gather your things. Come daybreak, Roy here is gonna drive you to Caliente and put you on a train."

"Plum assignment," Roy says.

"Better not touch her," I say but he only laughs.

Four more men arrive—including Anthony Cicero, that fellow from the White House lobby—and take up posts around Lila's apartment. The shoes of the fellow standing over by the bed are probably only inches from my revolver. Their clothes are identical: dark canvas dusters, bowler hats, and gloves. Cicero hates me with his eyes but otherwise makes no show of having seen me before. A man will eat a lot of crow to keep from being exposed as incompetent.

Limping back toward the kitchen, Curt stops at Lila's dressing table and scoops up a fistful of necklaces, rings, and bracelets. "Boss wants these back," he scolds her. "You didn't keep your end of the bargain."

I run my tongue over my teeth. One up top is already loose so I ought to keep quiet but the temptation is too great, "The rest of you, watch. Lipford will never see even half of what's in his hand."

No point in resisting now; I check out as Curt lays it on. He rages and sputters, cursing and coughing in my face even as he's punching me. He tears into me with such unrestrained fury that after only a few moments, two of the strangers intervene. Even Roy, who as far as I know has never been able to control himself, steps in and it takes all three men to pin Curt's arms to his sides. Spattered with blood, Lila screams until Anthony Cicero grabs her by the elbow, clamps a gloved hand over her mouth, and hustles her out the door.

Once Curt is subdued, I let my chin fall to my chest and take inventory. I can feel my pulse in every fiber of my being. Ears are ringing, too, and the pain in my head is worse than any hangover. Nose is bleeding, dripping onto my shirt-front; possibly broken, but since my face is already swelling, who knows? Doubt I'll live out this week so the only thing I have to look forward to is feeling like shit for the rest of my life.

∽

It's a short drive to City Hall. At five a.m., the cuffs are removed and I'm thrown into one of four holding cells in the basement.

A wooden bench projects from one wall. Settling onto it, I taste blood trickling down the back of my throat. Pull a moth-eaten blanket up to my chin but don't feel any warmer. Probe with my tongue and realize the tooth that was loose earlier is missing. Either I swallowed it or it's somewhere on the floor at Lila's.

Christ, I've stepped in deep this time.

Right before I black out, I remember something that's haunted me these past few weeks: Helen warned me I was on the wrong side but I wouldn't listen. Should've listened. Should've run. All these months, I've protected a beast. A monster that preys on this camp—protected Grendel, himself. For a long time, this monster had its way with Delamar but God help him, the villagers have finally taken up their pitchforks.

God save me, I'm a monster, too.

PART TWO

FUGITIVE

---

*"Those who are uninformed yet opinionated, incapable of self-restraint
and yet want to have their own way, and who feel beset by problems
yet refuse to learn from the past—all such people court disaster."*

—

Confucius, The Doctrine of the Mean

*"I want no prisoners. I wish you to kill and burn; the more
you kill and burn, the better it will please me."*

—

U.S. General Jacob H. Smith, 1901, in orders to
Major Littleton "Tony" Waller for the treatment of the
population on the Philippine island of Samar

SIXTEEN

I don't often think about China but here in this cell, I find myself thinking about lots of things that don't normally concern me. Memories of my year there don't malinger like those from the Philippines. A few things, sure. July's ungodly heat as we disembarked at Taku. The train station there, crowded with Russian Cossacks, Japanese marines, and turbaned Sikhs from British India. The earthshaking fireball when the Hsin Chieng arsenal in Tianjin blew—*that,* I remember clearly. The Boxers, themselves: wave after wave of men *and* women, punching, kicking, and spinning as they rushed our positions. Their leaders carried red or black banners; others had swords, spears, or bows and arrows. So many of them, too. Wave upon frantic human wave; how they didn't roll over us and wipe the whole international expedition off the map, I'll never know. We were beetles atop an anthill.

Mixed among the Boxers were imperial Chinese troops and they were fine soldiers. Carried modern Mannlicher rifles and pressed their attacks, even in the face of heavy German and Russian shelling. Sniped several of our number, including Colonel Liscum during an attack across a swampy area south of Tianjin's outer walls. All the same, as good as they were, they couldn't keep us out forever. After big Krupp guns set half the city ablaze, Japanese engineers blew the main gate and Chinese resistance crumbled. Then the looting began. Soldiers from every participating nation stole everything they could carry and pigs and dogs gorged on the dead.

Within weeks, we started for Peking and the legations. I remember marching for hours across hot, featureless plains, feeling half-dead from the heat and some nasty intestinal ailment that hit me once the fighting in Tianjin ended. Same thing overcame others in our regiment and we spent days in and out of a hospital train that was, if anything, hotter than marching out in the open.

Odd thing then: after serious resistance at Beicang and Huangcun, the closer we got to Peking, the softer Chinese defenses became. Might've been due to the rain that started falling in mid-August. Rain, we heard, or rather a lack thereof, is what sparked the whole rebellion in the first place. Drought and famine had led peasants to blame outsiders and missionaries for upsetting Heaven, and the Empress tried yoking this unrest in an effort to drive out the foreign legations. Once the skies opened, the Boxers began deserting in droves, yet we bore down with increasing cruelty. One correspondent wrote of our approach to Peking that "the line of march of the allies was a trail of fire and murder." He doesn't know the half of it.

⁓

I feel sick today. Weak. Low-grade fever. A little nauseous, even. Happens after a beating: the body treats all that bruising like a disease. I'm just lucky nothing vital was broken.

While it hurts to move and knowing nothing will improve, I shift from one position to another. Already, the swelling around my left eye is going down. That's good. Through a tiny air hole in the ceiling, I hear the muffled roar of a big crowd outside City Hall: shouting, voices chanting in unison, bits of song. I presume they're out there because I'm in here. Won't be long; walls can't keep out a determined foe forever.

⁓

Looking back, it's a wonder our final push into Peking succeeded at all. Eager to be first inside the Imperial City, each country's forces set out on their own in rain and darkness and attacked the walls piecemeal. The Russians tried first, got hung up, called on their Japanese rivals for reinforcement, and spent one whole day and part of the next trying to batter their way inside. The British attacked a gate whose defenders had re-deployed against the Russians; our U.S. Marines used ropes to scale another section of the wall; and other nations enjoyed varying degrees of success in their sectors. The following day, the Tartar Wall was taken and the Empress fled the capital. More fighting took place over the next five days, some of it pretty stiff, but generally that was all.

Apart from all the makeshift fortifications, walking into the legations was like strolling into a city park on a holiday. The trees were in flower and it was strange how unaffected the diplomats and missionaries were. One French bishop even lamented that a splendid opportunity for martyrdom had been wasted. Go figure.

Once we'd captured Peking, the orgy of looting that followed made the sack of Tianjin look like fair play. We took everything—*everything*. For God's sake, British authorities held daily loot auctions in their sector. Funny thing is, each country complained about the others' abuses, yet we were all guilty. All of us. I held out a few weeks before temptation got the best of me; like the water cure, perhaps the desire to take things that don't belong to us is impossible to resist. Most of what I took, I traded away for booze. The only item I kept was a small, horse-shaped vase made of gold and jade. Its eyes were rubies or garnets, I presume, and it's broken or buried in the ashes of Balangiga.

Otherwise, the American sector was well run. We established a medical clinic. I went on patrols with Chinese policemen and translators to try to clean up the streets. Even learned hand-fighting techniques from a reformed Boxer. Ordinary routine until a German general who was supposed to have led the whole expedition, but who'd been weeks late in arriving, showed up and tried to prod the *Schiltzaugen* into another fight. When that didn't happen, the Germans retaliated with some monstrous policies in their sector: goddamn, but something in the Hun soul is rotten.

The Ninth stayed in China for a year, standing guard inside the Forbidden City. Winters in Peking are brutally cold; a necessary counterweight to their brutally hot summers, I guess. In June of 1901, we shipped back to the Philippines and found things more or less as we left them: no large-scale fighting but every day, a thousand little skirmishes all over the islands. Filipino saboteurs blew bridges, cut telegraph wires, and assassinated collaborators. Ambushed our patrols daily. Knife attacks and sniping from the undergrowth, mostly. Another stirred-up anthill, if you please.

Manila was still exotic, still beautiful, and slightly less dirty than before although certainly just as hot. Baseball games and military-band concerts most every night. Watched Governor Taft's inauguration and fireworks on the Fourth of July, but we didn't stay long. In August, we shipped out for a village called

Balangiga on the southern coast of Samar, a big island about three-hundred miles to the south.

⁓

I hear keys rattling against the sheet-iron door. A young deputy, unarmed and apparently right out of high school, steps through with a tray of food: cold ham, fried potatoes, and coffee.

"Thanks," I say, even though I'm not hungry. It hurts just to sit up.

"Someone's here to see you," he says and I'd swear I hear a tremor in his voice. If the crowd outside riots and rushes the jail, it's clear *he* won't be one to prevent a lynching. Hands shaking, he sets the tray on my wooden bunk and leaves. "Ten minutes," he says and then Billy Meeks steps into my cell.

The door closes and keys rattle. For a short while, except for the kid's receding footsteps, it's quiet again.

"Hello, Billy," I say and he responds with coughing.

He turns to face the wall and braces himself with a forearm.

"You sound rough." He shows no sign of slowing down so I pick up the tray and start eating. Not the savoriest circumstance, but given what's liable to happen to me soon, I decide I don't care. Besides, although the ham is tough, the coffee's hot and the potatoes are salty and crisp; I could do with another whole plateful.

"Damn," Billy croaks. He clears his throat and takes a seat on the bench's far end. "Damn it."

"Want some?" I hold up the enameled tin plate but he waves me off.

He stares at the swelling and bruises around my eyes. "Jesus, Shep, they worked you over, didn't they?"

I take another forkful of potato and ham; wash it down with coffee. "What can I do for you, pard?"

"It's cold in here." Billy stares at the small, rectangular slit in the cell door and rubs his hands together.

I shrug. "Assessments are down; probably can't afford to heat the place."

Another bite, another sip of coffee, waiting for Billy to say something, except he doesn't. Merely stares at the little window, wearing an expression like he hopes someone else will show up and speak for him. Can't tell if he expects me to talk or if he's screwing up the courage to deliver bad news.

Tired of waiting, I go first, "Why'd you send me to Dunbar, Judas?"

Billy cringes and scoots away from me but he's got nothing to worry about. Given my condition, he's a bigger threat to me that I am to him. From outside, I hear the roar of the crowd, rising and falling like distant surf.

"Curt said he'd kill me if I didn't."

"Figured. He say I killed Joe McCuskey, too?"

"Didn't you?"

I shrug.

"Never mind," Billy says, "Don't care anymore. Only thing I care about is getting home to my wife and kids. Nothing else matters. I followed Curt's orders because I didn't see no other way. Sorry, Shep."

He wipes at his eyes.

Despite the pain in my neck and ribs, I clap a hand on his shoulder. "Don't apologize. God knows I've twisted arms all over Lincoln County, too."

"Sorry just the same."

"Wasn't your fight, Billy. We used you—I used you—so I'm the one who's sorry."

"Well, we're both in it now." He scratches his wrist. "Anyway, I wanted to say adios before I left town. Jerry Rosen's after me to come in and talk."

"Then you'd better leave before he finds you. Been down here three days and I'm surprised Jerry or Roy haven't bribed a deputy to say I was trying to escape so they could shoot me."

Billy shakes his head. "Garland's dead."

"What was that?" I'm sure the surprise on my face is plain.

"Went on a spree to celebrate your capture and the bastard ended up beating on a girl down in Red-Light. Seems she reached under her pillow, pulled out a derringer, and shot him right between the eyes."

"Know her name?" I ask, hoping to hear it was Fancy Pants who did me this favor.

"I don't. Whoever she was, they bundled her off to Pioche right quick. You're the only one down here."

"Figured."

"Must be lonesome."

"Don't rub it in. Thought by now Lila would've come to see me, but maybe it's too hot."

Billy shoots me a funny look. "Lila's gone, Shep. Cleared out the day after they dragged you in."

"Ah, Curt said Lipford was gonna run her out of town."

Billy shakes his head, apparently embarrassed by whatever it is he's about to say. "She left *with* Lipford. Climbed into his fancy green car with all her bags and they drove off together."

"No kidding? You saw them?"

"I did."

"Seriously?"

Staring at his boots, he nods.

How do you like that? You dupe, Shepard, you idiot. Hell, for a long time I knew how things stood between Lila and me—I *knew* it—but it seems wherever she's concerned, me and common sense part company. Time and again, she showed me how she ticks and time and again, I excused her.

Billy says something else but I'm so lost inside my head I can't be bothered to listen. Jesus, what a disappointment. Not her—not entirely, anyway; Lila's a feather in the wind—but *me*. I knew better—*knew it*—and still, I followed her around like a puppy. Now Lipford's gone to set her up somewhere or else plant her out on the desert. Either way, goodbye, Lila.

"Hear what I said?" Billy jostles my knee.

I admit I haven't.

He stands and cracks his knuckles. "Folks are interested in you, Shep."

"That so?" I study his face but still don't know what he means.

"Powerful people."

"Well, tell one of 'em to bust me out."

He coughs again but it isn't one of those horrible, incapacitating jags. "Don't know if I oughta…" Reaching inside his coat, he hands me a small bottle of whiskey. "What the hell, right?"

"Hey, Billy, thanks a million!" I take a quick pull before hiding the bottle underneath the bench.

Out in the corridor, I hear keys on the deputy's belt keeping time with his gait. "Time's up," he says through the window.

"So long, Shep," Billy says. He stands and takes a step toward the door. "I'm quitting Delamar tomorrow."

"You won't miss it."

Billy and I shake hands before he slips out into the hallway. The deputy takes my meal tray with him and the building goes quiet. Quieter outside, too, which I take to mean it's getting late.

❦

Stretching out on the bench, I wince at the soreness in my neck and sides, and now I'm doubly glad for Doctor Billy's prescription. Reaching under the bench, I take the bottle for another spin and stare at a water-stain darkening one corner of the ceiling. Gonna be me soon: an ugly stain in a corner. Just a matter of time. All I can figure is since his wife is still away, Lipford's taken Lila out of town to set her up in secret and it's kept him from discovering that I took those papers from his office. However unintentional, this might be the nicest thing Lila's ever done for me. Otherwise, by now, I'm sure Curt or Jerry would've come down here with heavy questions. Thank you, Button.

Already drowsy, I tip the bottle again and again and next thing I know, it's empty. Pity. Pain's better, though, and thank God for that. Might be enough to keep the nightmares at bay, too. Once the crowd outside City Hall thins, around two in morning, maybe Curt and Jerry or Anthony Cicero and the others will come for me. With any luck, I'll never even know what happened. That'd be fine: the best possible ending.

Feeling good and buzzed, I fall asleep.

∾

Sure enough, in the early hours, they do come.

Outside, I hear a scuffle. Shouting. Church bells pealing. Then the door bursts open and men with clubs and long knives surge into the room. Sergeant Martin has a fork halfway to his mouth when Pedro Avila brings a bolo down on his neck, killing him instantly. Turning sideways, Manire barely avoids having his own head cleaved from his body.

"They're in on us," someone shouts, "run for your lives!"

Some try to rise from the narrow benches surrounding the mess table but can't. They're slaughtered just where they're seated. Others of us manage to wrench our knees from beneath the table and run. Charlie Marak vaults clear over the table. Arnold Irish cracks one Filipino's skull with a heavy walking stick, giving me just enough space to slip past.

Since most of our weapons and ammunition are stored in the municipal hall, Henry and I run that direction, but attackers have seized the building's first floor and barred the main entrance. We circle back to climb a ladder to the second. Near the top, a Filipino leans out the narrow door and bayonets Hank in the shoulder. His foot slips from a rung and kicks me in the face but somehow we both hold on. Incredibly, Hank not only fights his way past this fellow but also wrenches the non-working Krag from his hands and clubs him with it.

I run toward the interior stairs, nearly colliding with Felipe, a local who interprets for us. Thank God, I think, because Felipe and I have become friendly these past few weeks and I figure he's come to help. Then he swings his bolo.

Barely missing my throat, the blade sinks an inch deep into the doorframe beside my head. I try to slam the door except Felipe wedges his shoulder inside the frame so that it won't close. Throwing all my weight against it, I shout for help but Hank's still fighting for his life with that first Samareño.

I stretch my hand toward another Krag standing against a wall. Shouldn't have, though, because once my weight shifts, Felipe manages to wedge the door open wider and wrench his bolo free. Abandoning the rifle, I press my full weight against the door, pinning Felipe's arm below the shoulder. He howls in pain but he can still swing the blade. He strikes my shoulder twice but since his arm's up high and I'm seated on the floor, these cuts are hardly more than scratches. Hoping to break his hand or the bones in his forearm, I throw elbows over my head but nothing connects.

Another Filipino rushes upstairs and throws himself against the door. It sways but thank God, they can't push me over…yet. Still, Felipe shoves his shoulder farther into the gap and now his arm moves freely.

The first cut takes off the top of my right ear and leaves a long gash in my scalp. I raise my right arm to protect my head. Manage for a second to pin the bolo flat against the door but cut my fingers in the process. They're starting to move me. Across the room, Hank finally works the Krag's magazine cut-off free and shoots the fellow he's been fighting since the outset.

"Hank!" I shout, "help me!"

Manire hurries across the room, sights into the gap, and fires. Although the second Filipino falls, Felipe swings again and this time the bolo sinks all the way to bone. While Hank works the Krag's bolt-action, Felipe draws the knife across my head like a cellist's bow. I try to duck but this only accelerates his cut and I can feel my scalp peeling away. Feels like my head's been doused with kerosene and set on fire.

Manire, God bless him, presses the muzzle right against the door and squeezes the trigger. Felipe's blade clatters to the floor, and as I lean away from the door, his arm slips back through the gap and his body tumbles down the stairs.

Pressing my hand to my head, blood pours between my fingers. "Bastard cut me!"

Manire slams the door. "Grab a rifle," he shouts, "here they come again!"

More footsteps on the stairs. Like hornets now—too goddamn many of 'em. I try to move but something's wrapped around my body. "He got me, Hank," I groan, "the bastard cut me!" Blood in my eye. I press my hand against the side of my head and stagger, landing with a thud on the floor.

"For God's sake," someone hisses, "get up!"

Cold concrete against my face. Heart's pounding and my head hurts.

"Wake up, dummy!"

For a long moment, I'll be damned if I can tell where I am or who's talking. I feel my scalp. Scars are still there but when I check my hand, what I thought was blood is only sweat.

"Are they gone?" I press my back against the wall. Unwrapping the blanket from around my knees, I throw it onto the bench.

"Settle down, hear?" A deputy scowls at me through the window slit. His eyes are unfamiliar and his voice deeper; must've been a shift change while I was sleeping. "Christ, you're a case. You kick over your pail?"

"What?"

Fully awake now, I notice it's brighter out in the corridor. Crowd outside is back at it, too.

"Your pail, stupid," he says.

I take a deep breath and look around the cell. In the opposite corner, a piss-bucket stands half-full.

"No. You ever gonna empty it?"

"Soon as you're gone," he sneers. "You got a visitor—fifteen minute limit. Now, keep away from the door and no sudden moves or I'll kill you like you killed those fellows out at Groom Lake, hear?"

The door opens and a well-dressed man enters my cell. Extremely well dressed; good Lord, there's hardly any mud on his shoes. Funny, discovering me in a disheveled heap on the floor doesn't seem to bother him.

"Fifteen minutes," the deputy says, pulling the door shut.

Ignoring my jailer, the well-dressed fellow turns to face me. "Mr. Sunday? Porter Nielsen. I've come from Salt Lake City. I'm your attorney."

I figure I heard him wrong. "My what?"

"Your attorney. I've been hired to defend you." His nose wrinkles at the smell in here and I can't say I blame him.

"Nonsense. Who are you, really?"

He looks around the cell, paying particular attention to the same water stain that captivated me last night. Runs a hand through his thin, blond hair, takes a seat on the bench. Sets his hat atop a thin leather satchel.

"Quiet in here."

"Everyone says so." Am I dreaming again?

He drums his fingers on the satchel. "Yes, well, time is short so I'll get to the point. My client, the Western Federation of Miners, believes you could be useful in their fight against Jack Lipford's Association. Accordingly, they've retained me to represent you in court and do all I can to secure your release."

I can't help but laugh. Me under WFM protection? Ye gods, what a notion.

"No, thank you."

"Mr. Sunday—"

"I said no, thanks. Won't testify against the Association."

"Your reticence is understandable, Mr. Sunday, but given your straits, you may want to reconsider."

His eyes are pale blue, about the same color as Joe McCuskey's. That's a bad sign.

"You're in Jack Lipford's doghouse—" he continues.

"Doesn't mean I've switched sides."

"Yet the tables have turned, Mr. Sunday. Rest assured, no one from the Association will lift a finger to save you. In fact, I'm sure they'd prefer you were silenced. Cooperating with us, then, is the only way you'll leave here alive."

"What about that mob out there? You're saying *they* don't mean to lynch me?"

"Probably more than a few have scores to settle, but we'll deal with them. The vast majority are demonstrators, Mr. Sunday. Union members, working-men, and they're all that stand between you and summary execution."

I still don't believe a word he's saying. The WFM is a hardscrabble outfit without the means to defend all its dues-paying members, never mind an antagonist.

"Look, pal, what can I do for you?"

Nielsen glances around the cell. "We'll see. Given your suspected role in quite a lot of nastiness around here, we believe you are uniquely positioned to help pry Lipford's fingers from our members' throats."

"A fishing trip, then?"

"If you like."

"You're working for Lipford, aren't you?"

He shakes his head. "I assumed you'd have questions…" His voice trails off while he retrieves a sheaf of letters from the satchel. "Which is why," he resumes, "I've obtained testimonies from persons known to you."

He hands me three pieces of paper. The first is a note from Andy Maguire, Delamar WFM No. 77's president, confirming Nielsen is a partner in the firm Nielsen, Cannon, & Pratt of Salt Lake City; that he represents the union's interests in Nevada's Lincoln, White Pine, and Elko Counties; and that he's been retained to represent me. Over the past few months, Billy Meeks let me read several of Andy's messages so I recognize his handwriting but as far as I'm concerned, his note doesn't confirm much. Next one is from Billy, himself, addressing Andy and me both, apologizing for spying on the union and swearing Nielsen's on the level. Again, the handwriting's genuine.

"You know Billy?" I say.

"Met him last night. Not in Union Hall, of course; Meeks is no longer welcome there. But before he went down to Caliente this morning, I asked him for an endorsement. Five minutes later, he handed me that letter."

"Say where he's headed?"

Home: Glenwood, Iowa. Mr. Meeks is in poor health, you know, so he's hastening back to say his goodbyes."

These details suggest either Nielsen's telling the truth or he's savvy enough to study up beforehand. Hard to say; Lipford has several lawyers on retainer who don't do much except lie.

The third message is from Helen Molloy:

❧

Dearest Shepard,

I've tried to come see you but the deputies won't allow it. I hope you weren't badly hurt. You can trust Nielsen. I've known him for some time and I'm certain he'll do his very best to secure your release. Let me know if there is anything I can do, whatever you may need. Please know you can trust me—the key's in its usual place.

Affectionately Yours,

H

❧

I glance at Nielsen. "How do you know Helen?"

"I was her father's attorney; I helped him purchase the lot beneath the Colorado Belle."

Well, well—small world.

"You read her letter?"

"It isn't addressed to me so no, I didn't."

I almost believe him. "Sure you didn't take it out of her? I'll hear about it if you did."

Taken aback, he stares, he stares at me, his pale blue eyes flashing with curiosity and contempt. "'Take it out of her?'"

"Don't be dense. Did you smack her around?"

Nielsen looks at me like I just spit on his shoes. "Oh, my heck, is that what your people do? Batter women to get what you want?"

"My people?"

"Formerly, Mr. Sunday, formerly. I didn't mean it that way."

I let it slide. "I don't hit women—surprised?"

"Pleasantly," he says, his tone drier than the desert. "I've run up against the Association in Ely so I'm familiar with their…tactics. But see here, I've fought them before—other businessmen's protective associations, too—and prevailed. In this case, there are certain particulars and less time to prepare so we'd better not waste any more." He takes a notebook from his coat pocket and clicks a mechanical pencil. "Mr. Sunday, you've been charged with ten counts of murder—"

"Framed," I correct him.

"We'll get to that." He reads the same list of names the stranger recited back in Lila's apartment, concluding with Joe McCuskey's. "First, I'll read these names individually. Tell me everything you can about each fellow, every interaction you recall. If you don't know someone, then say so. Don't speculate. If you're repeating hearsay, then say so and identify your source. Be specific with your descriptions—"

"Jesus, mister, I get it. You defend blockheads and Bohunks for the union but look, chief, that ain't me."

"Oh, I'm sorry." Nielsen closes his notebook and fixes me with an unfriendly stare. "You're an educated man?"

"No diploma but smart enough to recognize condescension."

"I'm not…" He glances at the tiny window and exhales heavily. "That's diligence, Mr. Sunday, not condescension. No matter who I represent, this is how I work. I'm good at my job, too, which, provided you cooperate, you may come to appreciate. I have degrees from Yale and Northwestern; President Roosevelt was a classmate at Columbia Law School; and I've argued twice before the state supreme courts of Nevada and Utah—"

"Did I ask for a c.v.?"

"—and won both times," he persists. "Forgive my failure to explain why I need so much information to defend you properly."

"Sure, so long as you understand that I hate condescension. From Salt Lake, you say? Jack Mormon or the genuine article?"

He sighs. "My work for the WFM leaves my standing with the bishops in question but yes, I am a Latter Day Saint. Does this bother you?"

"Nah, but it explains plenty."

"What do you mean?"

"You're as narrow a bunch as God ever made. Gentiles can't get fair shakes in the Great State of Deseret."

He exhales heavily. "Mr. Sunday, if you continue wasting my time—"

"Your time?" I interrupt. "Buddy, you're on trial, too. Answer my questions, I'll decide whether I think you're telling the truth and maybe then I'll cooperate."

Looking up from his notepad, his eyes turn cold. "Very well, I *do* consider my station higher than yours, but not for reasons you suggest. Unlike you, *I* haven't been arrested for murder, and *I* am not bloodied and bruised, lying in filth on the floor of a jail—"

"Go on."

"—nor am I *antagonizing* the one person on earth who can keep my head out of a noose. Is that honest enough for you?"

"Much better. See how easy that was?"

"I detest gutter-talk." He shakes his head and writes the date on a page in his notebook. "Can we get back to business?"

I pick myself up off the floor and stretch. Taking a seat on the bench's other end, I turn to study him. Nielsen's tall but thin. Soft hands: a desk-fighter, plainly, and I'd make short work of him if ever we scrapped. Boorish thoughts, I know, but that's generally how men size each other up. We wonder if we can beat the fellow across from us according to the standards by which we live. Men like Jack Lipford credit adversaries according to how much money and power they wield. Nielsen's made it plain he thinks he's smarter than me; a point I'll concede so long as he understands I know how to fight. My kind, we farm, we dig, we build, and when others try to take what's ours, we fight. Tooth and nail, we fight. Each group considers itself superior to all others, yet secretly fears them, too. Honestly, I don't know the man who perceives the world much differently than he did as a schoolboy.

"Mr. Sunday?" Nielsen says and I realize I've been staring this whole time. Maybe it's an acoustic trick, or maybe there's a thinness in his voice that wasn't there before. "In order to win your freedom—to save your life—you'll have to trust me. There's no other way."

"Got it." I lean toward him. "Do you trust *me?*"

He eyes me warily. "I trust you have your own best interests in mind."

Clearly uncomfortable, he leans away, which pleases me. At last, we've reached the starting line.

"Huzzah," I say. "Fire away."

His brow creases slightly but otherwise he reveals nothing of what he's thinking. It's a shame Mormons don't gamble: this fellow would make one hell of a card player.

I hear the deputy's boots thudding in the corridor just before he raps on the iron door.

"Time's up, counselor. Time to clear out."

Nielsen rises from the bench. "We've barely scratched the surface, Mr. Sunday. Do you accept our offer?"

"I'll think about it."

"Very well, though I shouldn't need to remind you we haven't much time. I'll return this evening at six."

"Lucky me."

Goddamn, I don't trust this fellow. Too slick, too condescending. Strikes me the way Lipford's attorneys did when they visited from San Francisco, looking down their noses at everyone. And those shiny shoes: no way he works for the WFM.

Nielsen covers me with that blank stare of his before turning to leave. Then the cell door clanks shut, the deputy's keys rattle, and I'm alone again.

For a little while, anyway.

∾

Without a watch or window, I can't be sure but I figure it's around noon when I hear a door open upstairs, followed by the low rumble of conversation. From out in the hallway, shuffling and scraping sounds are followed by the clatter of a wooden club against the door. Glancing through the tiny window, the big deputy's eyes dart around the perimeter of my cell.

"Visitor," he says but this time no keys rattle in the lock and the door stays closed.

"Thought you weren't coming back 'til later," I say, presuming Nielsen's returned to badger me again.

Curt Broe's eyes appear in the window and he takes a long moment to gloat. "Nice place. Suits you perfectly."

Seeing his face—a portion of it, anyhow—I suppress a bitter laugh. Even under the circumstances, Curt's still a joke to me.

He clears his throat. "Hear what I said?"

"Fuck off, Curt."

"Oh, hey, pard, don't be hasty. See, I'm here to admit I was wrong. I figured Lipford was done with your girl but it turns out he *does* want to keep her convenient. Took her to out to Long Beach and set her up sweet. How 'bout that?"

"Sounds like you hope he'll do the same for you."

"You're lucky they made me check my revolver upstairs, jackass."

"Hardly matters; I've seen you shoot."

Curt frowns. He stays quiet for such a long time I can hear the gears grinding inside his head. God knows how much sand is up there.

"Drive you out onto the desert, myself," he says; "see what you think of my shooting."

He tries to spit through the window, except it hits the upper edge, instead. For the rest of our conversation, this vile stalactite divides into halves what little I can see of his face.

"Won't get the assignment," I say. "Lipford hates fuckups, bub, and you're the undisputed king of fuckups."

Can't see his entire face but the way he's squinting suggests he's wearing that ugly grin of his. "Big talk for a man in a filthy cage."

"Jackass."

"Nah, son, *you're* the biggest jackass in camp. Your girl cheated, you lost your job, and now look at the fix you're in. Your arrogance done you in, boy."

So what if he's right? Damned if I'll give him any satisfaction. "Hell of a black eye there, bub: who gave it to you, again?"

Curt exhales heavily but otherwise contains himself. "Still don't see it, do you?" He leans from side to side, eyeballing the far corners of my cell. "You think you're still in control. Well, guess what? I don't give a *damn* what you say now. Ain't worth nothing anyway, understand? Hell, less than nothing: you're a mistake I'm gonna erase."

Christ, I wish I had my revolver. Better yet, a bottle. Already this morning I was feeling low, and for Curt Broe of all people to stand outside my cell and taunt me pretty well kicks the chair out from under my feet. Hate to admit it but he's right: I'm nothing but a whore, a demon on loan from hell. Nothing I've done here makes me proud, I've no achievements to my name, and I can hardly stand my own reflection. Big Stupid's right: I *am* a mistake.

"Hear me, Sunday?" Curt persists. "Gonna kill you slowly. Shoot both your knees and take my time reloading."

I'm so far down that by the time I find my tongue, the words don't sound like mine, "You're finished, too, jack. Nothing's gonna set you square again with Lipford."

Curt's face contorts and he averts his eyes. Perhaps he's thinking—as much a novelty as a bearded woman or a two-headed calf—and the hallway goes so quiet I can hear the deputy complaining to someone upstairs. A long while later, Curt coughs, spits on the floor, and looks back through the tiny window.

"Okay, listen, I think we can both get we want here. Gotta work with me, though, understand?"

He glances down the hallway and as he leans away from the door, I can see more of his profile than when he was pressed up close. Christ, he's ugly.

Returning to the window, he softens his voice, "Found your note at headquarters, bub. What papers did you take and where'd you put 'em?"

"Sorry, what?"

"Goddamnit, you know what I mean. Evidence, files, papers: if they mention our work—any of it—your name's gonna be all over 'em, a hundred times, minimum."

"Yeah, and you're gonna look stupid for failing to secure headquarters during a crisis. Prince Jack's gonna turn you out, too."

"Now *you're* being stupid," he counters. "Don't think you can turn state's evidence without implicating yourself in a hundred felonies. You'll hang for sure."

"I'm a mistake, Curt, remember? Does it matter who takes out the trash?"

"Gonna tell me where you hid 'em?"

"Hid what?"

He kicks the door in frustration. "Better tell me what you took!"

"Or what, you'll kill me?"

"You don't have no friends here, jack. Witherill, Fisher, and Thompson are all dead and your Injun deputy ran away. Jerry Rosen's *my* deputy now—"

"Go to hell."

He snorts. "Lipford's coming back soon and you know he'll want the heat turned up once he hears what happened. I mean that literally, Shep: ever seen molten copper poured over someone's feet? Nineteen-hundred degrees, right out of the furnace. Even thinking about it still makes me a little sick, but hey, you tell me where you hid whatever you took and I'll do what I can to cover for you. Even help you get a head start. We've had our differences, you and me, but everything don't gotta be rough. Make me look stupid, though, I'll tip that crucible, myself."

"You don't need help looking stupid. Go shit in your hat."

He sticks his fingers through the window, right through the spit-wad, and starts shaking the door so loudly the deputy comes running. "Motherfucker," Curt hisses, "I'll *destroy* you. I'll pull your eyes out, you rotten son of a bitch!"

"Get back," the deputy shouts, followed by the unmistakable sound of a shotgun's action. "Back!"

God, I pray, *make Curt keep rattling the door* but since the Lord and I don't keep regular company, like all my other prayers, this one goes unanswered.

Curt lets go of the door but I can still hear his heavy breathing out in the hallway. The deputy says something to him but I can't hear it. More shuffling and scraping.

Curt's left eye reappears in the slit. "See you real soon," he says before turning toward the stairs.

The deputy makes a brief reappearance. "Lunch in an hour, jackass."

Halfway up the stairs, both men start coughing. Like thunder, this sound rolls back down the hallway, echoing off the concrete walls. I clamp my hands over my ears.

Hope they cough up their lungs and die.

❧

Rising from the bunk, I pace my cell, punching at my shadow and wishing it was Curt's face. Son of a bitch, I'm out of time.

It isn't fear or the thought of being tortured to death that rattles me, although trust me, those things are lodged in my mind, too. It's more that Curt and I are essentially the same. No matter how stupid, violent, and unprincipled he may be, all these months we've done the same things. Inflicted pain and sown terror which makes me no better than him. We are attack dogs. Dumb brutes, nothing more. Everything I've done in Delamar has been a waste. Everything. Miners have blasted millions out of Ferguson Hill. Carpenters and stonemasons have built homes and business blocks. Physicians have set broken bones and healed the sick, and me, I've terrorized people so a selfish, unprincipled man could add to his overfilled accounts. I hate this. Hate it. Hate myself. Never should've taken this job. Never should've come to Delamar.

What have I done? My God, what have I done?

SEVENTEEN

——••◦⟨∞⟩◦••——

Escorted by the same deputy as before, Nielsen returns at six o'clock.

"Have you considered our offer?"

"Sure," I say, which is an understatement. It's all I've thought about for hours. I've considered whether Nielsen sent Big Curt to rattle my cage and move me along; whether the union wants to learn what I know before cutting me loose; or whether their offer is bona fide.

"And?"

"Let's talk and see where it gets us." As if I have options.

Nielsen retakes his seat at the bench's end while I pace the length of my cell, a grand distance of nine and one-half feet.

"We have an hour this time," he says, "so unless you object, let's revisit that list."

I tell him that's fine so he reads off those same ten names, all but two of which are unfamiliar. He makes notes as we talk, scratching the paper with such speed that I seriously doubt anyone but him will ever be able to read it.

"Sixth is C.B. Grimes," he says. He clicks his mechanical pencil, waiting for a new lead to descend.

Staring at the window in the door, I stop pacing and nod.

"Okay," Nielsen says, "why are you nodding?"

"Because I shot Cyrus Grimes. He's buried out at Groom Lake, or at least, he *was*. Maybe not anymore."

Nielsen exhales. "Who was he?"

"High-Con's surveyor—"

Nielsen raises an index finger. "Delamar-Highland Consolidated?"

"Correct."

"You concede involvement in this man's death?"

"Yes. I went to retrieve papers he was using to extort Jack Lipford. Grimes went for his gun but I had the drop and shot first. Drove his body out to Groom Lake and buried it."

"So, you were defending yourself?"

"Charitable use of the term."

"I've worked with less. So, Mr. Grimes threatened you and you shot him; what was the sheriff's opinion?"

I shake my head.

"No one ever investigated his disappearance? The town marshal? Sheriff's deputy?"

"Even if the sheriff himself had come down from Pioche—which he didn't— we made sure there was nothing to investigate. Charlie and I scoured Grimes' cabin and erased every trace of his time in Delamar. Even replaced bloodstained floorboards. Forged a letter of resignation and tucked it into his file at High-Con. Burned his personal effects, settled his credit account at Hunt's Dry Goods; tricks like that, and no one from back East ever came looking for him."

"Who's Charlie?"

"My old partner. Association murdered him."

"Sorry to hear it." Nielsen looks up from his notepad. "But why take Grimes so far out on the desert? Why not up in the hills, or throw his body into an abandoned mine?"

"Because no mine's abandoned forever and Groom Lake's desolate as hell. Nothing's ever gonna happen out there."

"This man's friends, his drinking buddies—they never searched for him?"

"Hardly anyone in Delamar has friends; no one stays here long enough."

Nielsen exhales heavily. "Details, then. Every interaction with this Grimes fellow, dating back as far as you remember."

As I talk, he scribbles with the same intensity as before. Going back months, I remember quite a lot I'd shelved. Little things that probably don't matter and others I wish were forgotten, still. At various points, we circle back over well-covered ground.

"Grimes shot first, you say?"

"No, he went for a gun lying on a table but I shot first."

"Where, again?"

"His cabin: a one-room place off Helene Road, just above the cemetery. It's vacant now."

"But he definitely fired this weapon, yes?"

"Put a bullet in the wall as he fell."

Nielsen flips back through his notepad. "What happened to his firearm?"

"Buried it with him. Smith and Wesson, .38 special as I recall."

"I'll send someone to retrieve that bullet."

"Don't bother: dug it out, myself."

"Then if his weapon can be recovered at Groom Lake, it'll contain, what, five rounds?"

"Presuming it was fully loaded in the first place, presuming whoever found it—*if* they found it—hasn't discarded it since."

"Valid points." Nielsen exhales. Scribble, scribble, scribble. "So, what was in the papers Grimes stole from Jack Lipford?"

I stop pacing. "A survey."

Nielsen stops writing and furrows his brow. "A land survey?"

"Correct."

"Describing what, exactly?"

"A ghost; an honest-to-God fortune."

"What do you mean?"

I take a deep breath. "There's a stray fraction up on Ferguson Hill. Unclaimed land between mining claims—in this case between Highland-Con's Hog Pen and the Black Tiger Mine. Mining claims typically border one another or even overlap—"

"Sure."

"—but not this time. Whoever staked the original claims up there missed a ragged swath between the two properties, about eight-hundred by two-hundred feet, right in the heart of the district."

"So Grimes used this survey to extort Jack Lipford?"

"Tried to. Neither company owns that ground but both are using it, understand? Anyone claims it, they'll physically and legally control *both* properties, including High-Con's sole point of access to the Hog Pen. It'd cost millions to acquire the surrounding claims and drive a new tunnel into their workings."

Nielsen stops writing and stares at me. "Why *hasn't* Lipford claimed it?"

"Trouble at the land office, trouble with another Association member, I don't know." Back to pacing. "Maybe his shysters need time to concoct a plan before he shows his cards—no offense."

"None taken."

I stop pacing. "I studied Grimes' map before I turned it in and it's a disaster for Lipford. Not just the unclaimed ground, but it also shows that High-Con drove its Zero-Level adit from Black Tiger's property. Struck highgrade, too, not thirty feet below grassroots."

"Highland's stealing ore?"

"Tons of it. Third quarter this year, Prince Jack wrote himself a bonus check for $80,000. You tell me how much they're stealing."

"'Prince Jack'—that's Lipford, correct?"

"Behind his back, yes."

"I like it." A minute later, Nielsen stills his pencil and stares at his notepad. "I'm curious, Mr. Sunday, why didn't *you* claim this stray? You'd be a millionaire."

It's a fair question: why *didn't* I file claim on the richest part of Ferguson Hill? Take Lipford down a peg? A chance like that will never come again and considering where I am now, I don't know if I could resist temptation a second time. But back then, I did. Who knows how, but I did. Whatever might've been, that way is closed now.

"Because I'm not Jack Lipford."

For a full minute, Nielsen covers his mouth with his hand and stares at the floor. I resume pacing.

"Incredible," he murmurs, "that something so crucial could be overlooked this way."

I shrug. "Fences were strung. Suppose everyone assumes they follow claim-lines."

"And Black Tiger—did Grimes approach them, too?"

"Don't think so, but Black Tiger isn't part of the Association. Couldn't approach them without showing High-Con's hand. Honestly, the two companies despise each other."

"So I hear."

Nielsen writes for so long that I pace off one-hundred and twenty-nine steps and startle when he speaks again.

"Did Grimes tell anyone else?"

"Might've. Grimes' chain-man was a fellow named Tubbs and we can't fix his whereabouts. Collected his time a week before this blew up and left town. Tracked him as far as Milford, Utah, where he stepped off a train and disappeared."

"Think Grimes accosted Mr. Tubbs?"

"Probably, given the stakes. Grimes told Prince Jack he wanted $50,000 or he was gonna file claim, himself, and sell the stray to Black Tiger or even George Wingfield. Lipford panicked because he's been feuding with Black Tiger's English owners since '06. I don't follow the markets anymore but everyone assumes they're setting up for a run at Lipford's company."

Nielsen stands, walks over to the door, and looks through the window. Evidently, no one's there because he turns back to face me.

"Were your orders to retrieve this survey, only, or to kill Grimes, too?"

"I don't really remember. That was two, three weeks after I arrived in camp and I was unsteady then."

"'Unsteady?'"

"Unwell…" It takes a moment to get my breathing under control; this is no time to break down. "Bad time in the Philippines." He'd better infer my meaning; I won't give him any more.

"Just tell me what you can."

I have to think for a moment. We were in the Association's offices: Lipford sat behind his father's desk; Sam Rice stood beside him. I take a deep breath and close my eyes. "Sam Rice was angry and embarrassed all this happened on his watch—"

"Who's he?"

"My predecessor. He wanted to make Grimes pay."

"So he chose an 'unsteady' man for the job."

"I heard it was Lipford's idea. Probably hoped we'd kill each other."

"How do you figure?"

"A fellow named Roy Garland told me Rice tipped off Grimes. Probably why Grimes had a loaded revolver handy the night I went to his cabin."

"Why would he do that?"

"Which man? Why would Rice tip off Grimes, or why would Garland tell me about it?"

"Both."

"Well, Garland was a sociopath, and maybe Rice figured I was getting too close to Lipford's old man. Or Rice and Grimes cut a side-deal, or if I'd been killed, the Association would've rented a jury and hung Grimes. Never found out: three weeks after I shot Cy, Rice vanished, too."

"Did you have anything to do with Rice's disappearance?"

"Honestly, nothing."

The attorney returns to his seat on the bench and stares at his notepad. "Jack Lipford's father—"

"Hiram."

"Was *his* death in suspicious?"

I can help but laugh. "No."

"Unusual, then? People don't usually laugh describing someone's death."

"Well, he was on a spree down in Red Light. Heart attack just as the parlor-jenny he'd rented began to—"

"Stop. I get the picture."

"Really? You don't want details?"

"No, thank you." Nielsen blushes, furrows his brow, and scribbles some more. After a while, he takes a deep breath and casts another look over the top of his notebook. "Mr. Sunday, you say you were 'unsteady'…"

"Hard to imagine, but things were even worse back then."

"Jack Lipford knew?"

"Everyone knew."

"So even in your agitated state, he and Sam Rice sent you where it was possible—no, *probable*—that you'd be shot?"

"Never looked at it that way."

"Well, you should've." Mid-sentence, Nielsen stops writing. Stabs me with that icy blue stare of his. "Given his appalling lack of character—how little he cares for anyone not named Jackson Lipford, why in Heaven's name would you work for him?"

Buddy, that's a question I've asked myself a hundred times and I *still* don't have an answer. As I stare at the floor, the seconds tick away.

At last, Nielsen clears his throat. "Very well. Unless there's more I should know, that's enough for now."

Should I tell him about McCuskey and me? About Lila and Lipford? Either subject could take the better part of an hour and our time is almost up.

Nielsen scribbles for several minutes before clearing his throat. "We are aware of Black Tiger's plans for Delamar," he says. "We've even met to discuss the changes we expect if Lipford can be made to sell. Are you willing to repeat in court everything you've just told me? His attorneys will do everything they can to destroy your credibility—"

"I'm sure they will."

"—so we'll need as much corroborating evidence as we can gather."

"Like Grimes' survey?"

Nielsen flashes a wan smile. "If only."

I look at him and shrug. We stare at each other for several seconds before he tilts his head.

"What are you saying? You still have it?"

"Sure, and if the Federation will, too, if they can get me out of here."

Nielsen stares at his notes. It's so quiet now I can hear his breathing quicken. I'll bet his imagination's running wild with possibilities; with plans for a weapon he didn't know he had. The odds of him sticking his neck out for me just improved, too.

Several moments later, he exhales. "Do you honestly mean—"

"Yes, I do."

"Why, Sunday, you devil." Nielsen folds his hands over his chin, perhaps to conceal a grin. "You magnificent devil."

I shrug as if I don't care but the fact he isn't pressing for the survey's whereabouts is the strongest evidence yet that he's trustworthy.

Another minute ticks by in silence.

"This changes everything," he continues, "root and branch. If I can arrange your release, do I have your word that you'll surrender this survey to the Federation?"

I nod.

"And you'll cooperate fully, including testifying in court, in order to help us break Jack Lipford's stranglehold on this district?"

"Nothing would make me happier."

"You're sure it's safe?"

"Safe as I could make it."

"But you can still get it, yes?"

"Yes, but I'll have to get it, myself. It's 300 miles away now and it's caretaker would sooner destroy it than give it to someone other than me."

"For everyone's safety, it'd be better if you left the district, anyway. You'll be accompanied, of course."

"Of course," I say, though I don't believe it matters: no one's ever broken out of Delamar's jail.

"Then I'll see what I can do. With Billy Meeks gone—"

"Meeks isn't our only snoop: Curt Broe handles a fellow on your finance committee named Dave Todd."

"Thanks for that." Nielsen shakes his head in disgust and scribbles again. "Thank you—truth will prevail."

I speak through a yawn, "That isn't how Prince Jack works."

"Oh, I've dealt with others like him. We'll buy two jurymen for every one of his."

Good. This fellow understands how decks are stacked around here. Some folks naively presume the county courts or the sheriff will protect them but they *won't*. Every table's in this casino is rigged in the house's favor.

Nielsen watches his condensed breath floating in the light beneath a ceramic fixture and shivers. "Freezing down here," he says.

I shrug. "It's jail."

Out in the hallway, I hear the deputy's heavy footsteps but before he reaches my door, he starts coughing. Hard, too. I hear jags like this daily but Nielsen stares at the tiny window, aghast.

"Widowmaker's hooked another one," I say.

Soon as his fit ends, the deputy shuffles up to bang on the door with a wooden club. "Time's up," he wheezes before spitting on the floor.

"My watch says I have three," Nielsen snaps and my estimation of him soars. "I'll knock when I'm ready." He turns back to face me. "We'll talk again after your arraignment."

"When's that?"

"Ten a.m. tomorrow. Merely a formality: a circuit judge will read the charges against you and ask how you wish to plead. I'll enter a plea of not guilty on your behalf and you'll answer 'yes' when he asks you if this is correct. He'll set your bail beyond reach and then I'm afraid you'll be returned to this place, at least until the sheriff arranges transportation up to Pioche."

"I've seen these hearings before."

"Good. I'll accompany you but I doubt we'll have time to talk beforehand."

Violent banging erupts on the door's other side. "Come *on*," the deputy rasps. "I gave you extra."

Nielsen and I shake hands before he steps out into the corridor. The door swings shut and keys rattle in the lock.

"Supper in thirty," the deputy says, commencing to cough even worse than before. There's Delamar's real work song: the sound of blood-tainted breath leaving a thousand lungs.

I've changed my mind: Delamar is a terrible place. I'm no longer proud of the role I've played in its metastasis and soon I hope I can help burn it to the ground.

This meeting with Nielsen leaves me feeling uncharacteristically hopeful. Feisty, even, so although I can do nothing, I doubt whether I'll be able to sleep. I spend the rest of the evening and on into the night pacing my cell and shadow boxing, trying to keep my joints loose and my reflexes sharp.

EIGHTEEN

Nielsen's right: my arraignment is strictly pro forma. A prosecutor down from Pioche states the county's case and Nielsen enters a not guilty-plea. Judge Faraday tells me I'm being held over for trial, sets my bond at fifty-thousand dollars—$5,000 for each body exhumed from Groom Lake—and gavels the whole session closed in under fifteen minutes.

The bailiff's there, of course, and one of the strangers from Lila's apartment—Shoe Polish, judging by the pitchy tint of his hair—but not Curt Broe, Jerry Rosen, nor anyone else from the Association. In fact, apart from Myron George, a writer for the Delamar *Lode*, the chamber is otherwise empty. Voices are clipped and answers are short. Even the streets outside are quiet, which adds to the tension in the room.

Minutes later, I'm back in my cell with unanswered questions. I know what's in store: I've seen how justice, official and otherwise, works in this dry corner of the republic, but I'd surely like to know why the prosecution seems so timid. Typically, those accused of murder are driven to Pioche within hours of their arrest, yet thus far I've heard nothing except vague declarations about moving me "once secure transportation can be arranged." That can't be the issue: there's no shortage of wagons or weapons in Delamar. All I can figure is that Lipford must still be out of pocket and no one knows what to do in his absence. I'm surprised someone else from the Association—Ed Conrad from the High Park Mine, or the Big Four's manager, Karl Wiltz—hasn't acted in his stead, but with the WFM threatening violence, perhaps no one's willing to shoulder that responsibility. Lipford's the sort of man who'd bankrupt his partners if anything to happened to his own properties.

I settle back onto the bench, pleased to find I'm slightly less sore than I was last night. Folding the blanket for a pillow, I stare at that water stain on the ceiling. Spreading from one corner toward the door, it has rings like a tree. Curious to know what's caused it. No running water in Delamar so it can't be a sink or fountain. No springs within five miles of town, either. Leaky cuspidor? Chamber pot? Gross. I waste two minutes counting rings—seventy-two—and several more calculating how long it'll take to reach the opposite wall. Camp started in '92 but burnt in '95 and this building's been here only since '01, so about one ring per month. Maybe ten, twelve months more and it'll cover the whole ceiling. Seems from the day it was built, this place has been rotting.

Basically true of all human endeavor. Weeks ago, the Tonopah *Sun* carried an item about an Englishman who'd obtained permission from an Afghani emir to excavate some Greek ruins on the desert, only to be killed by tribesmen who never got the message. No surprise. Royal tax collector's probably the only government official they've ever seen, and for what? Article said the Englishman had traveled for weeks on horseback to reach the ruins, suggesting the emir hadn't built any roads thereabouts. No roads, schools, or clinics: nothing to show a tribesman where his money's going. Such limited authority shouldn't need income, yet everyone knows that isn't how things work. Here in the U.S. our taxes and tariffs have paid for two wars of dubious value, lined the railroad and smelter trusts' pockets, and furnished funds for troops to crush anyone who dares to question these cozy arrangements. Hell, yes, something's rotten.

Another year, that stain will cover the ceiling. Weaken the joists and eventually bring this whole building down. Fall down, burn down—who knows? Doesn't matter. No matter how we scurry, in the end everyone and everything turns to dust.

∿

First I heard of President McKinley's assassination, we were standing on Balangiga's municipal plaza for evening roll and to collect our mail—the first we'd received in weeks. Captain Connell stood on a crate to make the announcement. Uncharacteristically, he hadn't even objected to the ensuing chatter, though Lieutenant Bumpus threatened us with work details if we didn't maintain order. We were up half the night debating what it all meant, which partly accounts for our fatigue and disorganization during the attack the following morning. Not many factor Leon Czolgosz in C Company's massacre halfway around the world but there are a few of us.

Most in our outfit were either jingoes or Christian evangelists, determined to drag the wayward Filipinos into the warm sunshine of Western democracy. Others figured it was all a misadventure—an attempt by corporate titans to align the nation's policies with their own. Me, I didn't feel like throwing in with either faction and even today, I still don't. Growing up in the country taught me that whenever possible, people should do for themselves. Of course, that isn't always possible; now and again, everyone needs their neighbors' help. Isn't that the point of human society? Yet the higher people climb, the more they benefit from 'us', the likelier they are to downplay or even deny they had help along the way. If the chips are down, you'd better turn to the poorest folk you know because suddenly your wealthy acquaintances will make themselves scarce. They'll claim they never even knew you, as if your hardship was contagious, and they'll complain that no one has it harder than they do—even those who've never heard hunger's bony fingers scratching at the door.

❦

Returning from the Philippines, I tramped all over the Great Basin looking for meaningful work. Tuscarora and Wonder, Kennedy and Bullion. Four months at Rockland, but it was on the slide and I couldn't find steady. Followed the crowd to Cripple Creek in 1904, just before the district went berserk with violence. Got lucky, I guess, and left Colorado three steps ahead of trouble instead of my customary one. Coming and going, got hassled everywhere I went in Utah. After that, I returned to prospect in Nevada, ran a Shoshone work-crew grubbing sagebrush for a rancher up on the Owhyee Rim, and spent an entire year in Edgemont, setting timbers at the Lucky Girl Mine.

Now and again I met other veterans, likewise burdened by conscience, and saw the things they did to get right again. Saw the effort it took to obtain uncertain results and I guess I got scared and threw in my towel. Still might've gone straight but Joe McCuskey, that old devil, showed up just when I didn't need him. I was drinking way too much and not only did I brush aside what'd happened on Samar, I let down my guard going forward. Julia tried her damnedest to set me square but I was weak and when she died, the grief was overwhelming. I am ashamed of everything I did afterward. Everything.

Without her around, no one could keep me in check and God knows I wasn't up to the task. Of course, Joe split and although I started after him, I couldn't stay dry long enough to catch up. Five months of near-misses and I quit again.

Without a clear target for my rage, I took it out on anyone convenient. Fairview was another disaster: got into a pointless brawl my second week there and had to quit town on the hop. Came to my senses and holed up in Manhattan for a while after that. Took a job working straight security but the big earthquake in San Francisco cut off outside capital and the mines there closed. Drank up most of my last paycheck before someone told me Delamar was booming over on the Black Belt's far side, so that's where I went. Any port in a storm.

Fought on my first night here, too, though the outcome was different. Jack Lipford's father, Hiram, had earthier tastes than his son (and cirrhosis of the liver, I'll bet), which is why he'd been watching from the crowd in a ragtown saloon. The next morning, he not only bailed me out but had me delivered to Association headquarters. Standing there in what is now Prince Jack's office, Sam Rice *strongly* advised the old man against hiring a hooligan like me.

"I don't like this," he said. "Not one bit."

"The hell do you know, Sam?"

"Nothing, Hi, and that's the problem," Rice answered, looking at me the same way people look at their shoe after they've stepped in dogshit. "We don't know anything about him except that he's a hooligan." What Rice *didn't* say was that Hiram's son, Jack, had already promised Rice a bigger role in running the company. Rice, in turn, was grooming Curt Broe as his deputy and here I'd shown up, threatening to spoil everything.

"Well, if I want your two cents, I'll ask for it," Hiram rasped. "I *seen* him fight and I *seen* he don't back down. Ever work security, son?" he said, turning to me.

"Yes, sir," I said.

"You heeled?"

"I can get my service revolver back from the marshal."

The old man nodded. "Put him on at the usual rate then. Have him watch the Highland change-house for highgraders. And Sam, don't you say another word or I'll kick you straight to the curb."

Reluctantly, Rice did as he was told but it's clear this meeting set me on a collision-course with Broe.

The night I kicked down the door to Cyrus Grimes' cabin, I caught him with his hands in a washbasin. He threw its contents at me before lunging for a revolver. I told Nielsen I'd shot Grimes because I was faster but that's only partly true; I was faster because I'd gone into Grimes' home *intending* to shoot him. I *wanted* to, and between my employer's orders and Grimes reaching for his weapon, I had all the setup I needed. Sure, Grimes squeezed off a round as he fell—that much is true—but it was a dying reflex; I was never in his sights and he posed no threat to me then.

Upstairs, the deputy coughs again, scattering my thoughts. Nine, ten months, he's gonna cough up his lungs—I've seen it before. Wads of pink, spongy tissue; face contorted in shock and pain. All because of dust. It's the real killer around here.

Crowd outside is so quiet today I figure they've given up. A mouse skitters under the door, thinks better of it, and scurries back into the hallway—no scraps in here. Haven't moved my bowels in days but the piss-bucket in the corner hasn't been emptied since the day I got here and the cell reeks. Heart's beating painfully against my ribs. Might as well be a clock winding down.

᠀

Sometime in the afternoon, my attorney returns. At first, I figure the noise in the hallway means a deputy's bringing supper early but it's Nielsen's lean face at the window, instead. This time, he's covered with dust and his hair's askew.

I must be lonelier than I realized because I'm oddly pleased to see him. "Counselor," I say, "you look rushed."

"Yes," he pants. "Have you heard anything? Anything unusual?"

I say no one has—that it's been quiet all day. Don't see the need to tell him about Curt's look-in yesterday. Clearly, that was personal.

"Something's happening," he whispers, alerting me to the fact that a deputy must be standing somewhere behind him. "An express driver is taking me to Pioche so I can try to stop your transfer to the county jail—"

"Why? What have you heard?"

"Around midnight, they plan to take you out on the desert and kill you."

"How do you know?"

"The Federation has spies, too, Mr. Sunday." Then he grins, maybe the first time I've seen him do so.

For days, I've resigned myself to a violent end but now that it's near, my stomach twists itself into knots. "Why are you driving up to Pioche? Can't you pick up a telephone?"

"I've tried but Judge Faraday left Delamar after yesterday's hearing and there's no line out to his ranch." Nielsen glances over his shoulder. "No one's answering the courthouse phone, either. I'm sure I could convince Judge Brown to issue a stay but I can't get through. Operators must be screening outbound calls, which means I can't delegate an associate in Pioche, either."

Sounds too well planned for Big Curt's handiwork; one of those imported fellows must've taken over. Or maybe Jerry Rosen's calling shots—he's pretty smart. This is awful news. Everything's down to the wire now and there's nothing I can do. Except...

"The S.P. yards in Caliente," I say. "The yardmaster there is a friend of mine—name's Frank Croft. He can patch a call from the their switchboard."

"You trust him?" Nielsen says, scribbling in his notebook.

"Yeah, Frank's good people—tell him I sent you. So long as you aren't on a party-line, you can bypass Delamar's exchange."

"Worth trying. I told Andy Maguire I'd do everything I could to keep them from taking you."

"Of course—Andy wants that job, himself."

"Mr. Sunday, honestly—"

I hold up a hand. "Lousy joke, counselor, relax. Midnight, you figure?"

"Or sooner, so I'd better be going. Already, two wagons and an auto-stage are parked across the street behind our protesters."

"Loosen bolts, flatten tires."

"Already have but we can delay them only so long. Deputies arrive in force, we'll have to step aside. If they do come down here, stay calm—"

"Oh, you know me."

"Exactly," he whispers. "Don't antagonize them. I advised against it but this afternoon, Andy sent the union's rifle club up north to watch the roads."

"Ah, that's no good."

He nods. "We can't let them get you beyond town limits."

Wasn't what I meant but I hold my tongue. I'd meant that a few men with squirrel guns and damaged lungs would be no match for combat-hardened veterans with shotguns, pistols, and more. It'd be a slaughter. The deputy's footsteps grow louder.

"Go see Helen Molloy," I whisper. "She knows where I sent that survey."

"Time's up," the deputy rasps.

"Yes, but what of it?" Nielsen whispers. "You said whoever has it won't give it to anyone but you."

He's right. My brother, Wade, would sooner toss it in a fire.

"Then bust me out of here."

Nielsen turns to study his pocket watch in the dim light. His eyes are nearly colorless. "I'm doing all I can. It's going to snow tonight so I'd better be going. If your friend in Caliente can't help, then I'll have no choice but to drive to Pioche."

"Thanks, Nielsen. Hurry." Don't know what else to tell a stranger who holds my life in his hands.

He turns his arm sideways and thrusts it through the window. The result is an awkward handshake but I appreciate the gesture.

"Miss Molloy speaks highly of you, Mr. Sunday."

"And I think the world of her" I say. "She deserves better."

"Then do better." He fixes me with that lawyerly stare of his, neither hostile nor friendly; merely curious to hear my response.

"Hope I'll get a chance."

"I'll see what I can do."

Through the little window, I watch until he reaches the stairs. Returning to my bunk, I take a seat. As their footsteps fade, I grope beneath the blanket for the bottle Billy Meeks gave me. Figure I can break it against the concrete floor if I have to. Less than six inches long, it isn't much of a weapon. Liable to cut my hand, too, but I like knowing it's there. It's something.

Nothing else to do but wait and worry and it's almost enough to drive me mad. For the rest of the afternoon and on into the night, I alternate between pacing my cell, shadow boxing, and trying to sleep. My dreams are wretched, though, filled with slashing knives and church bells summoning shadows from the jungle.

NINETEEN

Turbulent sky. Light snow falling. Crows high above a dry lakebed. Parked between the salt and a jumble of granite boulders is a Ford Model N and a mud-spattered Welch. Six men with shovels. None recognizable, their voices are unintelligible. Lots of talk, though. Harsh laughter, too. The dirt they throw on me weighs nothing; but the clay around my feet is cold. Cold and wet. As a boy, there was no better feeling than mud between my toes after a big summer rain but now it just feels cold. My vision fades but opening my eyes wider makes no difference: everything is dark. Darkness beyond sensation and without sensation, there is neither memory nor anticipation. Only paralysis. Dreamless sleep, waiting to be born.

"Sunday."

Something strikes my shoulder, like the blade of a shovel. Want to turn onto my side but can't. Again, I try rolling away but it's no use. Whoever's there won't leave me alone.

"Sunday," someone whispers, "it's time."

How does he imagine I can move? I think, although this is merely an idea behind a thought, like the farthest reflections in opposed mirrors, too dim and distant to recognize. Mouth's full of salt. Clay pins my arms to my sides. The shovel comes again, and again I can't make it stop.

"Come on, get up!"

The voice is so insistent that I inhale and with a jolt, I'm awake on the floor beneath a wooden bench. Blanket's twisted around my waist, my right arm pinned against my body. My left arm's asleep, having been folded beneath my head. A pair of boots stand inches from my face. Only one? Maybe others are waiting out in the hallway; that's how these jobs get done. So dark, I'm damned if I can tell who's there.

I roll onto my side. "Time is it?"

Soon as the words leave my mouth, my head clears. I pull my right arm free from the blanket and grope along the wall beneath my bunk until my hand closes around the bottle. Might be too late but I grasp the flask by its neck and try to gauge the height of this fellow's boot-tops.

"Nine-thirty," he whispers and in the faint light coming through the open cell door, I can just see the young deputy's face. "Come on, we gotta go."

Room stinks worse than usual, embarrassingly so.

"Get away from me." I scuttle backward until my spine touches the wall. With my free hand, I pull myself upright.

"Settle down," the kid whispers. "I'm here to bust you out."

Now, here's the funny thing: given what I'm seeing, he might be telling the truth. He isn't carrying a gun and he's let me get between him and the door—despite his guts, it's clear he has no idea what he's doing.

"My feet are wet," I say, as much to myself as to him.

Taking a step toward the door, he answers, anyway, "You knocked over your pail. Come on, we're in a hurry." He slips past me and steps out into the corridor.

God knows why but Jerry Rosen's name pops into my head and I hesitate, guessing this is a ruse to get me upstairs without a fight.

"Wait, who sent you?"

"Porter Nielsen—my name's Jordan."

"Nice meeting you, Jordan, but I need to know what's doing before I step outside. You're with the WFM?"

"Yes."

"Why didn't Nielsen tell me earlier?"

"Because everything came together at the last minute." He brushes his clothes with his hands. "Town marshal's out front, arguing with fellows from the Association—"

As the kid turns to glance down the hallway, I tuck the bottle into my waistband. The glass is cold against my hip.

"Someone spotted Jack Lipford at the Comstock Club this evening," he continues. "That's what set this in motion. Now, hurry up."

I have never been less sure of anything. For months, I wasn't wary enough and now I'm convulsed with suspicion. Kid isn't holding a weapon. Isn't hostile which is odd, given who he claims to be and what he must know of me.

"Porter Nielsen really sent you?"

The kid edges toward the door. "Look, follow me or don't but I'm leaving."

Hearing this, I won't say the fog lifts, exactly, but I recognize the situation for what it is. This boy might lead me to my death but I reckon that's preferable to waiting for it here.

"Wait," I say, pausing at the door to remove my boots.

"What are you doing?" he whispers. "No time!"

From the corner, I take the overturned bucket and set it beneath the bench. With the blanket over it and my boots protruding from the other side, from the window's limited vantage, it appears I'm still asleep on the floor. If anyone enters the cell it'll be obvious what's happened but if not, it might buy us a few minutes.

"That's enough," the boy says. "Let's *go!*"

He closes the iron door behind us and slides the key beneath it. Taking care to move quietly, we walk the corridor on the sides of our feet. We've almost reached the steps when a door upstairs rattles and cold air floods the building. Normally dull like the droning of bees, noise from the street explodes. Judging by the volume, there must be several hundred people out there and not one of 'em sounds happy.

Shouting at someone outside, Marshal Finch's voice carries above the racket, "No, goddamnit, I need papers! A writ of some kind. You bring me a court order, he's all yours, but not a moment before. Albert, Arthur: watch these fellows while I make rounds. Make sure they stay outside." From the sound of it, Finch is the only one who enters.

My heart's pounding against my ribs. Spilling over the rail, the light here is stronger. Glancing at Jordan, I gesture to suggest attacking Finch but the boy scowls and waves emphatically for me to stay put.

The marshal's shadow appears on a wall upstairs. He walks directly to the railing and braces his hands against it. The smell of cigar smoke wafts downstairs. I glance at Jordan and while it's too dark to read his expression, he seems awfully relaxed for someone on the verge of detection. Bits of ash from Finch's cigar land on the bottom step, inches from my feet.

"Five minutes," the marshal says before exhaling heavily and hurrying back toward the entrance. The door outside opens and shuts and another wave of cold air flows down the steps.

"Jesus Christ, you bought Shorty Finch?" I say but Jordan has already turned.

He unlocks a small door set into the wall beside the first cell. "Coal cellar," he whispers, unlocking a small door set into the wall beside the first cell.

It scrapes and groans the way rusty metal does but not so anyone outside could hear. Inside is a bunker five feet wide, ten deep, and five high, with a small, square hatch in the ceiling. More firewood than coal in here and not much of either, possibly confirming my theory about the town's diminished budgets.

"You first," Jordan says, pointing at the chute.

"This go to the alley?"

"Yeah, they're waiting for us."

No point in asking who he means since it's clear what kind of reception awaits out front. As the door closes behind us, the bunker goes as dark as a mine tunnel and it's every bit as suffocating. Opening the ceiling-hatch, little bits of tumbleweed and trash fall into the bunker. A gust of freezing air dusts us with powdered coal.

"Stand beneath it," Jordan says. "Raise both your arms."

Feeling my way forward, I discover that the chute rises vertically for about three feet before bending at forty-five degrees toward the back wall.

This makes my neck and arms ache but I comply. Directly beneath the chute, I can stand upright. Indeed, from the collarbones up, already I'm within its lowest reaches. Raising my right knee, the glass bottle falls from my waistband, hits the floor, and shatters.

"The hell was that?" Jordan hisses, properly suspicious.

"How would I know?" I lie. "Drunk tossed his bottle in the chute or something. Fell out when you opened the grate."

"Well, be careful," Jordan whispers. "You got no shoes and now there's busted glass everywhere. Okay, spread your arms until you're touching the sides. On the footwall, feel that seam in the concrete? Projects about an inch. Pull yourself up and I'll boost you from below."

Doing as I'm told, I wriggle my way to the bend where a square of red cloud is visible through another small opening.

Snow's coming—I can smell it.

Moving upward a few inches at a time, I use my aching back and knees as much as my hands and feet. My fingers are within inches of the opening when a gigantic man's silhouette blots out the sky. He reaches down, grabs my arms, and my heart surges. No use struggling. Either Jordan's on the level and this is one of his people, or I've been conned and this is the end. Whoever he is, his forearms are like braided steel cables and he damn near lifts me straight out of the chute.

"Jordan's behind you?" he says, depositing me on the ground.

I unclench my fists. "He is, yeah."

This brute with the big arms must be one of Nielsen's union boys—glad I never tangled with him. He turns his attention back to the chute; it's as if I'm not even here. If I still had my boots on I'd have run for it. As it is, I guess I'll ride this out and see where it goes.

Turning, I see a horse-drawn wagon blocking the alley from Juniper Street. Two men in heavy coats are seated on the box and once they see me, they begin talking quietly. One has a shotgun—glad I didn't bolt.

"Does he need help?" I ask the big fellow, gesturing toward the chute.

"Nah," the fellow says. "He's climbed out of worse than this."

Sure enough, within moments, Jordan's blackened hands grip the opening and he pulls himself the rest of the way. Covered with coal dust, he could be mistaken for a chimney sweep and I figure I must look about the same.

"Still good?" Jordan says and the big fellow tells him no one's come through the alley since he took up his post.

"Pushing ten minutes, though."

One fellow jumps down from the wagon to shovel coal into the chute. The scraping and banging are loud but hardly uncommon this time of night so no one comes to investigate.

"Can't take Main Street," I say. Underscoring my point, a scrum of men pass the alley, evidently headed toward the demonstration around front. We press ourselves into the shadows.

"Or Mazuma," Jordan's giant companion whispers. "Or Malapai, or—"

"Alleys," Jordan says. "Stay close, stay quiet."

Even before we reach the end of the block, it begins snowing. Just a few flakes at first but soon it's as if someone's dumping bucketfuls right where we're standing. Good—maybe it'll wash some of the stink off me.

"Would you look at this?" the big man says but Jordan scolds him to keep quiet.

Over the adjacent block's roofline, I see the White House's upper floors, blazing like a bonfire. In better times, I've taken comfort in this glare, even sort of envied its shamelessness, but tonight it just seems pitiful—like an old man on a spree, blowing his life's savings in a vain effort to convince strangers that he still matters.

We run across Portis Street with Jordan out front, me in the middle, and the big fellow hard on my heels. My bare feet are freezing and every pebble feels as if it's been sharpened for the occasion. Mercifully, Delamar's layout is long and narrow and it only takes a few minutes to cross most of downtown.

"Name's Beck," the big miner says, breathing heavily.

"Beck's your first name?"

"Not even my last. Call me Beck though; everyone does."

"Quiet," Jordan scolds, pointing at the last door on the left before Nixon Street. He looks around before crossing, unlocks the door, and slips inside. A moment later, he leans back out and motions for Beck and me to follow.

Inside is a long corridor. Office building, clearly. Names on the doors announce contract engineers, mine promoters—even a dentist. We stop at an unmarked doorway near the front entrance and Jordan knocks twice. A panel slides back so whoever's inside can see us. Locks clatter and the door swings open, revealing a windowless room containing a few pieces of cast-off furniture.

While Beck blows into his cupped hands, Jordan exchanges quiet words with the fellow who let us in. I notice he's holding a sawed-off shotgun.

Turning to face me, the boy nods. "Sunday, stay here with Mike while Beck and I go fetch the wagon."

"Wagon?"

"That's how we're smuggling you out of Delamar. No one's gonna notice a pair of wagons making an early run across the mountains."

"Nonsense. They'll search every vehicle, coming or going."

"Relax," he says, "we have a plan."

Nothing I've seen so far relaxes me but I keep my own counsel. Jordan and Beck step back out into the hallway and close the door. Shotgun Mike throws two deadbolts and takes a seat on a chair in the corner.

"You can sleep if you want," he says, settling the weapon across his knees.

I glance around the room. It's twice as large as my cell. One wall has shelves containing tinned food and secondhand clothes. A single bare bulb dangles from a loose porcelain fixture. From time to time, we've found WFM safe-rooms like this, a few of them occupied.

I glance at the pile of shoes.

"You mind?" I raise my bare left foot.

"Go ahead." Mike takes a plug of tobacco from his coat pocket and bites off a hunk. "It's what they're for, ain't they?"

Removing my wet shirt, I wipe days' worth of grime and coal dust off my face. I note the bruises on my arms and shoulders. Some have turned a revolting mustard-yellow, while others have retained their purplish hue, and I'm sure the rest of my face and body looks about the same.

"Jesus," Mike says. "Someone fucking laid into you, didn't they?"

"Yeah," I exhale, "they fucking did."

I find pants and a shirt that fits, plus a vest, and a nice, heavy coat. The socks have holes in them and the boots are scruffy but even so, they're better than what I had before.

"Better take a hat, too," Mike says. "Storm's gonna blow all night."

"Appreciate it." Among three hats on the top shelf, I'm pleased to find a black homburg that fits.

"Replenished from time to time by the Ladies' Aid Society. You get what you need?"

"I think so."

"Great." Mike snorts, leans over a brass spittoon, and makes a deposit. "Now, sit down so I don't have to track you all over the room."

Seems Mike's hospitality has its limits.

My gratitude has limits, too. Shotguns are touchy things so I'm unwilling to tangle with Mike just now but I've been observing his habits, watching for an advantage. He keeps his hand over the breech, for instance, instead of gripping it properly with a finger on the trigger guard. No sense fumbling for your weapon in an emergency but the bad habits people develop over time are funny like that.

∽

God knows C Company developed questionable habits during our garrison on Samar. Captain Connell put us through daily drills and exercise so it wasn't tropical lethargy or inattention that left us vulnerable but a complete misreading of the Samareños.

The atmosphere in Balangiga was always tense. Connell was a prig who, within a week of our arrival, banned cockfighting—a major entertainment throughout the islands—and forbade mixing socially with the townspeople. Up north on Luzon, we'd gotten used to bantering and trading with the natives but on Samar, they were profoundly conservative and wanted nothing to do with us. Even so, some in our company made advances toward young women that were hotly refused, once even resulting in one of our fellows being beaten by a woman's male relatives. Between this lack of deference, attacks on our patrols, and pressure from Manila to produce results, a week before September 28, Connell ordered every able-bodied male arrested and confined to a pair of Sibley tents we'd set up on the town's plaza. Eighty Samareños imprisoned in a space built for thirty-two. As well, we'd felled coconut trees, burned rice stores, and ordered all the camote and gabi growing wild around their huts cut down. These measures, plus confiscating the village's pigs, fish, and chickens were taken ostensibly to deny food to the rebels Connell believed to be lurking nearby, but the only practical effect was that soon the townspeople began to starve. Starving people are dangerous; you'd think we'd have learned as much in China the year before but Connell wouldn't hear it.

~

I stretch out on a cot and stare at the ceiling. No stains on this one.

Mike coughs into his fist but it sounds like garden-variety congestion, not miners' con like Billy Meeks, Curt, and Lipford all have. Don't know whether Mike's condition might not be worse—at least silicosis isn't contagious. He spits tobacco juice into the cuspidor and wipes his mouth with the back of his hand.

Ten minutes pass.

"Know how long they'll be?" I say, and Mike startles.

He rubs his eyes. "Not much longer."

The room is cold but Shotgun Mike is clearly drowsy. I watch him through slit eyes, noticing he's biting his nails and clenching his fists in an effort to stay awake. Anticipating an opportunity to move soon, my breath quickens, but footsteps in the hall and a knock at the door dispel any thought of escape.

Mike jumps to his feet and withdraws the bolts. I can tell it isn't Jordan or Beck in the hall, though, because Mike steps backward with his hands slightly raised. Like I said, bad habits will catch up with you.

Can't hear the full conversation but Mike's share is clear enough. "Take it easy," he says, followed by "Not yet," and "No, they didn't." He glances along the corridor, his gun still swinging on the cord around his neck. Emptyhanded, he steps through the doorway and disappears.

"Get lost," says an unfamiliar voice, "and keep your mouth shut, understand?"

Son of a bitch. Figuring nothing I want is heading my way, I step away from the cot and flatten my back against the opposite wall. Two men burst into the room, both carrying revolvers. Don't know why my mind fixates on this, but one has a tuft of snow like a rabbit's tail on the crown of his bowler.

"Don't move," Rabbit Hat says while the second fellow moves around Mike's empty chair.

Glancing toward the hallway, the second man motions with his head. A third fellow carrying rope jostles his way through the door. Some days I'll take 2-to-1, but 3-to-1, and two of them strapped, make for piss-poor odds in a fight.

"Turn around," this latecomer says and I comply, albeit not fast enough to suit him because he throws a lazy punch at my jaw.

I'm trying to stay calm, goddamnit, but my reflexes still work and I brush-block his fist without even trying. Counter with a back-fist and catch him in the temple but Rabbit Hat slams his revolver against the back of my head.

Three-to-one, stupid.

My knees buckle and I sit heavily on the chair. The second man lunges forward and puts me in a chokehold. Conjoined this way, we crash backward over the cot, upending it, and rolling into the opposite wall.

Not like I'm in fighting-shape, anyway, so I give up resisting. Exaggerate my stupor, even, just so the fellow who tried to punch me doesn't overdo tying my hands behind my back although he does, anyway. And somewhere between my reputation as a nuisance and wanting to delay these bastards for as long as possible, I pretend I'm too wobbly to sit straight, although I certainly could. Worst of all, they pull a dirty bandanna tight over my mouth and tie it even tighter than the cords around my hands. Damn it, they get me outside, I'm as good as dead.

They pull me to my feet.

"Come on, move!" Rabbit Hat snaps and punches me in the ribs.

Reaching the doorway, I stagger, slump against the frame, and drop to my knees.

"Son of a bitch can't walk," Sucker Punch complains, rubbing his head where I clocked him.

Rabbit Hat tells this fellow to fuck off. "You hadn't hit him first, I wouldn't have thumped him. Come on, Gene, help me carry this bastard."

Gene the Second stashes his gun in his jacket and leans down to snake his arm beneath my shoulder. Rabbit Hat does likewise and soon we're lurching along the corridor, my head flopping from side to side and my feet dragging.

Takes almost a minute to reach the door facing the alley and both of my caretakers are breathing hard. As Sucker Punch reaches for the knob, the door crashes open and Beck steps through, a double-barreled shotgun tight against his shoulder. His hat and coat are plastered with snow.

Rabbit Hat starts pawing his coat for his revolver but Beck covers him with the gun.

"Nope," Beck growls, "not unless you want some."

Gene the Second yanks his one hand from under my shoulder before raising both. Rabbit Hat, on the other hand, maintains his grip, causing me to turn so my back strikes the wall. He takes a step backward, trying to drag me with him as a human shield but a door at the hallway's far end opens and Mike advances, shotgun raised.

Gene follows Sucker Punch's lead and raises his hands, but Rabbit Hat won't release his grip. Keeping me upright is a chore, though, and forces him to press his other hand against the wall. Glancing between Beck and Shotgun Mike, he spits on the floor and finally lets me drop.

"You don't wanna do this," Rabbit Hat says, narrowing his eyes.

Holding a snub-nosed .38, Jordan steps past Beck and searches the others' coat pockets. "The hell we don't, jack." In short order, he confiscates their revolvers plus a knife from Sucker Punch's right boot.

"Think about what you're doing, kid."

"Remind Clayton the vote was fair and square," Jordan snaps. "You're out of line here and you know it."

"Take it up with The Ten," Rabbit Hat says. He jerks a thumb my direction. "Andy's gonna catch hell if he turns this one loose."

"Back inside." Jordan waves the revolver.

Gene and Sucker Punch comply but Rabbit Hat lingers a moment before stepping through the door.

"Better account, Jordan," he says. "Beck and Mikey, too. You think we'll take this lying down, then y'all are dumber than I thought."

Beck advances and muzzle-bumps Rabbit Hat's chest, hard.

"Shut up," the big man spits. "Get inside."

With Shotgun Mike on his left and Beck menacing from the right, Rabbit Hat thinks better of his stand and steps back inside the safe room. Mike kicks the door closed, takes a key from his pocket, and locks it.

"Someone will come along around midnight," Jordan says, pressing his mouth against the jamb. "Bust out before then and Mike's gonna give you a dose, understand?"

"Watch your backs," Rabbit Hat growls, his voice muffled by the door, as Beck and the kid walk back to where I'm seated and pull me to my feet. With Sucker Punch's knife, Jordan cuts the cords around my wrists and takes the bandanna out of my mouth.

"Can you walk?"

"Yeah, I'm fine." I stretch and crack my neck.

Jordan and Beck exchange glances.

My fingertips are numb and welts encircle my forearms, but I'm definitely getting off light. Head hurts, too, but not so bad I can't nod and thank the boys for coming back for me.

"Had to," Jordan says. "We swore to Andy we'd get you out of town."

"Aye," Beck seconds and opens the door.

The wind is howling now, driving snow sideways between the buildings.

I pull my new hat low around my ears. "Who were those guys?"

Beck shrugs and Jordan barely acknowledges the question, "Politics. I'll explain later."

TWENTY

Emerging from the same alley that swallowed us an hour earlier, Jordan glances around before waving us forward; Beck trails me by ten yards.

We cross Nixon. The streets are strangely quiet, or not so strange considering how hard it's snowing. The few people we see are carousers out making their rounds and they don't care about us, the weather, or anything else except their sprees.

Walking in silence gives me time to think. Why was Marshal Finch involved in my escape from his jail? I know Black Tiger Mines bankrolled Shorty's election—a fact that enrages Prince Jack—but he's still gonna catch hell once my absence is discovered. And when might that be? Once Lipford finishes supper? Midnight, per Porter Nielsen's warning? Not for the first time, I appreciate that no one here does anything except on Jackson Lipford's say-so.

West of Delamar Wash, the roads steepen and we enter the yards below Black Tiger's surface-works. We hop a wire fence, walk single-file below the sorting house, and regroup inside a small shed on the property's far edge. Inside, the walls are set with racks for various lengths of iron pipe and bins filled with couplings and fittings. Suspended over a workbench, bare lightbulbs hang inside green enameled fixtures. Through the corrugated walls, I hear teamsters readying the wagons for our drive to Stine Siding.

Jordan ventures off somewhere while I take a seat. Beck blocks the doorway, chewing tobacco and spitting in the snow outside.

"Those fellows say anything to you?" he says.

"In the safe room?" I rub the lump on my head where Rabbit Hat clocked me with his gun.

Beck nods.

"Not much. Gave me the bum's rush and then bickered once they realized they had to carry me."

"Why would they carry you?"

"Short one thumped me with his pistol so I pretended it made me shakier than it actually did."

"Did you really? That's great." Beck laughs. He spits again through the door. "Idiots."

Bracketed by gusts of wind, a short silence follows. One of the teamsters drops something and shouts.

"Jordan mentioned 'politics' there in the alley behind your safehouse and the short kidnapper said something about 'The Ten'…" I let this question die, unsure whether Beck will get touchy airing the WFM's dirty laundry.

"Factions within the union." Beck shrugs. "The Ten is nothing but a handful of fellows who think we oughta be more direct in dealing with Black Hand Jack and his Association."

"'Direct?'"

"Violent. They wanted to make an example of you."

"Andy Maguire doesn't?"

"We just want fair shakes—that's why we're backing Black Tiger. Clayton Hock and his Wobblies want a revolution."

"Hock's the new secretary, right?"

"Replaced Billy Meeks. Remember him?" He grins at me before turning to spit through the door.

Can't read this Beck fellow. I haven't exactly been a friend of the union, yet he's treating me well—better than many of my Association counterparts did, certainly. Angry or hostile I'd understand, but he isn't either of these things. I don't know how to function in this environment.

"Beck, can I ask you something?"

"Shoot."

I study his profile as I speak, "Know who I am? Why the Association's keen to put me out?"

"Sure." He glances my way. "We've been after you for months, too, but you're tough to pin down."

"Not hard enough."

"Well, now you're on our side of the ledger." He grins again.

I stifle a laugh. Of all the nonsense: I haven't thrown in with *anyone,* least of all the WFM. I'm here only until I can run.

"Then you know what I've done? On Lipford's behalf, I mean?"

His expression doesn't change. His head remains tilted as if he's more interested in sounds coming from the yard than answering my question.

"Yes." He takes a deep breath. "But Porter Nielsen says you have something that's gonna force Black Hand Jack to sell. If that's true, then there's a lot about you that I'm willing to ignore."

"Don't get your hopes up. Can't imagine what it'll take to break his grip."

He shrugs. "Odds are better than they were this morning."

I shake my head slowly. This blind, desperate faith—how bad are things that he'd look to someone like me for help?

"Are we good, then?"

He turns to face me and his voice hardens, "I said 'ignore,' not forget. So no, we aren't good—not yet—but Delamar's workingmen are on the ropes. Jack Lipford's beaten us down on safety, hours, wages—everything we have—so if you can help, we're on a different footing, aren't we? What idiot rejects good news because he doesn't like the messenger?"

Me, for one. For a long time, I've been that kind of idiot.

⁓

"Sunday," Jordan says, leaning through a door on the shed's far side, "someone's here to see you. Beck, come give me a hand."

Once Beck exits, Helen Molloy steps inside and I have to catch my breath.

"Shepard," she says and I thrill to the sound of her voice.

Walking toward her, I feel something I haven't in years—something between tenderness and lust, happiness and loss. Don't know why she'd come here or whether I deserve to see her at all, but I'm elated just the same. She's all I have.

"What are you doing here?" I say. "Are you okay?"

She doesn't answer. Instead, she wraps her arms around my waist and kisses me hard and damned if I'll stop her. Wasn't expecting happiness or pleasure tonight and since I'm unsure how to react, I figure it's better if I don't.

A long moment later, she lets go and steps back. "It's happening," she says. "It really happening."

"What is? What do you mean?"

"Last night, Beck told me a plan was underway to spring you. All day, I thought something had gone wrong but then a man came to the Belle and said you were out."

"Who's that?"

"A messenger, I don't know."

What's going on here? Why would the union go to Helen with plans and news of my escape? She rests her hands on my chest, derailing these thoughts. She smells so good I'm embarrassed thinking how I must stink.

"Can't stay long," she says. "It'll be dangerous on the streets soon."

As if it wasn't already. "You shouldn't have risked it."

"I had to—I brought your things." She reaches into a bag slung over her shoulder, rummages for a moment, and hands me my Colt revolver.

I don't believe it. First Helen, herself, and now this—I couldn't be more surprised if Charlie Witherill walked through the door. "How'd you get it?"

She reaches back into the bag and pulls out my old jacket, so thin it's been folded down to the thickness of a book on political ethics. Searching the pockets, I find Julia's photograph and my keys—but no envelope. No bonus cash. Gone. I search the pockets again.

Sensing my agitation, Helen rests her hand on my shoulder. "What is it?"

"Nothing." I stash my things in the various pockets of my new coat. "Thanks for these."

Helen withdraws her hand. "Didn't think to ask if she'd left everything alone."

"Ask who?" I say, still thinking of Julia.

Helen wrinkles her nose. "The stenographer."

I'm more confused than ever. "Lila brought you these things?"

Helen purses her lips. Outside, snowflakes fall through beams of light like sparks from a cold fire. For a long while, she says nothing and eventually I realize what a stupid thing I've just said.

"Jesus, of course she didn't. I'm sorry."

Even as dark as it is, I can tell she's looking at me. "No more lies, Shepard. I can take the pain, but not your lies—not anymore."

I get what she's saying but I'm unsure how—or even whether—I could ever do what she's just asked. I lie for a living, for survival, for my sanity. No such thing as truth in Delamar, anyway—any wonder the churches are empty and the brothels full? Hell, sitting in jail, it struck me: everything I've done these past few years is a lie. *Everything.* Maybe Thiel and Pinkerton men can separate their personal and professional lives, but not me. I've lived my job, so to speak, and now that it's been smashed, there's nothing left to lean on. No achievements, no connections—nothing I can point to with any pride. All the discord I've sown, all the pain inflicted: none of it means anything. Nothing good, anyway. Lipford's richer than ever, Joe McCuskey's been shelved, and *still* the tide is rising.

"I don't know where to start. I know I'm wrong—"

"About *everything*," she says, brushing aside my apology.

"Everything, you're right."

She backs away. "The morning after they arrested you, I went to Lila's apartment and demanded your things."

"Thank you. Was anyone else there?"

"Nobody. She handed me everything I just gave to you and kept packing. Never said a word."

"She was never in my corner."

"Didn't I say so?"

"Yeah, but I'm a fool."

"You aren't the only one."

I try to take her hand but she pulls away. I try again and this time, she relents. She's stiff at first, unyielding, but soon she leans and rests her head against my shoulder. I feel her breathing, her chest rising and falling with mine and it feels wonderful. Like standing close with someone ought to feel. Take this moment and multiply it a million times: this is what I want. Just this. Won't get it though. Not after all I've done. For all its warmth, this feeling isn't real; just a kinder version of loneliness. Ah, who knows? Despite our mistakes, we might still have something, her and me. From the way she's tilting her head, it's clear she expects me to say something—hell, I'd like to reassure us, both—but still the right words won't come. My thoughts are ugly, my voice is ugly, but I have to say...something.

"I hate what I do. Hate what this place has done to me. I want to get right again but I can't see how."

Snowflakes float slowly past the open window.

"This." She squeezes my ribs. "This is how. You can do something great here, Shepard—something that redeems everything."

"How do you figure?" I can't see what's happening as anything more than another transaction—Black Tiger and the Federation get some papers and I get to run.

"Porter Nielsen told me about the survey you're taking to Carson City."

"Did he?" I grit my teeth and swear to myself. A little careless aren't we, buddy boy? The less said the better, although who understands how the Western Federation conducts its business? Might be tomorrow's headline in their crappy little newspaper.

Helen leans into me. "The night you were arrested, is that what you wanted me to mail?"

"Yes."

"Then why did you turn away? You know I'm on your side, don't you?" She brushes my temple with the back of her hand.

"To protect you."

"I don't need protection, Shep."

"You say that because you don't know what's after me—after *you* if they ever learn you're involved."

"Oh, give me a *little* credit."

Out on the yard, a mule-team plods toward the mine, giant things with snowy backs and steaming flanks. Stones clatter beneath their shoes.

Helen sighs. "Why can't you trust me?"

"Other people—people I thought I knew—they turned on me."

"Don't you know I wouldn't?"

"I know," I say but stumble over words. "You're…You've been…"

"Never, Shep. I *hate* the Association, hate how they use up men and discard them—how they used you."

"It's just business."

"It's *criminal*," Helen snaps. "I run a business, too, and you don't see me cheating my employees." Her eyes flash with anger. "It's got to stop. He can't keep getting away with it and for once, we're on even footing."

Who's this 'we' she keeps talking about? I honestly don't know what she means. Hell, I didn't ask for this. Didn't ask for any of it. Then again, I've been so bad at reading signs lately, perhaps I did. Asked Nielsen to bust me out and this is the price.

"I'll do what I can," I say, "but don't set your hopes too high." I always feel a little confused talking to Helen. She drives me to distraction. I talk too fast and afterward wonder if I've said too much.

Taking the keys from my coat pocket, I spin the ring around my finger. One unlocks my room at the boardinghouse; another, the Association's offices on Malapai; and the third opens a lock on the explosives bunker up at the

Tomcat. I consider dropping them into a bucket of bolts on the ground beside me, but at the last minute, slip these relics back into my pocket. Call me quaint but I can never discard old keys, even when I've forgotten what they unlock.

My thoughts return to my cash-bonus, which I presume Lila pocketed. Either that or it fell out in her room. Don't think Curt's boys found it or they'd have searched the apartment for more, likely discovering my revolver in the process. Honestly, Helen might've taken it but I hate this thought and tell myself to knock it off.

Pacing the room, I'm in danger of slipping into a rage when Helen looks at me and smiles. Just like that, I am helpless.

"Remember how we met?" she says.

"At the Belle—you had me thrown out."

"Not first thing," she laughs. "You started a fight."

"I did?" I honestly don't remember. Been in so many over the years that only a few stand out.

"Yeah, you did," she says, "but it's *why* you were fighting that made me notice you."

"I forget."

"Two fellows from the Association came in looking for trouble. Picked on a customer, a skinny kid with a union pin and your boys didn't like it."

"Oh, yeah. Sean Foley and…" I think a moment before snapping my fingers. "Dan Rayland, no, *Dale* Rayland. That's right. Foley and Rayland."

"You wouldn't let them pick on the kid and I'd *never* seen anyone from the Association stick up for someone that way. Not for someone from the WFM, certainly."

"Sam Rice didn't like it."

"Well, *I* did. Even if you went about it all wrong, it was a decent thing to do. An honorable thing."

"That right? If you were so charmed, then why'd you have me thrown out?"

"You broke my rules." She squeezes my hand. "That man—one who'd protect a stranger—we need him."

Jordan knocks on the doorframe. His hat is caked with snow. "We're all set," he says.

Helen takes a step to leave but I grab her sleeve. "Wait, can I ask you something?"

She pulls on her gloves and says that'd be okay.

Don't want to upset her again but curiosity compels. "How'd you figure my things were at Lila's?"

"You're serious?" She elbows me in the ribs and steps through the door. "And here I thought you were going to kiss me again. I went there because you're more predictable than you think."

Funny, I was thinking the same thing.

Jordan waves us toward the sorting house. "Come on, you two, hurry."

TWENTY-ONE

My confidence plummets once I see where I'm expected to spend the next several hours. With a reinforced suspension, iron-rimmed wheels, and sheet-iron lining, the wagon itself is sturdy enough. It's my hiding space that leaves much to be desired. Seems the WFM's plan is for me to lie at the bottom of the wagon's V-shaped bed, cover this space with a reinforced lid, and heap broken ore on top so it looks like a normal shipment. I'll have five, six inches of clearance, at most.

Don't know what I was expecting but it wasn't this. This is an iron coffin.

"Union finally gets its wish," I say to Beck and he grins.

"You'll be fine."

"You'd get inside that?"

"If I didn't have a choice, sure."

The wagon's bed is wet with snow and freezing to the touch. At the bottom are two locked, hopper-type doors. Down at the rail siding, teamsters drive these wagons up onto loading platforms. The doors open and ore falls directly into railcars bound for the smelters in Salt Lake City. The mules up front—eight in all—are big animals, too: each pulls a one-ton load-equivalent. Can't imagine we'll run that heavy tonight. Hope not, anyway.

"Hi, howdy." An extravagantly bearded teamster steps forward and rests his elbows against the bed. "Name's Stub. You're the extra, I take it?"

I introduce myself. We shake hands and since I have a big mouth, I ask him if Stub is his given name.

He holds up his left hand and all the fingers are missing save for his thumb and about an inch of his pinkie. "Lost 'em in the Colton Mine outside Searchlight in '98. Had my hand on the gate over Number One compartment when the chippy went by. No rush of air, no bells on station, no warning of any kind. Lucky I didn't lose my skull, yeah?"

"No trouble handling a team?"

"None: I was born to drive, jack. Should've stayed up top where I belong. Might still have my fingers but everyone said the big money was underground. Believe you me, nothing good comes from going underground."

I couldn't agree more. "Really think this will work?" I ask.

"Should, but make yourself skinny," he laughs. "This ain't no Pullman car."

No kidding. Despite two-inch pipes welded to it for reinforcement, the sheet-iron separator they'll set over me is dented and gouged—deeply in places—and I'm no longer sure this is the best way to leave town.

The teamster clears his throat and spits. "Settle into the lowest part of the bed and we'll lower that separator. Then close your eyes, hold your breath, and cover your ears. Once those chutes open, it's gonna get louder'n hell."

"Thought you were gonna shovel in?"

"No time," Jordan says.

Helen glances at the gears and levers that control the doors on the wagon's underside. "Is it strong enough?"

The teamster shoots Jordan and Beck a look before turning back to Helen. "Of course it's strong enough. How many tons, Hugh? Four, you think?" He squats to check the locking mechanism holding the doors together.

Atop the ore bin, a chute-tender leans over the railing. "This is run-of-mine, headed for the mill in Pioche. Ain't as heavy as highgrade. Don't worry; we've done this before."

"With people?" I say.

He shakes his head. "Rifles and such. I'll keep it light."

"Nothing ever gets broken?"

Again, the teamster glances between Jordan and Beck before answering, "You'll be fine." He urges me toward the wagon.

"Where do I sit?" Helen says.

Stub looks around at Jordan, the others, and me.

"You ain't coming, miss," he tells her. "Ain't safe, ain't suitable. One of you boys wanna set her straight?"

Helen appears calm but her eyes blaze. "Don't talk to me that way—I'm going, too."

"Not on my rig, you ain't."

"Mister, you don't have a say."

Down in town, the bell atop City Hall begins ringing. Despite the falling snow, the sound comes loud and clear. Everyone here understands what it means, and me, I don't much like the sound of church bells.

"Ride with the others if they'll have you," Stub spits. "I'm washing my hands of this." He turns and stalks across the yard.

I glance at their faces. No one dares to cross Helen so I go to stand with her. "You don't need this," I say. "It's too dangerous."

"Can't stay, Shepard; I'm invested."

"Tomorrow morning, then—the auto-stage to Caliente. Don't put yourself in danger this way."

"Too late," she says, and for the first time tonight, her voice shakes. "What if Shorty Finch turns again? Took one bribe, didn't he?"

"Helen—" I start but she won't have it.

"God knows Lipford has a thousand times more resources than we do and he isn't above kidnapping or worse. It's all coming so fast now." With her head in her hands, she leans against my chest.

I can't argue with anything she's said: there are no good options now.

She looks back across the yard, back toward Delamar's dull glow. I'm desperate to know what she's thinking. I have so many questions but there isn't time and I bite my tongue. For a moment, the only sounds I hear are of the pealing bell, the champing mules, and the hiss of falling snow.

Helen straightens her back. "This is how it goes," she says, sounding calmer. She turns to face the others. "All of you, get going. Get Shepard away from here."

Somehow, this breaks the spell. The others turn to follow Stub, struggling to wrestle the heavy separator into position.

I take her hands in mine. "Low profile, yes?"

"You, too, Shepard. Run fast and don't stop." Then she kisses me hard—like she knows she might never get another chance—before turning and walking away.

Reaching the wagon, I look back over my shoulder. Helen's already in the darkness beyond the bins. Snow's picked up again and she's hard to see: a three-dimensional shadow.

"Think she'll be okay?" I say and Beck nods without conviction.

I turn to look again but she's gone.

"Goddamnit, come *on!*" Stub bellows. "That bell hasn't stopped and now I don't see how we'll get away."

∽

I climb into the wagon and wriggle around the half-set separator. The thin layer of hay beneath my back is wet, though I suppose I should be grateful for a cushion. The image of Helen as a shadow lingers in my head.

Beck looks over the wagon's edge. "Ready?"

"No." I'm lying in an iron box with a heavy iron lid teetering just a few feet to my left. This is insane.

He hands me a bandanna.

"What for?"

"Dust," he says and then he's gone.

Stub's silhouette replaces Beck's. "Someone stops us and paws through the ore, even probes it with an iron bar, it's gonna make noise but keep your mouth shut and they'll stop looking. Nothing can touch you, understand?"

"Got it."

The millhands strain to keep the sheet-iron from toppling into the wagon. Beck and Stub clamber onto the wheels and grasp two iron rods threaded through the reinforcing pipes. I hear them grunt and curse as they maneuver the separator into place. Inches at a time, the sky disappears. The wagon reverberates and sways as the loaded bars settle on the bed-walls. Dust swirls inside the compartment, making my eyes water and my throat burn.

"That was the easy part," Stub shouts. "Gonna pull the rods now, both at the same time, too, or the plate won't fall evenly. Crush the extra and we don't want that, yeah? On my count now, one…"

My pulse surges. I turn my head and press my back against the bed.

"Two…"

Close my eyes and hold my breath.

"Three."

With a huge, metallic clang, the plate drops into the bed. A blast of air slams my chest and pops my eardrums. For a second, I figure I've been hit by the separator, itself.

Metallic dust fills the compartment and my first breath is an unhappy discovery. My throat and lungs burn; feels like I've inhaled poison. I cough with the same ferocity I've heard elsewhere in Delamar and even after an unreasonable length of time, I can't stop.

"Hey, Sunday," Beck calls from somewhere on my left, "pard, how you doing?"

"Here," I wheeze between jags.

"Great. We'll take on ore now. Ten minutes more, I reckon."

The wagon lurches forward and sways on its springs before shuddering to a halt. Now there's barely any light in the compartment. Rivulets of snowmelt seep around the separator's edges.

"Sunday," Stub shouts, rapping on the iron six inches above my face. "The big fellow says you're okay so brace yourself, yeah? Close your eyes and hold your breath as long as you can; you ain't never taken a dusting like this."

"He gave me a bandanna," I say, still coughing.

"Sure, sure," he says, followed by an long pause. "Everyone, stand back!"

I screw my eyes shut, hunch my shoulders, and still feel exposed as hell. Above the elbows, my arms press against my sides but I can move just enough to clamp the bandanna over my mouth and nose, and rest my other hand atop Julia's photo and my revolver. While neither totem can protect me if something goes wrong, I still want them near. They're my lifelines now. Stub says something more but his voice sounds distant and I can't tell whether he's talking to me.

"What did you say?" I shout. "What?"

A loud 'ping' sounds as a rock strikes the iron separator somewhere near my feet. Just as I realize Stub's counting again, the gates go up and four tons of broken rock come roaring down the chutes. The wagon sways hard on its springs, knocking my head against the sides of this tiny prison. *God*, I think, but nothing more. No prayers for safety; no thoughts of loved ones. Only *God*— Alpha and Omega—because nothing else is anywhere near as huge as the sound that assaults me. Lying under that sheet-iron, all that noise—it's *physical*. The breath is ripped from my lungs and my eyes feel dangerously close to bursting. Tears freeze against my cheeks. All this continues for what feels like forever, like it'll be everything I'll know for the rest of my life. I am an upcountry Jonah, swallowed by the earth for my sins.

Eventually, the roaring stops but my body shakes as if fevered and my ears can't distinguish silence from sound. It's like trying to listen underwater. Voices are shouting at me from all sides, though they might as well be seals barking. Bits of rock and dirt trickle around the separator's edges and already I can tell that pounds of grit have worked their way into the space around my feet. Did the separator shift? Feels like it. Shit, it's pinched the left elbow of my coat and when I pull free, the fabric rips. Might've cut me, too, but who knows whether I'm bleeding or my elbow's wet from snow? Then stillness returns and since it appears nothing's been broken, a wisp of gratitude flits through my head: Thank you, God—thank you.

Too soon, though; too soon by half. All this while, I've been holding my breath and although I don't *want* to breathe yet, I've hit my limit. Inhaling, even with the bandanna, is like plowing a field with my teeth. Bitter, acrid, abrasive. I cough ferociously, unsure whether I'll ever stop. Lungs feel blistered. Crackling sounds inside my chest and rattling in my throat. Mud fills my mouth and there's no way to spit it all out. I wipe my face until the bandanna's a filthy, sodden mess and then I surrender and let it roll down the sides of my face. Claustrophobia grips me but as I thrash, I strike my head on the iron plate and this knocks a little sense into me.

I tell myself to settle down and breathe slowly, except the mere act of breathing is pain, itself.

"Sunday," Beck shouts. He raps on the wagon's side with a shovel. "Still in there?" Sounds like he's down in a well.

"Can't breathe," I sputter and cough again.

"Buddy," he laughs, "you can talk, you can breathe."

I can hear the gruff teamster's voice but not what he says.

"He's fine," Beck shouts. Goes quiet. Shouts again, "Okay, I'll tell him."

The wagon lurches forward and rubble spills around the separator's edges. A few moments more and we grind to another halt.

Beck speaks again from somewhere on my left, "Soon as we load the other wagon, we're off. Jordan's gone ahead to see whether anyone's watching the road. Presuming they aren't, we'll be across the range before daybreak. Unload you for breakfast."

"Beck…" I try to clear my throat and cough again. Can't even remember what I wanted to say. Swallowing hurts. "Too much dust," I rasp.

Beck laughs. "Pard, that's nothing but a day's dose in the mines. Hang tight, okay?"

I'm alone with my thoughts now, compressed into the tiniest space imaginable—Big Curt said I was gonna end up in a hole. Goddamn, this is a terrible plan; can't believe I ever agreed to it. Should've left Delamar long ago. Should've kept walking over Ferguson Hill with Warren Jim. Should've done a million things differently but here I am. God in Heaven, here I am.

TWENTY-TWO

It's freezing cold, pitch-dark, and for several moments, I've no idea where I am. Then a jolt knocks my head against sheet-iron and dirt trickles onto my face.

That's right: buried alive.

The wagon lurches again. Taking inventory, my list of complaints is long and pitiful. Chattering teeth. Hands and feet are numb, my body aches, and my lungs flat-out hurt. Every cough is like sandpaper on the back of my throat, though whether this is from dust or the biting cold, I cannot tell. So damn cold. I'd figure the wind whistling through all the little gaps would've cleared the air but no, not at all. No idea how long I've been asleep or how far we've traveled. Might've stopped once at a checkpoint, I don't know. Must be how Joe McCuskey felt there at the end.

Everything around me creaks and shifts constantly. Only difference since leaving Black Tiger's yards is our pitch. On the range's western side, my head was above my feet. Now everything's reversed: my feet are higher and blood's pooling in my head. Gallons, too, from the feel. Headache's worse and my face is so swollen I'm afraid that if I scrape against the iron around my head, I'll burst like an overripe berry. Apart from these discomforts, though, I've little to report. Wish I had a bottle, but that isn't news. The claustrophobia that gripped me at the start has passed. Mentally, I am reconciled with confinement. Just one more thing to endure, except now my sense of time is shot. The past, present, and future all commingle in such a way that no one vantage dominates. I wake, I doze, I wake. One minute I'm following a muddy trail in the Philippines and the next, I'm wiping actual mud from my face. I recall sitting beside Jack Lipford, listening to managers' reports on weekly tonnages. Julia's beautiful eyes and her soft, sweet voice. Helen's, too. Why did I take her for granted for so long? Should've treated her better. Should've seen Lila for who she is. Should've been man enough to choose. Never should've come to Delamar in the first place. Dozing off again, here come Charlie Witherill and Joe McCuskey. Everyone and no one, everything and nothing, all at the same time.

∾

Moving faster now. Feels like it, anyway, though it's impossible to measure from one minute to the next. Right hand rests on the revolver. Safety's on and I'm careful to keep my fingers outside the trigger-well. Lift it an inch above my chest. Set it down, but its weight brings no comfort. Given my situation—sealed in a box with a thin iron plate between me and tons of rock—currently it is useless. Unless I decide to shoot myself, that is. Always an option.

All I want is to get out but I don't know the plan for shaking me loose. Once we reach Stine, I suppose the doors beneath me will open and presuming the separator holds, I'll crawl to safety. Then Jordan, Beck, and I will hop a southbound as far as Las Vegas before transferring to a northbound headed for Beatty and Goldfield. At least, I think that's the plan.

Honestly, there is no plan.

∾

Faster now. Much faster: every sensation confirms it. The wind's pitch, the wagon's action on its springs, and the accelerated shower of grit inside the compartment. So much dirt around my feet now that I can hardly move them. I'm aware, too, that my heart's beating faster: no conscious effort made that happen. I tell myself to breathe slowly but this makes me cough. God, please don't kill me in a runaway. Every week, the papers describe gruesome deaths in wrecked wagons.

Someone shouts—at the mules or to someone else, I can't tell. Stub, surely, since no one else could be near.

"What's happening?" I yell although I can hardly hear myself. Have the animals spooked? Another roadblock? Creaking and scraping sounds fill my ears; the mules' hooves are louder than hailstones on a tin roof. No way he heard me.

A shotgun booms—a solitary thunderclap in a hurricane.

More shouting. We bounce in and out of ruts in the road—has Stub lost control? Press my knees and elbows against the compartment's sides but it doesn't help. My head bounces up and down, rebounding against the iron above and below. Can't anticipate which way the next jolt might throw me; feels like it did when Curt was pouring it on back at Lila's. Manic hoofbeats, metallic complaints. Dust everywhere. My stomach lurches.

Another gunshot, distinct from the uproar.

At once, the shaking goes from terrible to worse—must've left the road. For a second, I am weightless; my stomach dips and soars. Dust, always, but now I smell pine and sage: the team must be knocking down everything in its path. I hold my breath and *still* dirt finds its way inside my mouth. Hard lurch to the right; my nose smashes against the separator. Wagon lurches and lists—a wheeler must've tripped. The mules bawl and it smells like hot blood and bile. Rocks strike my chest and face and when I reach out to steady myself, something pinches the side of my left hand. Jesus, I—

Bang! A terrible jolt and wrenched metal. Wheel's off or a spring broke because the wagon lurches *hard*. Head slams against the compartment wall and most of my bodyweight follows, compressed into my neck. Stars dance and the sound of colliding trains fills my ears. *Bam!* Another violent lurch and the wagon slows. Slows and then jerks to a stop, rolling me onto my side. Baseball-sized rocks clatter into the compartment. Others tumble from the bed. The wind gusts hard and pushes little skiffs of snow deep inside the wagon. At last, everything stills.

Still but not steady. Even lying inside the rig, it's obvious we're balanced on a knife's edge. The mules are bawling hysterically. Spinning like a windmill, one wheel makes intermittent squeaks that keep time with my heart. Thankfully, while both slow, eventually only one stops. Before long, the ringing in my ears fades, too. I blink away tears and slowly, carefully flex my limbs, testing each one with the care a mother shows her newborn. My hands aren't moving the way I'd prefer and there's a sharp pain in my neck but it seems I'm still in one piece. Dizzy, but not so that I'm worried—too many other distractions.

I draw the thinnest breaths possible, trying not to let the rise and fall of my chest push me too far in any one direction. Head hurts. Everything hurts.

"Stub," I shout, choking on the scratchiness in my throat. "Anyone there? Jordan? Beck? Anyone?" Cough, cough. No answer.

New sounds fills the compartment, a wailing chorus that builds and builds until I'm drowning in it. Oh, God, the mules. They're screaming in agony and it's unbearable. More than once, I've heard dying men cry out for their mothers, but this might be worse. Whereas humans construct whole religions just to take the terror out of death, animals have no such balms. No delusions of afterlife, no hope for eternity. Just the abyss. From everywhere at once come whines and groans filled with horror and confusion; the sounds of betrayal. Of treachery. A horrifying, heartbreaking wail that rises and falls but never, ever stops. Can't think. Fingers in my ears can't stop it. The dust in here is suffocating.

Moonlight spills around the separator's edge. In this thin beam, I see my breath which is good, and that I have a fearsome cut on my hand, which isn't. Blood drips from the heel of my palm, soaking the sleeve of my jacket and spattering the lapels. Fear puts its claws around my heart and squeezes. Get out! *Out!*

I press against the sheet-metal with all my strength. The wagon trembles and shakes but the cover won't budge. Trying again, it actually rebounds an inch before shifting ore locks it in place. Now it won't even sway. Sweating despite the cold, I thrash like a madman.

Already terrified, the dying mules' wailings grow louder. For God's sake, why? Stop this! But He doesn't and they can't; this is all they have left. They're strong animals, bred to pull enormous loads, so they'll die slowly, too. One bucks in its halter and kicks the wagon and it's like cymbals crashing inside my head. All my life, I've lived with livestock—seen 'em die, sure—but never like this. Never so cruelly. Their screams fill my head until there isn't room for anything else.

More dirt spills around the separator, pelting my face and filling my ears. Fittings pop and snap like firecrackers. For a moment, I'm sure the rig's going over but after one sickening lurch, it catches against something and stops. The Colt tumbles from my hand. Doesn't go far, thank God, coming to rest against my hip, and I close my trembling fingers around the grip. Honey, don't leave me. Don't you dare—you're all that's keeping me sane.

"I see it!" I hear someone shout.

The wind gusts. Boots punch through crusted snow. The wagon shudders. Then I hear that same voice, "No, he's dead."

Does he mean me? "In here," I shout but it issues as a whisper, "I'm still here!"

More shouting but I can't understand it over the mules. Their cries fill the wagon, pinning me just as forcefully as the separator.

"Hold on," he says, "I will!" Now I can tell it's Jordan.

Even in my straits, I hear the panic in his voice. Must be awful out there—it's awful in here.

"For pity's sake," I cry, "shoot them!" although I doubt whether he hears me.

A rifle shot cracks and the wagon rolls back and forth like a rudderless ship—God only knows how it stays upright.

"I *know*," I hear Jordan shout, "I'm working as fast as I can!"

"Jordan," I yell, "I'm in here," but he doesn't answer. Must be talking to Stub.

Two more gunshots. The wagon settles against the hillside as the last animal expires. No more sounds; not from the mules, anyhow. The wind hasn't let up and the wagon's broken front axle makes a scraping noise as it finds repose, but at least the animals are out of their misery. Not me, though: dirt keeps filtering into the compartment and I have to writhe like a snake to stay atop the rising pile. My whole body shakes. Again, I realize how hard I'm breathing so I try to control it. Inhale. Exhale slowly. Cough. Repeat.

"Sunday?" Jordan shouts. He leans against the wagon, trying to see around the separator. "You in there?"

I tell him I'm alive but this makes me cough.

"Hey, good," he says, panting heavily. "Good, by God, but we're in some trouble."

"I'll say." More coughing. "Stub there with you?"

"Stub's dead. Bastard steered us into an ambush, Sunday. Dozens of lights down in the canyon and they're heading this way."

With something new to worry about, my head clears a little. "What lights? How far?"

"Steered us into an ambush, Sunday—"

"You sure they aren't your people?"

"Supposed to meet two men, not thirty." He steps up, wraps his fingertips around the sheet-iron, and pulls. "There's one auto, maybe two, and electric torches in the woods on both sides of the road. Figure they'll be here in twenty minutes if we don't get moving."

"Where are we?"

"Don't know." He grunts and strains, trying to loosen the separator. "We were gonna follow Taylor Canyon to Stine but Stub went right at the pass instead of left—"

"Springs Canyon, maybe?"

"Think so." He pauses a moment. "We're on a flat above some ravines. Cliffs on the canyon's north side; rolling hills to the south."

Thinking clearly now, I can picture where we are. "What's Beck doing?"

Jordan lets go of the separator. "He's still…still on the road."

"We need him."

"He can't…" The kid's voice breaks.

"Can't, what? Jordan, go get Beck," I shout, "We can't move this spacer without him."

"He can't walk!" he shouts back. "Can't move his legs, Sunday. He's bleeding bad."

"Then go help him!"

"Wouldn't let me; he sent me to help you."

This time, I'm sure the boy is crying and I don't blame him.

Stub, you bastard. How could he know the plan well enough to sabotage it like this? Must be more spies down at Union Hall than I knew. Here comes the war Prince Jack wants, rushing toward a whole class of people—people who already live and work with one foot in their graves—without the ways and means to defend themselves. He won't ever stop. Not until he owns everything. Not until everyone scrapes and bows. Not me, though. I've been through worse. I can handle myself, damn it, and I mean to handle Jack Lipford but first I need to get out. Nothing else matters unless I can get out of this cage.

"Jordan," I say, I say, "go try the doors but carefully, understand?"

No answer.

"Jordan? Pard, listen to me. Go look at the ratchet, okay?"

"On the underside?" His voice shakes like it did that first time I saw him in the town's jail.

"That's right. Can't tell you how it unlocks but it can't be too complicated. Go look."

"Hang on, that side's buried in sagebrush."

He circles the wagon and I hear him struggling to part the scrub. Three times, he yanks on a lever to release the doors. Three times, the rig shakes and shudders but the doors won't budge.

"Ratchet's busted," he shouts.

I brace my hands and knees against the separator and push with my back. No luck from this direction, either. I run my fingers around the separator's upper edge. If we can force it enough for me to squeeze through, I'm willing to live with cuts and scrapes.

"What's keeping this thing upright?"

His boots crunch in the snow as he ranges about. "A pair of junipers."

"Then as long as they hold, we'll dig like jackrabbits and try to pry this sheet-iron loose. Nothing else will do."

He claws at the pile. We agree that the corner of the separator nearest my head projects father than the other so I paw and scratch at the rocks holding it in place. Rough work. Between the tight confines and the ore's jaggedness, in minutes my hands are raw.

"How far are those lights now?"

Breathing hard, Jordan steps away for a look. "Ten, eleven minutes. They've cleared the switchbacks."

Despite the cold, I'm sweating like a pig—a pig who knows what happens on the killing floor. "Try again; I'll push, you pull."

He wraps his fingers around one of the bent reinforcing pipes. This time, the iron plate tips outward about three inches. For the first time since leaving Black Tiger, snowflakes land on my face. I feel better until a branch snaps and the wagon shifts. Jordan yelps and jumps backward. For a moment, I'm certain the wagon will tip but then the shaking stops and the whole rig settles and sighs. Releases its soul, I guess; don't know how else to describe it.

We dig some more. I've thrown about all the rock and sand that'll fit in the space beneath my feet so I ask him to try again. The separator tips outward another inch. My hands and the top of my head fit but damn it, there's no way I can squeeze through and keep my nose and ears. Jordan grasps my right hand but I shake him loose and pull back inside the compartment. We're out of time.

"Jordan, go help Beck," I say. "Get him to a doctor."

"Can't, Sunday. He said my *only* job was to get you out. Made me swear I would!"

"*Go!* They'll be here any minute." I can hear the vehicles on the road now.

"No," he pleads, *"dig!"*

He keeps pulling down rocks so I figure I should, too. What I'd prefer he do is let me end this on my own terms. Wait quietly until they pry the separator back and then raise the revolver. Take out two or three right there; make the others re-think their priorities for a while. Wouldn't last long, though, even inside a metal box. One will circle around back, or work his way toward the side where my feet are pinned, jam a shotgun's muzzle into the gap and...that'll be that.

Besides, I'm out of room. Jammed against the roof, lying sideways on a pile of rocks, there's nowhere else to put even one more handful. I'm done. As I begin a quick prayer to apologize for my prodigious sins, Jordan wraps his hands around the separator's edge.

"There," he shouts, "I see it!"

He braces one foot against the wagon's bed and kicks at a plate-shaped rock wedged tightly between the iron sheet and the wall. On the third try, it spalls rust from the bed before breaking in two and showering me with grit.

"Now, push!" he says.

It scrapes and groans like before but this time, the separator tilts outward by a foot. In an instant, I exhume myself from that upended grave, scratching my back and bruising my ribs in the process. Jordan tries to help but he needn't bother. With the revolver in my right hand and nothing in my left, I claw and scrabble faster over those wet rocks than any lizard ever crossed summer hardpan. Headfirst, I slip and tumble head-first into the snow. Up quickly, I glance wildly around the clearing. Stars! Snow! I'm laughing and snarling, giddy and furious. Feels like a win; like a giant first step on a run that ends on Jack Lipford's doorstep.

Jordan skates down the heap until he's standing beside me. "You okay?"

"Good enough." I clap my hand on his shoulder and pull him forward until my forehead rests against his. "Thank you," I say and let him go.

I'm grinning like a lunatic but I don't care. I want to cry, to curse, to shout for the mere thrill of being alive but there isn't time. Maybe later. This place smells like blood. Sobering quickly, I see a wide, dark trail of gore where the mules plunged headlong into the woods and for twenty, thirty yards the wagon plowed a deep furrow in the hillside. Clumps of juniper, sage, and dirt cover everything.

"Let's run get Beck while there's still time."

Jordan's eyes water and he shakes his head. "Too late."

"Nonsense! We can't *leave* him."

"He's dying, Sunday; no two ways about it. Stub caught him twice."

I'm ready to argue for going back—perhaps as much for water as for Beck—when Jordan grabs my arm and points across the mountainside. On a bend about four-hundred yards downhill, a car's headlamps wash the road with light. Several men are walking alongside, helping to push the vehicle up a steep, muddy stretch. Another vehicle, possibly a stakebed truck, follows closely.

Shaking, Jordan pulls on my sleeve and backs uphill.

Three electric torches are already in the woods on our right, even closer than the vehicles. These move in fits and starts, pausing to sweep the trees. Separate from the others, another man comes into view. He isn't looking uphill; appears to be studying the ground, in fact. And maybe it's only a trick of the wind but I'd swear I hear him shouting over the engines' grinding roar. He's one, two minutes away at most.

Crouched behind the wagon, I see no sign of Stub nor anything worth taking. No water, no shotgun. Nothing. Likely our little detour raked away everything that wasn't bolted down. Backtrack far enough, we might find Stub himself, his long beard entangled in a tree like Absalom's hair. Given how he got there, I say good riddance. Only one way to go: uphill, back along the wagon's tracks. I *hate* leaving Beck, although I admit this thought occurs as we're running away. If I had more time to think, I might reconsider how I faulted Joe McCuskey for abandoning John Covington and Pat Dobbins in Balangiga, or me at Lawaan. I will later—I swear I will, but not this morning. This morning, Jordan and I are running for our lives.

At last, we have a plan.

⁓

The clouds return and so does the darkness. We keep to the road, following channels scoured clean by the wind. In other places, we wade through drifts built up in the mere half-hour since the wagons rolled through.

Glancing over my shoulder, the lights are still there but they aren't moving. Must've found the wreck. Then they'll look for Stub and figure out what happened. Search the clearing with their torches, search for footprints. Quarry confirmed, they'll never stop baying. Lipford won't let them, the same way he wouldn't let me. And even if they do, he'll bring in others.

In the woods, a shotgun booms. Rifles and pistols respond: six at least, although it might've been eight. Wind, snow—it doesn't matter; I'd know those sounds anywhere. A few more rounds, I'd be willing to bet on the caliber and gauge. But what's their target? Probably spooked, jumping at shadows. Haven't spotted us, have they? Impossible. It's too dark and we're too far away. Then I picture Beck standing next to me in the shed at the Black Tiger. Beck shot first.

Between the wind and our exertions, I try to convince myself that I didn't really hear anything; that it's too far away to be sure. How conceited, thinking I could identify sounds under these conditions. One look at Jordan, though, and I know. Kid's sobbing as he runs, bawling and wiping away tears with his sleeves before they freeze to his face.

We left our partner.

TWENTY-THREE

How long have we been running? Five minutes? Ten? However long, it isn't enough.

Even so, we pause at a fork in the road. At this point, neither of us is moving very well. I'm cold, stiff, and crazy with thirst. The air is so cold it hurts to breathe and I need to keep muffling a deep, rasping cough with my sleeve.

"Where does this one go?" Jordan says.

I glance down the left-hand track. Relatively free of snow, it crosses another clearing before turning and disappearing behind a stand of pinyon.

"Booster station for the water pipeline."

Delamar's only steady water comes from Meadow Valley Wash, twelve miles east of town and 1,500 feet lower. From spring through fall, with the help of three booster stations, two three-and-a-half-inch steel pipes deliver a paltry forty gallons of water per minute, most of it destined for High-Con's mill. From November through March, they're drained before they freeze and split. Then the only way to get water is to bring it in by the barrel at fifty dollars per.

"This way, then?" Jordan points up the main branch. He adjusts the rifle slung over his shoulder and spits in the snow.

"Give me a second." My hands are freezing so I jam them inside my trouser pockets in a vain effort to thaw them out. At least the cut on my hand stopped bleeding.

Below us, lights are still in constellation on the clearing's far side. One or two are probing the woods nearest the road but it seems we've reopened a gap of fifteen minutes or more. Beck paid for this time with his life. He committed to Jordan and me like I've never committed to anything. Thank you, friend.

On my right, I trace the pipelines, straight as arrows and anchored by concrete risers as they pass over a rock sill. They look for all the world like narrow-gauge rails. About fifty yards uphill to the right, a wood utility pole stands against the clouds like a tall, short-armed cross. Tufts of snow have built up on the glass insulators. Where does that line go? The third booster station and...I feel the keys in my pocket and I remember.

"I know what to do."

I turn left and take steps down the side road. We start to run. This feels right.

❦

Daybreak soon or at least what'll pass for it, given this weather. Isn't getting brighter, exactly; more a dilution of shadows and besides, it's snowing again.

The wind has scoured short stretches of this side road clean. Narrow drifts have formed between the trees but we jump over these, trying not to leave tracks. Beneath the electrical lines, I wade into the snow at a right angle from the road, uphill, and motion for Jordan to follow. No time to rest. Despite my exhaustion, I know I can keep running because I've done it before and Jordan, well, he's seventeen. No one needs rest when they're seventeen.

"Hear any dogs?" I say, panting like one, myself.

"No."

"Me, either, so let's keep moving. They'll follow our prints as long as they can; with any luck, they'll miss our detour here and figure we're headed back to Delamar."

"But we are, aren't we?"

I shake my head.

"Hell, if I'd known, I'd have said more goodbyes. Packed a few things."

"Soon as things settle down, you can go back and do whatever you want."

He glances over his shoulder, maybe hoping for a glimpse of Applewhite Summit, where the road between Delamar and Meadow valleys crosses the range. If so, too bad; this morning, there's nothing to see but snow-covered mountains rising into heavy clouds.

He draws a breath and lets it out in one long, slow hiss. "Won't be the same," he says.

"Neither will you. Keep up."

∽

For ten minutes, we climb through deepening drifts. The wind never stops—just a little bit of this and they'll have a hell of a time following our trail—but the clouds break again, throwing one last bit of moonlight across the canyon.

Below a stairstepped rock, we catch our breath and glance downhill. The vehicles are moving again, grinding slowly uphill. Headlamps and torches wink on and off as they pass between the trees. Hard to tell at this distance but a few of the searchers could be on course to discover our detour away from the main road.

Jordan shoves a handful of snow into his mouth, waits for it to melt, and swallows. "We've climbed long enough," he says. "Let's go around this mountain."

"What do you mean?"

"South, so we can drop into the canyons that feed Cedar Wash."

"No cover down there; open desert."

"Where, then? They'll pin us down up here."

He's right. They're spreading out, casting their net wider and wider. Safe bet that another team is coming up from Delamar on the range's western side, too.

"Downhill again, heading east."

The boy shoots me a withering look. "You're kidding, right? We've been running due west for nearly fifteen minutes."

"This is a setup."

"For what?"

I gesture at the electrical wires suspended fifteen feet above our heads. "How's your pitching arm?"

"Good," he says. "Why?"

"Keep it loose. We'll follow this line for another two-hundred yards. The Tomcat Mine sits below that ridge there and I have a key to the bunker, see? Take a few sticks of dynamite and make a big show of fighting our way back into Delamar."

"For what?"

"So we can slip past, headed east."

"Hell, Sunday, why don't we just shoot ourselves and be done with it? Ever handle powder before?"

"Sure have," I say, cursing my sloppiness.

I forgot miners only ever call explosives "powder," whether it is, in fact, black powder, sticks of dynamite, or any other kind. And even if I hadn't just red-flagged myself as an amateur, his skepticism would be appropriate. While chemists have made it safer than before, dynamite cartridges are still affected by swings in temperature and shock, often with unpleasant results. On the hottest day of August last year, one of Curt's deputies drove a Ford carrying a case of powder into a washout and blew a crater in Burnt Springs Road ten feet deep and thirty feet across. Here, Jordan and I might have the opposite problem, since frozen dynamite is *too* stable and won't always detonate. No other option but to chance it.

"We'll only take a few sticks. Ones that haven't sweated nitroglycerin and if it makes you happy, I'll carry the blasting caps."

While dynamite's safer, blasting caps remain viciously unstable. I hate the thought of those little devils bouncing around in my pockets but what choice do I have? Without a cap to detonate it, a stick of dynamite is no more of a weapon than a snowball.

"Don't know why you'd risk it," he says.

"I know how these fellows think: they're focused on Delamar. That's what everyone does: they hide out in town. First, they run and then they double back to pick up money, or clothes, or a girl. And if they corner us, well…"

Jordan gestures at the lights in the trees. Snow is falling again, making them hazy and indistinct but it's obvious they're climbing again.

"Better be right," he says, turning to follow me uphill.

I couldn't agree more.

∞

Up here, we're *in* the clouds; snowflakes aren't falling so much as floating in the air. Visibility's down to twenty feet and I have to keep glancing overhead to make sure we're still following the electrical lines.

The Tomcat is sleeping. By now it's Sunday morning, so no one's on shift except a watchman and I know for a fact he's a lazy son of a bitch who drinks twice what I do and spends half his days sleeping it off.

Seeing the place, I get an unpleasant feeling in the pit of my stomach, which I fully deserve.

"Don't know anyone who works up here," Jordan whispers.

"You know me." He shoots me a funny look but there's no time to explain.

Only one light bulb burning over the office stairs. The surrounding woods are still and I'm confident no one will see us.

We skirt the main works and head for the bunker, which is nothing more than a small, concrete blockhouse located far enough away from the shaft that if there ever were an accidental explosion, it wouldn't damage the mine itself.

My key still works and once inside, we find it well-stocked. I break open a box with "Hercules" stenciled across the lid and grab four sticks. Although nitroglycerin can cause rashes, I slip two sticks inside my shirt, directly against my skin, hoping this will thaw them enough for detonation. Feels like I'm holding icicles in my armpits but I hook my thumbs into the armholes of my vest to keep them from falling out of my sleeves.

I take six blasting caps, too, careful to slip each one into its own individual pocket. Jordan coils about ten feet of Bickford fuse inside his jacket, plus four candles and a box of safety matches. All done, we retrace our steps, detouring only once toward the shaft-house to swipe a knife and pliers off the wall.

Only a couple of minutes and already our footprints are disappearing. Good. Come and find us now.

TWENTY-FOUR

Our raid on the bunker takes less than five minutes but by the time we cross back over the ridge, we've lost half of our lead. Even worse, it's quickly growing brighter. We'd better stick to the deep woods to keep from being seen.

Behind us, the electrical and water lines are no longer visible. We've reached the center of a steep triangle between the booster station, the turnoff where we first left the road, and Applewhite Summit. Powdery snow is falling again but the clouds have lifted. No blue sky anywhere but in places the clouds are thinner and pale light filters through.

"After this, no more talking; they'll be too close." I smother a coughing fit with my forearm; my lungs still ache from all that dust inside the wagon.

"So what's the plan?"

As I explain, he nods along.

Only once does he question me, "Why not south?"

"Because that was the original plan and the original plan is shot. I wouldn't get on a southbound now unless you could prove every one of those bastards was dead and gave me a hundred dollars walking-money, to boot."

He's wearing a strange look so I ask him what's the matter.

"Never killed anyone before."

"Not asking you to."

"They shot Beck," he says, studying his knuckles.

"Nah, you don't want—" I say but Jordan doesn't let me finish.

"What was it like killing Joe McCuskey?"

"Who says I did?"

Jordan shoots me a quizzical look. "Didn't you?"

"Ask me later," I say, not because I'm offended but because I want to think before I answer. "We get out of this, you can ask me anything you want."

What does it feel like to kill another human? Feels like a lot of things, except when it doesn't. Years ago, it was me asking the older fellows in our company this same question and their answers spoke volumes about what kinds of men they were. A few bragged in gruesome detail about the Spaniards they'd killed, or Indians, but these weren't fellows you could rely on in a pinch. They tended to linger inside our trenches or hide behind walls until someone else handled the problem. Their stories didn't add up. Others clearly *weren't* lying; something in their souls had curdled and they seemed altogether too comfortable with the act. Detached, even. But a majority by far merely shrugged and said it was a necessary evil: simply 'them or me.'

In San Isidro, Harry Wright pointed to campfires on the river's opposite bank. "Those fellows just want to go home, same as you, but someone important promised 'em something so now they have guns. You don't kill 'em tonight, tomorrow they'll try to kill you. Say your prayers and learn to deal with it."

To be honest, I haven't done either of those things.

∽

The flat light and fog make it hard to see. We run downhill in silence, stop to look, and then run some more. For several minutes, we work our way across the mountainside until we're back on the main road beside another utility pole. From the sound of it, the automobiles aren't far off. That old codger in Dunbar was right: you *can* hear these new vehicles from miles away.

Keeping an eye on the woods to our left, I gesture for Jordan to watch our right flank while I go to work. He unslings his rifle and hands me the coiled fuse and pliers. It's an aggressive distraction I'm after, not careful mining, so I follow only enough of the normal routine for handling powder to ensure my safety. No need to cut slits in the waxed-paper sleeves, for example, since I won't be compressing the charges into a drill-hole the way miners would to blast rock. However, I *do* take extra care handling the caps. Perhaps now more than ever, blowing off fingers simply isn't on the list of things I want for myself.

Despite the cold, I'm sweating again. Between my frozen hands and the roaring automobiles—still unseen but plainly audible—I'm as nervous as I've ever been. One stick takes its cap easily. I wedge this charge into a notch in the utility pole about a foot above the snow, but the second one, damn it to hell, won't cooperate. Dirt fills one end of the cap and while I'm able to scrape this out, the priming cavity in the powder is so shallow I'm afraid odds are no better than 50-50 it'll go off.

Behave, you son of a bitch.

Jordan nudges me in the back with his knee. Jesus, of all people, he should know better. I rest the blasting cap on my knee and turn to see what has him so worked up.

The boy is bug-eyed, clenching his teeth so hard I can see the muscles tensing along his jaw. He catches me looking and gestures south. A man with a shotgun balanced in the crook of his arm is crossing the clearing's lowest corner. Isn't looking our way, though, and doesn't appear to be following tracks of any kind. Honestly, he seems more concerned with keeping snow out of his boots than scouring a cold mountain for fugitives. I've dealt with this before. Deputized saloon brawlers are a blunt-force weapon, effective against the weak and unwary but just as often useless or even dangerous whenever they're really needed.

With the blasting cap in my left hand, I reach out with my right and tap Jordan's elbow. "No," I whisper and gesture for him to lower the rifle.

He doesn't look happy but at least he listens.

Across the clearing, the man disappears behind a stand of trees so I whisper again, "Candle."

Returning to my work, I insert one end of a second fuse inside the copper tube containing the blasting cap and crimp it carefully with the stolen pliers. At last, we have a connection. No way to tell if the powder is warmed enough to detonate, though I figure the itchy sensation on my arms where I was holding the sticks is a good sign. Even the tiniest bit of active nitroglycerin should do the trick. I hold up ninety seconds' worth of cord—about thirty-six inches—and Jordan nods. To expose the black powder inside, I cut the fuse's tail-end on the bias and reach back for the candle.

Now, here's a tricky bit: should've had him light two candles because sometimes burning powder will spit back and extinguish the flame. Provided the fuse catches, no problem, but if it sputters out we may not have enough time to try again. The autos are close now; the sound of men shouting to one another is unmistakable.

Hands are so cold I'm afraid I'll drop the candle but within seconds, sparks and flame erupt from the fuse. A steady hiss and puff of acrid smoke prove it caught. Burning powder lands on the back of my hand and I drop the candle but so what? Time to run like hell.

Glancing across my shoulder, I see movement—either part of an auto or someone's hat—above a dip in the road. No time for a second look, though. Soon as we cross the road, Jordan and I jump an embankment and slide into deep snow at the bottom of a ten-foot gully. We turn and scramble east, downhill, trying to gain distance before the powder detonates. This ravine is so steep and narrow that we run beneath the trees overgrowing it. We aren't actually running, per se: "falling directionally" is more like it. No dignity and no decorum.

Voices carry from the road; electric torchlight sweeps the trees over our heads. Glimpsing movement, I grab Jordan's arm and drag him beneath an overhanging rock.

On our right, the truck's exhaust backfires.

"Was that…" he pants, "the cap?"

"Backfire," I wheeze, still clutching his arm.

"Sounded…like a cap."

"Backfire," I insist. "Truck's…straight uphill; don't move…or they'll see you."

His eyes bulge. "Look up there," he tilts his head.

Christ, seventy yards *above* the utility pole, a dozen riders are dismounted and leading their animals into the trees before the larger party walking uphill can spot them. Must've come up from Delamar. Ten seconds more and they'd have caught us out in the open.

Closer at hand, I hear bits of shouted conversation, "…all these side roads. You see anything—"

"Hey, Phil," another man bellows. "Sonny found tracks heading south, away from the road."

Beside me, Jordan's still panting so heavily I can hardly understand what he's saying, "You crimp…the cap…around the fuse?"

"Yes." Now I smell smoke, or maybe that's just residue on my hands.

"If it fell out—"

The bomb detonates: a thunderclap that shakes the ground, splits the air, and thumps our chests. A wave of dirt, snow, and broken wood washes over and around the boulder, burying us up to our knees. Acrid smoke fills the gully, clinging to its contours before the gusting wind sweeps it away.

Beside me, Jordan shakes his head to clear it. My ears are ringing, too, but some in the first search party are so close I can still hear them shouting. A few are running away; others begin shooting or scrambling for cover—one tumbles headlong into the gulch about fifty yards above us. Happy to see we've sown a little panic. I press my shoulder against the slab and turn so I can see around its edge. Now driverless, the truck is idling directly uphill, its windscreen spattered with dirt. It's rolled backward into an embankment, its headlamps staring uselessly over the trees.

I cut twenty-five inches from the second fuse. It's primed to burn for only thirty seconds now. "Rifle," I say, handing Jordan the bomb.

Jordan unslings his weapon and hands it over. Funny thing, it's a sportsman's combined rifle and shotgun, one barrel each, side by side. I give it a quick once-over. The rifle is 38-55 and the shotgun's bored for twelve-gauge shells; both are single-shot.

"Granddad bring this from the Old Country?"

"Sears & Roebuck, twenty-three dollars."

"Is it any good?"

"Belgian-made and the rifle's sights are dead-accurate to three-hundred yards. You any good?"

"Good enough." After Adolph Gamlin, I was C Company's second-best marksman but there's no way I'd say so because bragging usually precedes an embarrassing failure.

More gunfire above the road but I can't tell who's shooting or what they're trying to hit. Here's our chance to run.

"Spit that thing and throw it in front of the truck."

Jordan lights another candle and the fuse catches like before, but instead of throwing the charge, he remains crouched behind the rock as seconds tick away. Smoke, flame, certain death.

"C'mon, throw it!" I snap, taking a step backward. *"Now!"*

Jordan gives me a sour look before turning and hurling the bomb. Hell, as hard as he throws it, he might have overshot the road but that's okay. Amazing what you can do when your blood's up. With the shotgun, I blow out the truck's windscreen. A rifle discharges, followed by others. With all the smoke and shadows up here, who knows what these boys imagine they're facing?

We turn and run, slipping and falling with every step. Rocks roll beneath our feet. A branch scratches my neck and Jordan hits his knee against a boulder but except for bullets, nothing's gonna stop us now. The gulch we're in joins another and with every step the walls rise and the floor widens. Behind us, the firefight intensifies.

When the second charge detonates, more than just a tree and some snow are between us and the blast. This time, the concussion is more of a slap than a punch and neither of us stumbles.

೦൦

We run for a long while, downhill all the way. At the dry falls, we slide down a slippery, thirty-degree face; no problem except for the rockpile at its base. Still, neither of us rolls an ankle so we pick ourselves up and continue running. The only thing unusual along this stretch is a short, sudden twang as if someone plucked the big E-string on a guitar.

"What…," Jordan rasps, "was that?"

I'm afraid it's a ricochet—afraid someone's spotted us—but no report follows. All I can guess is since we blew up the utility pole, a taut electrical wire must've snapped.

"How much farther?" the boy pants.

"Don't know," I say, because at this moment, I can't imagine a safe distance. Colorado, maybe? Kentucky? "Don't stop now."

"Don't worry about me," he says and passes me on my left.

೦൦

Down here our footing's better and the running easier. More sagebrush than pinyon. Less snow, too. Only in drifts is it deeper than an inch or two and although there are prints in it, all point uphill. The sound of gunfire still echoes down the canyon, though fainter by the minute and before long, it stops altogether.

"Recognize those riders above the gulch?" I say.

"Couldn't see clearly," he pants.

Me, either, but given the direction they were heading, I'd guess they were Clayton Hock's boys—maybe even Rabbit Hat, Sucker Punch, and Gene. I hope I never find out.

The wind picks up again, casting skiffs of snow around our shins. Hopefully, it'll fill our tracks before anyone discovers we've gone. Hope they're all still murdering each other in the woods, too, wondering where we went.

Jordan scans the broken woods on either side of the canyon. "Should we look for the fellows who were gonna meet us here?"

"No point," I say. "Ten bucks says they were driven off."

The clouds are breaking, revealing patches of pale blue. White trees, red rocks, and blue-veined skies. Another mile or so and we'll reach the main wash. Half a mile on and the canyon widens, but this openness unnerves me. I keep glancing to my right, knowing the road is somewhere up on the ridge, but for now it appears we're alone. Opting for speed over safety, we follow faint ruts through the sage at a dead run. Whenever possible, we keep to the shadows below the canyon's southern rim, sprinting from one stand of trees to the next. Slowly, the canyon walls close around us again—steep, jagged cliffs on our right and towering outcrops of white volcanic ash on the left—before emptying once and for all into Meadow Valley Wash.

TWENTY-FIVE

In a close-cropped pasture, we stop and lean against a boulder to catch our breath. Down here, bare cottonwoods and willows line a permanent stream, and despite hoofprints and dung everywhere, both of us drink for a long time from the clearest-looking channel.

"Now what?" Jordan says, wringing water from his coat sleeves.

"Ever jump a train?"

"Of course," he bristles. "Rode all the way from Cheyenne to Imlay over in Humboldt County."

I cough and wipe my mouth with my sleeve. "You from Wyoming?"

"Over the line in Nebraska. My folks homesteaded but they lost their ranch in 1905. Didn't want to move back to Lincoln so I headed west."

"Then you know what to expect. Stine's a half-mile that way but we can't jump there."

"Why not?"

"Too many eyes: a loading platform, power-plant, and a watchman's shack. Tunnels in both walls of this canyon, though, and trains slow to a crawl through here. Engine in one tunnel, caboose in the other, we can board unseen."

"What'll we do in Caliente?"

"Jump the Pioche Pacific and ride north. Hope so, anyway."

"Yard'll be crawling with Pinkertons."

"Nah, don't believe everything you hear. The Pinkertons are spread thinner than paint: maybe two agents per thousand miles of track. Probably even fewer on this part of the system."

"Company bulls, then?"

"The agent working the Caliente yards is a friend; he'll help us if he can."

"Know everyone in Pioche, too?" His voice has an edge to it.

"No. What's eating you?"

Jordan shoots me a look I can't read. "What were you so sore about back there?"

"Back where?"

"You honestly think I'd hang on to that charge? Blow us to bits?"

"Didn't throw it as fast as I would've liked."

"I know what I'm doing."

"Didn't look like it." I yawn so hard it leaves me with an aching jaw.

"I'm a hardrock miner, Sunday; I've spit more powder than you ever will."

"Don't bet on it."

"That right? Seems I don't know anything about you." He brushes his shaggy bangs away from his eyes. "Not one, single thing and I have questions."

Everyone has questions, kid: get in line. I glance up the canyon before turning to face him, except he's sideways to me now and I can't read his expression. Don't know why he thinks he's entitled to answers, except that he's stuck with me through situations that'd test anyone's resolve. Maybe he *is* trustworthy or maybe I've misread him, mistaking sophistry for innocence. Maybe I can no longer tell the difference.

I yawn again. "Listen, Jordan, we're stuck with each other. Next few days, I'll answer any question you have but right now, I need a little sleep. Think you can keep watch for twenty minutes before we trade? We missed the overnight runs; next northbound won't be through until about eight o'clock."

"Still don't see why we can't go south," he says. "Union friendlies in Elgin and Glendale will be looking out for us." He dips a hand back into the creek for more water.

I shake my head. "Association will look there, too, assuming we're trying to reach Las Vegas. Remember, they know our old plan but not that we've figured 'em out. That's our advantage, see? " Another yawn. "Come on, Jordan, I gotta get some sleep. Twenty minutes is all."

"Yeah, but *Pioche?* It's the county seat."

"Won't stay there, chief."

Jesus, was I this annoying when I was seventeen? Yes. Probably worse, come to think of it. There's a scratching inside my chest and I cough to make it stop. "You're sure you can stay awake?"

"What? Hell, yes, I can—I'm *wide* awake."

He stretches an arm toward me, hand open, and for the life of me I can't figure out what he wants.

"Rifle?" he says. "How else am I supposed to keep watch?"

I reach inside my coat for my revolver. "Take this, instead. Better at close quarters and it'll keep you from trying to pick off someone at a distance."

"Still don't trust me, do you?"

"Just handed you my revolver, didn't I? That said, I also remember what *I* was like at your age and in hindsight, I wish someone would've kept me in line."

"Already have a dad."

"He'd say the same thing."

"Yeah, yeah, go to sleep. I'll wake you in an hour—"

"Twenty minutes."

"—in twenty or if I hear anything. Jesus."

"Thank you."

"You're welcome."

Finally.

Without delay, I curl up in a dusty hollow beneath a fallen cottonwood and within minutes, I'm fast asleep.

∾

Isn't Jordan who wakes me, though, nor the rumbling of a train. It's a young man's voice: the voice of someone who manages to sound small and frightened even as he's making threats.

"Keep still," he says. "Move like that again and I'll shoot."

Who's this? Is he talking to me?

The sky is brighter—it must be nine-thirty or ten. Damn it, Jordan fell asleep. We've been out for two, three hours, minimum.

Still lying on the ground, I look through a hole in the trunk and see my young partner seated on a rock. Jordan's resting his hands on his knees and his head is bowed. My revolver's lying in the dust about ten feet in front of his boots.

A man in a tan canvas duster stands about twenty feet in front of him, gripping a revolver so tightly that even from my odd vantage, I can see his hands shaking.

What have we here? Someone from the railroad, or one of the Mormon ranchers from farther down the wash? Something's irritatingly familiar about this fellow's posture, about the sound of his voice, but I can't see his face to confirm his identity. All I know is that we're in one hell of a fix. Thank God, I still have Jordan's rifle.

"Look, what do you want?" Jordan says. He lifts his head but keeps his hands on his knees. Dirt on his sleeves, red eyes—looks as if he just woke up.

"Come down Rock Springs Canyon?"

"Nah, from Panaca. Headed south to see family in Logandale."

"Two sets of prints in the dirt."

"What can I say? Only half are mine."

"Got papers?"

"Yeah, I got papers," Jordan says, producing his union card.

The stranger says something else but it's too low for me to hear.

Jordan stands, raises his hands over his head, and moves ten feet farther away from me. He sets his card atop a rock, backs away, and the fellow in the duster steps forward to retrieve it.

"Sit down," he says.

Damn it, I know his voice! It's driving me mad that I can't place it.

Pushing Jordan's rifle with my hip and shoulder, I wriggle out from beneath the giant log on the same side as Jordan and the stranger. The dirt beneath my back is free of stones and soft as talcum powder; it makes no sound and moving across it is easy. Thousands of twigs on the ground, however, and I push them aside to keep from breaking any. Jordan, God bless him, is looking right at me but doesn't bat an eye.

"Why do you need to see my card?" he says. "You a deputy?"

"That's right," the fellow says, studying Jordan's identification. "Jordan James Barley, is it? Delamar Local 77, WFM…"

"'Til the day I die," Jordan bristles.

"Careful what you wish for. You said you're from Panaca; card says Delamar. What are you doing here?"

"I'm out of work."

"No, I mean *here*. In this clearing," the fellow says. "Who are you with and where did he go?"

Jordan yawns. "Told you, I'm on my own."

While Jordan's kept him talking, I've crept within ten yards of the fellow. With his back to me, I can see his jughandle ears, skinny neck, and, despite the overcoat, thin arms. Christ, he's just a kid, no older than Jordan.

I have the rifle trained on him—have him dead to rights—when a stick cracks beneath my boot. As he turns, in the same instant we recognize one another. It's Nicholas Reed, one of the eighteen-year-old twins assigned to my team late last summer.

Eyes wide, he sees me moving toward him but he hesitates with his weapon. "Sunday," he says and it's hard to tell what I'm hearing. Fear? Deference?

Doesn't matter. Whatever it is, it buys me a half-second and by the time he swings the revolver around, I've closed the distance between us. Knock his arm aside with barrel. Clamp the muzzle against my left shoulder and bring the stock up swift and hard, making solid contact with the boy's jaw.

Kid never gets his shot off. His head lolls grotesquely and he topples over backward, his body stiff and arms outstretched. The revolver he's carrying falls from his hand and the wind carries his hat into the weeds.

"Oh, *boy!*" Jordan leaps to his feet and crows as if he's just heard a terrific joke. "Oh, boy, yes! Gonna finish him off or what?"

"No."

"Come on, how'd you get your reputation if you aren't gonna shoot anyone?"

"Knock it off."

Jordan doesn't seem to hear. "Gotta teach me how to do that! So fast, I almost couldn't see it but bam! Honest to God, that was *amazing!*"

"I said knock it off," I snap. "I know this kid."

Kneeling, I feel along Nick's throat for a pulse. It's still strong but he's bleeding from his mouth. Broken jaw, certainly; concussion, likely. I turn his head so he won't choke on his own blood. Poor kid, he didn't ask for this. The boys' uncle is an Association member; runs the big silver mine up in Atlanta. Lipford told me I'd no choice but to take on Nick, never mind that he isn't cut out for this line of work. Now he'll wear scars and false teeth as proof.

Sorry, partner, but you can never let down your guard. Ever.

Lots of young men learn this lesson the hard way. I sure did. Nineteen years old, I fought with an old sailor in Manila. Had him beat, too, but I treated the whole thing like a lark and turned away after knocking him down. All in the same motion, the son of a bitch stood and punched me square in the face; broke my nose and knocked me senseless. If others in our company hadn't been there—Pat Dobbins and Ernie Ralston, among them—it's safe to say the old fellow would've stomped me to death. Corner an old man and he won't hesitate and he won't stop. I say this with certainty because now *I'm* the old man.

I hand Jordan his rifle in exchange for both revolvers. Dirt in the barrels but neither is any worse for wear. Search Nick's coat pockets and take every bullet he has. Wish I knew whether he was freelancing and followed us down Rock Spring Canyon, or if it was his lot to keep watch while the others went uphill. Can't ask him now.

I glance up the canyon again but same as before, nothing moves. No new prints on the road, no automobiles clanking down the grade. Only patchy snow in the wash, white hills above, and red rocks in the canyon. Except for Nick's prone form, nothing's changed. Still, someone will be along eventually so it'd be best if we didn't stick around.

From far to the south, a train's whistle echoes up the canyon.

"Let's go," I say. "See that tree with the dead crown? We'll hide there until the engine enters the tunnel. If it's pulling hoppers full of ore, guards will be riding along and that's no good. If that's the case, we're walking…"

On the tracks' far side, Jordan swings his rifle back and forth in a sloppy imitation of the move I used against poor Nick. Christ, he has it all wrong but what annoys me most is seeing him do it in the first place.

"Hey, junior, pay attention."

He lowers the rifle and throws me the same funny look he was wearing earlier. "I heard you: wait behind a tree."

"Which tree? What stock are we looking for?"

"Huh?"

"Rolling stock: what are we looking for?"

"Rolling—" He exhales heavily. "You got me, Sunday. I don't know."

"Of course you don't. You fell asleep on watch, jack! Hell, we're lucky it was Nicky Reed who found us and not Curt Broe—"

"I'm *sorry*! I didn't mean to."

I reach inside my coat to scratch where nitroglycerin has raised welts on my arm and Jordan takes a step back, gripping the rifle.

"Don't," he says, his eyes widening.

"I'm scratching an itch."

"Take your hand out so I can see it!"

The itching won't stop so I keep my hand inside my coat. "Settle down. If I wanted to shoot you, I'd have done it already. You ever get that drowsy again, go ahead and wake me up. I'll be a lot less angry than I am now."

Jordan's hands are shaking: not quite like poor Nick's were but enough so I notice. The train whistle sounds again, ringing off the canyon walls. Soon, we'll hear wheels on steel.

"Get your hand out of your coat, Sunday."

"Or what?"

"Or I'll shoot."

He raises the gun, still with that pinched expression on his face but I figure what the hell. Let's see where this goes.

Taking the barrel with my thumb and index finger, I lift the Colt from its pocket. Nothing in this gesture or the speed at which I'm moving is menacing, yet Jordan reacts as if I've pulled back the hammer and drawn a bead on his head.

"Drop it," he yelps, "drop it now!" The tremor in his voice is comical. He raises the stock to his shoulder.

"Check your weapon, kid. Couldn't shoot me if you had to." I set the Colt on a rock beside my hip and rest my hands on my knees.

The boy glances nervously between the revolver, the rifle he's holding, and me. He opens the breech and sees I've taken both cartridge and shell from their respective chambers. Locking eyes with me, he feels along the canvas sling for the shells he stored there.

Fishing around in my coat pocket, I hold up a shotgun shell. "Those, too."

"Ah, geez," he sulks, and the air goes out of him. "What do you want?"

"I want you to pay attention." I return the Colt to its pocket. "Slim-enough chance we'll get away from these animals, understand? Don't make their jobs easier."

"Yeah, I got it."

"Do this right, we can take down Jack Lipford and help your fellows down at Union Hall—payback for what happened to Beck. But if you aren't gonna pay attention, we might as well lie down in front of this train. What's it gonna be, Jordan? You with me?"

The train blows its whistle again and I feel the ground vibrate. The kid moves quickly to join me behind the tree.

"I'm in," he says. "I swore to Andy and I owe Beck."

"No hard feelings?"

"No hard feelings," he says but I'll bet he's lying.

Seems he can hardly bear to look at me but I don't care. Honestly, except for saying goodbye to Helen, abandoning Beck, a team of dead mules, and breaking poor Nick Reed's jaw, I'm feeling better and better about this whole morning. Feeling magnanimous, even.

The ground is shaking now, all that noise and energy amplified by the tunnel.

"Tell you what," I shout. "Soon as we get to Pioche, you can have your ammunition back. Local there keeps a safehouse off the Jackrabbit Road north of town."

"Is it secure?"

"Not really—it's safe because it's out in the middle of nowhere. And provided you're willing, I know where we can trade that strange gun of yours for something more practical. Pump-action shotgun, maybe. We'll hide out for a day or two before setting out again."

Jordan's still won't look at me but at least he's paying attention. "Can I think about selling my rifle?"

"Of course."

Moments later, a burly locomotive thunders from the tunnel, showering us with ash and soot. We crouch behind the cedar, waiting as the train rolls slowly across the canyon's mouth. One last, guilt-inducing glance at Nick Reed, still unconscious in the grass. Sorry, buddy. I'm sorry.

Thankfully, this is only a freight run. No hoppers, no guards, and it takes no great effort to clamber inside a half-empty boxcar. This time, I let Jordan sleep first.

TWENTY-SIX

Nevada keeps secrets. Natural, historical, political—secrets of every kind. Most hardly matter: local lore only a few people will ever know, forgotten after a generation or two. Some really *ought* to be common knowledge, while others are so awful it'd be best if they stayed hidden until the world ends. Maybe all these secrets are the reason I love it like I do. Outsiders generally misunderstand this state because most are merely passing through. Seated in their parlor cars, few bother to look up from their newspapers and of those who do, most are appalled by the vast, alkaline deserts outside their windows. Doesn't matter which direction they're headed; usually somewhere between Golconda and Battle Mountain is where they decide they hate it.

For those of us who know better, it's among the greatest places on earth. Isolated canyons as green as Ireland. Alpine lakes, teeming with fish. Aspen groves larger than some Eastern states, and remote hot springs where you can soak in perfect solitude while Orion chases the Pleiades across the sky. Some counties you can practically have to yourself and if salvation is found in silence, then Nevada might just be this country's grandest cathedral.

On the other hand, if emptiness unsettles you, then there are cities and camps on full boil, day and night. Gambling, dancehalls, and easy women— whatever suits your fancy. Chancy work, chancy play—a nod to the indiscriminate fates governing our lives. And if all this *still* isn't enough for you, we have violence enough for anyone's taste. Violence permeates everything here, from big-money prizefights to crimes against the land, itself—again, whatever you want, however you want it so long as you have the ways and means to defend your stake. Ever since white men arrived, powerful interests have fought to control Nevada's water, timber, and minerals, and lately some men want these things all for themselves. Anyone who says otherwise is in for a rough time.

I grew up in far-western Nevada. In a fit of jingo patriotism, I enlisted during my freshman year at the university and after a short walk out in the world, limped back home in search of the slower pace I remember from childhood. Honestly, it's probably gone now.

Like many with vague ambitions and no special talent, I've fallen into a role that leaves me frustrated and filled with a sense that I've wasted much of my life thus far. The only thing of which I am proud is that I've survived—I'm alive despite others' best efforts to show me the door. This is due partly to wits and a willingness to prepare—tenacity, too, but most crucially, I'm still here because of luck. Nothing else.

People like Jack Lipford hate to admit dumb luck played a role in their success. They'd rather believe they've made their own, but that's no more possible than creating your own weather. Whereas some folk are just born lucky, others can't ever get out from under the rain, and whether they see it or not, quite a few Americans are all wet.

᙮

Our first priority in Pioche is food. Well, first is not getting caught, but a close second is food. Figure we have about an hour to kill before sunset and then we can move around without drawing attention. As we're leaving the Pioche Pacific yards, Jordan catches me flat-footed, telling me he's carrying twenty dollars in gold. This improves our situation considerably.

What's more, I *like* Pioche. It's nestled into a northeast-facing canyon with fine views of Lake Valley—where there is no lake—and big, shaggy Mount Wilson on the far horizon. Well-provisioned shops and restaurants. Mines all around the canyon's upper reaches. Mills clanking away. Not a quiet place, but quieter than Delamar. Feels solid. Stable, which is a big change from how it was in the decade before I was born. Back then, Pioche and Bodie, California, were locked in a contest for recognition as the Murder Capital of the West.

In happier times last year, and I use that term loosely, I'd check in at the Association's office on upper Main, do whatever needed doing, and then head back to the Mountain View Hotel for a meal. Maybe wander down to the red-light district to see who had their shingle out. Other times, I'd meet my contacts in the two-story, brick courthouse—a building whose creation-story is a splendid example of civic ineptitude, if not outright graft. These days, Latter-Day Saints outnumber miners and the place is slowly assuming an air of respectability.

We set out for supper. There's a chophouse on the corner of Field and Main but it's too near the courthouse and county jail. Maybe no one here is looking for us yet but I don't want to risk it. Instead, we head downhill to Pioche's small Chinatown and duck inside a restaurant called Hang Chung's. The food is good, no one bothers us, and, praise Mormon Jesus, we have a quiet half-hour to figure out what to do. Jordan wants to go up to Local 263's hall and see if anyone will help us, whereas I figure the sooner we skip town, the better. In the end, we agree on an amalgamated plan to do both.

Stepping outside, the sky is the color of tarnished silver and growing darker by the minute. Pioche was spared most of that last snowstorm but who knows whether another one is lining up to take its shot?

Aren't many people out tonight: one couple walking arm-in-arm on Fourth Street and two fellows leaning against a painted advertisement for Old Plantation Whiskey, but no one else. All the same, I want to avoid Main Street so we skirt the cemetery and hike clockwise around Lime Hill on the town's south side.

Miners' Union Hall is on Cedar, a street that plainly serves as the dividing line between miners and management. With tarpaper shacks to the southeast and fine homes with wide porches to the northwest, it's clear who lives where.

Jordan goes inside the hall while I wait on its back steps. Nice view over downtown, with its opera house and shining lights. Quiet, too. Folks here hope new discoveries deep in the mines will revive the place but tonight, it feels as if it's resting. Not dead: resting. In Delamar, everyone understands that only one thing is keeping the lights on and as soon as the boom ends, the White House will go dark. Tons of low-grade ore remain locked inside Ferguson Hill but that's grunt-work for foreigners with no self-respect. Once the highgrade's gone, there'll be no more wildcatting, no five-figure bonuses, no overnight millionaires. You can almost smell it in the air: everyone's already nostalgic for something that hasn't quite vanished.

Not Pioche though. Say what you will about the Mormons—I sure have— but they build communities. They're survivors. Pioche has roots. Wish I had roots, too.

Jordan steps out the back door and taps me on the shoulder. "We should go," he says.

We start down a path between Miners' Union Hall and a couple of small homes fronting Meadow Valley Street.

"Any luck?"

"No." He glances over his shoulder. "Only one fellow inside. He asked me what I needed but I didn't want to say too much. Told him I was only passing through, headed south. Gave me a dollar, a canteen of water, and a timetable for the railroad but that's all."

"Just as well. Any news from over the hill?"

"Nah, the two locals don't often cooperate. Pioche is more conservative. Besides, Andy Maguire, Porter Nielsen, and the others in Delamar kept our plan a secret—"

"None too well," I scoff.

"Yeah, but..."

"Yeah, but nothing." I spit in the dirt but even this small effort makes me cough. Jesus, nearly eighteen hours later and I'm still coughing up mud.

"Who do you think sold us out?"

"Clayton Hock, Andy Maguire—could've been anyone."

"Not Andy; he's true blue—"

"Sorry, kid. Until we're sure, we'd better assume we're on our own, understand?"

"Yeah, okay."

"Someone sure told that fellow, Stub, and look how that turned out. Ever work with him before this?"

"A few times, yeah. Never had a problem until last night."

"Well, someone got to him."

For a long while, neither of us says anything more. We hike back around Lime Hill and re-enter the lower part of town, careful to avoid the yards with barking dogs. We retrieve Jordan's peculiar rifle from the weeds along a ditch below the depot.

"Thought we were gonna try to trade my gun," he says, even as he slings it across his back.

I glance back uphill at Pioche, its lights spilling down the canyon. "Knew a fellow who dealt in weapons but I'm not even sure if he lives here anymore." I shrug. "Don't want to go knocking on doors in the dark." What I keep from adding is that for once, I don't want to drag my sordid business into this peaceful little town. For once, I want to leave something alone.

TWENTY-SEVEN

⸺⁜⸺

For twelve miles, the Jackrabbit Road runs atop an abandoned narrow-gauge railbed. It's ruler-straight, slashing north between the trees and paralleled by sets of wagon tracks. No lights out this way and no houses, either. Nothing but unbroken forest. About a mile north of town, we duck into the piney woods as a solitary buckboard rolls past. Otherwise, we're on our own.

With clouds moving in, the woods are pitch-dark. The only way to find the safehouse is by counting telephone poles between Stampede Turn and the recently-revived camp of Jackrabbit. Just past the fiftieth one, a narrow road dives west into the scrubby woods. It enters and exits a shallow wash before ending at a miner's tiny cabin. No mine though; merely two or three shallow prospects in the surrounding woods. Whoever took their stand on this hillside busted in a big way.

Again, no lights out here but we weren't expecting any. The door is unlocked and opens onto a single room. A thick layer of dust covers everything and it's obvious from the smell and piles of twigs that packrats have taken up residence. Indeed, once we step inside, so many little claws go skittering across the tin roof that for a moment it sounds as if a rainstorm has cut loose.

"Hope you don't mind company."

"Damned pests," Jordan grumbles, "get into everything."

The furnishings are one step below spartan. Two bed-frames with wooden slats and plywood—no bedding, of course—a washstand with an empty basin, and one chair so ready to collapse I wouldn't sit on it for less than ten dollars. In one corner, a box contains tins of food so old I'm sure they're poisonous.

Warmer tonight than it's been in weeks so I drape my coat over a square nail stuck above the single window pane.

"Safe for a candle," I say.

Jordan sets one inside the chipped enamel washbasin and lights it. Even with a little light, the place looks no better. Old newspapers have been pasted over the walls for insulation. I love reading these but the only one the packrats left intact is a January 20, 1888, issue of the *White Pine News*, printed up in Cherry Creek. It sports the usual front-page items: bullion quotes; a fire in a Milwaukee high-rise killed sixty—all either "burned to death or dashed to pieces on the pavements"; and rising beef and hay prices. Meeting notices for various societies: the Grand Army of the Republic, Odd Fellows, Masons, and the Cherry Creek Miners' Union. Saloon ads by the fistful: The Star, Weber's Exchange, the Palace, and my favorite, Jim Henry's, whose proprietor declares that on and after Monday, July 1, he will "reduce prices to ONE BIT—For Everything passed over My Bar." Wish I could go back in time and drink with Jim Henry.

As it stands, the only drink we have is Jordan's canteen of union water, yet I'm glad even for that. Back at Hang Chung's, we both pocketed a couple rolls and these are all we have to eat. While Jordan takes his supper on the bedframe's edge, I go to the washstand and fish around in my pockets for ammunition. Taking inventory, we have two sticks of powder, four blasting caps, and around six feet of fuse. There's Nick Reed's H&R revolver and a box containing twenty .38 cartridges, plus a dozen .45 cartridges for my revolver.

I hand Jordan his four rifle cartridges and five shotgun shells. "Sorry I took these. That was no way to treat my partner."

"I shouldn't have fallen asleep."

"It's alright; just don't do it again. Speaking of sleep, we haven't any books or cards so we might as well hit the rack. You wake and don't see me, I'm outside either listening or taking a leak."

"Hunky-dory."

"Sleep as late as you want. We both need it."

"Sure."

"You okay going back into town tomorrow for a couple days' provisions?"

"Yep." He cracks a huge yawn, brushes aside rat droppings, and stretches out inside the bedframe.

"We'll rest all day tomorrow and the next. Head north after that, okay?"

"Crackers," he says but who knows whether he's heard a thing I've said. The kid's beat and within a minute, it's clear he's asleep.

I tip the piece of plywood atop my bedframe and hundreds of rat turds fall onto the floor. Back over to my coat, I take out my revolver before turning to extinguish the candle. I lie inside my bedframe and for half an hour listen to the sounds of scurrying rodents and the wind in the trees. One branch scrapes against the tin roof and while I consider going outside to break it off, in the end, I lack the energy. Eventually, after thinking about Helen and wondering if I'll ever see her again, somehow I fall asleep.

∾

I wake before Jordan does, pull on my coat, and step out onto the cabin's tiny porch. Sun's below the horizon still, but already the sky is turning yellow. Someone cut a short piece of railroad tie for a chair so I take a seat on this and prop my back against the wall. It's cold but not bitterly so, and last night's potential storm blew out without dropping any snow.

We're up high enough here I can see the Jackrabbit Road's tenuous slash through the trees and the Paradise Mountains, pale blue at this hour. A small dust cloud rises above what I presume is a wagon rumbling south toward Pioche. My stomach rumbles, too. Need to send the kid back into town for food but for the time being, I'm content to watch the sun rise over Lake Valley.

Before long, I hear Jordan bumping around in the cabin. I consider picking up my revolver in case he comes out with that rifle of his but when the boy steps outside, he's empty-handed and I'm glad I didn't let suspicion muddy the waters.

"Morning, Jordan," I say. "All quiet."

"Morning, Sunday," Jordan mumbles. He rubs his eyes and yawns.

"I'm a lousy host: no coffee, no eggs, no nothing."

"S'okay. I'm not hungry," he says but again, I'll bet he's lying.

I notice someone's nailed a mule shoe to the beam above the door. Glad to see its points are up to keep all the good luck from spilling out. I know it's only a superstition but whenever I see a horse or mule shoe improperly set, I spin it so that it can fulfill its intended function. Guess that's just my way of spreading sunshine and love all around the great State of Nevada.

Jordan looks so groggy I hate to say anything but if we're gonna keep the good luck rolling, we'd better prepare.

"Think you're okay for a walk back into town? We'll need three, four days' provisions. Prospectors' fare: canned meats, dried fruit, and crackers, mostly. Three tins of water, minimum."

"Sure." He yawns again.

"Look for a market at the corner of Lacour and Airshaft Road. Three miles past Atlanta Siding but you don't need to go all the way back to Main Street. Make sure to eat something while you're there."

"Top of my list," he says.

∾

Once Jordan leaves, there isn't much for me to do. I go back inside and doze but every little sound startles me awake. The other problem is that with the sun beating down, the cabin heats up and its ratty smell intensifies. Window's nailed shut so I prop the door open with that chunk of railroad tie. No wind, though, and it barely makes a difference.

Taking a cloth scrap from a packrat's midden, I disassemble and clean our weapons and re-sort our ammunition. There isn't much to sort. If we're cornered, I don't think we could hold out more than five, ten minutes at most. Happy to leave the blasting caps outside in the shade but I want our guns and bullets handy.

Around ten or so, I hear soft footsteps out in the gravel. Grabbing my revolver, I kneel inside the open door and watch as a herd of mule deer move uphill past the cabin. They glance and sniff at me as they pass but their pace doesn't change.

My heart's beating so fast now I'll never get back to sleep. Might as well walk around and stretch my legs. No sense stewing over when—or even if—Jordan will return. Hell, if I were him, I'm not sure I would. I start up the wash after the deer but never see them again. No surprise. To their ears, I probably sound the way an approaching train sounds to mine. After a few hundred yards, I circle back, picking my way over shattered limestone and drifts of pine needles. Hardly any snow out here although I see some higher in the Bristol Range. A bluebird darts past my head, startling me, but otherwise everything is perfectly still. I'm the only thing out of place in these woods.

Back at the cabin, I scan the road in both directions but there's nothing moving anywhere along its length. Not sure what Jackrabbit was like before it revived but I can't say I'm impressed by the traffic headed there today. Then again, another road runs parallel farther downslope, too low for me to see. Could be more travelers take it, instead. What do I know? I don't live around here.

I go back inside and try to catch more sleep.

$\backsim$

This isn't the first time I've been run out of town, yet now that we've put distance between Delamar and us, it might be the most leisurely.

In 1905 I left Edgemont on unhappy terms, sure, but twice the following year, I ran for my life. Up on Cripple Creek, so many people were traveling to and from the district that skipping out was relatively easy, but in Fairview, my escape was nothing short of a miracle. I'd only put in one shift in at the Nevadahills Mine when a company bob demanded to search my coat and lunch pail. This seemed unreasonable to me, given that I was working topside, tramming timbers from a stockpile over to the shaft-house. When I said so, he grabbed the lapels of my jacket and tried to throw me into a wall. Now, grabbing lapels is an amateur's move—might as well handcuff yourself while you're at it—and second, the easiest chore in the world is to counter a half-assed assault. In this case, too easy. Took nothing more than clamping my right hand over his, pivoting to drop my left elbow onto his forearms, and finishing with a left elbow to his jaw. He was out like a light and my belongings went unsearched: all fine and dandy except it turns out he was the nephew of someone important. One of the Churchill County Commissioners, as I recall.

Soon as word of what I'd done went 'round, a law-and-order committee went to my dugout, unloaded shotguns through the door, and lobbed a gasoline bomb inside. It was one of those times I'm glad I'm so high-strung because I'd known better than to stick around. Animal instinct or a blockhead's common sense, I don't know. I'd grabbed my revolver, a bindle of clothes, and set out before sundown, destination unknown. Hell, I didn't even learn about my dugout until a week later when I'd picked up an issue of the Manhattan *Mail*.

This episode revealed a truth to me; the Fairview Miners' Union, they were no help whatsoever. Downright hostile, in fact. Although this same detective had shaken down their rank-and-file for months, sometimes at gunpoint, my little dustup undercut a cozy arrangement wherein he would look the other way so long as the union's leadership allowed him to make an occasional show of "confiscating" ore from whoever was on the outs with the FMU. I threw away my union card in one of the gulches leading north from Fairview Peak.

Somewhere around Manhattan's town limits, I also decided that I belonged on the surface, figuring it was better to enforce rules than obey them myself. A company detective's wages are usually better than a miner's and while both lines of work have their hazards, a detective's rarely require him to go underground—something I genuinely dislike. Miners say the profession gets in the blood and maybe that's true. You'll see generations follow each other underground, but the only way I'll follow my father into the earth is in a pine box.

෨

Mid-afternoon, I spot a figure on the road, carrying something and moving fast. Based on height, thinness, and gait, I believe it's Jordan, though I wish I had binoculars or a glass so I could be sure. Turning north, I see a pair of southbound wagons but these are miles away and moving slowly. Five minutes and a thousand yards later, I'm positive it's him. No one's following. Good.

Soon as he reaches the wash, I walk down to meet him. He's sweating profusely but otherwise looks none the worse for his long walk. I, on the other hand, must look a mess because as soon as he sees me, he points to my shoulder.

"You're bleeding," he says.

I crane my neck so I can see what he's talking about and, sure enough, a bloodstain has spread across my collar.

"How about that?" I feel along the side of my head. More blood comes off on my hand.

Jordan falls in as I start for the cabin. "What happened?"

"Tree branch or something. I don't know."

"You don't remember doing it?"

"Nope."

"Looks like it hurt."

"Well, it didn't; scalp on that part of my head is numb. Got slashed in the Philippines and a surgeon tied everything down, but the nerves never regrew. No big deal." We step carefully around the cabin's trash-pile—tin rubbish and broken glass, mostly. Jordan reaches down, pulls a sharp piece of metal from the heap, and slips it inside the burlap sack slung over his shoulder.

Back inside the cabin, we dump the bag onto my bedframe so we can sort through everything he bought. Nice haul, too: tinned beef and ham; two pounds of evaporated apples, one of apricots, and one of raisins; two boxes of Nabisco soda crackers; green beans—

"Why?" I ask, holding up a can.

"Twenty-five cents for three. Don't like 'em?"

"All yours."

—pinto beans, and peaches; one pound of walnuts; two loaves of bread; a sack each of coffee and sugar; one box of ginger snaps; and, best of all, a small sack of oranges.

"Well done, son." Opening the sack, I raise one for inspection. "These look good."

"Fifty cents for the bag," he says but I wouldn't care if they'd cost a dollar apiece.

He also bought four half-gallon tins of water: a good start but not nearly enough, which means we'll need to travel spring-to-spring across the desert. That, or melt snow, provided any's available. No matter. Jordan did a fine job and I'm perfectly happy.

The boy's awfully quiet, though, and once or twice glances through the open door.

"Something the matter?" I say, taking a half-step toward the corner where the guns are laid.

He walks past me to the doorway, puts a hand on each side, and leans through, turning his head to observe the road. I glance over at the bedframe strewn with our food and see the metal scrap he picked off the dump is still there.

"Something happen in town?"

He turns to face me. "Saw two fellows I worked with over in Delamar."

"They see you?"

"Couldn't avoid 'em: they were outside the grocer's. Wanted to know what I was doing in Pioche and why I was storing up so I said I was gonna go try Fay but of all places, they said that's where they were coming from. Said the big mine there busted last month so I shouldn't bother."

"So, then what?"

"Asked where I was camped. Offered to let me bunk at their place but's Jon Linna's a thief—he and Mat Pakkila, they watched me pay for everything and damn near counted my change. Figured they were trying to bracket me so I went farther into town. Ducked into the Silver Café for a cup of coffee, you know, to wait 'em out."

Glorious. I sent Jordan into town because I figured he was less likely to attract attention.

"Get away clean? Run into someone else? What?"

"Went out the back and I don't think they saw me leave town. They *did* see me coming south toward the grocery store in the first place. Might figure I'm camped north of town."

"How well do you know them? Think they'll come looking?"

"I don't know. Maybe."

I step out onto the porch and trace the road south. No one on it; no one at all.

"Isn't as if we're barely over the limit; we're six, seven miles outside town. Think they'd come all this way to look for you?"

Still inside the cabin, Jordan takes a seat on the rickety chair and rubs his face with both hands. "Maybe."

"They say anything about Delamar?"

"Only that it's quiet. All the marchers went back indoors. Said deputies set up a cordon: no one in or out without being searched. Black Hand Jack made a plea for federal troops but the governor's agents found everything quiet and the request was denied. Too much going on over in Goldfield now."

"Good for Andy, keeping a lid on things. Lipford must be losing his mind."

"What should we do, Sunday?"

The kid's jittery but that's no surprise. Knowing someone's tailing you is like carrying a boulder. Every step takes concerted effort and you tire more quickly than usual. Even me, I can't say I'm used to it but maybe I know better how to handle the pressure. I go to the corner, take up Jordan's rifle, and step out onto the porch.

"Get something to eat and then rest. I'll keep watch while you sleep." Still cradling the rifle, I peel an orange.

"Sorry, Sunday; didn't think I'd see anyone in Pioche."

"Call me Shep and don't apologize. You made it back in one piece *and* you bought us enough food to cross the state. Far as I'm concerned, that's a fine day's work."

Looking over my shoulder, I see Jordan's already lying on his bedframe, chewing bits of evaporated apple and staring at the ceiling. He must be exhausted.

"Set out tomorrow?" he says.

"Tonight. Don't need anyone nosing around, looking for us."

He goes quiet for so long I assume he's drifted off.

Although it's still daylight, shadows are gathering deep within the woods. High on my right is a notch in the mountains called Stampede Gap, where the main road crosses between Pioche and the camps on the range's west side. We'd have gone that way if it wasn't for Jordan's misadventure. Now we'd better get as far away from here as quickly as possible.

Behind me, Jordan rolls onto his side. "Stinks in here," he says and he's right. Haven't seen a packrat since yesterday but doubtless they were enjoying the place for a long time before then.

"Go to sleep," I say.

Another minute passes before Jordan speaks again, "Shep, you said I could ask you what it felt like to kill someone."

Shit, I did say that, didn't I? "Why do you want to know?"

"Curious is all."

"I was in the army. Fought in China and the Philippines."

"So, you shot people?"

"I did. In Tarlac, a bullet punched a hole in my hat. Saw the fellow who'd done it, too, so I lined him up and brought him down. Honestly, it was like playing catch, except my throwing arm was better than his."

"That's what it feels like?"

"Just that once."

"What about the others?"

What does killing someone feel like? Honestly, there's no emotion I haven't felt about the things I've done. Elation, pride, guilt, horror, sometimes all at once. When it's kill or be killed, the act is easy enough to justify. That fellow in Delamar who shot at me on the boardinghouse stairs? For him, I feel nothing. In other cases, matters of necessity, retribution, and legality don't square with my conscience. These memories are the basis of my nightmares.

I can practically feel Jordan's eyes on the back of my head so I guess I need to give him an answer. "It's a burden, pard. A cancer. It fills your heart and your head until everything hurts."

∽

I haven't talked to anyone this way since Edgemont. Back then I'd cry for no reason—no reason I'd admit to, anyway—and my head hurt so badly I'd curl into a ball and clutch at my temples. Not everything on my resumé is justified and I hated thinking about it.

Julia, though, she sat beside me on the floor and rested her hand on my head. She gave me the civilian's version of what Harry Wright told me in the Philippines, "You did what you had to, Shep. What's done is done."

"Ah, don't think about it," I said, desperate to forget, myself.

"Don't try carrying these things by yourself, Shep. I'm not leaving—I won't ever leave you." Her father fought for the Union at Spotsylvania and Cold Harbor; she well knew why old soldiers thrashed and shouted in their sleep.

Sometimes I yelled at her to leave me alone. Said worse things, too: baseless accusations, blame for things that couldn't have been her fault. Eventually, though, I began to relax—to look away from the void and focus on the warmth of her hand on mine.

"Tell me what happened," she said. "Please, Shep. Nothing bad can happen while I'm here." And for a while she was right.

I'd pull myself closer to the edge of the bed and rest my head on her knee. Sometimes I cried, overwhelmed with grief. Other nights I'd empty my heart, or wrap my arms around her waist and stay awake just so I could listen to her breathe.

Before Julia came along, nothing except another crisis could distract me, and nothing calmed those gusts of anger and blood except when I drank enough to pass out cold. For a while, I thought I might turn a corner but in the end, it turns out Julia lied to me, too: she said she'd never leave me, but she did. As swiftly and completely as anyone has ever gone out of my life, she left me. She deserved better. A better suitor, a better life. She didn't deserve to die.

∾

December 31, 1904, Joe McCuskey walked into the Buena Vista, where Ed Hansen and I were counting down to New Year's. That night, I busted McCuskey's lip but over the next several weeks, I decided I liked Edgemont enough to tolerate his presence. A few weeks later, we squared off in another bar but before things got out of hand, he got me talking. Like I said, Joe's a talker and I guess I was drunk enough that he disarmed me with his words.

"Why are you so bent?" McCuskey said. "You weren't the only one who got nicked." He'd pulled up his sleeve to reveal a mass of scar tissue running from his shoulder to his elbow. Looked as if a dog bit off half his triceps muscle.

"Congratulations. Get that at Lawaan?"

"Come on, pard, I thought you were dead, honest."

I shook my head in disgust. "Charlie Marak didn't."

"I'm telling you, Shep, honest Injun, I never saw you move. We'd lost Armani and Buhrer; I thought they'd got you, too."

~

In some ways, our retreat from Balangiga was worse than the initial attack.

By seven a.m., Sergeant Betron had organized C Company's twenty-five survivors—only four of whom were uninjured—on the town plaza. Those of us who could still walk spent the next forty-five minutes searching for bodies, weapons, and materiel. Gathering on the beach, Taylor Hickman and others brought boats from the river landing down to the beach and we rowed out onto Sua Bay just before eight in the morning. Attackers kept sniping at us from the jungle, even after we'd launched. A few tried to follow but we drove them back with rifle fire and eventually, they gave up.

The most severely wounded were loaded into the largest boat, commanded by Sergeant Betron. Walter Bertholf captained ours: a long river-canoe carrying a Macabebe scout named Francisco, Litto Armani, John Buhrer, Joe McCuskey, Charlie Marak, three others, and me. Our little flotilla stayed together as far as Capines Point but out on the rougher waters of the gulf, the tides, wind, and relative strength of each boat's crew left us strung out along the coast.

Our boat eventually foundered and the seawater burned like acid on our wounds. Francisco stopped paddling so he could keep John and Litto from drowning in the bottom of the canoe. Others came back and Floyd Shoemaker, Richard Considine, and Jerry Driscoll were transferred to other boats but it was no use. Ours was half-sunk, unwieldy, and we drifted slowly back to shore. Sergeant Betron and the others promised to return, as there was nothing more they could do.

After nine hours in the blazing sun and sixteen without water, we were all delirious, although Litto, with an open abdominal wound, and John, with his eye socket crushed, were the worst-off. Around midnight, we grounded on a coral reef and waded ashore above the village of Lawaan. Joe and I carried Litto, and Francisco and Walter carried John Buhrer. Francisco saved our lives by climbing a tree to bring down coconuts—the first food and drink we'd had since our abbreviated breakfast the morning prior.

At daybreak, we found the tide had lifted our boat off the reef and carried it out to sea. Litto and John broke down and begged us to kill them before the natives did. It took all of us to calm them before we decided to venture up the coast in search of another boat. We'd made it about a mile to some tall rocks when Litto and John declared they couldn't move any farther. I volunteered to stay behind as a guard while Joe, Charlie, Walter, and Francisco went on. We three sat between huge limestone boulders, watching the others move slowly north.

Not two minutes after our comrades left, Filipinos with bolos and spears charged us from the jungle above the beach. The Krag I carried had been soaking in the canoe and wouldn't fire. Thank God, while we emptied the armory in Balangiga the day before I'd grabbed a .45 Colt New Service—a sidearm technically reserved for officers—plus a box of shells. I shot two Filipinos within feet of our position but there were so many of them, one got through and bashed my head with a club.

Can't tell you everything that happened then because I was face down with blood and sand in my eyes. What I *do* remember is seeing the Filipinos falter and fall back after shots came from farther up the beach. Lifting my head, I saw the natives hadn't run off completely; they were still lurking in the trees above the sand. One threw a spear at me but missed.

Turning again, I saw Walter and Joe advancing with Krags held tightly to their shoulders. Charlie was holding his rifle awkwardly, balancing the fore-stock on his left elbow, his forearm having nearly been severed at Balangiga. Joe looked skittish as hell, firing randomly into the bush until Walter shouted at him to stop.

"Can you see John?" Walter shouted. "Is he moving?"

"Dead," Charlie shouted back.

No one asked about Litto; I presume there was a reason.

"Joe," Walter shouted. *"Joe!* What about Shep?"

I looked Joe in the face, and while I grant I was on my side and covered with sand and gore, I'm sure he saw me. Even raised my hand to him.

"Dead," he said, turning to look toward the sounds of movement between the trees.

"No," I shouted but so weakly that the sound died somewhere between the wind and the surf. Tried to raise my hand higher but my arm was shaking and I couldn't lift it more than four or five inches above the sand.

Walter and Joe were backing north along the beach when Charlie Marak shouted, "Wait, Shep's moving—he isn't dead!"

He and Walter ran, shooting as they came, and lifted me by my arms. Joe stayed where he was, still firing into the trees.

"Can you walk?" Walter said and a few moments later I told him I thought I could.

A few wobbly steps and I had to lean against a boulder. While I recovered, the others kept firing, slowly driving the Samareños away from the beach. Shots from deep within the woods made us believe we were about to be overrun until the attackers fled and Francisco reappeared, firing into their backs.

After that, the five of us started back up the coast, stopping occasionally to snipe at natives paralleling our course. After four miles or so, we found an outrigger near some huts and once again put to sea.

Still without water, that leg of our escape was even more painful than the first. Our tongues were so black and swollen we couldn't help but drink sea-water. Charlie's arm ballooned to twice its normal size and hurt so much that he begged us to shoot him. I drifted in and out of consciousness, occasionally coming around to help paddle until I'd pass out again. Charlie said at one point I'd nearly toppled overboard. I was unconscious when we were rescued by the USS *Pittsburgh*, steaming south toward Balangiga with G Company and the few C Company survivors who'd made it all the way to Basey.

໑

In Edgemont, curiosity got the better of me. "Okay, what happened to your arm?"

Joe rolled his shirt-cuff back into place. "In Tacloban, some Visayan greaser leaned out of a crowd and stabbed me—lucky it wasn't my chest or stomach. Surgeon stitched me up in the field-hospital there but it got infected; spent two months in a Manila death-ward."

"What a shame," I'd said. "Still doesn't bring you square for what you did."

"What are you talking about?"

"Balangiga. Down by the river, jack: you never even fired your rifle. Dobbins and Covington's boat capsized, Samareños in dugouts surrounded 'em, and you ran away. I heard everything. You abandoned them, Joe—same way you turned your back on me."

"Bullshit," he'd spat. "Who said that?"

"It's in the action report, bub. Klaas and Cliff Mumby both swore under oath they'd watched you run away without having fired a shot."

"That ain't fair. I was in a hospital in Manila so I couldn't testify, understand? Goddamn Krag I was carrying jammed so I threw rocks until it was clear the gu-gus weren't stopping, and then I ran to look for others. Hell, *I'm* the one who dragged Mumby and Irish back to the river."

I stared at him, unsure what to say. That morning in Balangiga was such a whirlwind I'd figured it was possible for stories to get twisted. Certainly, I'd told others who were there what I remembered—things I *knew* I saw—only to have them contradict me, too.

"You know Mumby hates me," Joe said. "I'm not saying he's lying but I'm positive things didn't happen the way he told you. I didn't leave Dobbins, pard. Swear to God, I didn't abandon your pal."

After that, I was friendlier toward Joe. We weren't first-rank buddies but I didn't mind seeing him around and more than once, we'd stepped outside a bar and felt the rising sun on our faces. He'd found work at a small outfit in Dunn Canyon; I'd hired on as a timberman at the Lucky Girl and apart from working underground, for a while there my life got better. Julia still didn't care for Joe but she was a kind soul and tolerated him for my sake. Wish she hadn't.

In March 1905, about two weeks after a snowslide wrecked the aerial tram between the Lucky Girl Mine and the mill, miners broke into a twelve-inch seam of phenomenally rich ore. Free gold—none of your low-grade, refractory ore—so rich you could see stringers of it running through the quartz. So rich it bent rather than broke under the miners' hammers. All at once, people—and money—started pouring into camp. Lots of money. Money that wasn't meant for hardscrabble outfits like the one where Joe worked, so he started scheming to get his hands on some.

Joe loved cards and like most poker players, he was up to his nuts in debt. Tried to hire on at the Lucky Girl but by then there were thirty applicants for every position. By late May, he must've grown desperate because late one night, he asked me to help him plan a holdup.

I wasn't interested; not even slightly. Julia and I were happy, I was making good money, and for the first time in a long time, my head felt like it was on straight. I'd cut back on drinking and my nightmares were becoming less frequent. Joe wouldn't have it, though. First, he made appeals based on our time in the army. When that didn't work, he started hanging around all the time, pestering Julia for information. He knew she clerked in the Lucky Girl's offices and therefore knew when payrolls were scheduled and what route they'd follow.

There he was, his motives out for inspection, and I didn't pay attention; didn't take him seriously. Julia was no dummy—far smarter than me—but in a misguided effort to make me happy, she answered Joe's obnoxious questions, thinking this was what I wanted. The payroll that month was a monster, too: $11,000 in gold eagles and Joe went mad thinking about it.

Once he figured I wasn't going to help, he recruited two lowlifes: one, a cook at the mine where he worked, and the other, nothing more than a drinking buddy he'd met in a bar down in Flat Town. These idiots, they missed their chance to ambush the pay-wagon on the road from Aura so they hustled over the ridge and in broad daylight tried to shoot their way into the Lucky Girl's offices. True to form, as soon as security started shooting back, Joe slunk out of town, stole a horse from the Seven J Ranch, and rode for Idaho. His accomplices, on the other hand, made a stand before they were killed, firing more than fifty rounds into the office. Three people were hit: a clerk, a mine manager, and Julia. Julia was the only one with serious wounds. She lingered for five hours in the company's two-bed hospital before her heart stopped.

൭

Opening my eyes, I'm back on the porch of a tiny, ramshackle cabin in the woods north of Pioche. My heart's beating faster but otherwise, I'm not too rattled and I figure I'd better speak before my nerves give out.

"You wanna know what happened to McCuskey?" I turn to face Jordan.

He rolls onto his side, stirring the dust inside his bedframe. "Yeah," he says although his voice is groggy and eyes stay closed.

"Last month, my counterpart followed a tip that McCuskey was over in Caliente—"

"Who told you he was there? Billy Meeks?"

"Curt Broe from the Association said he intercepted a telegraph, but I don't know if that's true." I stare out the door. "We figured one of your officers requested McCuskey for a job in Delamar." Jordan doesn't say anything then so I continue, "Broe drove me to our workshop up in the range east of Delamar so I could…work him. Wanted to know what he was doing in Lincoln County. Afterward, I drove him out to the Association's dumping ground at Groom Lake. There at the last, he and I talked. Talked about things that made me realize how far I've strayed. Hell, for a while, I even thought I'd let him go but he wouldn't stop talking."

I pause, listening to a bluebird twittering on a branch outside. Jordan stays quiet but I'm talking now for my sake more than his.

"Dug a hole in the lakebed and rolled him into it, trying to scare an apology out of him, but the son of a bitch still wouldn't act right…"

I stoop to retrieve the Colt, gripping it with my right hand. I inspect the sights, still as clean as the day they were forged. The finish is nicked and scratched, especially the grip, but it's still a fine looking piece. You are my savior and my burden, old friend. A terrible burden.

"He said something I couldn't forgive so I took this…took this revolver and I…"

My throat tightens and I can't get the words out. Can't get the words out but why? Why should I feel badly about Joe McCuskey? Why should I care? Only the Devil has a stake in our next meeting.

I look over and try to read Jordan's expression but he's fallen asleep.

Thank God.

Sprawled across the bedframe, his limbs are askew and he's draped a coat sleeve over his eyes to block the dusty sunlight slanting across his body. Looks even younger than he is. Still just a kid. I was just a kid, too.

I wipe my eyes, pick up the rifle, and step back outside. It's getting old saying this but the road's still deserted: no one's on it, no dust anywhere along its length. Couldn't have found a better place to hide than this cabin. Wish I could stay here forever. The afternoon sun feels good and with a weapon handy, I'm confident there's no harm in a little siesta.

Taking a seat on the porch, I press my back against the wall, feeling the logs' roughness through the fabric of my vest and shirt. By design, my coat is still inside, hanging from a peg. I figure once the sun sets and the temperature drops, that'll be my alarm clock. Or maybe I'll close my eyes and never wake up. That'd be okay, too. The view from up here runs on and on and it is so very good to just sit for a while.

TWENTY-EIGHT

I never do fall asleep. Not fully. Too much on my mind, I guess, and I've rested long enough. Like I said, we haven't much to pack so within minutes we're ready to go. Weighing about thirty pounds, the burlap sack has most of our food in it and we'll take turns carrying it. Jordan has his rifle and I have the two revolvers, plus the powder and blasting caps. These last items are wrapped inside a scrap of cloth carried hobo-style at the end of a long stick; no point blowing a hole in my side as we stumble through the woods.

We sit on the porch, awaiting nightfall. Door behind us is closed—the packrats have free rein again. Moon's a day or two away from full but already it's sailing high above the eastern horizon.

Jordan leans back to look at the emerging stars but I keep my eyes on the road. No need to tell him yet, but I see two lights moving in and out of the trees about a mile south. For the longest time, their approach suggests they're following the Jackrabbit Road. Then they turn and start uphill. I don't think they're coming our way but given Jordan's encounter earlier, they bear watching.

They move east again, downhill toward the road.

"Hand me the rifle," I say and Jordan complies.

"What is it?"

I point to the lights and sight them in. Way too far for a shot.

"You said the sights on this thing are good to three-hundred yards."

"Gonna wait until they get that close?"

"Won't be necessary: look."

The lights are moving south now, away from us. A few minutes later, they turn again and start back uphill. Either they're miners, trying to make their way to diggings up in the hills, or else Jordan's former comrades, stumbling about like idiots.

The boy seems awfully nervous, though, so I say something to boost his pluck, "Hundreds of little mines throughout this range; likely just prospectors headed back to camp."

We watch the lights wink out behind a ridge before reappearing higher on another.

"Prospectors," Jordan says but he doesn't argue when I suggest we should make our way north toward Jackrabbit instead of southwest to Stampede Gap like we'd planned. "Think they told anyone they saw me?"

"Probably did."

With this, we hoist the food and our belongings and make our way down to the main road.

∾

It's still warm out but then that's why so many miners come down to Lincoln County for the winter. It's uncomfortable and expensive to overwinter in the state's northern ranges: snow ten feet deep and roads closed for weeks at a time. Oh, it gets cold here, too, but nothing like they deal with up north. Can't say I miss it.

Tonight's so warm that before long, I unbutton my coat and Jordan takes off his and ties it around his waist. We cover seven miles in near silence—nothing more than "watch out," or "duck,"—until we see Jackrabbit's scattered lights. Here, the road angles harder to the northwest but between barking dogs and our need to pass unseen, we detour east and then north around town before striking the road to Bristol Pass. Dozens of side roads depart this stretch, all leading south toward various mines and prospects, and at last, we encounter supply wagons moving between Jackrabbit and the big Bristol silver camp on the range's western side. Noisy things, though, and each time we manage to duck into the trees before we're spotted.

Sometime after midnight, we reach Bristol Wells. It's a battered-looking place, a milling center from the district's pioneer days, and its stone buildings— plus a line of beehive-shaped charcoal ovens—are all deserted and beginning to collapse. We rest a while on the steps of one and listen to coyotes sing to the waxing moon.

"How are you holding up?" I ask.

Jordan finishes his drink of water. "Hallelujah, I'm a bum," he says, quoting a song WFM-types sing to tweak the mine owners' noses. "Hallelujah, bum again."

I remember a little, "Oh, why don't you save all the money you earn?"

"That's right," he laughs, singing, "If I didn't eat I'd have money to burn. Hallelujah, I'm a bum, Hallelujah, bum again."

"Hallelujah, give us a handout to revive us again."

He looks as pleased as I've ever seen him, clearly glad to remember happy hours spent in fellowship at Union Hall. He beckons with his hand, trying to draw out the next verse, but all I can do is shrug.

"Sorry, that's all I know." I take a drink.

He glances at the moon, directly overhead. "Association have any songs?"

I choke and spit out my water. "What? No. *No!* It's a commercial concern—they don't sing *songs.*"

"If there's no camaraderie in it, then why'd you work for 'em?"

"Jordan, that's a question without an answer." I screw the lid back on the water-tin. "Come on, let's get moving."

The boy's shoulders sag but he hoists his bag without complaint and we set off again.

We follow the road northwest along a low divide between Dry Lake Valley on the left and Muleshoe Valley on our right. About thirteen, fourteen miles later, we reach the Schell Creek Range, here only a welter of modest hills. Down on the valley floor, it was nothing but sagebrush, but now that the road is climbing, junipers and pinyon are closing in around us.

Tired and footsore, I'd love to prop my feet in front of a fire and sleep for ten hours but we're too exposed up here. Even a small fire would be visible for miles. No fire. No water, either. The soil here is powder-dry and dust-devils spin across the road like ghosts in the moonlight.

"How much farther?" Jordan says, sounding about as tired as I feel.

"Only to the top of this pass."

"How far have we come, you reckon?"

I attempt some verbal math, "Set out at six o' clock; Jackrabbit was around six miles. Six more to Bristol Wells. Maybe thirteen, fourteen here. Jesus, we've covered twenty-five, twenty-six miles in about eight hours—no wonder we're beat. Once we reach the summit, we'll get off the road. We can sleep until mid-morning and then figure out which way to go."

The view from up top is broad but uninspiring; another moonlit basin hemmed in by another moonlit range. More mountains on the horizon. That's Nevada for you: an armada of rocky battleships steaming south toward the Gulf of Cortez.

My feet are in terrible shape. Jordan isn't as beat but he still looks miserable. At this point, I'm not sure why I thought we could hoof it all the way to Goldfield but we'll take up that problem tomorrow.

Jordan holds up a nearly empty tin. "Last of our water."

"Finish it."

I motion for him to drink it all but he shakes his head.

"Take some yourself. No way I can carry you if you collapse."

"Not gonna collapse from thirst," I scoff. "We're only four, five hours from water tomorrow. Gonna sleep thirsty is all."

We take a mouthful, each, though I delay swallowing mine. Didn't realize how thirsty I was but again, that's a problem for tomorrow. Within minutes of stepping off the road, we curl up under a break of twisted pinyons and neither of us stirs until the following day is well along.

TWENTY-NINE

❧

We rest all day and set out again only an hour before sundown. The wind is up and the air's turned colder. No clouds but that doesn't mean a storm can't come roaring in within hours.

Somehow I'd imagined walking downhill would be be better, but with my toes pressing against the tips of my boots, I can feel blisters growing atop my blisters. Probably lose my toenails, too. I keep reminding myself we have a lot in our favor—food and fair weather—but with my feet hurting the way they do and now that we're out of water, optimism is getting harder to sustain.

We've covered only a mile or two when the road forks. The main branch continues northwest toward the White River marshes while the other bends north toward a gathering of low red hills.

Maybe fifty feet in front of me, Jordan stops and points. "Which way?"

A hand-lettered sign points north to Silver King, a small district that's floated along for years on rumors of rich silver ore. Despite decades of gophering, though, not a damn thing's come out of it.

"Straight," I say. "Might not reach the marshes tonight but that's our goal." Even thinking about water makes my thirst worse.

"Why'd we come so far north?"

"One, no one's out here. Two, White River is the only sure water in this part of the state." That's where Warren Jim said *he* was going and if anyone's advice is worth a damn, it's his. "And three, it puts us on a beeline to reach Basin Creek."

"Know someone there?"

"No, and I want to keep it that way."

A couple of minutes later, we spot two log cabins: one at the base of a ridge and another near its top. Is this Silver King? Not much to recommend it, if so.

The pain in my feet has made me inattentive. I'm limping along, feeling sorry for myself, when Jordan steps off the road. Only after seeing him crouch and point does it occur to me that something's amiss.

I advance and kneel beside him. "What is it?"

He gestures toward a point where the road enters a wash. My eyes are as good as anyone's but for the life of me, I can't see what's spooked him.

"Right side of the road," he whispers.

"Can't see anything."

"A *body!* Right by that little juniper."

I squint and by damn, he's right. About fifty yards ahead, a body lies at the road's edge. Its feet are bare and the head and torso are partially concealed by weeds.

My heart surges and I forget how much my feet hurt. Jordan tries to rise but I set a hand on his shoulder.

"Wait," I whisper, motioning for him to unsling his rifle.

I draw my revolver from a coat pocket and make sure a round is seated.

"Wait for what?" Jordan whispers.

"See if anything changes. Wait until dark if we have to."

We've seen no one since Jackrabbit but that's scant consolation now. For all we know, someone's been watching our shambling approach for a mile or more. I tell myself there's no way Curt Broe or a Thiel would think to wait for us here. This is something else; random coincidence. It has to be.

For ten minutes we watch the road and surrounding scrub, and for ten minutes nothing happens. Not a damn thing. The wind stirs the grass but that's it. I trace every ridge, every gully with my eyes. Nothing.

I tap Jordan on his shoulder. "Follow me. Don't get separated and for God's sake, don't get ahead of me; I plan to shoot anyone who crosses my sights, understand?"

We move farther off the road, trying to keep the body in view without presenting our profiles above the ridge. Nearly sunset and the day's last rays have turned everything red and orange—lovely, except this cast of light makes it harder to distinguish between form and shadow. For staging an ambush, you could hardly ask for a better setting.

"Look." I point to a reddish-brown spatter on a sandstone slab. A few feet away, I spot another. "Whoever that is, they staggered downhill until they collapsed."

"Down from where?"

Shadows are crawling up the hillsides but higher in the wash I see footprints and another red stain on a patch of whitish soil. This evidence lines up with the cabin at the foot of that low ridge.

I gesture toward it, its reddened tin roof a dull imitation of sunset.

"Stay close," I say, inching forward between clumps of sagebrush.

I crawl through the weeds until I'm close enough to touch the body, although I don't. Instead, I reach out with my revolver and jostle his shoulder. He doesn't budge. A reddish stain darkens his shirttail but I can't tell if he's been stabbed, shot, or something else. Not gonna roll him over, though; he's a mystery unsolved.

Jordan crouches beside me. "What happened?"

"No idea, although I'm surprised the coyotes haven't found him yet."

"He shoot himself?"

"If someone else did, they're long gone by now. Dust on his trousers, see? Been here three, four days, I'll bet."

"Indians, maybe?"

"Jesus, no." I shoot him a scornful look. "What century do you think this is?"

"Just a thought." He sounds sheepish.

"Well, keep that one under your hat."

"Hadn't we oughta bury him?"

I stand and look around. No lights in either cabin, no sign anyone's around. Looking north, I see no other buildings. I'd heard Silver King was home to sixty, seventy people but damned if there's anything here resembling a town. Just these two homes. I'll bet it's tucked up in the hills farther north. Above a clump of brush, something metallic flashes, like someone's trying to signal us with a mirror. Scrambling higher for a better view, I realize these are reflections off a windmill's spinning blades. Set back among the trees, I hadn't noticed it before.

"Leave him," I say. "The less time we spend here, the better."

Jordan doesn't like my answer. "Leave him to the elements? To the animals? That ain't right, Shep."

"He's none of our business," I insist, "and if a crime's been committed, the sheriff oughta see it. We bury him, we're burying evidence, too."

Starting uphill, I tell him to keep his rifle ready.

"Where are we going?"

"Windmill." I point toward the first cabin. "Water, I hope."

We follow a footpath through the sage, past a dugout roofed with sticks and clay, to the first cabin. The second house sits directly uphill from the windmill but since it's back on a ledge, it's hidden from view. A doorless, lean-to shed is partially embedded in the hillside behind the first cabin and inside is an autocar, partially covered with a tarp.

I glance through a window into the cabin and although it's dark in the corners, nothing seems amiss. Pots on the woodstove; a table with two chairs, and a short stack of plates in the cupboard. A thin layer of dust covers everything.

Outside, the hills have gone red. The cabin, the trees, the windmill, all burnished by the sun's last rays. Every tuft of grass, every stone—the sun itself is a perfect red ball.

Thank God, the windmill's operational and although water in the galvanized tank is brackish, enough splashes from the pump for us to refill our tins and drink for a long while. Hoofprints converge here from every direction. I'm a little surprised cattle aren't bedded down beneath the surrounding trees.

We drink and drink again.

"Hell, that's better," Jordan says, and I agree.

"And none too soon. White River's farther than I reckoned."

I say we ought to walk due west from here and stay wide of that corpse on the road. One windstorm and I'm satisfied our tracks will vanish, but given what's after us, it's better we take as few chances as possible. Jordan agrees, so I rebalance our food bag to accommodate the water tins while he washes his hands in the stock tank.

He cocks his head to one side like a dog. "Hear that?"

For several moments, I listen carefully but can't hear anything over the wind and the windmill.

He shrugs. "Animal, maybe."

"Windmill." I kneel to repack the bag. Honestly, unless it's an autocar, horses' hooves, or human voices, I'm too beat to care what he hears.

Jordan walks over to the cabin, peers through a window, and steps around the corner.

Squeak…squeak…squeak…the windmill spins. Must've been what he heard.

I set cracker boxes and dried foods on top the water tins and pull the drawstring closed. Again, I think how much my feet hurt, poor me. Temperature's gonna plunge once the sun goes down—

Still inside the house, Jordan shouts; something wooden—a chair, a table—clatters to the floor. Pop-pop—one gunshot, followed by another.

I drop the bag and run. Door's open. Jordan's leaning against a wall, gripping the rifle's stock with one hand and clutching his side with the other. Revolver drawn, I scan the kitchen. Can't see anything in the shadows but damned if I'll wait for my eyes to adjust. Grab the kid by his collar, yank him through the door, and deposit him in the dirt at the base of the steps.

"Who's in there?" I kneel and raise the revolver, ready to plug anything that shows.

"Right side," Jordan wheezes. "Door."

Jesus Christ, this is nothing we need.

"Are you hit?"

The boy says nothing; just stares at his hand. My eyes dart back and forth between him and the cabin door. Nothing moves.

"Jordan, are you hit?"

The kid's eyes are wide and he won't take his hand from his side so I can have a look. Blood seeps between his fingers.

"Let me look at it. Move your hand and let me look, okay?"

Glancing up, I notice a mule shoe nailed over the door but its heels are pointed at the ground. Damn it, should've been more attentive. Should've made sure no one was here before going for water. Did everything backward and now look at the fix we're in.

Jordan pulls himself onto a bench at the steps' base. Still won't speak: he's probably in shock. With gunshots, the bullet's energy opens a larger, temporary cavity along the route of the 'permanent' hole, disrupting everything—nerves, heartbeat, organ function—everything within the confines of our skin. Some people recover from this jolt; others don't.

I pull the kid's jacket tight across his chest. "I'm going in there. Anything happens, get yourself back to Jackrabbit, okay?"

He nods.

In Delamar or back in the army, I wouldn't have tried to clear a room without the help of at least one deputy, preferably two. No choice here. Immediately inside the doorway, I stand with my back against the wall, waiting for my eyes to adjust and trying to control my breathing. I'm telling you, more than once

I've figured where men were hiding in adjacent rooms by the hiss of air rushing in and out of their noses.

Soon enough, I see what Jordan meant: only one door through the right-hand wall. Isn't pitch-black in there: twilight spills through the doorway, which means there must be a window.

Once inside, rules call for me to clear the nearest corner before running a wall to the next; worst thing I could do is stand still. Likely what Jordan did; his silhouette in the doorway made a fine target and whoever's in there obliged. Neither of the other rules apply: don't overlap your partner's field and maintain communication—here, I'm on my own.

At last, my eyes adjust and I can see each fork and knife on the washstand—the stripes on a flannel shirt draped over a chair. Heart pounding, flooding me with adrenaline, I inch toward the door. Counting backward from three, I turn and step through.

Swing my revolver from side to side. Near corner's empty. Move along the longest wall toward the second. No one standing, no one crouched. Room *stinks*. Chest of drawers against one wall. Dried blood on it. Thin mattress halfway off an iron bed. Chair in one corner.

Shoes: the soles of a pair of shoes protrude from behind the chair. Little .32 revolver on the floor, a feeble hand groping for it.

I kick the chair, knocking over whoever's there. My heart races and my finger's inside the trigger-well but the man there merely groans. Doesn't fight back. Doesn't rise from the corner; doesn't even try. Maybe he can't. Bloodstains on the floorboards. The stench hits me again, stronger than before—he's been here awhile.

"Bastard," he croaks, "I knew you were still here." His voice is brittle like morning ice.

"Your partner's dead," I say, guessing he means the body down on the main road.

He doesn't answer. Spit rattles in his throat.

I kick his .32 toward the doorway and back out. Picking up the gun, I step into the kitchen. Don't think he'll ever rise from his corner but I close the door and wedge a chair beneath the knob. A healthy man could kick his way out, easy, but that fellow's nearly dead—I'd know that smell anywhere.

Back outside, I shake out the .32's chamber and eject three cartridges and two casings from the cylinder. These I hurl into the sagebrush across the road; the weapon itself goes into the stock tank below the windmill.

Out of sheer frustration, I'm tempted to go back and shoot him, anyway, but honestly I don't want anything more to do with this place. It reeks of bad luck. Don't care why a man down on the road is dead and another inside the cabin is dying. Double-cross? A partnership gone bad? None of my business. Jordan's my only concern.

The boy's hunched over but I can hear him breathing.

"How is it?" I lay my revolver on the bench beside him and kneel in the dirt.

He's still got a hand pressed to his side, which is good, and coughs, which isn't.

"Hurts," he whispers. "Can't hardly breathe."

With luck, the bullet might've only passed through the muscles above his left hip. If it punctured his abdominal cavity, though, any number of problems could result: organ damage, internal bleeding, and septic shock, among others.

"Does your gut feel tight?"

"No," he says. "My side and back—like the worst cramp imaginable."

Leaning forward, I find a bloodstain on his jacket about seven inches higher than the wound in his side, but no hole in the garment. Peeling off his coat for a closer look, a .32 slug tumbles out and lands on the bench. Assuming that specter in the cabin fired from a seated position, this trajectory makes sense.

Already the wound in Jordan's back is clotting. He pulls his hand away from his side and in the dim light, I can see a small entry-wound and a fair amount of blood.

"Want your lucky souvenir?" I point to the bullet.

"Don't feel lucky."

"You are. Another inch toward your centerline and who knows? Keep pressure on it and I'll see what I can find to patch you up."

Re-entering the cabin, I hear nothing from the other room. Grab a dishtowel and that flannel shirt off the chair. Back outside, listen again. Nothing. Duck around the corner for clean water from the pump. Tear the shirt into strips, fold the towel, and make a rough field dressing around Jordan's midsection. Just a trickle of blood now. Similar treatment for the wound higher on his back with the added benefit of pressure from his jacket.

"Press hard," I say. "Lousy bandage but it's all we have. Can you walk?"

He stands without difficulty but catches himself against the cabin wall. "Feel sick."

"Go slowly. I'll help you."

He glances at the closed door. "Is he…"

"Don't worry about him. Take your time; don't move until you're ready."

With one arm over my shoulder and the other pressed against the wall, Jordan holds his breath and takes a step with his right leg. No problem there, but his left buckles and I barely catch him before he collapses.

Resettled on the bench, he coughs into his hand. "Can't put weight on it—can't breathe right, neither."

Maybe he wasn't so lucky. Even with my help, he'll never manage forty miles to Basin Creek. Hell, it's twenty-five back to Jackrabbit, and I doubt we'd find a doctor there. Could go north to look for signs of life in Silver King but that'll sink us deeper in whatever happened here at the cabin. All options are bad.

Despite the fact that no one's after us now, my heart won't stop hammering. The night's gone silent: no wind stirring, no sounds from the cabin. I'm as wound up as I've ever been, feeling about like I did back in Delamar's jail. Trapped, only this time, my cage is 300 miles wide.

I step onto the road and glance uphill. The second cabin's roofline is barely visible but no light colors the surrounding trees. Wonder if that's where the dead man down on the road lived? Or are there more bodies up there? I hate this place.

In the shed behind the lower cabin, a perfect, shining circle catches my eye. Takes a moment before I recognize one of the autocar's brass headlamps.

⁓

The car is fairly new—probably only twelve months from the factory—yet typical of vehicles out here, already it's in rough shape. The passenger-side running board has been torn away; sagebrush pinstripes along both sides; and the right front fender is badly dented. The top's in good order, though: the struts are sound and I see only one small rip in its oiled canvas tonneau. These injuries notwithstanding, it's still a pretty thing. Even in the dim light, I appreciate its olive-green body and wine-red running gear.

Opening a door, the wind spills a stack of maps on the passenger's seat, their edges warped and curled. Below these is a folded newspaper: the *Ely Mining Record* from late November. In the back seat is a kit for several days on the road: a bundle of replacement tubes, a can of grease, and seven one-gallon tins of gasoline. Another bag contains a plaid shirt, two sweaters, and two pairs of trousers—someone was ready for a getaway.

I step around the other side to look on the floor below the rear seats. Dust covers everything, including a rock-hammer, two canvas sample-bags of rocks, several empty bags, a bundle of wood survey stakes, and a flat-bottomed gold pan. A geologist, maybe—geologist or prospector. Hardly matters now.

Jordan coughs. "You sure about this, Shep?"

I presume he means taking off with someone else's automobile and not my fitness to drive. "Hell, yes, I'm sure. No one here needs it now."

I help Jordan into the front seat and stuff a horse-blanket between him and the door. He winces and holds his breath but his pallor's returning to normal. We may get out of this yet.

Stash our things in the back. Hesitating, I search inside our bag for the powder and blasting caps I've carried since our raid on the Tomcat's magazine. These I leave on the floor of the shed. With all we're up against, I'd hate to add explosion or fire to the list, especially with gasoline tins nestled in the back seat. I fold the windscreen so Jordan has an unobstructed view of the yard.

"Gonna try to start this thing. Here's my revolver. Excluding me, shoot anything that moves, understand?"

He takes the gun but his hands are unsteady. "Said I didn't need to worry. You didn't kill him?"

I ignore his question. "Don't get caught off guard again."

The boy can't be shaken so easily. "You didn't kill him?"

"That's between him and God, not him and me."

Jordan slumps against the seat.

I empty one tin of gasoline into the tank and walk around front. Dropping the crank handle on the ground beside my boots, I set the choke and spark valves where I figure they ought to be and glance over the hood.

"Know where the hand-brake is?"

"Never been in an autocar before."

"Next to the, no—other side. Long lever with a release on the handle."

"I see it."

"Is it pointing at two o' clock or noon?"

"Noon."

"Good. Now, keep watch."

If this car won't start then we're stuck walking, so for several minutes I turn the crank like Jordan's life depends on it. All the while, the engine sounds as if it's about to start but never does. All I get for my efforts are blistered hands and a sore back.

"Son of a bitch," I hiss, ready to give up. "Maybe there's a spare dry-cell in the back."

I tinker with the valves, turn the handle ten or fifteen times with my left hand, and spit on the ground in disgust. Sweaty and cold, I climb into the driver's seat.

"You want to try?" I say.

"Okay," he says, despite being unable to sit up straight. "Does it matter which direction?"

"Clockwise, as fast as you're able. Don't grip it with your thumb; all your fingers on one side. Damned thing ever starts, the pistons could throw the handle backward and break your hand."

He fumbles for the door but I reach across and stop him.

"I'm kidding."

"Don't mind trying," he says, coughing again.

"Offer's appreciated but you're in no shape for the job."

I step back down and retrieve the crank. Three or four revolutions in, the engine coughs and sputters to life. Oh, thank God and whoever built this autocar. I open the throttle and soon, all four cylinders are purring like well-fed tigers.

Back behind the wheel, I nod to Jordan. "Watch the cabin door until we reach the main road." Not sure why I bother; kid's hands are shaking so badly I doubt he could pull the trigger.

"Maybe it needed to hear you complain," he says.

"What?"

"The car." He coughs and winces. "Some machines need to hear how badly you need them before they'll work properly."

I stare at him a moment. "Something they teach you in the mines?"

He shrugs. "Nah, but I think it's true."

Whatever its motivation, the car is running well now and I ease it out of the shed and onto the road below the cabin. Unchallenged, we coast downhill to the main road and turn west toward a pale horizon and the Grant Range's black teeth.

Jordan falls asleep quickly and I don't know what to think. His wounds aren't catastrophic, yet he's awfully lethargic. Need to check on him regularly. Inspect his bandages and make sure he stays warm.

We bump along in the darkness. Only slightly faster than I can walk, true, but we're moving again and that's something. As the distance between us and Silver King grows, I start to feel better, like a pebble's been removed from my shoe. That place was cursed.

Before long, I'm feeling sharp again. Focused. Every rut, every bit of brush overhanging the road, is clear to me. Clear, too, that I can't permit any more delays. With luck, we'll reach White River before dawn.

THIRTY

I sleep for three, four hours atop the pass but Jordan is down most of the night, waking only once to drink some water.

Roads west of the mountains are rougher and Jordan doesn't look so good. Here in the early-morning sun, he's deathly pale, his forehead's hot, and he can't stop coughing. Not harsh, wracking fits like you'd hear in Delamar—just a nagging wheeze like he can't clear his throat. At least the weather holds and the last miles unspool quickly.

Basin Creek looks nothing like I remember it. When I rode this way in '03, the place was dead. There was a small store and three other buildings, all either vacant or collapsed. I stayed at the big ranch higher in the canyon. Foreman there said the entire population had moved out in the span of a week and he didn't think it was ever gonna revive. Now thirty or forty wood-frame buildings stand in various states of construction and twice as many tents are scattered across the surrounding hillsides. Right at the canyon's mouth is a new hotel, a hardware store and post office, four saloons, plus a dozen other businesses fronting a wide main street that ends at the base of a cliff. People walking everywhere, too. Basin Creek is booming.

A wagon loaded with ore rumbles down-grade, its team shying away from our noisy vehicle. Another man reins in his horse as we approach; the animal hops nervously as we chug past. People stop what they're doing and stare at us—not the reception I was hoping for—but at least no one recognizes us.

The crowd parts as we pull up before a brand new, blindingly white, two-story hotel. A man on a ladder is hanging Christmas greenery from the hotel's balcony. Another wraps red bunting around its posts.

I lean over and shake Jordan's knee. "Basin Creek, partner. Cross your fingers there's a doctor here."

Jordan grunts in return. He's been coughing more this past hour but I confess I'm focused on other things, like keeping a sharp lookout for familiar faces. God knows where Lipford has operatives watching for us.

A crowd of men and women gather around the automobile's front, looking it over and talking among themselves. I worry that whoever owned the car in Silver King might've driven here before but it seems these people merely want to gawk. Cars are still enough of a novelty here in the interior West that it isn't unusual for people to want a closer look.

"Fine looking machine, mister," one fellow says. "What is it?"

I'm filthy and probably stink to high hell but anyone who arrives by auto-car—even one in pitiful shape—is someone to be reckoned with. Brand new, I'm guessing our automobile would cost around $2,700, far beyond the means of everyone except bankers, stockbrokers, and mine owners. In Delamar, Lipford keeps a half-dozen autocars around for his enforcers to use because more than anything, he wants people to know he has the money to do as he pleases.

"Iroquois Type-D," I say, "all the way from Seneca Falls, New York." I know this only because I read a manual in the tool kit. "Say, can you tell me—"

He whistles. "Rough roads don't give you no trouble?"

I'm trying hard to sound casual but one glance at Jordan and I cut him off, "Sorry, but my nephew isn't well. Any chance there's a doctor in town?"

I brace for the answer, expecting him to say I'll need to make for Tonopah or Ely but thank God, he gestures up the block.

"Office near the end of this street."

The man hanging pine garlands steps down from his ladder and pushes his way forward. "That boy don't look so good. Want me to fetch Doc Robinson?"

"Yes, thanks." I hand him a few coins.

Garland Man steps into the street and heads north toward a cluster of one-story, false-fronted buildings.

The fellow with the questions repeats himself, "Rough roads don't give you no trouble?"

"Two flat tires and some scratches," I say, watching Garland Man's progress along the street. "Otherwise, no: this car's a champ. Thirty-five horses under the hood, forty-inch wheels. Can't open up the way I would on graded roads but we haven't had any problems, either. Pard, what did we reach going around that lakebed? Forty, forty-five miles per hour?"

Jordan coughs and runs his fingers through his dusty hair. "Fifty-three."

"Good-*ness,*" the man says. "Hard to breathe at that speed?"

"Exhilarating, sure, but no trouble breathing." Saying this, I cough twice to clear the scratchiness inside my chest and Jordan follows with a gust of his own.

I stand on the porch, admiring the view. Basin Creek sets at the mouth of a hanging valley carved into the Grant Range. Like castle walls, snowcapped peaks rise on three sides; the fourth one is open and the effect is like sitting in an opera box overlooking the dun vastness of Garden Valley. The cottonwoods along Cherry Creek are barren this time of year and the pinyons dull with dust, but the sky is such a clear, crystalline blue that any artist who'd dare to scrape this tint across canvas would be scorned as an amateur.

Don't have long to appreciate the scenery, though, because Jordan grabs my elbow.

"Can you help me into the hotel for some water? I'm parched."

I whisper that we can't go inside because his coat is bloodstained. I beckon to Ribbon Man on his ladder and ask if he'll fetch a glass of water. He agrees, though with less enthusiasm than Garland Man showed in going for the doctor.

The crowd around us drifts away—all except for Question Man, who appears to be an autocar fanatic cut from the same cloth as Jerry Rosen. He squats on his heels to study the Iroquois' undercarriage.

I press my hand against Jordan's forehead. He's running a fever and sweating like a pig, worse than he was an hour ago.

Garland Man returns. "Doctor will be along shortly. Says he just needs to wash up."

A moment later, his counterpart emerges from the hotel with a glass of water for Jordan. The boy takes the glass and downs half before coughing again and slumping against the seat.

I circle around the car and lean against a fender. Don't know what I'll do if Jordan takes a turn for the worse. My instincts for solitude and self-preservation tell me that delivering him to a doctor is all that's required and I can leave—*should* leave now, but my damned conscience won't listen. At least, no one from Delamar is here—not as I've noticed, anyway. We are far off the two main routes between Pioche and Goldfield so I wasn't expecting familiar faces. Basin Creek's an obscure camp, though not as obscure as I expected.

Maybe we'll head northeast to Ely and catch a train to Carson City. Bypass the southern camps entirely.

Question Man circles around front to study the car's instrumentation. Irritated, I've half a mind to shove him to the ground. Lost in cruel thoughts, I'm late noticing a man in a brown suit and blue shirt approach from the street. This new fellow walks right up to the car and leans inside.

"This him?"

He's shorter than me. Blue eyes, an intense stare, and short, brown hair. He looks so young that at first, it doesn't occur to me that he could be the doctor.

"Who are you?" Imagining how that sounded, I wince.

He takes out a pocket watch, checks Jordan's pulse, and holds his hand against the boy's forehead. "Jim Robinson," he says, sounding equally irritated. "Who are you?"

Question Man looks my way, evidently interested in my answer.

"Charlie Witherill," I say, fumbling for cover. "This boy's my nephew, Casey."

Robinson pulls a stethoscope from his coat and listens to Jordan's chest. "How long has he been like this?"

"Since this morning."

"Coughing?"

I nod. "Figured it was on account of the dust. We drove here from Tybo, took a wrong turn in Railroad Valley, and had to backtrack across the playa. Started coughing after that."

Question Man glances at Jordan, grins, and goes up the stairs and into the hotel. Goddamned weirdo.

"Isn't dust," Robinson says. "Casey's breathing is shallow and his pulse is elevated. You say he fell ill this morning; did you encounter anyone in Tybo who was ill, or did he eat or drink something you didn't?"

I glance around, judge no one else is near enough to hear, and lower my voice, "Look, my nephew shot himself cleaning his revolver. Didn't want to make a scene, understand?"

Robinson leans away from the car. "Is that really what happened?"

Don't know if he's speaking to me or Jordan but the kid glances up and nods. I help him lean forward, pointing to the bloodstain on the back of his jacket.

"How'd he shoot himself in the back?"

"Exit wound; bullet went in above his left hip."

Again, Jordan nods.

Robinson keeps glancing between the kid and me. "I'll do what I can," he says, "but I don't want trouble, understand?"

"No one does."

Robinson steps backward, still glancing between Jordan and me. Then he looks over the Iroquois, dented and dusty, but still smart in the midday sun.

"Gonna walk to my office?"

"How about a ride? The kid's legs don't work so well."

"Fine," Robinson says, "but so you know, there isn't much I can do for bullet wounds."

"Great," I say, "keep your voice down."

Robinson opens the rear passenger seat and climbs in. "Stitch him up as best I can. Some medicines in my stores. Bayer's aspirin for his fever and as much water as he'll tolerate."

I step around to the autocar's front and start cranking. Hopefully this won't take long. All at once, I'm seized with a burning desire to get the hell out of Basin Creek.

∾

Turns out, we could've just as easily carried Jordan to Robinson's office—it isn't more than a hundred yards beyond the hotel. The only thing noteworthy during our short drive is that another auto—a Ford Model N and the first I've seen since leaving Pioche—passes us going the other direction. The driver acknowledges me with a wave.

"Two cars in a single day," Robinson says; "there's a first."

Maybe the first but surely not the last. Won't be long until everyone gives up and goes horseless. Can't see this nation of strivers going any other way.

Inside Robinson's office, we settle Jordan onto a table in the examination room. The shelves are crowded with boxes and tins containing powders and compounds. Most are brown and murky and look as though they'd taste awful. I help Jordan remove his coat and shirt. The doctor sets a panful of water on a woodstove before rummaging through drawers and cabinets around the room.

"Take these," he says, handing the boy several tablets and a glass of water.

The wound in Jordan's back, about an inch below his scapula, is small—the bullet must've traveled through his body intact—and no longer bleeding. The entry wound is clean but slightly depressed and still leaking. Not badly, but now more than twelve hours after his 'accident', it shouldn't be at all.

After cleaning Jordan's side with soap and water, plus a thorough dousing with iodine, Robinson spends a long time pressing on the boy's abdomen and listening to his chest with a stethoscope. He makes notes on a small paper tablet, consults a book, and listens some more.

"Okay," he says but doesn't elaborate.

I study his face for answers. "What?"

"Not sure."

Continuing his examination, he rolls Jordan onto his right side and briefly studies the entry wound, poking at it with a steel stylus. He goes to his desk, takes out a protractor, and makes several measurements, jotting these down on his tablet.

"Wound's dirty," Robinson says. "Nothing you could've done out there but it needs a thorough cleansing." He measures and mixes compounds in a vial before retrieving a steel syringe from a tray.

"What's that?" Jordan says, his face sagging.

"Anesthetic: one per-cent Stovaine in a physiologic saltwater solution. You'll feel a sharp pinch at first but then the area around the injury will quickly go numb. You—" he gestures to me, "—grab the whiskey on that table, would you?"

I hand him the bottle. "For you or him?"

"Him." Robinson shoots me a sour look. "Stovaine's physical but whiskey helps with the mental. Take as much as you want; we're in no hurry."

Jordan takes a solid pull on the bottle and winces. "Gah," he sputters.

A minute later, the doctor makes several injections around the entry wound. Jordan flinches and groans but otherwise rides it out. Soon as Robinson finishes, the boy gestures for the bottle and takes another aggressive swig.

"Sit tight," the doctor says. "Once the anesthesia takes effect, I'll get to work."

๑

Thirty minutes later, Robinson finishes and goes to wash the blood off his hands. I help him roll Jordan onto his side and within minutes, the kid falls asleep beneath a blanket.

"Staying here in Basin Creek, Mr. Witherill?" Robinson says.

"Rather not. What's his prognosis?"

Robinson dries his hands on a towel. "Casey's lucky; the bullet missed nerves and arteries on a course between his hip and its exit between the fifth and sixth ribs on his left side. Based on how he's moving, I don't believe he'll suffer any neurological impairment, but that cough…" His voice trails off and he stares out the window.

"Kid works in the mines. Isn't silicosis, is it?"

"No." He turns back to look at Jordan. "Based on what I've heard, the bullet might've injured the pleura or even the lung, itself."

"Meaning what?"

"Meaning I'd like to make sure his lung doesn't collapse. I'll need to keep an eye on him here for at least twenty-four hours. Ideally, it'll heal on its own and you'll be back on your way; otherwise, I'm here to treat him in case his condition worsens. Bullet wounds are always serious—"

"I was in the army," I say.

"Then I shouldn't need to explain why he can't travel, should I?"

Although I shake my head, inside, I'm seething with frustration. "Guess I'll head over and get a room before the hotel fills up."

"There are two in camp: the Basin Creek, where I met you and your nephew, and the Delmonico House. The Basin Creek is nicer but more expensive, though maybe a man like you won't mind."

Odd thing to say. Perhaps he's mistaken me for a speculator or a bank robber, but I keep my mouth shut and nod along. Can't tell him how I've come to possess an automobile, or that I'm really just a fraud who's running for his life. Given how people tend to react to news like that, he can mistake me however it suits him.

"Come back at six," he says, opening a side door to throw a basinful of pink water into the sagebrush.

I say okay, retrieve my hat, and head for the street.

⁊

A room at the Basin Creek Hotel sets me back three dollars and fifty cents but since I pay with Jordan's pocket-money, this is a bearable hardship. I take a seat in the lobby while the clerk busies himself with paperwork. Out of nothing more than rude curiosity, I peek inside the boy's wallet, wondering if I'll find a photo of his sweetheart from wherever he lived before Delamar. Or maybe I'll find one of Lila Hannigan—wouldn't that be something? Instead, I find it packed with cash-money, so much, in fact, that I close it and stuff it back inside my jacket before anyone else sees.

Sweet Jesus, the equivalent of half my yearly salary's in there.

Since there's no one around except the preoccupied clerk, I venture a look inside that bag from the Iroquois' back seat. This time, no surprises: same shirt, sweaters, and trousers as before. A prospector's sample-logbook is underneath these, and while the numbers it contains mean nothing to me, I tuck it inside my jacket.

Collecting my room key, I hustle upstairs for a better look inside Jordan's wallet. Counting the cash into thin stacks on the bed, it adds up to $675. No wonder the kid didn't flinch when I sent him to Pioche for supplies, and no wonder he was so nervous that his former companions might rob him.

Even more bizarre, I'm certain I recognize a mark on one of the bills. It's a ten-dollar gold certificate, defaced with ink. In block print, someone's written HOLD in letters so large the H touches the United in "United States" and the D splits Michael Hillegas's face in two. Believe you me, back in Delamar, I'd never seen so much money in one place and I counted and re-counted every bill in that bonus Prince Jack paid me. I'm sure I recognize this one, but how in God's name did it end up in Jordan's wallet? Helen collected my things from Lila's but never mentioned money; did either of them take the envelope from my old jacket? Think I can rule out Lila, as there's no evident connection between her and Jordan. Helen, on the other hand, clearly knows the boy. Both have union ties and they seemed to know each other there at the Black Tiger. Did she ever mention finding my money, or more specifically, *not* finding my money? Damn it to hell, I can't remember.

My head hurts and I worry this is something I *ought* to know—that I knew once but have forgotten since. Again, too many knocks on my head and it scares me to think I've begun forgetting such things as may keep me alive. Believe I'd rather be legless and confined to a wheelchair than lose my mind, though I might not have a say. I stare at that marked-up bill, frightened by what it could mean. Stare at it for so long my vision goes gray and next thing I know, I wake up facedown on the bed.

Outside, shadows are stealing across the canyon. I transfer the cash to my wallet before washing up and heading downstairs.

༄

After a shave at the barber's and a new shirt from the store next door, I feel calmer. Calm enough to realize I'm famished, anyhow. Time for a quick supper before heading uphill to check on Jordan.

The hotel's dining room is simple but spotless. Plank floor; white ceiling, white walls, and white tablecloths. The place is packed and I seat myself at the only open table. A waiter arrives with a pitcher of water—an extravagance in most parts of Nevada, though maybe the high mountains surrounding Basin Creek catch enough snow to keep this valley wet.

"Evening," he says. "Welcome to the Basin Creek. Tonight, we're serving fried chicken, pan-fried trout, and quail on toast. All our plates come with buttered rolls and winter vegetables."

"The trout and coffee, thanks."

The room is buzzing with conversation and judging by the sound, all anyone's talking about is mines and mining. Figures in the tens of thousands are swirling around like leaves on a breeze. Perhaps only a few of these deals will ever pan out but merely imagining the possibilities is intoxicating.

Soon enough, a fellow seated at the table next to mine leans over and offers his hand. "Hello, friend," he says. "A.L. Hart—Abraham Lincoln Hart—from Reno."

I introduce myself using the fake name I gave Doc Robinson.

"Pleased to meet you, Mr. Witherill. Where are you from?"

"Illinois but I spent most of this past week in Ely."

"Still copper-mad up there?"

"Madder than ever."

"I keep offices in Tonopah and Goldfield," he says, "but all folks there can talk about is Basin Creek, so here I am."

Don't know why but I decide to play along. For once, I'm glad Lipford had me sit in on his business meetings. Think I've picked up enough jargon to keep from exposing myself as an impostor.

"Prospects here as good as I've heard, Mr. Hart?"

"Call me Al, won't you? And opportunities in this district are better than anything you've heard," he grins. "Far better. Why, this is my second week in town and I've optioned at least one property per day. First hour in town, I bought ten lots for $1,000, total. Already, I've sold five for four-hundred apiece and just this morning, I sold another one for nine-hundred."

"Like the sound of that."

"A speculator's heaven." Al grins. "What's your interest, Charlie? Mines, real estate?"

"Mines. Officially, I represent an investors' group from Chicago by way of Ely but since I'm here, I also want to carve off something for myself. All above board, of course."

"Of course." Al winks at me. "Everyone represents someone, don't they? But then who's looking out for you, right?"

"That's right, Al."

"Well, it just so happens I might have what you're looking for. Upstairs, I have a map of the claims I've obtained. If you don't mind, I'll bet I can fetch it before the waiter comes to take your order."

"If it isn't too much trouble."

"No trouble at all, Charlie. Back in a jiffy."

"Say, can I buy you a drink while you're gone?"

"Whiskey, sure." He claps a hand on my shoulder. "Back in a jiffy."

Soon as he's gone, I consider getting up and walking away. I have time to kill, certainly, but this is stupid, pretending I'm a high-roller. I've almost convinced myself to leave when another fellow from an adjacent table leans over and sets his business card on mine.

"Pardon me, mister," he says. "Couldn't help overhearing your conversation with Mr. Hart and I want you to know he isn't the only game in town. You can kick around with prospectors out in the hills or come straight to me. I control more than forty superior claims—gold, silver, antimony, tungsten, and fluorspar—all of which I will let on time, percentage, or sell outright. Moreover, *I* don't ask for a ten-thousand percent return on my options the way some fellows will. And finally, if you own any claims you'd like to sell, I pay cash."

"Thank you, Mr.—" I pause to read his card. "Carson Foster from Spokane, thanks, because I plan to investigate as many opportunities as time and circumstance permit."

"Good plan, given union troubles in all the big districts. Get in here on the ground-floor. Delamar, Tonopah, Goldfield, they could go up in flames at any moment."

Don't I know that for a fact? "Mr. Foster, will you have thirty minutes the day after tomorrow?"

"Certainly will. I'm staying at the Delmonico House at the other end of this street, Room 202. Feel free to leave a message with the desk."

"Much obliged." I pocket his card.

Since I plan to be there soon, I need to consider conditions in Tonopah and Goldfield. If things there are as touchy as this man, Foster, suggests, then maybe it's best to avoid them altogether.

Al Hart reappears with a rolled-up map and stack of assay reports. "That your autocar out front, Charlie?"

The waiter returns and sets two whiskeys on my table. We raise our glasses and drain them.

"Yep," I say, guessing that whatever prices Al had in mind five minutes ago just doubled. "I'm rigged out for a good long trip."

"That so? Where are you headed next?"

"Oh, I heard rumors about doings in Tybo. New prospects in the mountains east of Duckwater. Then it's back to Ely and Salt Lake City, where we'll catch a train for Chicago."

"Tybo, you say? Hadn't heard anything new up there."

"Might be nothing," I say, trying to sound like someone who's trying too hard to sound nonchalant.

"Ah, don't bother with the old camps; all the good ground has been claimed for decades. Only ones getting rich there now are lawyers."

"Too true."

"Gotta find virgin ground. These claims," he says, unrolling the map and pointing to a series of red rectangles on a hilltop, "are everything you want. Vein's traceable along the surface for a quarter-mile. Made an open cut about two-hundred feet above West Pine Creek. Four feet down, my boys struck a ledge about five feet thick. Had Crampton & Crampton in Goldfield run the assay and it's a crusher. Here, read this."

He hands me a sheet of paper. Columns show the ounces per ton for gold, silver, lead, copper, zinc, silica, and iron. The gold values are astounding. From ten different locations along the vein, sample results range from a mere 0.85 ounces per ton up to a staggering two-hundred and four ounces per ton. At $18.93 per ounce, that's roughly $3,862 per ton in gold alone; maybe $4,200 including the other metals. Factor out half for expenses and still you'd net nearly $65,000 on a thirty-ton carload of highgrade.

"May I keep this?" I say.

"It's a copy, sure."

I calmly fold the sheet and tuck it inside my jacket. No point in getting excited. Even if these figures are legitimate—and it's unlikely they are: salted claims are epidemic and highgrade pockets often pinch out after only a few feet—I don't have the money. Not five figures' worth like I've heard from others around the room.

"Might have another Mohawk on our hands," Al says, referring to the richest mine in Goldfield.

"No offense but I've heard that before. I'd want to look it over first. Study the survey. Sample it."

"Sure, sure. Hell, if you'll shake on it, you can go up there yourself. Knock off pieces to take back to your clients, although I can't guarantee these claims won't sell before you return, understand?"

"Are they even accessible?"

"Won't be able to drive your autocar all the way," Al says, "not even with chains. You can walk in, though, certainly. Look, friend, here's something else you might want to consider." He leans in and lowers his voice so that I, never mind others nearby, can hardly hear him, "That ledge continues uphill, see? I had that part of the hilltop staked off separately. Now, Charlie, what's the controlling feature of a vein or ledge in Nevada?"

"The apex."

"Right, and if you'll partner with me on the claims above the block I sell to your backers, we'll be in the driver's seat. Airtight and perfectly legal. Control the entire deposit, understand what I'm saying?"

I sure do. Mining law gives whoever holds a vein's highest outcropping—the apex—the right to follow and mine wherever it leads, even if it extends into or beneath other mining claims. Al's proposal is thoroughly underhanded but so what? Hell, I wish I *was* representing Jack Lipford here just so someday I could pull the rug out from under his feet. I'm so wrapped up in this little revenge fantasy that I'm late to realize Al's still speaking.

"…sell your client the lower six claims for $20,000 cash plus shares in any company that mines there," he says. "I've capitalized the May Queen Mining Company at one million shares with a value of one dollar each. I could place these with the John S. Cook Bank in Tonopah—"

The waiter arrives with my food and sets it on the table.

"Don't mean to cut you off, Al, but I'll need to take this to my client before I can gauge their interest. Don't suppose there's a telephone exchange in town, is there?"

Al shakes his head. "Three or four more weeks, I'm told."

"Day after next, I'll send them a telegram from Ely, okay? I'll do my part but whether they'll do theirs', I can't say."

"Understood. You have time tomorrow to go look?"

"Might. My nephew, Casey, fell ill during our drive today; he's up at the doctor's as we speak. Need to finish here and go see how he's doing before I'll know what tomorrow holds."

"Sorry to hear it, friend. I'll leave you alone."

"No bother, Al: it's been a pleasure speaking with you. I very much want to see what's doing with this property. You'll be around tomorrow afternoon?"

A waiter clears the dishes from Al's table and sets a cup of coffee on mine.

"After 1:30 or 2:00, sure. I'm rising early and taking a runabout over to the district's eastern side. Grubstaked a prospector there who says he has something to show me."

"I'll leave a message at the front desk if I haven't seen you before then."

"Great." Al rolls up his map. "Need me an automobile like yours, Charlie. Get more done in a day. Geez, my manners—I'm just so excited about this opportunity. Please, enjoy your supper."

Throughout my meal, I'm aware that others around the room keep looking my way. Maybe Al has an outsized reputation here, or maybe they figure he's caught another sucker. Or it could be they're waiting for a chance to ply me with treasure-tales of their own. Regardless, it's more scrutiny than I'd like and I have no one to blame but myself. The trout's good, too. Wish I had time to savor it but instead I eat quickly, tip squarely, and leave to check on Jordan.

༺༻

Asleep on the table, Jordan looks pale. Dr. Robinson doesn't have anything good to report.

"No improvement?" I say.

"A little, but honestly I expected more. You say your nephew shot himself cleaning a handgun; did you happen to retrieve the bullet?"

"Tumbled from his coat but no, we left it."

"I'm worried a piece might've broken off and lodged somewhere inside his chest. Do you recall if it looked deformed in any way?"

"Don't think so but the light was bad."

Robinson scratches his chin. Scribbles another note on his tablet. Jordan coughs but doesn't wake.

"Might've nicked his left lung."

"Meaning what?"

"Air is leaking into the pleura. One or both lungs could collapse. His heart could be impaired. With rest, sometimes these small ruptures heal themselves but right now, your nephew's struggling. I strongly advise you to stay here another day so I can monitor him."

Damn it. Every day we're on the road gives Jack Lipford more time to plot and Curt Broe more time to search. We have so much ground to cover, I don't know how much longer we can go without being spotted, even in a region as thinly populated as this.

"What happens if we leave?"

"His lungs could collapse. Pressure on the mediastinum could compress blood vessels or even his heart. Either he'll suffocate or die of organ failure."

"And if he improves overnight?"

"You continue on your way. You're in a hurry, I take it?"

"Big one."

He glances warily between Jordan and me. "I can't make you do anything, of course."

I stare at Jordan for a long time. Funny, a few weeks ago, I could just as well have run him down if Jack Lipford gave the order. Beat him to a pulp in some back alley or worse. Now I'm tearing my hair out, trying to decide whether to risk my life in order to save his. When I was his age, I thought I was invincible, capable of handling anything thrown my way. Balangiga and Samar stripped me of that conceit. Looking at Jordan, heavily bandaged and lying on his side, I imagine until recently he was thinking the same way. Nothing in the world was gonna slow him down. Kid was strong and sure, pulling gold from the basement of Ferguson Hill and smuggling messages into Delamar's jail on the WFM's behalf. Think of the nerve it took to slink in there and spring me loose. Now look at him, as helpless as a newborn.

On Samar, I must have looked as young to the old Indian fighters as Jordan does to me, and there at Lawaan, just as helpless. And who was watching out for me? Watching even after Joe McCuskey gave me up for dead? Even though others were trying to kill him, too? Charlie Marak, who was so much older than me we'd hardly spoken more than three or four times in the six months prior to the massacre at Balangiga. So, whose example should I follow, Joe's or Charlie's? Which man would I rather emulate? In this light, my decision's already made. Isn't so much a decision as an acknowledgement of obligation.

"Of course we'll stay," I tell Robinson. "What do you need me to do?"

"Nothing tonight." The doctor exhales and clears his throat. "I'll come get you if anything changes."

I take my hat and coat and step outside. Lights shine through the windows of every building in town and only the brightest stars are visible. The good people of Basin Creek are doing their part to beat back Heaven. Figuring I should do my part, too, I head back to the hotel and don't leave my seat at the bar until a little after three a.m.

THIRTY-ONE

Nine o'clock the following morning, I down several strong cups of coffee and hustle over to the doctor's. The news is neither good nor bad: just more of the same.

"Cyanosis," Robinson says, gesturing at Jordan's faintly bluish lips. He runs a stethoscope back and forth across the boy's chest and makes notes on his tablet. "Hard to say what's happening. Jordan presents several symptoms but in other regards, his functions are perfectly normal. Skin's cool but his blood pressure's right where it should be."

"Meaning what?" I speak softly because my head hurts like it hasn't in a while. Suppose I should be upset with myself for falling off the wagon but for now, my physical torments are punishment enough.

"No difficulty breathing, no distention of the veins, especially along his neck. He's sleeping peacefully."

"What about when he's awake?"

"He's only stirred once to ask for food and water. Even made a trip to the outhouse: all positive signs."

"So, what now?"

"Wait. Observe. Maybe this is how his body heals."

"Or not."

Robinson shoots me a cutting look but I don't care. I'll do everything I can to help Jordan along but unlike Doctor Candide here, I see no point in pretending everything must get better. In my experience, that's rarely the case.

Robinson advises me to lay off the drink and come back after lunch so I head back to the hotel, stopping in the lobby bar for a double before collapsing in bed. Some getaway this is.

∽

It's four-thirty when I step out onto the hotel's wide porch. Uphill, the false-fronted buildings cast long shadows across the street, yet Basin Creek remains squarely in the middle of a workday. Dozens of people are moving up and down Canfield Avenue, but no sign of that promoter, A.L. Hart. No message for me at the desk and the one I left for him last night hasn't been claimed. So much for getting rich here.

Walking uphill, I pass Doc Robinson's building and a shoe store housed in a canvas frame-tent. Next to these is a small, false-fronted lunch counter. Near the end of the street are the Delmonico House Hotel and the Belmont Saloon, a shoebox of the kind that's absorbed an awful lot of my time and money these past few years.

Its front door is wide open and although I look away, the smell of spilled beer and cigar smoke nearly brings me to my knees. I hear the buzz of conversation, glasses clinking, and from a table near the front, a faro dealer chatting up his customers. Crackers, I need another drink. Something to take the edge off. Two fellows step around me and go inside. I want so badly to follow them but I remind myself I'm leaving town in a couple hours.

Think of something. Anything. Anything but a drink.

Before I went down to the bar last night, I spent the better part of an hour studying a roadmap, trying to guess which passes and towns Curt Broe might watch. Trying to formulate a plan. Wondering what's happening in Delamar. For all his acumen, Lipford doesn't improvise well—he likes to work from a script, and I'm sure these past few weeks have tripled his blood pressure. With any luck, he'll have a stroke.

Someone inside the saloon laughs and I shake my head. Would the Belmont extend credit to someone like me? Probably would've if I'd pulled up in the Iroquois. Son of a bitch, I'm sweating now. My skin itches. The spirit is willing but the flesh is weak, or is it the other way around? Not since I was young have the Bible and I kept regular company. With my foot, I gather sawdust that's drifted through the door and with a kick, scatter it across the boards. One drink would mend this headache, you bet.

Stop it—settle down.

Someday, I bargain with myself; someday, I'll have more time and fewer responsibilities. Some place like the Belmont will be handy—jinks like the Belmont are *always* handy—and I will cut loose with everything I have. They'll have to roll me out the door and leave me in an alley. Won't care. Hoods can riffle my pockets. Won't care; every last cent will be gone.

My jaw hurts from clenching my teeth. Another man emerges from the bar, blinks to shield his eyes from the light, and stumbles as he steps into the street. Disgusted and a touch envious, I watch him weave his way toward the center of town. I *can't* give in. Can't.

A terrific crash follows from the hillside behind the saloon as a counterman throws out a crateful of chipped glasses and broken bottles. He wipes his hands on his apron and picks his way downhill through the sage, leaving behind a mound of sparking glass, like diamonds in the afternoon sun. Who knows why, but I take this as a sign and start walking.

Directly across the wide street is a well stocked newsstand. Tobacco, hard candy, chewing gum—I buy five pieces for a nickel and jam them all into my mouth—plus racks bristling with magazines and lurid dime novels. Dozens of newspapers from across the country, too. Among these are weeks-old copies of the national rags so I mingle with a small crowd scanning the headlines. The San Francisco *Daily News* gives an account of the rebuilding effort since last year's great earthquake. The *Chicago Tribune* reports the Standard Oil Company has asked for more time to defend itself against a federal grand jury's indictment returned last August. And the *Idaho Daily Stateman* has an article about jury selection in the trial of WFM Secretary George Pettibone for collusion in the assassination of Idaho's governor, Frank Steunenberg.

The local paper is flimsy: mostly boosterism for Basin Creek's matchless mineral wealth and unlimited future—pretty much what you'd read in any boomtown—plus advertisements and social news. The editor's message is an admonishment for citizens to stop dumping garbage into the "crystal-pure waters of Cherry Creek" and a reminder to spend their holiday dollars in town instead of with mail-order outfits.

The papers from Reno, Tonopah, and Goldfield, though, are all about the unrest in the latter. Federal troops have been there since December 7 but since a Presidential Commission visited and found scant evidence of riots, vandalism, or union-sponsored beatings—all things the mine owners cited in pressing Governor Sparks to summon troops—Roosevelt has demanded the governor convene a special legislative session, both to authorize the army's continued presence and pay for at least some of the associated costs. Some papers, such as Lindsay Branson's *Tonopah Sun,* brim with invective against the WFM and IWW and call for forceful intervention by the government.

Jack Lipford loves the *Tonopah Sun.*

Others, like the *Reno Evening Gazette,* are incredulous that the President of the United States of America was duped into sending the military to perform police functions on behalf of a private corporation. I ask the vendor if he sells the *Delamar Lode* but he says he hasn't received an issue in weeks. Pretty sure that isn't a good sign and not for the last time, I wonder what's become of Helen Molloy, Nick Reed, and all the others.

Helen most of all. Did she stay in Delamar or is she on the run now, too? Did she hear how that fellow, Stub, double-crossed us? Or was she in on the cross-up, herself? I still have feelings for her so I hate to think that way, but ever since I found what I'm certain is *my* money in Jordan's wallet, I'm not so sure I ever really knew her. How I made it out of Delamar alive I'll never know.

I pay ten cents for the *Goldfield News,* make a wide swing around the Belmont, and stop at the lunch counter. Twenty-five additional cents get me a lunch-plate consisting of fried eggs, sausage, stewed prunes, and coffee.

Stories in the *News* are about the same as those in the *Sun,* minus the shrill, anti-WFM tone. Even so, given the unrest there, plus the fact that the Goldfield Mine Owners' Association—George Wingfield and Senator Nixon's machine, and every bit as predatory as Jack Lipford's cartel—has brought in hundreds of deputies to enforce a lockout at the mines, I can't think of a worse place to go.

Back in Delamar, that was our plan: Jordan, Beck, and I were to cross the state to Goldfield, where friendlies in the local would ride with us to my family's ranch in Esmerelda County and retrieve Lipford's problematic survey. From there, Nielsen would've pulled strings to get it into the hands of Governor Sparks and Black Tiger's directors, thereby forcing the prince to sell. After that, I don't know. Put me on trial, buy a jury, and let me off as a thank-you? Or leave me to twist in the wind? Ideally I'd have slunk off somewhere knowing I was temporarily in good standing with the people I've abused for the past year and a half.

Frankly, seated here with money in my pocket (my money?) and an automobile parked a block away, I'm tempted once more to get up, drive off, and disappear. East to New Mexico or north to Montana—somewhere far, far away—and find work on a ranch, maybe. Write for a paper, or become a cop, even. Shucks, I still don't know what I want to be when I grow up. What I do know is that we *can't* go to Goldfield now. Too risky.

If it turns out Jordan needs big-city medicine or even hospitalization, then I'll deliver him to Tonopah or Ely. Might end up dumping him on the local's doorstep with a note but at least I'll get him there. My conscience needles me again: can't maroon the kid here in Basin Creek. Ought to see how he's doing and then make plans. I leave the newspaper folded beneath my plate. Exiting the lunch counter, I scuffle back along the street, raising little dust storms with every step.

⁓

Jordan's asleep but Dr. Robinson isn't there. I settle into an uncomfortable chair and brace my feet against the examination table.

Listening to the boy's shallow, rapid breathing, I feel a twinge of guilt. I didn't shoot him, certainly, but if anyone knows a crime scene has to be treated like it's red hot, it's me. This is all my fault; there's no one else I can blame. Andy Maguire and the Delamar stiffs who sent him—him and Beck—to watch me? Nah. Or what about Prince Jack? If not for him, none of this would've happened. But so what? He wasn't in that cabin so once again, this is all on me. Hell, if Lipford's to blame, then why not unspool things a little farther and throw it on Leon Czolgosz again? Because nothing comes from bringing the dead to book, that's why. In time, even tyrants are forgotten. Forgiven, perhaps, but forgotten, always.

Me, I choose to believe that experience has tempered me to walk through fire. My scars are lessons and I won't forget what they've taught me. Others may disagree and shrink from the wisdom of pain, but not me. I see this all the time. Mine owners' colleagues send their clean-cut, college-age sons inland for the summer, figuring a season in the camps will toughen them up for their predestined roles as bankers, attorneys, and captains of industry. Most of these kids manage capably and some even thrive, but I've seen plenty of others waiting at the Caliente depot, sobbing into their hats, terrified to discover that the world doesn't find them exceptional. Problem is, no train can take them back to innocence. Cloistered hours at Harvard or Berkeley will not dull the shame of irrelevance. Pity, too, because instead of crawling home to brood, they might've come to understand that anything is survivable. Nearly anything.

What I mean here is that I *do* see how my childhood tempered me for conflict and cruelty. Dad thrashed me whenever I got hurt and beat me when I sought comfort, and this hardened me for the things life has thrown at me since. Helped me hone an instinct for survival and to understand that caring for others is to admit heartache into your life.

Problem is, he didn't beat all the empathy out of me. Listening to Jordan's labored breathing, the need to see him better hits me with unexpected force. Wouldn't have thought I had any tenderness left but here it is. I'm not nearly old enough to be his father, yet that's the only way I can describe what I'm feeling. I have to look after him—to see him well again. I can't leave.

༄

Not sure what startles me awake: Dr. Robinson barging into the examination room or Jordan gasping for air.

Robinson quickly sets a plate of food on his desk. "Why didn't you come get me?"

"I was asleep."

"Bullshit. You're hung-over and your nephew's suffocating." He hustles around the room, opening cabinets and pulling down supplies. "This is an emergency: I need your help now."

The wall clock reads twenty after six.

"Right." I rub sleep from my eyes. "What can I do?"

"Open his shirt and swab him with iodine. Clean towels in there," he says, pointing to a drawer. "And the big brown bottle—no, *that* one—is iodine. Yes, his entire chest, twelve inches below his collar bones."

Jordan sounds like an automobile's parked on his sternum. Every breath is a titanic effort with little result and while his eyes are wide and searching, I can't tell if he sees me. Then he turns, focuses on my face, and gasps my name.

"What's wrong?" I ask Robinson. "What's happening?"

The boy grips my arm without strength. His hand slips and his arm falls off the table.

"Tension pneumothorax," Robinson says, laying several large needles plus what looks like an ice pick on a side-table. "He's suffocating. Air is trapped between the lung and the pleura and it's crushing everything inside his chest."

"What can you do?"

Robinson keeps working as he talks, "Decompress his chest." He takes a rubber glove, snips one fingertip, and tapes this tiny cap so that it partially covers one end of a short tube.

"With an ice pick?"

"A trocar. It's hollow—I'm threading a rubber tube through it."

All this while, Jordan thrashes until he can't; his skin grows cool and clammy. He isn't looking at me anymore, isn't looking at anything. Like I said, I can handle just about anything thrown my way. Staying calm under pressure is a point of pride but Jordan isn't me and I'm no doctor, so that's all gone out the window.

"Hurry," I snap, "he's fading."

"I *am* hurrying," Robinson snarls. "Ten seconds."

Looking at the boy, I feel my own chest tightening. His eyes are closed and already he looks dead.

Can't have this. Can't.

If he dies here, I'll drive straight back to Silver King, bad luck be damned, retrieve those two sticks of powder, and beeline for Delamar. Then I'm gonna blast Jack Lipford back to hell or else die in the attempt. With any luck, Curt Broe will circle back and I'll deal with him, too. I'm so wrapped up in these thoughts Robinson needs to elbow me aside so he can work.

"Hold his arms," he says. "He's weak now but he may thrash in a moment."

While I move around the table, Robinson presses Jordan's upper chest with his fingers, evidently feeling his way between ribs. At a point several inches to the right of the kid's sternum, he stops, plants the trocar, and pushes hard.

I feel my lunch churning so I turn my head and look away. Helps some but my stomach lurches again when pressurized air hisses through the rubber tube. The kid's chest literally deflates.

Jordan takes several small, shallow breaths and then a huge gasp. I catch his arms before he can push Robinson away.

"Hold him," Robinson barks and I say that I am.

He withdraws the trocar, leaving the rubber tube protruding from the boy's chest.

"Hurts," Jordan groans, "oh my God, it hurts."

Robinson sets to work taping the rubber tube in place and securing it with gauze.

"Hang on," I say, "he's almost done. Don't think, just breathe. Nothing else: slowly in, slowly out."

Wincing at the effort, Jordan inhales slowly. Tries to, anyway, but he coughs and makes the flutter-valve at the tube's end burp.

"Great advice," he says. He squeezes my hands and I feel his strength returning.

"Hell, don't listen to me. Do what you have to."

I help the boy sit upright so the doctor can wrap his chest. As soon as Robinson finishes, I help lower Jordan back onto his side. He gives the kid an injection plus another shot of whiskey and within minutes, Jordan is asleep again, breathing normally.

"Good," Robinson murmurs, wiping his brow and throwing a blanket over the boy. "Good for now."

"Thanks," I say. "Thank you for saving him."

"Glad to." He picks out trash from among his supplies and gestures around the tiny room. "This is all I have. Few years ago, I owned a practice in Seattle. Fine home overlooking the Sound. Then I married a lovely young woman from Bremerton, but she wouldn't leave her family so I came down here with everything she left me."

I rub my eyes and yawn.

"That's a joke," Robinson says. "Dear girl didn't leave me *anything.*"

"Sorry to hear it."

"Don't be. Living with her family would've been worse." He shudders at the thought.

Jordan shifts but doesn't wake.

"Now what?" I say. "Stay another day?"

"Just the opposite. Whatever injury he sustained, it isn't healing. He needs a surgeon's care as quickly as possible and I'm no surgeon."

I glance out the window. Sun's setting and the sky is clear but the wind is rising. Smells like weather. Hate to get caught out in a snowstorm, but that risk is gonna linger until May.

"Where, then?" I say. "Ely?"

"They don't have the apparatus necessary to treat him."

"Where, then? Reno? San Francisco?"

"Wouldn't make it that far. Goldfield's the only place now."

"How's that?"

"Their new hospital," Robinson says, shaking his head in wonderment, "has every piece of equipment you'd find in New York or San Francisco." He smiles dryly. "One advantage of building a city atop the world's richest gold deposit, right?"

"What can they do there that they can't in Tonopah or Ely?"

"Mine Operators Hospital has the only differential pressure respirator between San Francisco and Pittsburgh. And where better, what with all the chest wounds inherent to mining—ruptured alveoli, punctured lungs, and so on. The patient's body rests inside an airtight chamber while their head remains outside, secured with an airtight neck cuff. Electrical valves control the pressure inside this chamber—"

"Honestly, Doc, I don't understand anything you're saying."

Robinson shrugs. "Goldfield's hospital has the one device in all Nevada that can save your nephew's life. It's our best option now."

"'*Our* best option,'" I say. "Does that mean you're coming with us?"

"No, I can't."

"What if he takes a turn between here and there?"

"Drive faster."

"That's it?"

"Mr. Witherill, I can't leave these people; I'm the only doctor within a ninety-mile radius."

"I don't know anyone in Goldfield. What am I supposed to do—roll up and insist they stuff the kid inside this chamber?"

"No, I'll write a letter of introduction."

"Can't say I share your confidence."

"Never said I was confident." He crosses the room to rummage through a cabinet. "Your nephew's condition is desperate; you can't let anything delay you."

"Got it."

"Understand what I'm saying? Lay off the bottle."

"Yeah, I got it."

Robinson studies me a moment before turning to wash his hands in a basin.

Huzzah. Just like that, the one place I didn't want to go is back on the itinerary.

A knock on the door startles us both. Hat in hand, a grubby young man steps inside.

"Doctor," he says to Robinson and "Beg your pardon, mister," to me.

"What can I do for you?" Robinson says.

"Accident up on White's Grade. Ore wagon overturned: the mules are all dead and the driver's hurt bad."

Recalling how I left Delamar, my lip curls.

While Robinson and the young man talk, I turn to look at Jordan. He's pale but his breathing's normal. Why isn't he healing? Whatever's wrong, it should've happened to me. Should've died a dozen times before but here Jordan's had his ticket punched, instead. What did I say? It all comes down to luck.

"Mr. Witherill?" Robinson steps back into the examination room. "I'm going to my house to change clothes and write that letter. It's up to you whether to wait until tomorrow or start for Goldfield tonight."

I look at Jordan again. His face is tight with pain.

"What would you do?"

Robinson glances out a window. "Weather's good. You okay to drive at night?"

"I'll manage." I hand him eighteen dollars. "Appreciate your help—sorry for causing trouble."

"No trouble at all. Good luck out there."

We shake hands and he goes outside. I bundle the kid's scarce belongings and run them out to the automobile. Mercifully, Jordan wakes easily and with considerable support, manages to stagger this short distance.

"We're leaving?" he whispers.

"To Goldfield, sure. Surgeons in a hospital there are gonna patch up your lung."

"Sorry, Shep, putting us off-track."

"Don't apologize."

Jordan shrugs, curls up in his seat, and goes back to sleep.

∾

At the hotel, A.L. Hart comes bounding into the lobby.

"There you are!" he exclaims. "Sorry I took longer than I said I would."

Seeing as I was lying last night, what I ought to do is 'fess up and send him on his unhappy way. Ought to. But like I said, these days, everyone in Nevada—and here I include myself—is angling for their shot. It's harder than you'd think to come clean. Even if Al's proposition is a lie and what's keeping him interested in me is another, it's all preferable to reality.

"Change of plans, Al. Jordan's in a bad way and I need to get him to a hospital in Goldfield. We're leaving now so if there's anything you want to tell me, you'll have to do it on the run."

"You aren't going to Tybo?"

"Not now. Doctor says it's life or death."

"Gee, tough break, Charlie. Need any help?"

I say no so he tells me he'll wait in the lobby and walk with me to the car. On the way upstairs, I wonder whether the hotel has a back entrance. Seeing him waiting there in the lobby, I wish I'd looked for it. He holds off while I settle my bill but as soon as our feet hit the porch, he opens up with both barrels.

"Listen, Charlie," he says, "you're up against plenty so don't think I'm looking to cause trouble."

No one ever says that unless they're looking to cause trouble. I bite my tongue and start toward Dr. Robinson's.

"I have to ask: do you honestly intend to option those claims," he says, struggling to keep pace, "or are you stringing me along? I mean, I'll wait a couple days until you reach Goldfield but should I even bother?"

Again, I ought to come clean but honestly, I'm having too much fun. Yes, Jordan's situation is foremost in my mind but this is something else.

It's a genuine pleasure to be trailed by someone for reasons other than them wanting to kill me. I know I'm weak. I understand the Golden Rule and all that but damn it, I've never been mistaken for someone with legitimate authority. Never had someone bow and scrape except that they were afraid of me. I ought to come clean—I *ought* to—but dammit, *I don't want to.*

"Yes, I'm still interested."

"Well, pard, here's what makes me wonder: when I met you at supper yesterday, you said your nephew's name was Casey. Call it a blessing, call it a curse but I never forget a name and a minute ago, you called him Jordan."

Damn it, I did slip up, didn't I? I stop walking and turn to look at Al.

"Yeah, we used fake names—so what? Said I wanted some action for myself, right? Don't you figure I'd like to know who I'm dealing with? Make sure you're not also one of my client's agents?"

I resume walking. Although the sun's already set, I can see Jordan slumped in his seat.

Al hustles after me. "And I thought I was clear that I'm here for the deal. If you swear you'll bring someone to the table for those six claims, I'll name you, your nephew, or even Teddy Roosevelt as co-owner of the apex, understand?"

Jesus, these big-wheelers. Sell the rings off their dead mothers' fingers.

"Much appreciated," I say, "but Jordan's sick and I doubt whether I can bring anyone along soon enough to suit you."

"Listen, Charlie, shake on it and I'll hold out a while longer."

Reaching the car, I throw my bag into the back seat and take the crank handle from its cradle.

"No guarantees, Al. Hell, after this trip I can't guarantee my employer won't fire me or worse."

He's still looking my direction but his eyes are unfocused, as if looking through me while he's thinking.

"I figured that boy ain't your nephew," he says, "but I don't care, see? Can't figure out your angle but I recognize a fighter when I see one. Faded bruises on your face. Scars on your head. You stood out in that roomful of shirt collars and stick pins—that's why I went to you in the first place."

I turn the Iroquois' crank a couple times, stopping to adjust the throttle.

"You'd cut me in on a million-dollar deal because I look rough: is that what I'm hearing?"

"I could use rough help."

"Well, I'm trying to get out of that line of work. Honestly, I don't think I can get you what you need."

"$4,200 per ton, Charlie: think about it. Money enough to do whatever you want."

I stand to look over the hood and shrug. "What can I tell you, Al?"

"A thousand dollars and I'll deal you in."

"Don't have a thousand."

"Come on, I can't give these claims away. Maybe you're worried about me but I feel like *I'm* the one who's getting skinned here."

"You know I'll find you if you're lying, right?"

"Yeah, I figure."

What the hell am I doing? It's pure foolishness but there's something so irresistible about the idea of making a killing that I can't help myself. Regardless of whether he's on the level, I reach inside my jacket and take out my wallet.

"Hold on," I say, turning my back to him as I count out $500.

For someone who deals in high-pressure situations, it seems I'm no more immune to get-rich-quick enticements than anyone else is. By handing cash to a big-talking stranger, I tell myself I'm investing in the potential for things to get better. Potential and finality, too; more than anything, I want to end this conversation and get moving. Maybe that's what Al's been counting on this whole time.

"Five-hundred," I say, handing him twenty $20 certificates and ten bison $10 bills. "Take it or leave it."

"I'll give you a six-month option. Another five-hundred gets you twelve full months." He reaches out and shakes my hand. "Here's my card; wire me about your clients' money for the other claims. What name do you want on the contract?"

"Wade Aaron Sunday, Sweetwater, Esmerelda County."

"That your real name?"

"My brother's."

I get that I'm acting recklessly—that the odds of finding another $500 inside of six months, never mind convincing someone within twelve to entrust me with $20,000, are slim—but this is Nevada. People with less have made more than I stand to collect. Far more. Hell, maybe I'll take the Standard Trust survey and sell it to the highest bidder. I know for a fact it's worth more than $20,000.

Producing a fountain pen from his pocket, he lays papers on the Iroquois' hood. "Sign here, and here."

I take the pen and scratch my name across the paper. "There you go."

Al grins. "Ever notice your brother's initials are W-A-S?"

"Are we done?" I turn the crank handle again.

"Don't get sore," he sputters. "Wade Aaron Sunday, it is."

"We're done," I say but he doesn't seem upset.

"Send me a letter," he says. "You won't be sorry."

Like hell, I won't. I throw Al's card inside the glove box, snap it closed, and crank the engine. The car's a beast and turns over after only four or five revolutions. Haven't had a problem with it since our first encounter back in Silver King. By the time I circle around and climb into the driver's seat, Al's already started back toward the hotel. I'm tempted to hustle after him and retrieve my cash but then I hear Jordan groan and figure I've already wasted too much time.

Fools and money weren't meant for each other, anyway.

Ready to walk over to Robinson's house to ask about that introductory letter, I notice an envelope lying on the dashboard. Opening it, I find a note that says exactly what the doctor said it would so I fold it and tuck it into my coat alongside A.L. Hart's dynamite assay report.

Down to the stables to buy tins of gasoline before heading north over the pass.

On our way, we pass a buckboard bringing in the injured teamster. Good thing we're leaving; appears the good doctor has another long night ahead of him. Hope the mules didn't suffer.

Beyond Basin Creek's limits, the road begins climbing. I'm guessing it's almost nine when we round a curve high in the mountains and the town's lights disappear for good. At once, the stars come out in force. Shadows on the snow lay dark blue on light.

Maybe a thousand feet higher and already the air is colder. Still climbing, the road is dark and dusted with snow but the tires hold and I feel okay pushing our speed. Don't have a watch but it feels as if time—Jordan's, mine, this world's—is running out. Like there's no choice now except to push the car and myself to our limits. Despite the danger, I shift from first to second and mash the pedal to the floor.

THIRTY-TWO

Two hours pass quickly. On the range's northern side, beyond a set of tight curves near the summit, the road is one long, straight descent into Railroad Valley. No settlements out here and no mines—only a few small ranches. Less snow, too. No light beyond the Iroquois' headlamps: darkness and stars rule the night. Jordan sleeps the entire time.

My eyelids are getting heavy, too, and not long after we reach the valley floor, I stop. No need for shelter and good thing because there isn't any. No trees anywhere: just wide open country, flat as a billiard table. Somewhere west of here, Hot Creek breaches the Pancake Range and dumps tons of muddy water into the valley's southern end, but I've been that way before and it's treacherous. Instead, we'll bear southwest around Red Hill and cross the Reveille Range. Skirt the Black Belt's northern fringes on our way to Goldfield. Not yet, though. If I don't get some sleep soon, we're gonna leave the road in an inconvenient way.

An hour or so later, I'm jolted awake by the sounds of movement all around us in the dark. On reflex, my hand goes for the Colt but soon it's clear these are nothing more than cattle walking through the brush. Soon as I step out of the car, they flinch and scatter. Doubt anyone's riding herd this time of night but just in case, I crank the car back to life and resume driving with the lights off.

Isn't hard to do; between the straight road and the newly risen moon, I hardly even need to steer.

With little to command my attention, I have time to think. Not about home, or the Philippines, or even Edgemont so much as Delamar. How did I fail to see everything hurtling toward me? A few things gave me heartburn, sure, but I failed to connect these clues in any useful way. Big Curt delivering Joe McCuskey like a present; all those false reports on Francis Boudreaux; and Lila's trips all coinciding with Lipford's. Any one of these red flags should've held my attention. Didn't though—not hardly. Too busy being angry and miserable. Stumbled along exactly the way Curt would've, lashing out blindly and afterward scrambling to figure out what'd happened. Could be why these past few days have been so quiet: I didn't stick to the script. Didn't go after Prince Jack or Curt Broe, and I didn't loiter around Delamar looking for an opening.

Nielsen's plan—or was it Andy Maguire's?—was blown, that's for sure, but I'll bet they'll still watch the train stations in Goldfield and Tonopah: can't get anywhere in western Nevada without passing through one or both. Beyond these cities, though, they'll have no idea where I'm headed.

Unless Helen told them, that is. She's the only one who knows I mailed Lipford's survey to my family's ranch in far-western Esmerelda County. Would Jordan and Beck have tried to kill me there? To tie off one loose end so the WFM could focus on its fight with Lipford? Possibly, though I can't picture Jordan pulling the trigger. Maybe that was Beck's role—maybe he was acting friendly to get me to drop my guard. If so, I'm afraid it worked.

Ah, what does it matter, all this is all conjecture? Now that the kid and I are in a situation no one could've imagined, everything going forward will be off the cuff. That's good. Only wish Jordan hadn't run into those two knuckleheads in Pioche. That's bad.

An hour later, we cross the valley's axis and the Iroquois' wheels sink into mud. Fortunately, Nevada has rocks in abundance, so I stack several under the tires, roll out of the mire, and launch the car forward for a hundred feet before it sticks again. Repeating this process five times, it takes us an hour to cross this depression, maybe two-hundred yards in all.

Mercifully, the soil beyond it is firm. As soon as we reach dry ground, I park the car and go back to sleep.

THIRTY-THREE

This time, Jordan's coughing wakes me. He's sitting upright with a tin of almonds in his lap, coughing like mad.

"You choking?" I say.

He holds up an index finger before coughing and groaning some more.

"Sounds like quitting time back in Delamar." I thump him on his back before remembering why I shouldn't. "Sorry."

Once his fit subsides, he spits weakly over the door. "Ugh," he moans and wipes his lips with his sleeve. "Ouch."

I yawn, stretch, and step down from the car. Cold this morning; probably no more than thirty, thirty-five degrees. The rising sun breaks the horizon and out on the flats, shadows stretch away from us for a hundred feet. I relieve myself in the frosted grass before unwiring a fuel tin from the running board and refilling the Iroquois' tank.

"No Joshua trees," Jordan says and he's right.

Nearest trees are some cottonwoods around a spring, more than five miles to the south. "None since Bristol Wells, yeah?"

"Funny." He looks the other direction, where banded mesas glow orange in the morning light. "I kinda miss 'em."

Seems Joshua trees only grow within very specific limits: too low and they disappear; too high and they're crowded out by pinyon and juniper; up north is too cold and any farther south, they can't take the heat. Within their range, though, they are the toughest damn things God ever put on this planet. Spiny and dense, they thrive on limited water and in alkaline soils that'd kill other plants. Honestly, most everything is tough enough where it belongs—people, too. Problem is, hardly any of us bother to stay there.

"Feeling better," Jordan says, "'cept I can't get enough air, no matter how I try."

I circle to the passengers' side. My hands are freezing but I place the back of my hand against his forehead, anyway. "Fever's down. How's your strength?"

He raises both hands a few inches, rotates his wrists, and slowly lowers them onto his thighs. "Weak as a newborn."

I swab the end of the tube protruding from his chest with rubbing alcohol and tie a clean towel over it. I can still hear Dr. Robinson's voice, "Keep it clean, understand? It's a pathway straight into his chest and anything foreign that gets inside could kill him."

"We'd better get moving," I say. "Need water?"

"Hurts to swallow." This frigid air can't be helping.

"Skip the dry fare next time. How about an orange?"

"Couldn't reach 'em."

I reach into the back seat and rummage through our bag for an orange. Partially frozen, it's difficult to peel. I hand him sections but he moves like he's handling gold bricks; he needs his right arm to help raise his left to his mouth.

Son of a bitch, this is bad.

❧

An hour later, the car begins climbing a debris-fan that skirts the Reveille Range's eastern side. No wide-open anymore: here, the road points straight toward an unbroken wall of dark volcanic rock. This one of the desert's favorite tricks. Old fellows who've worked in the Arizona and New Mexico territories call these 'habras,' where water cuts narrow entrances into wider canyons above. Soon, we'll round a hill or drop into a gulch and *that* road will enter these mountains. These ruts must mean something; every road goes somewhere.

Forty minutes later and I'm not so sure. We've rounded dozens of hills and at certain points, followed side roads up side-canyons, yet all have dead-ended within a few hundred yards. Some lead to small prospectors' pits; others have petered out amid rocks and brush. Backing down one, the Iroquois' undercarriage strikes a rock and I imagine the worst—a busted axle or wrecked transmission—but when I get out to look, everything appears as it should. Scraped metal but no real damage.

Slack-jawed, Jordan stares at the dun scenery, slowly opening and closing his hands. Every furrow, every bump in the road throws him against the door, the dashboard, or my shoulder. Poor kid's gonna be black and blue when this is all over. Me, too, for what it's worth.

"Wanna lie down in the back?" I ask.

"No."

I turn the wheel hard to avoid a large rock and Jordan slams into the door.

"Was it like this inside the wagon?" he whispers.

"Dustier." I spin the wheel the other way but can't avoid scraping the sides against a thorn-brush that's overgrown the ruts. "Speaking of Delamar, where do you think Helen might've gone?"

"Helen Molloy?" His breath steams like smoke.

Emerging from shadow into brilliant sunlight, I squint to protect my eyes. "You saw her start for town, right?"

"Nah, Shep, I didn't. Think she went into Black Tiger's office there at the mine."

I stop the car. Jordan tilts forward slowly and has to brace his hands against the dashboard.

"Why would she do that?"

"Honestly, I wasn't paying attention. Helped the others set that sheet-iron but then Beck sent me off to see if the road was clear. Pretty sure I saw her turn for the office there below the sorting house."

"You walked ahead and Beck picked you up?"

"That's right."

"He say anything about Helen? Once you were riding with him, I mean?"

"We hardly spoke until Stub went off-course."

I sit a moment with my hands folded over the steering wheel. Hardly anything I thought I knew has survived these past few weeks and now another piece has crumbled.

"Think she's still in Delamar?"

Jordan shrugs.

Damned if I know what to do with this information. "Who is she, Jordan?"

He stares straight ahead, his chest rising and falling rapidly. "What do you mean?"

"I mean, what am I missing? I've known her for over a year and it never occurred to me she could just walk around inside a union operation like that."

Jordan shrugs again. "Helen's our eyes and ears."

"Billy Meeks never told me she carried that kind of clout."

"That's because Helen gives Billy money to help his family."

Jesus. I scramble to recall anything I might've told her about my cases. No wonder Nielsen went to Meeks for a testimonial letter. And more than once, she saw me pass him messages there in the Colorado Belle.

"Donated lots of money lately," Jordan says.

"As charity, or ..?"

"No, to the general fund. With layoffs and wage reductions, not everyone pays their dues. She's propped us up for three, four months now."

"Goddamn, where does she get *that* kind of money?" I'm sure the Belle turns a profit but not so she can carry the entire union.

"I don't know."

I grip the steering wheel with both hands and stare straight ahead. "That cash money in your wallet: where did you get it?"

The boy eyes me nervously. "Nielsen said $20 would get us across the state, but because that survey was so important, we should have more in case big trouble found us."

"Did Helen give it to him?"

"Don't know, and why are you asking me? Aren't you the one courting her?"

"Courting…" I wince and shake my head. "No, courting takes decency and dedication. She and I keep company once in a while."

"Huh." Jordan cuts loose with a yawn. "Beck figured she knows more than she lets on 'cause she's sweet on you."

"Is that right?"

The boy closes his eyes and slumps in his seat.

Now I know less about Helen than I did five minutes ago and even less about myself. For as long as I've been in Delamar, I've taken pride in seeing the angles others miss—on tying down loose ends so that I'm the one who's in control. Who knows where his enemies sleep, where they stash their weapons, and how they take their whiskey. Not anymore. Here at last, I realize I've been sleepwalking.

I tap the accelerator and the car lurches forward. "You ever see her again, tell her I wish I'd done better. Tell her I hope she'll give me a chance to work things out."

I glance over at Jordan but he's fallen asleep. Probably just as well.

⁕

Reaching another junction, I take out the map again and weight its corners with rocks. The sky is clear but it's windier now. Fingers crossed, maybe one more day of good weather before the curtain descends.

I trace a dashed line across the map. Paper says the road we're on is true but we don't seem to be getting anywhere. That's a problem out here: maps show routes and features but they can't convey scale. Only reason I'm not panicking is that this sort of thing has happened before. Summer before I turned eighteen, I got good and lost in Mud Spring Basin south of our ranch. My brother, Wade, and I were cutting timbers for a new corral. Driving up from our campsite to get him, I couldn't believe the turn was as far as it actually was and I must've wheeled the wagon around three or four times, certain I'd missed it. On the fifth pass, I went a little farther and sure enough, there was the road I wanted. Wade was mad as hell, certain I'd been loafing, but on the way back, he saw all the tracks I'd made and realized I wasn't lying.

"Maybe you aren't lazy," he'd said, "but you're definitely an idiot."

I didn't even argue.

⁕

Far as I know, the town of Old Reveille is dead, a relic from the '60s, but the pioneers beat good roads to it and I simply need to keep my wits and carry on. Jordan's asleep again so he doesn't have to witness any more of my sorry navigation through one of the state's smaller ranges. Thank God we aren't crossing the Toyiabe or Toquima over in western Nye County. Hell, compared to those, the entire Reveille Range would be nothing but a single spur among many.

Ten white-knuckled minutes later, the road finally turns west. Descending between volcanic mesas, it joins a larger track—one I'd thought we were on all along—that snakes along a wide, sandy wash. I stop, look at the map again, and see where I went wrong. Nine years on and I'm still an idiot.

I see patches of snow on the north-facing slopes but otherwise the dirt here is so dry it rises behind the Iroquois in a long, high cloud. Even so, it must rain sometime because cobblestones litter the road, some with sandbars trailing like comets' tails. Creosote and grasses up on the hillsides and dense stands of juniper on the higher peaks down south. Not here, though. This is wasteland.

Sure enough, Old Reveille's a husk. Three or four habitable buildings. A dozen more in various stages of decay. Widely scattered piles of lumber and stone poke through the grass alongside several impressive trash heaps. Mine dumps and weathered headframes dot the surrounding hills. Shirts and overalls hang on wash lines behind two houses, but only one old man steps out to greet us.

"Hello there! How does your machine like these roads?" he shouts as the Iroquois chugs to a halt.

"Same problems you get with a team," I say. "Mud and breakdowns and such, but it doesn't eat as much as a mule."

"Sure, sure. You looking for claims, mister? There's good ore here, still."

"Sorry, just traveling through, bound for Goldfield. My nephew's ill and needs medical care."

"'Ill?'"

"Nothing contagious."

"Pity," he says but he looks relieved. "Anything I can do to help?"

"Water for my auto. I'm carrying some already but I'd like to conserve as much as possible."

"Sorry." The old man pauses to remove his bowler hat and scratch his head. "I'm all out and here's why: we get our water from a spring about four miles that'a way—," he points north, "—and late yesterday afternoon, two motorcars came through and emptied my barrel. Gonna hitch up later today and go refill."

"Cars, plural?" I try to sound only mildly surprised. "Isn't that unusual?"

"Sure is, but more and more common every year."

"Speculators? Politicians?"

"Pinkerton or Thiel agents, I figure." He spits on the ground. "Six fellows chasing a fugitive. Said they were deputized in Lincoln County but I never seen deputies follow someone a hundred miles into the next county."

"That *is* unusual."

"In every way. Said they were going over the hill to New Reveille before continuing on to Clifford and Tonopah. Likely stayed in the Liberty Company's little six-room hotel there."

"They told you all this?"

"Some of it—the rest is speculation. That's what old men do."

I know better than to ask questions. All at once, I'm certain Big Curt Broe is just over the mountain on my left. Of all places to cross paths. I take a long, slow breath to clear my head. My first thought is to turn around and return to Basin Creek but news has a funny way of traveling out on the desert. Better make myself as forgettable as possible.

"Sorry if that sounded rude; only meant there's safety in numbers out here. Guess we'll follow them and try to catch up. Is the road through Clifford the fastest way to Goldfield?"

The old man resettles the bowler over his wild gray hair. "Don't think they want to be followed, son. Besides, Clifford's out of your way—that's the way to Tonopah. If Goldfield's your destination, you'll save forty miles taking the Reveille Valley road south to Cedar Pass."

"Could you show me on a map?"

"Suppose I could, sure. Mind if I go get my glasses?"

While the old man ducks back inside his home, I reach into the back seat for Jordan's rifle and check that it's loaded. Close the breech and set it on the floor beside the gearshift and hand-brake. Both revolvers are handy, too: my Colt is in its usual place in my coat and Nick Reed's .38 is in the Iroquois' toolbox. Damn, I wish I knew whether Curt and company were already on their way north.

I unfurl the geologist's map over the hood again. Tracing lines with my finger, I curse my carelessness. Should've gone farther north. Old Reveille is where all three roads that cross this part of the state—from Dunbar, Hiko, and Basin Creek—converge like the neck of an hourglass.

No one's on that road up the mountain; everything on this side of the range is still. Tire marks in the dirt but I couldn't tell you what type of car made 'em. Jerry Rosen probably could: the man's obsessed with anything automotive. *Obsessed.* Even keeps a scrapbook of manufacturer's advertisements, dreaming of a day when he'll own a car of his own. Jerry has his quirks, certainly, but he's a company man, through and through. Odds are, if Curt's over that hill, then Jerry is right there beside him. Bastard was on my team but he always seemed to show up alongside Curt. Maybe Jerry's my blind spot. Hell, I have so many: Lila, Curt, Lipford, Billy Meeks, and possibly Helen. In time, likely others will be revealed; seems my whole life is a blind spot, three-hundred and sixty degrees.

"Found 'em," the old man says, startling me.

I'm so riled thinking about Jerry's treachery I'm late to realize I've reached inside my coat for the revolver. With the old fellow watching me, I make a show of scratching my shoulder.

"There a restaurant or grocer's in New Reveille?"

"No longer. You go that way, you'll see it's an insubstantial place. So much for reviving the district."

"How long will you stay here?"

He turns and looks downhill toward Railroad Valley, framed by low, volcanic hills, and the Grant Range, glittering white on the far horizon. "Probably forever," he says. "Got nowhere else to go." He pulls his glasses on over his ears and bends to study the map.

THIRTY-FOUR

The higher we climb, the colder it gets. The main road over the range follows a twisting canyon but Curt and company have done us an inadvertent favor: every washout is shoveled down and every soft spot loaded with cut brush. Hell, they've practically paved our way up the mountain. Even so, we eventually reach a fork where their tracks disappear. Bearing left, the road leading to the true pass looks so trashed by mining activity that I worry whether the Iroquois can handle it. Then again, the right-hand branch begins at such a steep pitch that I don't like its look, either. Which one did they take? According to the map, both eventually cross the range, although the left fork descends much closer to New Reveille. On this basis, I turn the wheel right, engage first gear, and gun the engine.

Terrible decision. This way is unmaintained, choked with sage, and brutally rough. It's like driving atop rails, keeping our wheels aligned with the corrugations between washouts. Must be ten, ten-thirty by now and I can't see reaching the valley floor any time before one p.m. Even worse, Jordan takes such a beating that I stop and move him into the back seat so he can lie down.

The car crawls along a steep, narrow shelf, and time and again I step out and roll away boulders that could smash the undercarriage. At one point, I exit across the hood because we are too near the cut-slope to open the driver's door and too close to the edge to use the passengers'. More than once, the wheels slip toward the shoulder and I'm afraid we'll roll. Thank God, there isn't any snow on the ground; if there was, there's no way we'd have made it even this far. That's how it is with bad mountain roads. Sometimes, no matter how frightening, going forward is the only option.

Below a towering ledge, we come to a stretch that honestly, I can't see how we'll cross. It's off-camber, raked by washouts, and who knows whether it even continues around the corner? I stop the car and kill the engine. The Iroquois has taken everything I've thrown at it but this may be the end. Down below, I see the main road from New Reveille: only a hundred yards as the boulder rolls but given our situation, it might as well be Washington Street in Carson City for all the trouble it'll take to get there. Exiting the car, I take extra care setting the hand-brake.

"Jordan," I say, "I'm going to scout ahead. You okay?"

No answer.

I scoot sideways between the cut-slope and car, scraping my backside against rocks until I'm standing beside the rear door. Looking inside, Jordan's sprawled across the floorboard. His breathing is rapid and shallow and his mouth has fallen open.

"Jordan?" I say again, louder this time.

"We there?" he moans.

"Not yet. Feeling any better?"

"No," he whispers.

He looks exhausted and sounds as if he's breathing through a straw. He struggles to rise and I lift him gently by his arms so he can look around. He glances over the side, blinks once or twice, and slides back onto the floorboard.

I rest a hand on his head. "I'm going to look ahead, okay?"

"Sure."

"Back in a minute."

Walking toward the curve, I want to thrash and pull my hair out—I *hate* trouble like this. Surprises jump up, your reaction's your answer. Easy enough. Fixes like this, on the other hand, are the result of conscious choice. Of poor judgement and arrogance. Old fellow *told* me the road would be rough but not to worry—it definitely went through. Didn't trust his advice, though, or to be honest, I thought I knew better. Now I may have stranded us.

The biggest washout is about three feet deep, three across, and cuts from left to right. The ruts beyond are littered with boulders of the three-hundred-pound variety. I can address all this with a half-hour's work but the slope is such that even with repairs, we still might slip off the edge. Situation calls for a mule team with a steel scraper, not some gangly son of a bitch with a shovel and pry-bar.

To my immense relief, the road improves immediately around the bend. If I can fill in those washouts and hug the inside corner, we might be able to put this mess behind us. Who says God doesn't look out for drunks and idiots?

I turn back toward the car. Green-on-green, it's practically invisible. Cedars hem it in, some growing so close to the road they're guaranteed to scratch the hell out of the car's sides. Don't care, though. I'm willing to degrade the Iroquois' good looks if it abets our escape.

Walking back, I hear the faint sound of a motorcar somewhere down in the wash: a low-pitched thumping that echoes off the rocks. This noise ebbs and flows according to the canyon's contours, and more than once it sounds as if the auto has turned and gone another way. Maybe I'll get lucky and it's someone I can flag down for help. Turning, I see a black touring car—a Pierce-Arrow—emerge onto the flat below Redstone Canyon, followed by a second.

No one's coming to help, stupid. That isn't your kind of luck.

Rounding the corner, I duck between the trees and run. Five minutes more, they'll be directly below us on the main road.

The kid's so groggy he doesn't ask why I fold down the windscreen or lay branches over the brass radiator. I take both revolvers plus Jordan's rifle and lay them all in the shadow beside a large boulder. Now I wish I hadn't discarded those last sticks of powder.

"Hey, buddy?" I glance inside the car. "Jordan?"

Kid's out cold, breathing through his mouth in shallow gasps. Poor fellow may not live much longer no matter what I do.

Taking a prone posture beside the boulder, I run through my options. Hell, maybe that isn't Curt and his team driving toward us; all this sweating and fidgeting may be for nothing. No, that's him. Has to be. Not like he followed us, but since every road across this part of the Black Belt converges here, it's just shit-bad luck that we arrived here at the same time.

With the low winter sun, we're still in shadow while the road below is about to be bathed in full, blinding light. Set above their sight-lines and surrounded by trees, I hope they'll roll on by, having seen nothing. Hope is nothing to count on, though, so I grip Jordan's rifle and balance it across my forearm. It's a short distance downhill and no wind is blowing. Wish I'd taken the time to zero in this thing but based on riflemen's rules and a short lead, I should be able to hit a slow-moving target. Only thing I don't like is that Jordan's fancy rifle is single-shot; if I miss, I won't have much time to re-load. Given its steepness, I like my odds if they try to charge this hill. Wish I had more cartridges for the shotgun, though. I wipe my brow and blink to keep my eyes clear.

The first car comes into view. Even at this distance, I can tell it's the same machine Curt and I took up to the Tomcat last month. Can't see the driver yet but I'll bet it's him; he loves that car. Personally, I think it's too heavy for a four-cylinder but to each his own. I'd sure like to kill him in it.

Looking through the rifle's iron sights, I follow the lead car as the road dips and turns. The second vehicle—a Ford, from the look of it—is following so closely that I can barely see it through the dust. This is good. So long as no one in the first car spots us, I doubt whether anyone in the second car will.

The road dips into a wash and both vehicles disappear. Even so, the droning cough of their engines grows louder. I wipe my forehead again. Dismayed, I notice a large boulder crowds the lower road directly below us. Isn't enough of an obstacle to stop them completely, but if it slows them enough, they'll have extra seconds to spot us.

The Pierce's canopy appears above the wash, followed by its big, bug-eye headlamps, and finally, its red undercarriage and wheels. Now I can see the driver clearly and to my surprise, he isn't Curt. Might be one of those drones from Lila's apartment but I can't be sure. Maybe that fellow, Anthony Cicero. Same with the passenger. Both are wearing goggles and heavy coats, and the passenger has a black bandanna tied over his face.

Then I see him. In the rear compartment, his back against the passenger-side door, Curt is turned sideways with his feet propped across the seat. His hat's pulled down over his face and he couldn't present a finer target, especially once the driver slows to a crawl between that boulder and the cut-slope.

Sunlight spills over the ridgeline. Even if any of them look up here, for the next minute I don't think they'll be able to see anything. I move the rifle's sights off the driver and settle onto Curt's head. It's a low angle and some brush is in the way but it's as clear a shot as I've ever had in my life. A trophy shot.

Right there.

The bastard's *right there* and my finger's heavy on the trigger. I exhale all the air from my lungs and my body stills. Base of his skull is in my sights. *Shoot, shoot, shoot,* I tell myself but the thought of taking on the others all by myself makes me hesitate.

Come on, *shoot.*

Sweat beads on my temples.

Come on.

If Jordan were well enough to fight, I'd have done it—ended one sordid chapter and leapt into the next, but a few seconds later the Pierce-Arrow disappears behind a cedar and my chance is gone. Gone and I'm left shivering in the shadow beneath a stone. Damn it, Shep, you idiot.

I spot Jerry Rosen in the Ford's front passenger seat but let him pass, too. A few seconds later, both cars disappear behind a curtain of dust. I release my grip and the barrel comes to rest in the dirt.

Shit.

I lay there for ten minutes. The cars reappear at the top of another rise and then they're gone. The sound of their engines lingers long after they've disappeared, slowly fading until the desert's stillness returns. Five minutes more and a dust cloud appears out on the flats, rising to stain an empty sky.

I stand, dust off my sweat-soaked clothes, and walk back to the Iroquois. Set the rifle on the floor between the front seats. To my surprise, Jordan is awake, leaning on one elbow.

"Who was that?" he says.

"Nobody. Investors on tour, maybe."

He closes his eyes. "Then why'd you take the rifle?"

I look out over the valley and see nothing—nothing but that receding dust cloud. The road to Clifford crosses the northern Kawich Range before dropping into Stone Cabin Valley; by now, they're miles away.

"Precaution," I say, wiping dust from my face. "Still need to fill a few washouts, move some rocks off the road. Probably take thirty, forty minutes. Want anything to eat? Some water, maybe?"

"Water," he whispers so I help him with the lightest tin.

Damn, look at that: storm clouds on the far horizon and they're building fast. Now I really want to hurry.

"Not much farther. This is the last bad stretch and then we'll be down, okay?"

While I inch past the wheels to untie the shovel from the car's back, Jordan sinks back onto the floorboard.

Moving forward, I lean over the door. "Won't be long, okay?"

He doesn't answer.

THIRTY-FIVE

Halfway up Cedar Pass, it starts to snow. Scattered flakes at first. The clouds are broken and it's still light out but we are miles from the summit and I'd rather we'd crossed over into the next basin before it cuts loose.

I don't get my wish. Within minutes, it's coming down so hard that our speed is halved and a small drift accumulates on the front passenger's seat. No goggles, so all I can do is duck below the windscreen, nearly opaque with ice.

Even so, apart from one flat tire, the car's held up well and I wouldn't be so apprehensive if I knew the route better. That, and it's quickly growing dark. As it is, I can't tell you what the surrounding country looks like; can't see more than a hundred feet in any direction. Leaden sky. Mounded snow on sage and cedars—that's it. All I want is to get over the pass and make camp somewhere on the west side. Or not. So long as the car will move, I'd better keep pushing.

Stopping to refill the tank, Jordan asks me to help him into the front seat.

"You sure?" I shout. "Wind's terrible up here."

"Tired of sleeping. Want to see something, anything before I go."

Before this, neither of us has mentioned the possibility that he might not survive.

"You're gonna make it, understand?"

No answer, no sound of any kind.

I do most of the work to get him settled. He can hardly sit upright so I pack the blanket and all the extra clothes around him to keep him from toppling.

Poor kid's shivering, too. Debatable whether it's better to push ahead or stop and make a fire.

Soon, the road flattens and becomes less rocky. We're down from the mountains—that range, anyway—so I tighten the chains around our tires and drive on.

Jordan tries to turn his head to look at me but his stiffening muscles won't let him. "If I ask you something, swear you won't get sore?"

I stare ahead into the gloom, trying to anticipate what in the hell he might ask. The car is climbing again and our wheels spin before catching and pushing us over a steep rise. "Okay, sure."

"Who's Pat?"

Without context, it takes me a moment to recognize the name. "Only Pat I know was my army buddy, Patrick Dobbins. He was killed in the Philippines; how would you know about him?"

"Back in that safehouse outside Pioche, you were mumbling in your sleep."

We slip and skid farther along the road, fishtailing around a curve. Now that we're headed downhill, all I'm doing is over-steering. The headlamps are almost useless in these conditions.

Jordan coughs weakly. "You said, 'What have they done, Pat, what have they done?'"

Ah, yeah: what have they done? A question for the ages. I wrinkle my nose and wipe at my eyes, whether from the falling snow or from crying, who cares? Jordan's chin is on his chest so he can't see me but it wouldn't matter if he could. Crying over a pretty tune or because it's New Year's and you're drunk is silly but shedding tears for dead friends is a holy thing—maybe the only religion I follow.

⁓

I lean over the USS *Pittsburgh's* port railing, five-hundred yards offshore, watching Balangiga burn. We've returned to bury our dead and recover any weapons the insurrectos might've missed. The *Pittsburgh's* 3-inch guns shell the jungle surrounding town for an hour before a relief expedition goes ashore. Some of my fellows from C Company stand alongside me—Arnold Irish, George Allen, Taylor Hickman, among others—and I'll admit we're glad every time the *Pittsburgh's* guns go off. We cheer every time a flash appears on shore and smoke rises above the trees. Clifford Mumby points as flames pour from the municipal building: the same building where Henry Manire and I fought our way down from the second floor a mere 48 hours earlier.

The bandages around my head are painfully tight, although my ferocious headache may have more to do with the twenty-seven stitches a navy surgeon used to reattach my scalp. Before long, I don't care to watch anymore. Maybe it's the guns' concussions or maybe I'm just sick of death and devastation. Don't know. Isn't my place to know.

Not much of a relief expedition; there's no one left to relieve. Going ashore with Captain Bookmiller's G Company, the town resembles hell itself; the smell of death and rot is overpowering. Our companion's bodies are still sprawled everywhere, most stripped of their clothing and some horribly mutilated. Someone's burned papers over Lieutenant Bumpus' face, gouged out his eyes, and filled the sockets with stones and raspberry jam. Some had their fingers cut off; others, their genitals. A work party pulls Dennis, Dent, and Gordon's bodies from the well before the municipal building. Even the company dog has been hacked to pieces. God knows how but we survivors keep our emotions in check. All the enraged shouting comes from the boys in G Company.

Major Surgeon Combe paces back and forth with a notepad, recording names as bodies are discovered and brought to the plaza for burial. Occasionally, guns bark in the jungle as villagers who stayed too long try to run. No one buries them.

The attackers lifted most of our stores and emptied the armory: maybe a hundred rifles, at least 25,000 cartridges, and more. As a domain of the United States government, the barrio of Balangiga, Samar, is a total loss.

Between my wounds and the sweltering heat, I move slowly—too slowly for those in our group wondering who might be lurking in the jungle. Preparing to guide a search party down to the river where he'd last seen Covington and Dobbins, Arnold Irish tries but can't talk me out of going. In the end, he relents because he understands; he's volunteered in order to look for the body of *his* friend, Frank Voybada.

Down on the riverbank, I find Pat's cartridge belt and Covington's haversack, both empty, but no sign that either man survived. I offer to guide another search party through the palm groves north of town but Captain Bookmiller details four men from G Company to help Arnold and I into a launch and row us back out to the *Pittsburgh*.

"Rest up, soldier," one naval officer tells me. "You'll be back here before long. Help hunt down and punish whoever did this."

I salute and thank him, tell him I can hardly wait, yet in all honesty, I never want to set foot on Samar again. Man was right, though. Before the month was out I was back, so filled with hate and sorrow that even six years on and 8,000 miles away, it still threatens to drag me under.

Back onboard, I stand by myself along the rail, watching launches moving back and forth between the *Pittsburgh* and the beach. Frenetic activity all around. The men of G Company are practically vibrating with rage—rage tinged with embarrassment, as if they don't know what to make of us survivors. Perhaps they're relieved it wasn't them, or maybe they're wondering what we did wrong. I hear mutterings: who got careless and how could self-respecting White men let savages get the upper hand? Despite the chaos and close quarters, they give us a wide berth as we stagger past.

A fresh plume of smoke erupts from somewhere along the village's southern fringe, towering over the tree line.

"What have they done, Pat?" I whisper, "What have they done?" Honestly, I don't know which side I'm panning.

Walter Bertholf, Charlie Marak, and Francisco—the Macabebe scout who'd defended us there at Lawaan—are aboard the ship, too. All three move along the railing until they're standing beside me. Francisco looks battered and bruised and Charlie's arm is in a bloody sling, but not Walter. Jesus Christ, Walt looks as if he got away without a scratch. Hasn't said anything, though, so I can't be sure. Some wounds can't be seen.

"Shep," Marak croaks, his voice comically hoarse. "Any luck?"

A navy corpsman arrives to escort us below-decks. "Only the bad kind, Charlie. Only the bad."

⁓

"Shep?" Jordan says as I jerk the steering wheel to keep our tires from leaving the ruts.

"One second; let me get past this turn."

I've only ever talked with Julia about what happened in Balangiga and the reprisals afterward. Once or twice, I tried opening up to Lila but she wouldn't hear it. One night last July, I started spilling my guts but she told me she couldn't stand hearing such talk because her high school sweetheart went off to Cuba and never returned. That's what she said, anyhow. Probably just as well. God knows what she might've told Lipford—intentionally or as pillow talk—and what he might've done with the information. I was wrong to trust her. Don't know if I can trust Jordan with my story, either. Now I'm the one who doesn't want to talk.

"Hey, Jordan, you know what day it is?"

Don't know if he's thinking or gathering his strength to answer. "I've lost track."

"Christmas Eve. Almost Christmas, buddy. No presents, though. Sorry."

"I won't—," he wheezes but doesn't finish his thought. "Merry Christmas, Shep."

Stomping the brakes, the car jerks to a stop above a washout. Its edge is so abrupt that the car's headlamps shine out into darkness, illuminating nothing but falling snow. I step out.

Standing above the embankment, my heart drops. For the last mile, the track we're on has grown rougher as it's dropped and now I see why: the road itself channels water flowing down from this side of the valley. Here at the wash's edge, runoff surging over a steep gradient has caused the road to collapse; now it's nothing but a twenty-foot gash filled with jumbled boulders and uprooted brush. Holy hell, we'll never get past this.

I lean against the passenger door and tug on Jordan's lapels, partly to keep snow from blowing inside his coat and partly to help him sit straighter so he can breathe. His face is ghostly and his lips are blue, although from cold or a lack of oxygen, I cannot tell. Death may run him to ground no matter what I do.

"Jordan?" He doesn't respond. "Jordan?"

"Shep?" he whispers.

"Gonna look for a way down, okay? I'll be right back."

No answer.

My hands are freezing so I jam them into my coat pockets. God knows I'm in better shape than Jordan and still I'm none too comfortable. Everything hurts.

Downstream, the embankment grows taller: a sheer thirty-foot drop into the wash. Not good. I work my way back along the edge, past the Iroquois, looking for openings in the sagebrush and kicking rocks away from the likeliest route. I've gone thirty or forty yards when I spot what I hoped I'd find. I've seen this elsewhere: cattle, accustomed to following their usual routes, must've found this same blowout. Looking for a way into the wash, they've trampled a formerly-sheer embankment into a steep, muddy ramp: still treacherous but potentially navigable. Some sections are more abrupt than others; hit one wrong and the car could roll. From rim to wash, I hike this slope twice until I'm sure of the route. Back on top, I take two mullein stalks and thrust them into the dirt as something to aim for above the edge.

Another tin of gasoline into the tank and we're ready. Leaving the road, the car bumps and scrapes along about the way it did when we were *on* it. I line up the radiator cap on the first stalk, except that falling snow makes it hard to see. After getting out and checking one last time, I'm confident we're on the right angle. Still, with the headlights shining out into nothingness, it's hard not to feel anxious as the hood plunges over the edge.

The Iroquois' back end skids right but I over-steer, keeping my foot off the brake, and after a jolt or three, we're down. The wash's floor is mostly sand and mud and while the going is slow, it isn't the worst stretch we've driven today. The exit on its west side is in substantially better shape; merely tapping the accelerator puts us back onto relatively level ground. Within minutes, Jordan's back asleep and then there's nothing to think about except the road, darkness, and snow.

∾

My head aches and my eyes hurt but for another hour, I keep driving. We pass several unmarked side roads. Abandoned buildings at Cactus Spring. The map says several small camps lie to the south: Jamestown, Trappman's Camp, and Gold Crater, but I've heard none among 'em are worth a damn. Not yet, anyway—maybe someday soon a prospector will crack open a seam of rich ore and the world will whisper these names. Or not.

At one prominent fork, I stop to read a weather-beaten sign that points north to Tonopah, 37 miles, and west to Goldfield, 30 miles. Thirty miles. Two hours if everything goes right, yet what are the odds it will? That said, all this will be for nothing if I don't get Jordan to the hospital in time. If only I hadn't wasted hours there in the mountains above Reveille. No, if we'd gone the other way, we'd have reached the main road only minutes ahead of Curt Broe's crew. They'd have spotted our dust for sure and likely given chase. Aggravation and all, that awful little detour was for the best.

I *need* to get Jordan to the hospital, though. Nothing else matters: not Curt, nor Helen, nor anything else. This kid—this *stranger*—has done more for me than I deserve. More than some of my so-called friends. I need to repay my debt.

Don't know what'll happen once we reach Goldfield. Other than Mine Operators Hospital, I don't know where else to go. It's Christmas Eve. Does that mean everything will be closed or in full swing? From all I've heard, probably the latter. Can't imagine a place as important as Goldfield closes for something as trifling as Christmas.

Up ahead, I see a break in the clouds. The road vanishes at a point on the horizon where the Milky Way stands on edge, so bright it casts shadows across the snow. Beckoning, beguiling, this pillar of fire is guiding me across the desert.

Finally, the storm lifts. I push the car from ten miles per hour to fifteen— even twenty in places where I can see far enough ahead. After one nasty jolt, the exhaust pipe comes loose and I stop to lash it in place with bailing wire. Takes ten minutes and leaves me soaking wet from crawling around underneath the car but this is merely an irritant. Won't let it or anything else stop us.

Road here is as straight as milk and cookies, but it enters and exits so many gullies that after a while I feel a little nauseous. Up and down, over and over: this is the closest I've come to seasickness since boarding a troopship for the Philippines six years ago. In one low spot, a coyote runs through the light from our car's headlamps, barely scampering out of our way in time. Crazy beast.

I'm nearly delirious with fatigue, biting my frozen fingers in an effort to stay awake. The western sky reddens. Can't be sunrise. Even in my condition, I know which direction we're facing. Then I see a ridge silhouetted against the reddened clouds and I realize it must be the glare from Goldfield's lights. Nothing yet of the city itself—a jagged ridge stands in the way—but now that the road is climbing, it's clear we've made it across Stonewall Valley.

"See those lights, Jordan? Almost there, buddy."

Jordan groans. Not much of an answer but better than nothing.

Hold on, kid, hold on.

Around another bend, we pass a miner's shack with a lamp glowing through the window. Its occupant steps outside to wave and stare as we pass, perhaps wondering who in the hell has come in from the east on this holy evening. Only me: an unwise man, bearing no gifts. I sound the horn as this light slips from view. The headlamps pick out tall, shaggy plants alongside the road: Joshua trees again, their arms upraised to God. It's a sign—must be a sign.

Less snow here: only a few inches and the road is a clean white stripe between the hills. We pass another shack, then several clustered together. Oddest thing, a sudden flash reflects off the low clouds, followed by a muffled boom. Another follows, and another. Sounds like artillery: sharp thunderclaps echo off the surrounding hills. A trail of sparks disappears into a cloud before the entire mass pulses with light from within.

"Jordan, are you awake? We made it, pard; made it to Goldfield. They're shooting off fireworks for Christmas."

Jordan opens his eyes just as another skyrocket explodes.

"Nice," he wheezes. Then he closes his eyes again and resettles his chin on his chest.

More lights now, shining down from houses, mines, and structures I can't identify. Then we top a rise and the road descends into a broad basin filled with more points of light than the skies above.

Goldfield, at last.

The clouds swallow another skyrocket. As it explodes, the whole basin is illuminated so brightly I can see the flat-topped Malapai west of town and the sloped spur of Mount Columbia to the north. A second flash follows, revealing a forest of headframes stretching in an arc around the city's eastern edge: the famed "Golden Horseshoe," where all the district's monster properties are located. Goldfield is *gigantic,* too—far larger than the last time I came through. Every available space is jammed with buildings of every size and description. More lights, more people, more possibilities. To hell with Lipford and Big Curt and everyone else who tried to stop me. I can't be stopped. Not tonight.

Near the center of town, I see the hospital: a two-story, tan brick building lit up like—hell, from one end to the other, the entire town is lit for Christmas. Delamar's White House Hotel, geez, Goldfield has dozens of buildings just like it. This place is dazzling; too bright by half.

Jordan gasps for air and in response, I mash the accelerator to the floor. He can't give out; not after all we've been through. Won't let him. I run my fingers through his blond hair the way I remember my father would on nights when he hadn't been drinking. There aren't many, but those are among my fondest memories of the man.

"Come on, Jordan, stay with me."

The boy gulps and gasps but he's still breathing. God, I hope the doctors know what to do with him. Hope the WFM's Goldfield Local picks up the tab, too.

Another skyrocket soars into the clouds, followed by lightning and a rain of golden stars. This might be the strangest, loveliest thing I've ever seen. Wish Helen was here with me to see it. If only.

Although we've only just met, Goldfield has restored my optimism. For the first time in a while, I can imagine better days and think beyond mere survival. Already, I'm strategizing weeks ahead, planning my return to Delamar. Planning to redeem all the markers on my account. Not tonight, though. Tonight, Goldfield is whispering that she's been expecting me and by God, I will not let her down.

Tires spinning as we round a big curve, we top a rise and nearly plow into a roadblock. With cribbing on the left and an embankment on my right, it's too late to turn—nothing to do but stomp the brakes. The car skids, arriving at the sandbagged barricade on an angle. A spotlight blinds me. Fumbling with the shifter, I search for reverse but my foot slips from the clutch pedal and the engine stalls; stalls but chugs and sputters a moment before dying.

"Don't move!" someone shouts, his voice amplified by megaphone. "Don't move—stay where you are!"

The hell is this? I shield my eyes with my left hand. We've seen almost no one since Reveille. How could anyone know we'd come this way? Hell, I'll shoot someone—shoot myself before they take me. My right hand goes toward the revolver in my pocket.

"Sergent Armstrong," someone shouts, high on the hill to my left. "No others: road's clear."

"Kinser," another voice calls, "the light! Driver, keep your hands on the wheel and don't move."

"My passenger's hurt," I shout, careful to keep my hands visible. "It's an emergency."

"Stay where you are and don't move!"

Three men in green wool emerge from behind a makeshift fortification. Winter service coats with stand-and-fall collars and canvas leggings over their boot-tops. They're carrying M1903 Springfield rifles; I'd recognize those anywhere. More ominously, on the right, I catch a glimpse of two others seated behind a tripod-mounted Maxim machine gun. Even with all the muzzles pointed at us, considering who I was expecting, I'm a little relieved to recognize United States infantry.

The spotlight's beam settles onto the road between our car and the road-block. A tall noncom emerges from behind the barricade, silhouetted by another skyrocket exploding over the city. A crackling boom ripples across the desert.

The sergeant's boots crunch gravel. He sweeps a small electric flashlight over the Iroquois. "Rough night for travel," he says. "Where are you fellows from?"

"Basin Creek, over on the Black Belt's eastern side. My passenger's injured; I have to get him to a hospital."

"That's absurd—roads east are impassable." Shining the flashlight in my eyes, he notices Jordan slumped in his seat. Its beam lingers on the boy before returning to me. "What's this about your passenger?"

"Shot himself cleaning his revolver." I grip the wheel, mostly to keep my hands from shaking.

"Shot himself?" The light returns to Jordan. "Either of you with the miners' union? WFM? IWW?"

"We're investors. Mining properties and real estate."

"Identification?"

I pull out the business card that fellow, Carson Foster, gave me back in Basin Creek, plus the envelope containing Dr. Robinson's testimonial letter.

By flashlight, the sergeant studies these bits of paper, pausing once to glance at Jordan. I see a bronze insignia on his collar—the number '22' over a pair of crossed rifles—and chevrons on his sleeve. Soon as he finishes reading the doctor's letter, he glances back at Jordan.

"He's Casey, I take it?"

It takes a moment to recognize one of the fake names we used with Dr. Robinson, but I don't think the sergeant catches this—thank God for the darkness. I turn to look at my young friend, too, and maybe it's only the light reflecting off the road but his face is grotesquely pale. His chest barely moves and if it weren't for the thin vapor he exhales I'd figure he was already dead.

"That's right," I say. "I need to get him to a hospital, fast."

Another skyrocket explodes over the city.

The tall sergeant turns back toward the barricade. "Private Curran, Private Riggs, take the truck and escort these fellows to Mine Owners." Turning back to me, he thrusts my papers over the door. "Welcome to Goldfield, Mr. Foster," he says. "Watch yourself, though; this town isn't safe."

Hearing this doesn't make me happy, but it comes as no surprise. Can't be worse than Delamar.

∽

GOLDFIELD, Nev., Dec. 22. — Gov. Sparks, it was said to-day, is preparing a statement of present conditions in Goldfield to be telegraphed to President Roosevelt. He is not satisfied that the President understands the situation, not with standing the report of his commission. The communication to the President will, it is said, contain a request for the retention of at least a portion of the troops now here after Dec. 30, the date now set for their going.

———

©The New York Times   September 30, 1901

PART THREE

HOMECOMING

"Hell is empty
And all the devils are here."

—

William Shakespeare, The Tempest
—Act 1, Scene 2

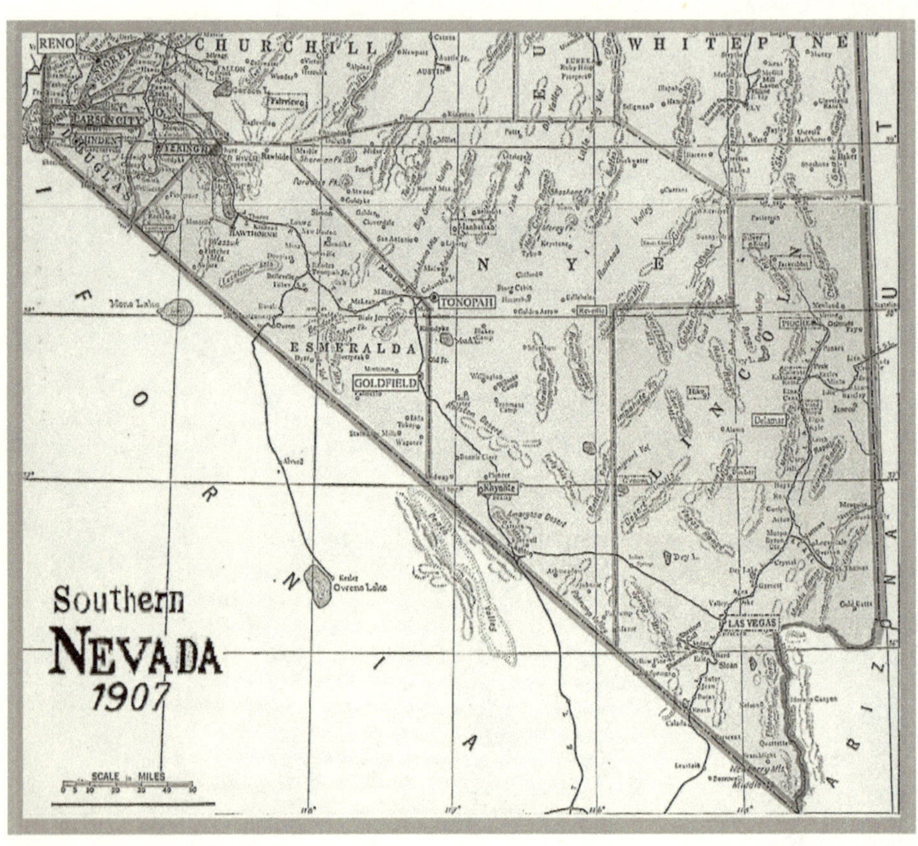

RENO
CHURCHILL
WHITE PINE
AUSTIN
CARSON CITY
MINDEN
YERINGTON
DOUGLAS
HAWTHORNE
TONOPAH
N Y E
LINCOLN
ESMERALDA
GOLDFIELD
PIOCHE
Delamar
Mono Lake
Rhyolite
LAS VEGAS
Owens Lake
CALIFORNIA
ARIZONA
Southern
NEVADA
1907
SCALE in MILES

THIRTY-SIX

A brass bell startles me from my trance. Looking up, I catch my reflection in a tall mirror on the opposite wall. My *full* reflection: mud-stained clothes, unkempt hair, and haggard complexion. A little over a month from now, I'll turn twenty-eight but to be honest, I look like I'm fifty. A fifty-year-old bum. Maybe it's fatigue showing, or maybe it's dry-rot coming to the surface.

From where I sit, I can't see the ward's far end and this makes me uncomfortable; Nemesis always enters through an unwatched door. I'd like to move my chair but seeing how a staffer kindly dragged it in here for me—and how it's much more comfortable than the pine benches in the lobby—it'd be rude to move it someplace where I might be in someone's way. On my right, a valve clicks open. Low hissing sounds and a faint antiseptic smell fill the air. A motor whirrs and stills. Then the only sounds in this long room are of another patient coughing, a door closing, and my young friend's shallow, rapid breathing.

My friend. I barely know Jordan Barley but consider him a friend. Born in Nebraska, a miner and member of the WFM since '05, and almost quaintly wedded to the notion that all men are created equal—this much I picked up on our long walk across Lincoln County. Then everything went to hell.

Another valve clicks open, followed by a second rush of air as the pressure inside the box adjusts itself.

I want to sleep but my brain won't shut down. Back, neck, everything hurts.

Another door creaks, this time followed by a cadence of shoes across the wooden floor. Recognizing a physician who'd come around earlier, I unhand the revolver inside my coat. He crosses the ward, accompanied by a woman dressed in white and armed with a clipboard.

"Still up?" he sounds surprised. "Then Merry Christmas to you." Of medium height, the doctor is heavyset, with white hair, a white mustache, and gold-rimmed glasses. Add a beard and a red hat and he'd look like Thomas Nast's famous cartoon of Santa Claus.

"Awake, yep." I stifle a yawn with my sleeve. "Merry Christmas."

"I'm Dr. Weston, chief surgeon here. This is Nurse Atchison, in charge of this ward. Sorry but I've forgotten your name."

"Carson Foster."

Several beds over, a man with bandages on his face and hands cries out in his sleep.

"Very good, Mr. Foster. Let's check on your friend, shall we?"

The doctor eases Jordan's mouth open and wedges a mercury thermometer beneath the boy's tongue. After a minute, he holds it near a green-shaded lamp and squints.

"One-hundred." Dr. Weston straightens his back and stares through his reflection in the window.

Damned if I can read his expression in this light. "That's better, yes?"

Down on Oak Street, a noisy auto-stage backfires and rumbles downtown.

"Better, but not good." He takes out a pocket watch, checks it against a wall clock, and turns to face me. "I read the letter Dr. Robinson wrote in Basin Creek—hats off for his skillful intervention, and to you for bringing him here quickly—but the boy's injury persists and he needs to regain strength before I can operate. We're scheduled for tomorrow afternoon, but that's tentative. Does he work in the mines?"

"He did."

"Henceforth, I doubt whether his lungs will tolerate conditions underground. I'm sorry."

Jordan, I'm sorry, too. Sorry you got mixed up in this mess. If anything reinforces my belief that it all comes down to fate, it's injury and illness. In the Philippines, a private in our company, Ernie Ralston, caught something—camp fever, malaria, I don't know. Whatever it was, poor Ernie couldn't stop shivering and his skin turned the color of butter. Mid-September, 1901, he was evacuated from Balangiga to a field hospital in Basey. We figured we'd seen the last of him, but after the massacre, I ran into him in Tacloban. Still looked like hell but by then, so did the rest of us. There's the rub: in a sense, did malaria save

Ernie's life? He transferred to Manila and rotated back to the States ahead of me so I don't know whether his poor health persisted, but I *do* know he wasn't in Balangiga on September 29th, 1901, and, by God, I'm not so sure I wouldn't trade a tropical disease for what happened there. Now here's Jordan: comatose and confined to a mechanical lung awaiting surgery. And for what—a claim survey? Higher returns? The world's gone mad.

"Mr. Foster?" Weston says and I realize I've been stewing too long.

"I'm with you. Anything more to do before you operate?"

"No. Already we've removed the catheter from his chest and strictly speaking, the boy can breathe on his own but this apparatus makes it easier."

He peers at a gauge over the top of his glasses, nods at the result, and mumbles to Miss Atchison. She scratches a pen across her clipboard.

"By reducing stress on his system, I hope he'll regain his strength faster."

"How long will he be here?"

He says that depending on how well Jordan tolerates the insult of surgery, the boy will be hospitalized at least until January first, a week from Wednesday. Jesus, what am I supposed to do until then?

Another patient shifts and moans loudly. Finished writing, Miss Atchison turns and crosses the room to look after him. A valve on the respirator clicks and another rush of air gusts around our knees.

"Any friends or family here?" Weston continues. "Somewhere to stay while the boy recovers?"

"I'll find something," I say. "This is Goldfield, right?"

"So I hear," Weston says, cracking the faintest hint of a smile. "I can loan you some money if you need. And if you'll come by my office tomorrow, I can suggest places to look for work. I'm on the boards of several mining companies—perhaps a manager can put you on for a few shifts, although with the new card system here, you may not want to disclose your membership."

"'Membership?'"

"You belong to the WFM, do you not?"

"No."

Dr. Weston raises an eyebrow. "I was told you wanted the local notified of this boy's situation."

"*He's* with the Federation." I point to Jordan. "It's a long story."

The doctor studies me a moment. The WFM is like a religion and it's rare for adherents to fraternize outside the faith. Guess he expects an explanation but I'm out of my mind with fatigue and damned if I'll show my cards to a perfect stranger, even one who's just offered me all kinds of help.

"Perhaps you'll tell me tomorrow. My midday rounds end around 12:30; come by my office at one o'clock?"

"Here in the hospital?"

"The administrative annex. Sure you don't need funds for the night?"

I shake my head. "I'm covered, thanks, but if you'd recommend a hotel without bedbugs I'd be grateful."

"The Casey Hotel is excellent—pricey but excellent—or the Grimshaw. Both are about two blocks west on opposite corners of North Main and Miners Street. Good day."

❧

Stepping outside, I feel snow on my face again—the really fine stuff you can't see unless you stare at a light fixture for a while. No challenge there: Goldfield is electrified on a scale that makes Delamar look like a charcoal burners' camp way back in the hills. Strings of bare bulbs form canopies over all the major streets, as well as a surprising number of minor ones. The big saloons are so brightly lit they cast shadows clear across the streets. This town is a temple of light, a monument to excess; no other description fits. Last I saw a clock it was two-thirty in the morning on Christmas Day, jack, yet the streets are bustling with what'd be a respectable workday crowd in any big city.

Here and there, soldiers observe passersby although their rifles are slung and their bayonets are covered. The troops look bored and no one's paying them any attention; at least, not in any way that interferes with the pursuit of pleasure.

Downtown is a hodge-podge of every kind of business. Banks, brokers' offices, livery stables, the stock exchange, and saloons—saloons, everywhere— all mixed like pebbles in a pan. Most are festooned with holiday banners or greenery. A laundry service stands next to a hotel still under construction; a Western Union office abuts the electric company's handsome stone building; and the Elks' Club shares a wall with a mechanic's garage. Did I mention the saloons? Advertisements and signs are everywhere: banners, flush-mounted boards, and projecting from façades at heights and angles that surely must cull drunks and the unwary. Quite a number are for nationally-branded products, confirming Goldfield's status as a cosmopolitan center. The sidewalks are so crowded that many—men and women alike—simply walk in the muddy streets.

Two beautiful women stroll past, arm in arm and wearing long fur coats and muffs, and the murmuring crowd parts so they can pass. Starlets in from San Francisco? If so, I confess my ignorance. Farther down the block, a shoving match breaks out between two men, but cooler heads prevail and the revelry continues as before. Newsboys and cigarette vendors dart in and out of the crowd. This place is a circus; a freewheeling riot of impulse and speculation. Don't imagine anyone here ever sleeps.

Hell, I'd better, though, or I'm liable to wander in front of a buckboard or pitch headfirst off a sidewalk. After a short stroll to see the crowds around the famous Four Corner saloons—Tex Rickard's Great Northern, the Palace, the Hermitage, and the Mohawk, whose combined nightly take is said to run upward of $30,000—I turn to shuffle up Main to seek lodging. Despite feeling like a kid in a candy store, this kid needs sleep before sweets.

One block east of the Palace, I see the upper floors of a titanic new hotel but it's still under construction and hasn't opened yet. Farther north, I reject a second hotel, figuring the noise and smoke from its main-floor saloon must make sleeping upstairs difficult.

At last, I reach the Casey. It's nicer—that is to say, more expensive—than I'd prefer, but with more than a hundred dollars left, I'm feeling swell. For once in my life, four dollars-fifty per night doesn't strike me as extortionate.

"Merry Christmas," the clerk greets me, and I mumble the same in return.

"Welcome to Goldfield, Mr…?"

"Foster."

"Yes, sir. No baggage?"

"It's in my car."

"Very good, sir. If you'd like, we provide a private garage for our guests' motorcars. I'll have a mahout fetch yours and a bellhop will bring your bags to your room."

"Great," I say. "It's an Iroquois, green with plum-colored trim, over in front of the hospital." Seems he's mistaken me for a gentleman.

"Which hospital, sir?"

"Couple of blocks that way." I gesture across the lobby. "Mine Owners', is it?"

"Mine Operators, sir. Would you like your automobile washed, as well?"

Is that what people do here? Maybe guests at the Casey, all bankers, brokers, and speculators, from the look of it. Hate blowing money on frivolities but if that's what it takes to blend in, then maybe this once I should.

"Sure, knock the dust off."

"Very good, sir. I'll see that it's ready by nine a.m."

"Noon's fine, thanks."

"Of course, sir. Would you like your travel clothes cleaned and pressed?"

He glances at my jacket and trousers, still damp and mud-stained from making repairs under the car. I'd figured I would wash everything in the basin but the Casey isn't that sort of establishment and I can't go tripping all over town like I just came off shift in the mines.

"Send up my bag and I'll hand over my laundry. Cleaned but not starched, right? I don't need creases where I'm going."

Honestly, I'm not comfortable with this kind of fawning; it's un-American, or at least it should be. Walking around Delamar, lawyers and shopkeepers alike fell all over themselves trying to get an audience with Prince Jack. Unctuous handshakes, gratuitous discounts, and so many free cigars that once we returned to the Association's offices, depending on his mood, he'd either hand them out among staff or simply toss 'em in a wastebasket. Hell, if there was anyone in Lincoln County who *didn't* need charity…Of course, there's no telling whether some gesture will turn a rich stranger into a patron, but the moral inversion of it irritated me. Still does, even as the recipient.

The clerk reaches for a ledger book under the desk. "And do you want a listing in the *News* or the *Chronicle's* hotel arrivals?"

It's common for businessmen visiting Nevada's camps to list their names in the papers so that anyone wishing to do business with them knows where to go. Me, I don't want *anyone* to know I'm here but neither do I want to object in a way that draws attention to this break from custom.

"Not this trip, thank you."

He smiles and returns the ledger to storage. "Whatever your preference, sir. You're never a stranger at the Casey."

I hope that's not true. Glancing over my shoulder, I notice a man seated in an overstuffed chair beside the fireplace. He's staring at me over the top of his paper. Seeing me turn, he lowers his eyes and raises the paper so all I can see is his hair. His clothes and shoes are finely made—too fine for a company detective, certainly—and while it's possible someone's watching for me in Goldfield, it's unlikely they'd be snooping around a high-end outpost like the Casey. Likelier to find a working-class fugitive asleep in the sawdust beneath a pool table or in a ragtown hotel on the city's outskirts. That's where I'd look, anyway. Still, wariness has me calculating angles and distances to the nearest exit. Glancing in a mirror, I'm relieved once this fellow stands and exits the lobby. Probably nothing more than a nosy bastard.

Probably.

Before the clerk hands me my room key, two army officers enter through the main doors, shaking snow from their hats and shoulders. They cross the lobby to stand behind me, speaking to each other in low tones. Can't hear everything they're saying but combined with what I've read in the papers, it's enough to figure they must be aides-de-camp to Colonel Reynolds. No surprise finding high-brass quartered in the priciest hotel in town. In Manila during the war, Governor Taft and our generals all billeted in Malacañan Palace, upriver from the walled barrio of Intramuros. I'm told the palace is beautiful inside although I never saw it; livestock like me weren't allowed anywhere near the place.

∞

Key in hand, I turn, set my feet on carpeted stairs, and climb to find Room 305. Christ, too, it's *huge*—ten times the size of my digs back in Delamar. I spend five minutes simply walking around—barefoot, because my socks are wet and my boots caked with mud— soaking in the oak-and-marble opulence, flipping light switches, and turning faucet handles merely to see the water coming out. Hayseed behavior, I'll admit.

I stretch out on a wicker lounge chair to think. I'd like to go to bed but first I need to stand for the bellhop. Check my pockets for tipping-money. Yes, covered. But what about tomorrow? And the day after? Then what? From what little I've seen of it, Goldfield is wickedly expensive. Do I skip town and make a run for Esmerelda County? I need to get ahold of that survey; it's my only leverage against Prince Jack; the only possible reason he'd recall Big Curt. And who's gonna pay Jordan's hospital bill? The WFM? Their Ladies' Aid Society? Not sure I can, even if I'd shown restraint and stayed someplace less expensive than the Casey.

The bellhop delivers my bag and palms his tip.

"Taking my laundry?" I ask.

"No, sir. Someone else will be along shortly."

"I see. Give him these—," I hand him more coins, "—and tell him I'll leave everything outside my door. They'll clean my boots, too?"

"Yes, sir." He backs through the door and closes it.

Damn it, forgot to wish him a Merry Christmas. So tired I'm probably forgetting plenty. My body aches all over and I'm in desperate need of rest, even one night's worth. Or maybe I'll snug up here in Goldfield and let things blow over. For weeks, I've been running like every dog and devil in Nevada knows my name but here, I feel anonymous. Blissfully, blessedly anonymous. I know better than to pray for wealth or safety but I'm okay with begging for anonymity.

Taking off my jacket, I hear papers rustling in the pockets. First is a carbon-copy of Dr. Robinson's letter describing Jordan's injury and suggesting use of the hospital's depressurization chamber. Second is the notebook full of numbers I found in the geologist's bag. Third is Julia's photograph, and fourth is a folded copy of A.L. Hart's assay report for those claims outside Basin Creek.

Seeing this, any levity I was feeling vanishes. I really am an idiot, buying a golden pig in a poke. Hell, Al Hart wanted a whole lot more but opportunists take what they get and idiots can't keep what they have. Ergo, I am now the owner of an expensive sheet of paper, nothing more. Regardless, there's no point in getting overworked tonight. Tomorrow afternoon, I'll head over to Hart's offices or the Crampton brothers' assay. See whether I'm holding trash or treasure.

Stripping naked, I set my laundry and muddy boots outside the door. Glancing inside the wardrobe, I find a cotton bag with LAUNDRY stenciled on it. Oh, of course. I shuffle back to retrieve my things. Hate to expose myself as a rube who'd dump muddy clothes in a heap outside his door. Without a stitch on, I'm glad no one's there to see me.

I plug the washbasin and soak my head and hair in warm water for as long as I can hold my breath. Dripping on the tile floor, I drag a piece of soap across my face and dive back in. Within seconds, the water turns browner than the Humboldt River in springtime. Ought to take a full bath but I don't have the energy.

Yawn so hard my jaw aches. Lying in bed, I hear people milling about on the street below, though not so many as before. The fireworks stopped a long time ago and the city's gone quiet. Quieter, anyway. The saloon two doors down still simmers and every few minutes, a wagon or auto-stage rumbles past, but I can filter out these sounds. At this point, I think I could ignore just about anything. Almost anything.

I retrieve the assay report from the nightstand and read it again. $4,200 ore. Half a million—Lord, the things I could do with money like that. Double my family's holdings over in Esmerelda County. Go look for Helen. Or hire my own operatives, return to Delamar, and settle accounts with Jack Lipford. I like this last one best.

Without even realizing it, I fall asleep.

THIRTY-SEVEN

Light through the blinds nudges me awake. A quick glance at the wall clock averts panic: only 11:27, so I haven't missed my meeting with Dr. Weston. The glare outside is terrific. Reflection off the adjacent building's windows? I'll look in a moment. Feet on the floor, I stretch for several minutes to get my body back in working order. Unused to sleeping so soundly. No nightmares, no waking fits—practically a miracle.

The stand surrounding the sink holds toilet and medicinal sundries, among these Sears, Roebuck & Co.'s Mexican Headache Cure; this in particular, I appreciate. A folded paper stuck halfway beneath the door turns out to be a statement from the hotel's laundry service; $2.50 has been added to my bill for the cleaning of my garments.

I open the door. My boots, cleaned and shined, and a paper-wrapped parcel lie outside. Inside it, my shirt, trousers, underclothes, and heavy winter coat, have all been cleaned, pressed, and mended. Fine work, too. Even that big rip in the coat's elbow: nearly as good as new.

Glad to have it back because looking outside, I see the storm must've picked up again and dropped nearly a foot of snow on the city. Maybe more in store later, since the sky is hazy.

A radiator comes on and warm air gusts around my feet. Honestly, given my circumstances these past few years, I have to pinch myself to be sure this is all real. Is this how rich people live? Beats the hell out of a filthy boardinghouse with a leaky roof. I throw all my money on the bed and count it. Minus hotel charges, I still have more than a hundred and fifteen dollars. Clearly, I'm not wealthy but it's enough to keep me in tall clover for another week, at least. Goldfield is starting to grow on me.

∾

After a quick breakfast downstairs, I stand at the desk behind an army captain. His boots are even shinier than mine, although it's clear he isn't enjoying his stay here like I am.

"When?" he asks the clerk. "*When* will it be fixed?"

"Sorry for the inconvenience. Telephone company says the problem occurred somewhere near Tonopah. Seems a motor truck left the main road and hit a pole, which snapped the supported lines. I imagine they're making repairs as we speak."

"Well, what's taking so damned long?"

Different clerk behind the desk. Younger. Less polished.

"It's Christmas Day. I'll bet they're doing everything—"

"It's been three hours already!"

"I'll send a message to the colonel's suite once the phones are working again."

The captain rests his hands on the desk's edge and shakes his head. "Think I can't pick up a handset and learn as much, myself? Look, one of our officers is gravely ill and we need to coordinate his *immediate* evacuation."

"Sorry to hear it, sir—"

"Then *do* something," the captain says, turning and stalking past me toward the stairs.

"Sorry, I'm new here," the clerk says but the captain merely throws a backhanded wave and continues walking.

The clerk side-eyes the officer before turning to me and nodding. "Morning. What can I do for you?"

Suppressing a jibe about officers' high-strung ways, I stick to business, "Like to extend my stay."

"Excellent, Mr…"

"Foster."

"Carson Foster, right." He pauses only for a moment but it feels funny. Like he's studying me, trying to commit my features to memory. "What room, again?"

He works here; shouldn't he know? "Three-oh-five. Hasn't been reserved, has it?"

"305—no, it hasn't. How many days?"

"Three for now," I lie. "Depending on business, maybe longer."

"Excellent. Got it." He writes "my" name on a piece of paper but not in the ledger.

I remember Al Hart saying he keeps an office in the Rhyolite Block so I ask for directions.

The clerk points with his hands as he speaks, "Out the door, west two blocks to Second Street, then south to Ramsey. Three-story building on the southwest corner. You headed there soon?"

"Yeah, I…" Hold on, I'm not giving this dupe my itinerary. "Yes, soon."

A grandfather clock by the fireplace chimes once for 12:30; time to start for Dr. Weston's office at the hospital. Goldfield and I were getting along awfully well, but all on his own, this clerk has soured me on the place. Crossing the lobby, I catch his reflection in a mirror. He's holding a telephone earpiece in one hand but keeping the hook depressed with the other, like he's waiting for me to leave before placing his call.

So much for laying low. Someone knows I'm here, whether it's Curt's spotters or the WFM's. I *did* ask Dr. Weston to notify the union that Jordan was in the hospital—chalk that up to fatigue-induced carelessness.

I can feel the clerk's eyes on my back as I step outside, and while I can't see him through reflections in the window, I'm sure he's watching as I turn left toward Third Street. I stand my collar and fall in with a crowd moving west through muddy snow. Now every gaze I meet is that of an adversary, every glance hostile.

Cornish miners brought a superstition about tommyknockers—little imps said to inhabit the mines—here when they emigrated. Beyond stealing tools and other mischief, they believe these creatures also try to warn humans when danger's nearby, provided they'll listen. Tapping on pipes, sudden gushes of water, and so on. Plenty of stiffs will tell you when the ground *stops* making noise, *that's* when you know something's about to happen—all that rock is gathering itself to move. Tradition shapes so much of what goes on underground that these beliefs persist, even among men without a drop of Cornish blood in their veins. And while I scoff at the idea of watchful gnomes, I respect the wisdom in listening to the noises around us. For too long, I ignored things I was hearing in Delamar. Loud, clear signals—ignored 'em until it was too late. Better not do it again.

At the corner of Second and Miners, I realize I'm walking the exact wrong direction for my appointment at the hospital. Only one minute lost and it's no great shakes re-crossing Miners, but this slip-up rattles me. Feels like everyone's got eyes on me. Taking note of my face, my clothes, my gait. Can't imagine I stand out here—Goldfield's too large for that—but who knows what months of labor strife and military occupation have done to the place? Maybe newcomers are suspect until a local vouches for them; that's how it is over in Lincoln County.

I pull on my collar and walk faster, partly to get off this street and partly to keep pace with traffic. The sidewalks are crowded and everyone's hustling. If it weren't for frequent shouts of "Merry Christmas," I'd swear it was just another workday. You can tell who's in a union because they append these greetings with "brother," and even the army troops appear to be in good spirits, nodding and chatting with passersby.

While I don't believe in tommyknockers, I'm told miners heading into a mountain above Potosi, Bolivia, leave booze and other offerings for statues of the Devil. This makes sense to me, since I can't imagine God spends much time down in the stopes. Mines are darker and dirtier than whatever's in your imagination and I hate going underground more than nearly anything. Now, not even gold could tempt me into the cages. Don't know why this occurs to me except that Gold Avenue angles northeast, directly toward the Mohawk Mine: the richest of many rich properties here in Goldfield. Two years ago last July, miners working the Hayes-Monnette Lease broke into a subterranean chamber literally lined with gold. From a claim with a surface expression of just 373 by 250 feet, the Hayes-Monnette partnership extracted nearly $5,000,000. One 50-ton shipment alone netted over $500,000. Think about it: all that wealth underfoot, with no sign above. What a colossal stroke of luck.

Less than a mile away, I see the Mohawk's headframe and sheave wheel, stilled for Christmas, and marvel at the wealth this one little plot created. For a long time, I've told myself I don't envy my former boss's money, though perhaps I do. Not for the reason he loves it; not because I could bend others to my will but because for once, I could outrun everything that's after me. Money gives a fellow wings and so help me God, if that claim above Basin Creek proves up, I will vanish from sight faster than frost before the rising sun.

THIRTY-EIGHT

Jordan looks peaceful. The mechanical lung keeps whirring and hissing and the boy is still alive—all fine things, though I don't like that he hasn't stirred even once since we arrived.

"He's resting," the nurse says, shooing me off the ward. "Leaving him alone is the best thing you can do."

Seeing me standing over Jordan, a man at the far end of the ward turns and leaves. I leave, too.

Dr. Weston is in his office, writing notes and slipping them inside stacks of paper folders. Behind him is a roll-top desk, its compartments crammed with medical books and papers. He seems improbably alert for a man who's been working nonstop for at least fifteen hours.

I knock and he glances at his watch. "Mr. Foster. Found your way in, did you?"

A cloud crawls across the sun, throwing the office into gloom. Weston pulls the chain on his desk lamp.

"Stopped in to see Jordan. Nurse said he hasn't budged."

"Close the door, won't you?"

Uh, oh.

Weston lowers the window blinds halfway before taking off his glasses and polishing them on his shirtsleeve. "Jordan's condition is stable," he continues, "although his surgery has been postponed until sometime early tomorrow. Hopefully, the perforation of his lung is small and easily repaired. Fever's down and his pulse and breathing are regular. I even turned off the respirator for a half-hour this morning and detected minimal impairment. All things considered, he's doing well."

I glance beneath the partially-drawn blinds, straining to see through my reflection. Across the street, an icicle beneath a gutter on the Red Front Mercantile has reached gargantuan proportions. Bundled against the cold, two little boys are attacking it with sticks.

"You aren't worried he hasn't stirred?"

The doctor resettles his glasses on his nose. "If he hasn't roused by six this evening, we'll have cause for concern, but not yet. The boy's taken a terrific beating."

"That's what worries me."

Weston turns and follows my gaze out the window.

"Pardon my curiosity but what were you doing in the Black Belt?" His voice has a funny shake to it, like a schoolboy on his first trip to the principal's office. "You're lucky to have made it here."

"Got that right. We were in Basin Creek, checking out the boom, when Jordan accidentally shot himself."

The doctor purses his lips but doesn't speak, so I continue.

"Dr. Robinson said the situation was crucial so I didn't see any option except to push ahead."

"It's well you did."

"He said your mechanical lung here was just the ticket."

"Well, we *are* the most up-to-date facility between San Francisco and Denver," Weston says, puffing his chest so the fabric of his vest strains against the buttons.

Noise filters up from the street. Some commotion down south siphons off most of a crowd outside the Pearl Restaurant. One man shouts, beckoning for others to follow him.

"Mr. Foster…" Weston clears his throat and turns his chair to face me. "I hate to go back on my offer but I don't think I can help you now. You seem like a decent fellow—"

"Don't recall any offer, doctor."

"Finding you a job?"

"Oh, yeah. I figured you were just being polite."

Weston glances back through the window before taking off his glasses and rubbing his face with his palm. "Yes, well, it isn't that I have anything against you, personally."

"Is it the bill? I can cover some of it now—"

Hearing footsteps in the hallway, he looks over my shoulder.

I hate sitting with my back to a door. Don't want to appear skittish but Dr. Weston's framed diplomas reflect a shadow in the hallway. I push my chair back, turn quickly toward the door, and reach inside my coat. Through frosted glass, the shadow wavers, its hand poised as though whoever's there is deciding whether to knock.

"In a meeting," Weston says. "Come back in a bit."

The shadow departs.

"That was Miss Atchison," he says, looking at me in a way that confirms he no longer thinks I'm a decent fellow.

No point stringing this out. "I can't pay for all of Jordan's treatment. Not yet, anyway."

"The WFM will cover it."

"Is that right?"

Weston pushes back his chair. Doesn't reach for his telephone or reach inside his desk but I can tell he's had as much of this meeting as he can take.

"No matter what you heard," I say, "I'm not here to cause trouble."

"Well, you have." Weston adjusts his glasses. "I'm leaving soon to celebrate Christmas with my family and I want no part of this."

"Part of what?"

"Whatever brought you here."

"Jordan. Jordan brought me here. I have no problem with Goldfield's unions, or didn't think so until now."

"Well, they're convinced George Wingfield and Jack Davis brought you here to stir up trouble."

"Really?" I laugh at this; can't help it.

Once a triggerman for Governor Sparks, these days "Diamondfield Jack" Davis is a bit of a bad joke. He styles himself as George Wingfield's chief enforcer but my buddies who work for the Goldfield Mine Owners' Association say he's a blowhard who shows up armed to the teeth only once the dust settles. Nips at the union's heels in view of the press, yet he's never around for any real work. And if anything, union-types think even less of him because last year, he perjured himself during the Preston-Smith trial. Davis' lies helped the DA cast a self-defense shooting as premeditated murder, sending two union delegates to the state pen for life. Hearing that the WFM thinks I'm in Goldfield on his behalf would be hilarious except it's given them cause to run me down.

Outside, a momentary break in the clouds lets in a little sunshine before the darkness returns. I'm looking at Dr. Weston; he's looking out the window again. Should I try to explain? Explain how everything he's heard is wrong? If I had it in for the union, why would I risk my life to bring one of its members here? Wouldn't I have abandoned him somewhere in the Black Belt? Not bothered with Goldfield in the first place? None of this matters, though; Weston's only a bystander.

The doctor stands and gestures toward the door, pre-empting any protest. "Please take your business outside this hospital." His voice trembles, "Already, I've said too much and I'm sure I can't help you."

As if anyone could.

"Take care of Jordan, okay?"

I leave his office without looking back, but despite the risk, I *do* stop by to see the kid. Probably for my sake rather than his, given that he's still unconscious and confined to a mechanical lung. Looks better now: the color's returning to his face. I lean over to whisper my situation and tell him the Goldfield local will cover his tab. Can't tell whether he hears any of this but even so, I'm glad I came to say goodbye. Don't want to but I'd better. Before I leave, I tousle his hair.

"So long, partner. Full recovery, hear?"

I leave through the back door.

∿

Down on Oak, men are streaming south toward Miners Avenue, individually and in groups of four and five. Most wear union pins backed by little sprigs of juniper or holly so I keep my turned and stand aside to let them pass. Per Dr. Weston, any of these fellows could be looking for me. Soldiers, too, although there aren't as many of them. They keep to the street, acting as a fence to keep this boisterous tide moving south. A few exchange words with the miners; others maintain a wary silence. Their bayonets are no longer covered.

Can't go back to the Casey. I duck into the nearest store, Maglio's Esmerelda Mercantile, mostly to escape the herd but also to stock up on ammunition. The mood outside suggests I'm gonna need more than I have.

"Merry Christmas," the counterman says, "I'm closing in five minutes."

I tell him I'll be done in four. The sporting goods section is small, no more than ten feet of shelving plus a locked gun cabinet. Boxing gloves and baseballs. Fishing gear—odd, given how dry the country is here—and bicyclists' gadgets, too, plus one whole shelf of boxed ammunition. A 50-count, two-and-a-half-pound box of .45 shells costs two dollars. Jesus, these boomtown scalpers, but what choice do I have? I grab a box, a ninety-cent Texas shoulder holster, and some crackers and other packaged food on my way to the front.

Reaching the counter, I gesture at the surging crowd outside. "Any idea?"

Old fellow glances through the window and shakes his head. "Bums. Hooligans meaning to lynch someone. A killer working for the owners, I hear. Funny thing, just this morning the Businessman's Association printed a bulletin warning that union saboteurs had slipped into town."

"Terrible."

"Nothing shocks me anymore." He eyes my pile of goods. "The army wants to be notified whenever anyone buys powder or blasting caps. Everyone's on edge, I tell you. These strikes are gonna be the death of this camp and all because those animals out there want a free hand to highgrade."

He isn't even looking at me; his attention is focused through the window. Safe guess he doesn't care for unions but I choose my words carefully. The surest way to earn a fat lip is to come down too strongly in front of the wrong audience.

"Army has things in hand, don't they?"

"The army," he spits, "should round up and execute every last socialist in Esmeralda County."

"You don't say?"

"They struck twice in '06 and *five times* this year. We lose our electricity at least once a week because the WFM organized workers at the power company's Bishop Creek plant and construction there stopped. Maybe with their commissar, Vincent St. John, out of the picture, the union's wobbly element will knuckle under, but who knows? Run one out of town and another arrives to take his place."

I remember thinking the same thing back in Delamar. "Never ends, right?"

"Oh, it's gonna. St. John was shot by one of his comrades last month and now that he's gone, they're starting to crack."

I study his profile while he counts my money. Plain features. Tufted gray hair and gold-rimmed spectacles. Placards declaring Mr. E.G. Maglio's membership in the Businessman's Association and Goldfield Citizens' Alliance hang on the wall behind the cash register but nothing from any other conservative fraternal organization that might explain such a dim view of his fellow residents.

"Picketed my store last spring," he continues. "I wanted the roof rebuilt and some Wobbly delegate storms in and tells me I can't hire the carpenter *I* want because *he* wouldn't join St. John's Big Union. Damned if I'll knuckle under, though—can't tell *me* who to hire. Picketed for a month before they decided there were bigger stakes elsewhere. Mark my word, George Wingfield's gonna show these thugs where to go, and God bless him, too. Soon as President Roosevelt recalls the army, Wingfield and Senator Nixon will bring in the Nevada State Police, deputize a thousand toughs, and the era of mob law in Goldfield will end."

Pretty sure he misses the irony in that last statement. "Do any miners shop here?"

"Sure do." He points to a shotgun on the back counter. "That's why I keep it loaded. Anyone comes in looking for trouble, they know I'll use it."

He counts my change, hands me a paper sack containing my goods, and wishes me a Merry Christmas. As I step outside, he locks the door behind me, turns a sign from OPEN to CLOSED, and I realize how just weeks ago, I worked for a fellow who'd agree with everything I just heard.

Outside, I turn left, away from downtown. At the corner I ask an old man sporting a GAR pin if he knows where to find the Casey Hotel's garage. He points west toward the corner of Third and Hall, more or less the direction I don't want to go.

Even more men are running now, surging around me like whitewater. I keep my hat low and my collar up. Glancing south along Second, I see a huge crowd coalescing a couple blocks south. Trying to recall a framed map of Goldfield in my room at the Casey, I figure it must be the Rhyolite Block they've surrounded: A.L. Hart's office. Time to make myself scarce and not a moment to spare.

THIRTY-NINE

Inside the garage—a large wooden building originally constructed as a theater—two mahouts slouch before a woodstove, their feet propped up on empty crates.

"Merry Christmas," one in a blue pea coat says, rising to his feet. "What can I do for you, mister?"

"Need my car." I hand him a ticket the desk clerk gave me when I checked in.

Pea Coat takes the ticket and checks it against a ledger laid out on a folding desk. He takes a long time with his finger beside my name.

"Sure you don't want to wait at the Casey, Mr. Foster? More comfortable there and we'll bring it to you."

"No, thanks."

"Alright." He motions for the other man to go get my car. "Lonnie, stall twenty," he shouts and the fellow waves to show he heard.

I stand near the door, blowing into my cupped hands. Men are still running south, converging on Second Street. My bag—more accurately, the bag of clothes I picked up in Silver King—is still in my room but isn't worth the risk to retrieve it. My bill's unpaid but I plan to rectify that here in the garage. Can't leave Goldfield fast enough to suit me.

Not sure what makes me turn—a sound of a shadow, perhaps—but as I do, Pea Coat is mid-punch. Can't deflect it entirely but I duck and turn just enough that his fist grazes my crown instead of connecting with my jaw. Planting my right foot, I pivot and catch him under his chin with an open palm. Lifting hard, I drive his head back so he can't settle his feet. Clawing at my arm, he tries to shake loose but I keep pressing, driving him backward until he stumbles and falls. His head smashes against an auto's headlamp and he's out. His hat rolls to the center of the driveway and stops.

Fifty feet away, the second mahout steers the Iroquois down a ramp, sees me standing over his bloodied comrade, and slams on the brakes. The car skids on the icy dirt, clips a Ford Model S, and chugs to a stop. Its left-front wheel crushes the unconscious man's hat.

I draw the Colt. "Hands up, *now!*"

Advancing at an angle, I circle the hood and motion for him to climb down.

"Mister, don't shoot," he pleads, hands still raised but frozen in his seat.

"He attacked me, not the other way around. Get out of my car."

I back away and motion again with the Colt, mindful of the wide-open garage door. This would be a particularly bad moment for the 22nd Infantry to amble past. Thankfully, the mahout slides meekly from the seat and steps away from my auto.

"Inside that landau. Back seat, lie down on the floor. If I see you outside before fifteen minutes are up, I'm gonna shoot you dead, understand?" Pretty sure I'm lying now. I don't *want* to shoot anyone in Goldfield but I'd rather he didn't know it. "Say you understand."

"I…I understand," he says, voice trembling.

"Here." I toss a $10 certificate and $5 bank note onto the ground. "Covers my bill for Room 305." Don't care how odd this seems; I won't be known as a welsher.

Meek fellow won't look me in the eye.

"Three-oh-five. Turn that money in at the front desk, hear?"

He still won't look at me. I'm pretty sure he's pissed himself. Without another word, he clambers inside the other car and closes the door.

Keeping my head on the swivel, I crank the starter, stow the shaft, and clamber inside the Iroquois. Releasing the hand-brake, it rolls past Pea Coat's prone form and when I pause to wipe what I presume is sweat from my face, my hand comes away red. Feeling along my hairline, I discover a scratch about two inches long. Son of a bitch must've clipped me with his ring. For a moment I'm tempted to stop and back the car over his legs but since we both have problems enough, I ease the auto onto Third. Weaving between a handful of preoccupied men, I steer west toward the LV&T railyard.

Beyond town limits, I slow to a crawl approaching another army checkpoint on the Tonopah road but once I reach the barrier, a bored-looking troop waves me through. Glad I'm not southbound; wagons and autos awaiting inspection are backed up for a half-mile.

Some Christmas this is.

Ten minutes after leaving the garage, I pull abreast of Goldfield Consolidated's gigantic new mill, still under construction on the western flank of Columbia Mountain. Glancing over my shoulder, the road behind me is empty. Icy and snow-packed, too, and while I'm not moving as fast as I'd like, I doubt whether anyone following me will manage any better. All the same, I should assume that by now the phone lines between the two cities have been repaired and therefore news of my arrival will reach Tonopah before I do. Hate to say it but this means I'll need to abandon the Iroquois somewhere along the way. Splendid thing saved us on the crossing from Basin Creek but it's also brought unwanted attention, something I can no longer afford.

A few miles later, I decide going afoot might not be so bad. This road's like a washboard, even worse than some of the isolated stretches Jordan and I followed across the Black Belt. Serpentine, too. These curves are a feature of auto roads everywhere across the desert; every time a driver swerves even a little, the ruts deviate from true. After months of this, even the straightest roads are remade as a series of broad S-curves. Only happens to roads built expressly for automobiles, go figure. There are other, straighter tracks bracketing this one, but since these carry everything from two to twenty-horse loads plus the occasional tractor-train in from Gold Reef, I won't take one for fear of getting jammed.

Near Ramsey Well, the road reaches the lowest point in a broad, shallow basin and the snow disappears. Ground's dry but no less corrugated. Low, gray clouds obscure the surrounding hills, making it impossible to tell whether more or less snow has fallen on Tonopah. I've heard this twenty-eight-mile run has been made in as little as thirty-five minutes but my speed today is nowhere near that. Even so, Brougher, Siebert, and the other jagged peaks south of Tonopah appear sooner than I was expecting so I turn west before the city's limit. Here on the basin's northern edge, the road rises and the clouds descend as fog.

A mile farther, I have to stop. Nearly colliding with a trash-wagon in the mist, I pull off the road and park amid a sea of tin cans, broken lumber, and shattered glass. This is Tonopah's dump, possibly the largest in Nevada, and a thoroughly unfit place to leave something so magnificent as the Iroquois. No choice though. If it weren't for this cloud cap, already I could see the town's mines, houses, and railroad depot.

Can't see that trash-wagon now but somewhere behind me, I hear it being emptied into one of the ravines here west of Brougher Mountain. I rummage around for useful things but there aren't many: the two sample-bags of ore, food from the mercantile in Goldfield. One tin of water. Nothing else.

I tie the sample bags' ends together and sling these over my shoulder. Maybe thirty, thirty-five pounds, total, so not too bad. The tin will be heavy in my hands but despite this cold, cloudy weather, I wouldn't go anywhere in Nevada without water. Everything else, including Jordan's rifle and Nick Reed's .38, I leave in the car.

Five minutes on, I see a woman and her two young kids down in a ravine, sorting through the mounds of trash. One child, a girl, maybe six or seven, sees me up on the road and stares.

"Hello," I say, and she responds with "Allo."

Curly, dark hair, she's an adorable thing but dirty and her clothes are shabby. She's collected a small mound of copper scrap on a piece of lagging.

Her mother looks up, sees me, and pulls her children closer.

"Back that way," I say, "I left a green automobile with a rifle in it. A handgun in the glove box, too. Take 'em if you want. They're all yours. The gold pan and pick, too—anything at all. Hell, you can even take the car if you know how to drive it."

The woman says something in reply but I can't understand her. Serbian, maybe, or Hungarian, I don't know. Likely a miner's widow; Tonopah has a silicosis problem, too. Not as bad as Delamar's, but horrifying in its own right.

I smile and repeat the offer, pantomiming driving and holding the rifle. The shivering kids grin broadly but the woman merely stares and I realize it might look as though I'm shooting a car. In any event, she must not understand me; the gulf is too broad to cross. I smile, wave again, and start walking.

"Goodbye," I say and the girl responds with "'Bye."

A hundred feet down the road, I glance behind and see she's standing on the road, watching me go. I wave, she waves back, but a few steps later and she's gone, swallowed by the fog.

Merry Christmas, kid.

⁐

Houses on both sides of the road now. Miners off for the holiday, drinking. Women pulling frozen laundry from the lines between houses. One beating the dust from a rug. Even a few people packing up their households, getting ready to move. I'd heard Tonopah was especially hard-hit by the financial panic last autumn. Here's the proof, perhaps.

Glad I decided to carry the ore-sample bags, as they've dusted my clothes and made me look like some desert rat in from his prospect. In fact, whether due to my appearance or the bitter cold, no one pays me any attention. Even so, I'm sweaty, nervous, and apprehensive. Only two, three-hundred yards from the rail station now, which strictly speaking, I mean to avoid. God knows if Curt's here, the depot is one place his crews will watch like hawks.

This fog is freezing. Thin frost covers everything and icicles dangle from the wires overhead. Two of these lines lead directly toward the Tonopah Extension's hoist house: my cue to turn left, west toward the open desert. The slope here is gentle but with every step, the elevation decreases and before long, I am back below the clouds. Glancing over my shoulder, I can see nothing of Tonopah or the mountains surrounding it; as far as I can see in the other direction, there's nothing but broad, scrubby flats cut by narrow ravines.

I stop to shift the sample bags. Again, they aren't too heavy, but ninety-five percent of their weight lies narrowly across my shoulder. Lunch consists of canned ham, crackers, and water.

About two miles ahead, a Tonopah & Goldfield train comes into view, eastbound on the wye that divides traffic between its branches. A black car follows the service road alongside it, at least until it reaches the trestle over Slime Wash, so named because it's the outlet for Tonopah's silver mills and therefore choked with fine tailings, or "slimes." The car disappears inside this wash before emerging upstream, behind the train and now on its opposite side. Kneeling beside a tall greasewood, I watch this procession until it climbs and disappears within the clouds. Were those Curt's boys or union stooges, following a false lead about me jumping a train outside Goldfield? Whoever they are, I assume they'll stake every crossroads between here and Carson City. Now I'm kicking myself for coming this way. Should've taken the car west into California; gone up to Sweetwater from the south. Still, that's a long, desolate route and the roads are terrible. I'd figured jumping a train in Tonopah would get me home quicker but it might get me killed quicker, too.

☙

Keeping an eye out, I continue downhill, west toward the branch that leads to Hawthorne. Beneath the trestle, I see the black car's tire-tracks. Water's pooled in places along the wash's floor and the slimes here are soupy like quicksand; judging by the S-shaped ruts, the car must've dug in for a moment before pulling free. Good thing for them and me, both, because otherwise I would've had to hide and wait until they dug themselves free.

Guess it's a good thing. Don't know. Tired. Demoralized. Again, I regret the decisions that brought me here. Regret not asking for help. Honestly, I never thought it was an option. For one thing, I was broke. Hadn't received my severance pay; hadn't seen—no, still haven't seen—my veteran's bonus. Guess I figured I could either starve to death waiting for a check or head out and see who was hiring. In hindsight, it might've been best if I'd just stayed put and starved.

Veterans take an awful lot of their pay in lip-service. Other than parades and pro forma gratitude, this country has curiously little use for us. Only skills I learned in the Philippines involved guns and knives, and no one puts out MEN WANTED signs for that—you have to slip through the cracks first to pick up that kind of work. Like Jack Lipford, I should've just taken up theft. If I had, I might already be in Congress.

❦

Four miles on, I reach the railroad's westbound branch, clamber down a tall trestle, and wait. Spend a couple hours shivering with my back against the timbers before they begin to shake. Scrambling up the wash's side, I spot a mixed train coming from the south—no autocar following this one. Fifteen minutes later, I run alongside it, take hold of a grab iron, and pull myself onto the blind.

I ride this way for hours as the train clanks slowly through Millers and Coaldale. A few miles south of Mina, the haze disappears. For the rest of the afternoon, the wind roars and cloud-shadows race across the desert floor as we roll through one dusty supply-center after another. Outside these towns, and even out on the wide-open desert, I see rats like me hopping on and off, each one a potential threat. My hand never strays far from the revolver. So many of us on the bum, though, that before long I figure I'm nearly invisible. Big Curt doesn't have the manpower to stop us all; must be driving him crazy. We are an army of rolling stones.

South of the Nevada & California division yards at Thorne, several of us jump down and scramble into the salt-scrub growing alongside the railbed. I fall in with a group of six and we cross open ground beyond the yards' northern end. We can see a railroad bull with a shotgun stalking the fence-line, though, so we continue across Ryan Wash, around some clapboard houses and a new saloon built to waylay the rail crews' paychecks, and on toward the next trestle.

"Lord Almighty, they're watching like hawks," one man says.

"Like this for days," says another. "Holdup at one the big mines, maybe."

Others mumble in agreement and I nod along so I won't stand out.

Anxious to contribute, the youngest member of our company—a red-headed boy, no older than fourteen—chimes in, "Man in Lunning said the Wabuska yards are crawling with Pinkertons; said they're watching for someone come up from the southern camps."

"Hell," the first man says, pronouncing the word as though it has two syllables: hay-yull.

For a long time no one speaks. Could be there are those among us with reason to believe *they're* the intended target of this dragnet. And maybe there are: this country's a mess right now. We plod along, perspiring despite the cold, squinting to shield our eyes against the glare. Caked with salt, our shoes grow heavy.

I think about what the boy said. I'd planned to ride to Wabuska, continue on foot to Yerington, and then follow the East Walker upstream to our ranch but now I'm not so sure. Glancing at Mount Grant, it's clear the storm last week buried its highest slopes under feet of new snow. That means the stock trail up Cat Creek will be impassable. Farther south, they'll watch the old Bodie Road, since that's the shortest route from Hawthorne. North of Walker Lake, I could try to swim the river and follow Reed Canyon through the range, but the marshes there can be treacherous and the river runs cold and fast. Lots of bodies—mostly corned-up Indians, I'm sorry to say—are fished out of Walker Lake and damned if that's how I'm gonna die. Christ, home is about twenty-five miles west of where I'm standing but it's starting to feel as if I'm trying to reach the far side of the moon.

"Any work up north?" I say, trying to get a sense of where the others are headed. "What's doing at Olinghouse?"

"Don't bother," someone says. "Crooked management."

"Dixie?"

"Dixie busted months ago. Copper boom throughout the range west of Yerington, though."

"Shoot, yes, there is," a tall, lanky man says. "Hiring anyone with two feet. That's why me and Bill here left Goldfield. Manager at the January Mine wanted to pay us in scrip and we said 'hell, no.' Like we ain't got options." This fellow and his friend both look to be about 20, and both are exceedingly thin.

"That's right," Bill says. "Won't take conversation money just so Wingfield and Nixon can defend their bank."

"The hell with money-men."

"Straight to hell."

Judging from his accent, the tall fellow's from somewhere down South—his friend, Bill, too—though damned if I can tell a Texan's accent from a Carolinian's.

The others all begin a rambling conversation about the depressed economy, the President's trust-busting efforts, and how a railroad strike has left hundreds in places like Goldfield and Tonopah on the brink of starvation. Me, I hear what they're saying and speak up just often enough to fit in but to be perfectly honest, I'm preoccupied with my own plans. Have to avoid Yerington now and make a wide swing around the western side of Smith Valley. Adds thirty crow-miles to my journey, but I don't imagine Curt's boys will think to watch the roads from that direction. Hell, I don't know what I'm doing; I'm making this up as I go.

FORTY

North of Thorne, we scale an embankment and swarm aboard a northbound. A boxcar's door is open which makes getting inside a cinch but also leaves us visible should an overzealous bull decide to walk the tops. Although the car's already occupied, the woman and two men inside it are so glad we aren't security that they're happy to share what little they have.

"Coffee?" one offers and I accept, although it's cold.

"Bread and hard cheese if you want any," says another, holding what looks like dried-up turnips. Hungry and not wanting to seem ungrateful, I lob these delicacies into my mouth and, in case I need to spit them out, mash them against my teeth with my tongue. Not half-bad, though, especially after a slug of whiskey from a flask tendered by one of the Southern boys. Under the circumstances, it's a feast.

Dark now and the next forty miles slip past in peace. No towns and no stopping at the far-flung sidings. Everyone except the original Boxcar Trio and our ginger-headed mascot plans to step down at Wabuska so I take the opportunity to close my eyes. The booze and the car's gentle swaying puts me down and keeps me there for more than two hours. Next thing I know, Southern Bill's elbowing me awake in darkness.

"Crossed the river," he says. "Next station ain't but a little ways off."

Underscoring his words, the train's whistle sounds, signaling that we're two miles out from the next station. Through the door, I see starlit farm fields crisscrossed with ditches and canals. This is the Mason Valley's northern end, a relatively well-watered part of the state, and in summertime these fields will ripen with hay and clover, fed by snowmelt from the High Sierra. Orchards and beehives, too, but here at year's end, everything is pale, cold, and dormant. Can't see much in the dark, of course, but I know the area well enough to picture sunnier days. I also know that currently the Southern Pacific is re-gauging its lines through here, and therefore all trains must stop and transload their cargoes onto standard-gauge equipment for the last leg into Carson City and Reno. Bigger locomotives, bigger cars, heavier loads; we've reached civilization's edge.

"Best we jump now," I say. "This stretch runs uphill from the river, but we'll pick up speed again in the last mile before the station."

Everyone agrees, though it means a longer walk into town. The train is crawling now so the leap down is hardly more difficult than stepping off a porch.

"Y'all headed north?" Southern Bill says, adjusting his cap.

"Yes, we are," says the woman. Her name is Eloise, I believe. "And you boys?"

"West, ma'am," the lanky Southerner says. "South and west to the copper mines."

"I have a cousin in Reno," the kid volunteers.

"What about you, Foster?" Southern Bill looks my way.

"Sister lives in Markleeville, California," I lie. "So long as you don't mind, figure I'll tag along with you for a ways."

Fumbling in the darkness, we circulate and shake hands, wishing each other safe journeys. Can't say why, other than I imagine it must be hard going alone in the world at such a young age but when the kid shakes my hand, I palm off a five-dollar gold piece and tell him to stay wary. The kid's a pro and makes no fuss or show that anything unusual has taken place. There's someone who's gonna turn out okay.

Reaching a crossroads, six of us turn south while the others start north. Behind us, another whistle signals that the train is one mile from the station. Bill passes around a plug of tobacco but I decline. We stumble westward in the dark, dead-reckoning our way across fields from one landmark to the next. Sometimes, it's the bare, white branches of a giant cottonwood; other times, it's a lamp shining through a farmhouse window. Dogs bark and snarl as we pass, while horses, curious to see what's stirring in the night, stand close against the fences and watch.

"Hey, Bill," I ask, "where'd you say you're headed?"

Bill glances at his tall, lanky friend. "Ray, where are they hiring, exactly?"

"Camps throughout those hills," Raymond says, waving his hand toward a stubby range visible only in silhouette against the lowest stars. "Hear tell Morningstar's the sun and moon just now, and Buckskin's kicking, too. Hottest over on the western side."

"East side, they're hiring at the Bluestone," another man offers. "That's where Kearney and me are headed."

We've come to a north-south road, the main track on this side of valley and a branch of the old California Trail. Traffic here is heavier; two wagons rumble past, followed quickly by a third. Lanterns hung from the drivers' benches sway in time with the mules' hoofbeats.

In the mid-distance, Yerington's lights shine and beyond these, confined within a rising canyon, the lights of Mason—another ranching and mining center below the Bluestone Mine.

"Boys," Kearney says, "there's our destination. Better days through Socialism." He produces a small flask of whiskey from his bindle-pack and we all take a drink. Then he and his partner shake our hands and set off in the darkness, talking and laughing.

Our group trudges west, footsore and shivering, until Raymond, Southern Bill, a dark-haired fellow named Gillis, and me all agree that we're tired and cold and ought to find somewhere to settle for the night. Passing a ranch house without lights or barking dogs, Southern Bill spots a haystack, so we burrow into it like mice. I dig a skylight above my face just large enough to breathe through. Luckily, nettle rash doesn't afflict me, though evidently Raymond is susceptible because he sneezes every few minutes until he falls asleep, and afterward snores like a bear. Doesn't matter. Soon enough, my eyes grow heavy and I, too, fall headlong into sleep.

❦

I wake to the sounds of an idling autocar and murmured conversation. My pulse surges, jolting me to alertness. Without a watch, I can only guess it's around six in the morning. Light enough to see, although the sun has yet to crack the horizon. Careful to keep the hay from shifting, I grope for my revolver. The grip is cold, almost painful to the touch, though I'm glad it's there. That Colt is the axis on which my confidence turns.

Peering out from my burrow, I see a man in a brown duster standing beside a black Ford Model N, talking across a barbed-wire fence with Southern Bill.

Bill points south toward Yerington, where woodsmoke rises above a canopy of leafless elms. While I can't hear what they're saying, neither man seems agitated. Indeed, the fellow beside the car nods amiably and tucks his hands deep inside his coat pockets. A minute later he climbs back inside his automobile, turns the wheel, and drives east while Bill ambles slowly back toward our camp.

Raymond speaks before I can, "The hell was he, Billy?"

"Quiet," Bill growls, continuing his slow shuffle toward the haystack's far side. "Not yet."

None of us inside the stack dares to move or speak. I stare through my skylight in the hay but now instead of stars, I see hundreds of tiny salt-and-pepper clouds. I hear Bill puttering around, trying to revive our fire, and the clank of a tin coffee pot. A wisp of smoke curls across the sky. Otherwise, the seconds tick by in silence. No matter. Even if I knew what that stranger at the fence told Bill, all I can do is guess what my new companions will do with the information. I'll know soon enough. The sun casts its first rays across the valley floor, turning the dead fields red and burnishing the mottled sky and the vapor rising from the fields. Frost on the grass shines like rubies. Disturbed as a piece, hundreds of little birds rise from the trees and turn directly toward the water, passing over us in a tittering, pinwheeling cloud. They vanish within the sun's searing light, a vision of life and vitality unmade by fire.

Bill coughs once and clears his throat. "Y'all can come out now."

We must look like ants burrowing their way out of a hill, emerging as we do. Takes a long while to brush the hay from our clothes and hair.

The field where we've camped is small, no more than two poorly-cleared acres. A few sections of fence are still standing but the rest has either fallen or been engulfed by sagebrush returning to its former range. To the east, the ranch house's roof has nearly collapsed. Red sun, red shadows. The hills to the west are red, too, and there isn't a single tree growing upon them—only rocks, sage, and dried grass. This is no-man's land.

Southern Bill stares without hostility, but neither does he look away when I stare back. Raymond sneezes. Realizing I've been holding my breath, I exhale heavily and the cloud lingers around my head.

Raymond notices his friend's posture and takes a half-step away from me. "What is it, Bill?" he says so quietly I almost miss it.

"Nothing," Bill says, shifting his gaze between Raymond and me. He crouches over the fire, takes a short branch, and stirs the paltry coals. "It's nothing. Hey, Gillis, you care to fetch more limbs for the fire? Deadfall under that cottonwood yonder. Nothing too big, though. Ain't much needs cooking."

Gillis strikes me as a shabby, simple fellow; he hasn't said more than a dozen words since Hawthorne. He nods and sets off across the field.

Raymond keeps glancing between me and Southern Bill and it's making me edgy. Don't like being out in the open like this. Bill turns to look south, which is, I believe, the direction in which that stranger and his Model N disappeared. Don't know who might be watching us; don't know what to do. A good twenty feet lies between me and the Southern boys—absolutely, I can squeeze off three or four rounds if they try to rush me. With my arms folded across my chest and my right hand inside my jacket, my fingers slide along the revolver's grip.

"Bill?" Raymond says, sounding confused.

Southern Bill rubs his stubbled chin. "Ray, ever walk away from two-hundred dollars?"

Raymond looks alarmed. "How do you mean?"

Bill glances between the two of us. "Pard, that fellow at the fence was a Pinkerton. Asked if I seen a man he figured might've gone through Wabuska; said the fellow was using the name 'Carson Foster.'"

"Lord Jesus," Raymond whispers. Turning to stare at me, he sneezes again.

"Said there's a two-hundred-dollar reward for information leading to Foster's arrest."

I clear my throat. "You plan to collect that reward, Bill?"

"I…" Bill falters, his shoulders slumping. "I told him I knew where Foster was."

I yank the revolver from its holster. Raymond winces and turns away. Bill stays rooted but inhales so sharply that his back arches.

"Lord, don't shoot," he says. "Hear me out, pard, hear me out."

"Raymond, don't move. Bill, talk." I glance around but can't find Gillis.

"Told him I come down from Fallon. Said I met a man last night who *might've* been you, headed south along the river with others. Said I was out here on my own—see for yourself, pard."

Glancing left, I see he's right; the Pinkerton and his car have long since melted into the haze.

"Why didn't you turn me in?" Two-hundred dollars is no small sum to men like him.

"Don't care for the Pinkerton's blood-money," Bill says and spits. "We're workingmen, Ray and me."

"Gospel," Raymond says although he's a little hard to hear. "Company men toil for the Devil, himself."

Goddamn, ain't that a fact?

"Hell, any man at odds with Pinkertons and Thiels is okay by me," Bill adds. "An injury to one…"

"Is an injury to all," I say, which is Wobbly claptrap for "we're all in this together." I lower the revolver. "He say why he'd look out here?"

"Caught a kid in the railyards at Wabuska who said he'd seen you. Meant that ginger-headed boy who rode with us yesterday, I reckon."

Yeah, I reckon, too. Wish I had my five dollars back.

Bill shakes his head. "Seen trouble, myself, brother. Highgrading, mostly, but I was near beat to death for it and run out of Montana. That's why I come down here."

"Yessir," Raymond says, glancing cautiously over his shoulder. "Company men in Silver City, Idaho, broke four of my ribs." He sneezes twice.

"Yeah, I heard they'll do that," I say. "Either of you furbished?"

"Knives," Bill says. "Can't afford no gun."

I return the revolver to its holster. "Sorry, boys, honest," I say. "You can put your hands down."

"These times make fellowship difficult," Bill says, stretching his neck and massaging his left shoulder. "No hard feelings."

Raymond glances at Bill, who nods in a way that seems to let him know the crisis has passed. More than once, I remember exchanging similar looks with Charlie Witherill back in Delamar so I think I understand how these two work. I may have poisoned the well but since we'll part company soon, I hope it won't really matter.

Raymond scratches his ear. "What did you do, Foster?"

"I stole from a thief."

He looks as though he's dying to ask more questions but doesn't.

Bill crouches beside the fire and holds his hands near the boiling coffeepot, trying to warm them. "Fine start to the day."

Feeling sheepish, I nod. "Soon as Gillis returns, let's have our coffee and clear out."

"Well, he's back," Raymond says but his voice sounds funny.

I glance at Bill, who stands and raises his hands again. He's staring past me toward the haystack. Turning, I see Gillis with a black pistol braced across his left forearm. Damn it all, doesn't this figure? I raise my hands, keeping my elbows tight against my body. There's no sense in going for my revolver: he's got the drop on me.

"I know who you are so don't move," he says. "I *will* shoot you."

"Traitor, Gillis," Bill snarls. "This ain't right."

"You two, back off." Gillis waves his pistol at the Southern boys before drawing a bead on my chest.

Best I can see, it's a .32 Colt Hammerless he's holding. Military issue; an officer's sidearm. Officer or a cop. Gives me a sense what I'm facing. I take a deep breath, pull my raised hands closer to my centerline, and root my feet in the frosted dirt.

"Get that pistol in the Army?"

"Shut up," Gillis says, advancing until he's no more than five feet away.

"This ain't right," Raymond says. He sneezes again and rubs his eyes.

Gillis reaches inside his coat and produces a pair of nickel-plated Bean-Cobb handcuffs—tools of the trade, I've used 'em, myself. Holding the pistol with his right hand, he advances slowly and steadily—he appears to know what he's doing.

"Kneel. Put these on past the third ratchet," he says. "Quick and correct or I'll shoot you in the leg and do it myself, understand?"

Raymond sneezes and spits in the dirt.

"How come you didn't say nothing to that fellow in the car?" Bill asks.

Still looking at me, Gillis scowls. I watch his every move. Angles, distance. Left on right, I tell myself—*left on right*. He's holding his weapon with one hand—that's a mistake.

"I don't share," Gillis spits. He wants to stare me down but with the Southern boys moving around, his eyes dart left and right. "You two, quit moving; this don't concern you."

"Company man, I wouldn't take that reward even—" Bill says, but Gillis cuts him short.

"You ain't heeled so don't be stupid. Go stand over there."

As he's speaking, he watches Bill instead of me so I rotate my torso slightly. My hands are still raised so I doubt I'll look any different once his attention returns. Why hasn't he thrown the cuffs at my feet? Another mistake.

Left on right, *left on right*.

"Mister, we don't want no part—," Raymond says but Gillis interrupts him, too.

"Good," Gillis snarls. "Sunday, quit stalling."

He reaches forward, dangling the cuffs in front of my chest and raises the pistol so it's pointed at my face.

Now, most people are more afraid of guns than knives, but firearms only shoot in one direction. Unless it's a shotgun or Gatling across from you, the danger, while acute, is highly localized. We'll see, anyway. My nerves are humming and I feel like I could catch lightning. My gaze is unfixed, my shoulders loose. I inhale slowly through my nose. Feels like the world's holding still; holding its breath, waiting to see how this ends.

Raymond sneezes violently.

"Goddamnit, Sunday, take the—" Gillis says, but I move before he finishes.

Isn't much of a move—just a quick lean of my head so I'm off the line. Simultaneously, my left hand strikes and closes over the slide as my right strikes the frame, except the first two fingers on my right hand catch in the cuffs. Gillis jerks his left hand toward his body but just like mine, his hand's entangled—for an instant, we are linked. The pistol fires: a thunderclap, like a sledgehammer striking steel, and while I haven't been hit—*cogito ergo sum*—my right eardrum might've burst. Slide's action gashes my hand, too, but that's nothing compared to my ear. Jerking free from the link, my right hand closes tightly around the pistol's grip. Two hands to his one. I lift and push, pressing so that the barrel points away from me. Still inside the well, his right index finger breaks, but not before pressing the trigger again.

The round hits Gillis right below his Adam's apple and he collapses, pulling me down with him. I wrench the gun free and throw it aside. Thrashing in the grass, sputtering horribly, he clutches at his neck. Gripping his knapsack with both hands, I climb on top of him and press it tightly against his face. He claws at my face, my eyes. Tries to reach around the satchel, tries to grasp my hands, but he's losing blood fast and his strength quickly fades. Fifteen seconds later, his hands and feet go slack and he's gone.

I squat on my heels, resting one hand on Gillis's body to maintain my balance. My chest heaves and I feel gingerly around the right side of my face. Spattered blood and flash-burns, too. Nothing mortal, but my eardrum, Christ, it hurts like the devil and I can't hear anything.

Back on my feet, I'm neither elated nor relieved. Exhausted, maybe. Despondent, too, because they'll never stop coming. Never, and I just want this over. Another one. Another stone on my back. Not even sure I care anymore. One more death—mine—and this whole debacle ends. Don't care. Not about me, or Lipford, or even Helen, wherever she is. Whoever she is. Too tired. Too tired to feel anything now, and that might be most worrisome of all. A human can't see as much death as I have and go on thinking there's a Plan, or believe there's a god who cares. I left the garden a long time ago and there's no going back.

"Foster?"

Noises in my head like voices. I stand and take a step backward. Shake my head to clear it. Bad decision: my ear doesn't improve and now I'm dizzy. Gillis is on his back in the haystack's shadow, arms outstretched, his face and head covered by the bloody knapsack. The sun on my face feels good so I take another step backward into the light. My foot bumps against the pistol so I pick it up, wipe my fingerprints, and drop it exactly where I found it. I left the army before they began fingerprinting soldiers in 1905 and not every sheriff has the means to check, but the world's changing quickly and I figure it's better not to take chances.

"Foster, help!"

Is Bill speaking? Turning, I see him kneeling over Raymond, pressing on his friend's neck, and my heart sinks. Guess I do still care.

Raymond's alive, but in shock. The round that missed my head clipped him above his right collar bone. Clean pass through the trapezius: small entry and exit wounds, only, and while it must look bad to Bill—hell, it looks bad to me—I've seen others take theirs the same way and they're still alive.

"He's gonna live," I say, staggering across the clearing. "Didn't hit his throat, didn't hit his face. Looks like he's bleeding out but he isn't; already be dead if he were."

"Bill," Raymond groans, "oh, Jesus, I don't wanna die. I'm sorry. I'm so sorry."

"Pard," I say, resting my hands on Bill's shoulder, "make up your mind to stick around and you *will*, understand?"

Raymond doesn't answer. He leans away from Bill and vomits.

"Bill," I shout, waving toward the fire, "no coffee in that water, is there?"

"Not yet."

With my ear ringing, I can't really hear. "What's that?"

He leans away from me—evidently, I'm shouting at him. "Said no, not yet."

"Okay, then fetch it, will you?"

I take over pressing on Raymond's neck with a cloth so blood-soaked I can only guess at its former use. Undershirt? Washcloth? God only knows but it's keeping Raymond's lifeblood where it belongs. Bill takes his own blanket and wraps it around his friend, who's shaking something awful; the big nerves that run along the neck must've taken a jolt.

I lean close to Raymond's ashen face. "This'll hurt but we have to clean the wound, okay?"

"Okay," he whispers. He says other things, too, but I can't hear what.

Taking the bloody cloth by its corner, Bill douses it with boiling water until it's merely pink. Scalding my hand, I take the steaming cloth, clean both his wounds, and then clamp it tightly over both. Within moments, it turns red again. We rinse it a second time and repeat the process. Raymond writhes and moans but he doesn't shout and doesn't struggle. Not knowing what to think, I ask Bill to find another cloth and he sets off running.

"Raymond, where are you from?"

"Lake…" he whispers, "Lake City, Florida."

I'm positive he said 'Florida' but the rest is a guess. "Headed back someday?"

"Want to."

"Home is home, right?"

"Yessir."

"Family's there?"

"Mother, Father, and my two sisters. We're cotton farmers."

This is good. As he talks, his breathing returns to normal and beneath the bloodstained cloth, his pulse is settles. He still needs a doctor but I'm certain he'll live. At least he isn't sneezing anymore.

Bill returns with a another shirt. It's reasonably clean but we douse it, too, before pressing it against Raymond's wounds. He winces and groans but doesn't speak. For several minutes we sit like this, holding our collective breath, waiting to see how Raymond responds.

I turn to Bill. "Nearest doctor's in Yerington. Let's go."

I'm looking south and Bill's looking north when Raymond speaks, "Not there."

I shrug. "Have to. I know a doctor there, or I did when I was younger. "

Raymond snakes his hand out from under the blanket and grasps his friend's forearm. "Can't. Yerington—company men."

"Swell gesture, Ray," I say, "but we're short on options. Bill, let's get him moving."

"Bill can take me, right?" Raymond says. "We made it this far."

I shake my head. "No, pard. Workingmen stick together."

Bill looks pained but nods. "Brother, I can't carry you by myself. I need his help."

Raymond stares at the sky, still flecked with cloud but quickly growing brighter.

"What about Gillis?" Bill jerks a thumb over his shoulder.

"Leave him," I say. "Far as we know, he's a suicide. Shot Raymond before killing himself." My pants, shirt, and jacket are splashed with blood, though—Gillis's, mine, and Raymond's, too—and no lawman worth his bond would buy that story.

"What about his pistol?"

"Want it?"

"Definitely don't."

"Then leave it where it is. That's trouble you don't need."

I keep the cloth tight to Raymond's neck while Bill ranges around our campsite, quickly collecting our things.

"Ore samples?" he says, hefting the sample bags I took from the Iroquois.

"Yeah, I did some prospecting a few months ago. Never got 'em assayed."

"You'll want to. Heavy rock."

Hope I'll get the chance. We slide our arms under Raymond's and raise him to a seated position. He shakes and needs help staying upright, but he doesn't pass out—that's good.

"Feel okay?"

"Sure."

"Just a few steps, then."

Bill and I lift Raymond to his feet. He's taller than either of us but doesn't weigh much so he shouldn't be too difficult to carry. Shouldn't, except I'm carrying the bags over my shoulder and Bill has to twist in a way that lets him hold that cloth tight against Raymond's neck. Poor Ray can barely keep his head upright.

"Can't cover five miles like this," Bill says.

"Won't need to," I say. "Back on the main road, we'll flag a ride. Hope so, anyway."

∞

We manage only a quarter-mile before we have to stop and lower Raymond to the ground. Between his wooziness, our knapsacks, and the rough terrain, we're in pitiful shape. We set him with his back against a boulder. Bill and I are breathing hard.

Bill brushes dirt from Raymond's face. "How do you feel?"

"Poorly."

"Not much farther," I say. "Bill, want to run ahead and catch someone's attention? I'll give you money for negotiations."

"Keep it," says Bill. Facing east, he looks over my shoulder and exhales. "Someone's already coming."

Turning, I see four, maybe five men on horseback followed by two others driving a wagon. They're shaded by the trees lining the road so I can't tell much about them except that they're definitely headed this way. I step away from my companions. Bill watches Raymond while I shield my eyes against the low sun. These riders fan out on both sides of the narrow lane, which tells me they've spotted us. Nowhere to run, nowhere to hide, and a man in the open is no match for mounted rifles and shotguns.

"What'll we do?" Bill says. He stares at me but damned if I have a good answer.

"Go see what I'm in for, I guess." I shrug and start walking. Must look like a butcher.

Another cloud of birds takes wing, churning like smoke. Swooping low as it crosses the lane, it rises and falls as it passes over the trees. Hundreds fall out over the larger cottonwoods, but others rise to take their places. First east, then north; south, and then west, this frantic host rushes over the riders' heads and moments later, ours. Chirping and fluttering as it goes, it makes one pass over the field and the haystack before circling back to settle across the empty field.

I check my revolver and tuck it into my waistband.

Still coming, the wagon lurches along the rutted track and now I can see the rider's faces. Dark coats, dark hair, broad-brimmed hats pulled down low. Paiute farmers or tribal police, I figure. No surprise. At this end of the valley, everything between Carson Hill and Walker River is part of Yerington Colony. If it weren't for Gillis lying dead by the haystack, the worst thing I'd expect would be a gruff request to leave their reservation. Now I don't know. They aren't moving with any haste, and if they're armed, they're carrying their weapons discretely. Most crucially, they aren't Pinkertons or Big Curt and his wrecking crew.

"What do they want?" Bill shouts.

"For us to leave." I watch them ride, hoping they'll turn but they keep coming, directly toward us.

Glancing at Gillis' body, I wish I'd covered him with hay but it's too late now; the nearest rider is a stone's throw away. The first two continue past me, as does the wagon. The last three rein in and look me over. Backlit by the sun, I can't see their faces.

"You're trespassing," the shortest one says.

"Not looking for trouble—we're only passing through."

"You hurt?" says the fellow in the middle. His voice is familiar.

I tell him no, but my companion is. Then it hits me: "Warren?"

"Hello, Shep."

My old friend dismounts and wades though the sage to reach me. Removes his cowhide gloves and extends a hand, pausing once he sees my condition. "You look worse up close. What happened here?"

"A bounty-hunter fell in with us and tried to cuff me; we wrestled for his gun and that fellow there was hit."

"What bounty-man?"

"Over there." I point toward the haystack, where Gillis' body lies. "Demised."

Their heads turn to look and for long while after confer in low voices. One gestures south, while Warren, looking pained, points east, back across the valley. I study my old friend discretely: Warren's wearing a collarless shirt, overalls, and brown suitcoat. His black hair is cut square with the bottoms of his ears. I know better than to interrupt deliberations but a sense of urgency overcomes me.

"Warren, can you get that fellow to a doctor? He needs help, fast. I can ride along and explain what happened."

Warren glances south. "Can't go to Yerington, pard."

"They set up a cordon?"

"Couple miles south; whole valley's in an uproar. Saw Jerry and Issac in Nordyke yesterday. Had to hustle to keep from being spotted."

"What about Curt?"

"Didn't see him but I'll bet he's around. Can't believe you made it this far."

"Me, either." I glance at Raymond. "I need your help, Warren, please. I'm trying to get back to Sweetwater. I sent something there that might break Lipford's cinch on Lincoln County—keep him from killing me, too—but only if I can get there before he does. Now there's this," I say, gesturing toward my companions.

Warren takes his time answering, glancing back and forth between the boys and me. "Yeah, I'll help. Gonna be careful about it, though. Real careful, understand?"

Not sure how he means this but I say I do.

Raymond and Bill are still seated beside the road. One of Warren's companions inspects Ray's wounds. He says something to Warren in Numu and they speak together for a long time before Warren turns to me.

"Harris thinks your friend will recover. He and Claude are my cousins—they and their friends will bind this man's shoulder and take him to the Taivo doctor in Yerington. You, Russell, and I will cross the Singatse from here and ride toward Sweetwater."

"Long ride—you sure?"

"No other way. River road's no good."

Claude grumbles some but Warren says something that seems to bring him around; that plus the ten-dollar bill I give him. We all agree Gillis should be left as he is. Once Raymond's loaded into the wagon, the groups talk among themselves, occasionally turning to the others for confirmation.

"Bill, you're okay with this?"

He doesn't look happy but he nods. "Whatever Raymond needs."

I slip him my last $10 bill; I have only a couple $20 gold certificates left. "Sheriff asks, you tell him it was me. Don't take fire on my account."

"Brother, we'll think of something. Workingmen stick together."

"Workingmen, right." Of all things, this gives me a pang of guilt, trading on fraternal bonds I haven't earned. "Sorry I got you fellows into this; especially you, Raymond. You'll be okay, hear?"

Warren's brow creases but he doesn't say anything.

Raymond's lying in the wagon bed on a mound of netting. Maybe he doesn't see me, or maybe he can't stand to. Either way, he doesn't answer. Warren's cousins and their two friends wheel around in the field, scattering the birds there. For another minute, we watch them both—riders and birds—head east, past the ranch house. Bill tips his hat and I wave back. Claude, who's loaned me his horse, government coat, and broad-brimmed black hat, might've nodded—hard to tell from this distance—but he sure didn't wave. Can't say I blame him. Don't think his horse likes me, either. Given how I must smell, I can't say I'm surprised.

恓

We follow trails along a sinuous gulch up into the Singatse Hills. Wind bends the spindly cottonwoods growing there and stings our faces with bits of sand. We spot two men high on a ridge prospecting with picks and shovels, but otherwise we are the only souls around.

Rounding a bend I tap my heels and push Claude's horse closer to Warren's.

"Pard, what made you think I'd be out here?"

"Didn't." Warren removes and resettles his hat. "We were heading up to Campbell's to trap jackrabbits. Heard gunshots and rode to investigate. Poachers all over the valley lately. Now Pinkertons and Thiels, too."

"Well, I'm glad it was you."

He nods in a way that suggests he isn't especially glad it was me.

We ride in silence for several minutes, the horses' shoes scuffling over loose rock. A jackrabbit bursts from beneath a clump of sage and races uphill.

Russell says something to Warren in Numu and Warren nods. "Yeah, I know."

I notice Russell's hat has three porcupine quills stuck in the band. He's eating something from a small bag—pine nuts or other seeds, probably—and while I don't usually crave Indian fare, I wish I could ask him for some. All I have is the crackers, though I ought to be grateful I have anything at all.

Warren shoots me a glance. "We go way back, Shep—our families, too—and I'll help you, sure, but things are getting hard around here. Hard to feed our families."

"Miners?"

He nods. "All throughout the Singatse, even on the valley's eastern rim, looking for copper. Disrupting things. Everything, really. Gotta be honest, pard, I don't really want to do this."

"I'm sorry, Warren. Sorry to drag you in."

"Me, too. That dead Taivo means big trouble but since he's on your account..."

His voice trails off but he doesn't need to finish. We both know how things are.

Perversely enough, the way things are is something we're counting on. It isn't right but even here with their reservation close at hand, Indians are practically invisible. White eyes might regard them for a moment but so long as they keep moving, only a few are ever paid much attention. Like tumbleweeds crossing a road: briefly noted and just as quickly forgotten. Keep moving, we figure, and hopefully no one will pay us any mind.

Looking south from atop the range, I see what he means. For miles in that direction, the hills are swarming with activity, every road jammed with traffic headed for the mines. Six months ago, I read in the Delamar *Lode* that geologists think the copper deposits previously discovered on the range's eastern flank continue westward beneath it. Now the boom is on. Towns like Morningstar, Camp Gallagher, and Shamrock—each a frenzied hive of activity—have sprung up overnight and Artesia and the other farm-towns in Smith Valley are exploding right along with them. Land prices have quintupled since last summer and the Indians have been shut out completely.

In the gulches above the camps, trenches have been sunk along all the surface outcrops and every so often, an explosion raises more dust and shakes the air. One group of miners shoos us away from their prospect and calls us racialist names but we just pull our hats lower and ride on. More than once, I'm sure we'll be stopped but it seems that everyone here is too intent on getting their share to pay us any mind. All these miles give Warren and I a chance to talk. Old times and local news, mostly, but the conversation is strained. I still think of him as a friend but I can tell it's getting harder for him to say the same of me. Too many changes, too many wounds, and here I've shown up with another burden. Same thing I should've learned with Joe McCuskey: sometimes, it's better to just cut troublesome friends loose. I'd sure understand if Warren did.

We ride for hours, stopping only once to water the horses. Afternoon now and the cold sun on my shoulders makes me tired. That, the constant travel, and limited food and sleep. Can't stop, though. Not yet. Maybe closer to Wellington, south of the river. Hope we're far enough off the main road into Yerington to escape detection. Only one way to know.

We reach Hudson Bridge at sundown. I dismount and hand Russell the reins to Claude's horse. His coat and hat, I give to Warren. "Thanks for bailing me out, pard. If ever I can repay you, I sure will."

I pull on my own jacket, still warm from where it lay across the horse's back, and note that Gillis' blood has dried to a brown color nearly indistinguishable from the canvas.

"Sorry to leave you this far from Sweetwater," Warren says, handing me a moth-eaten blanket. "Sure you're okay?"

I shake my head. "Pard, you've done more for me than I deserve. Maybe now that I'm gone, things will settle down."

He glances over his shoulder, where the western slope of the Singatse, once a blank spot on the map, is now studded with hundreds of tiny lights.

"Maybe." Warren leans down to shake my hand. "Maybe they will. Don't let anyone see you, Shep."

I consider saying the same thing in return but that seems unkind. "Thanks again, Warren."

With this, he and Russell turn the horses and ride back north, quickly disappearing against the silhouetted trees.

FORTY-ONE

Stumbling along in darkness, I walk south on the old Aurora road until I can't anymore. Stop to sleep in a willow thicket along Desert Creek. Sometime after midnight, clouds roll in and even after daybreak, the weather stays cold and wet like it did at Tonopah. No matter. I bathe in frigid water, scrubbing my hands and face with wet sand. Scrub my jacket with wet stones, too, trying to remove as much blood as possible. I linger for an hour beneath overcast skies, shivering and wishing I could light a fire.

I've no idea what time it is when I see two men over near the road, tracing and re-tracing a path beside one of the canals that gird this part of the valley. Whether they're farmers making repairs or hunters looking for deer, ducks, or me, I cannot tell. Locals or the law, armed or unarmed, I cannot tell, and while I'm sure they haven't spotted me, the sight of them is spooky. Soon as they depart, I start upstream carrying Warren's blanket, the water-tin, the Silver King ore, the Colt, and the clothes on my back. Everything else, I throw into the swiftly flowing creek. Can't leave Smith Valley fast enough.

All morning, I follow Desert Creek south into the Wellington Hills. Around noon, I see an Indian fisherman on the opposite bank. Since he, too, seems to want to mind his own business, neither of us even acknowledges the other. Higher up, the fog lifts but a cold wind blows directly in my face. Patchy snow requires me to break trail. I walk all day and on into late afternoon, pausing for ten minutes every few hours, and hide under an embankment when a horse-drawn stage rolls past on the Sweetwater road.

By the time I reach Salt Canyon, long shadows fill the valley. The Three Sisters are backlit by the setting sun and the wind near their summits unfurls long plumes of snow—"spoondrift," my Scottish grandfather used to say. Closer at hand, Sweetwater's lights appear: one church, a small hotel, one saloon, two stores, and seventy residents. Looks about the way it did the last time I was here and now I feel like I did outside Pioche. The valley looks so peaceful this evening, I hate to think what's followed me here. Only thing now is to retrieve the survey and leave these people alone.

❦

My brother Wade is known locally as a healer, willing—for a fee—to concoct remedies for whatever ails a body. Rheumatism, dyspepsia, tuberculosis, jaundice, dysentery: name the affliction and he'll gather wild herbs, brew tinctures, or press lozenges big enough to choke a mule. Several of our neighbors swear Wade's rude medicines kept them alive, even after doctors wrote them off as hopeless cases.

The irony here is that he has a darker reputation, too. It's common knowledge around Sweetwater that Wade beat a man to death over in Silver Peak. When I was a kid, troublemakers usually left me alone for no reason other than Wade was my brother. Gruff. Taciturn. He was so much older than me—nearly sixteen years—that I never really talked to him about it. Wasn't an appropriate subject, he'd say, so that was that. I'd seen him angry and I knew better than to press.

While I was overseas, Dad disappeared and Mom's health deteriorated so Wade started running our spread more or less on his own. There were hired men, sure, but he made every decision. Everything rode on his shoulders, so much so that by the time I returned, Wade seemed like he'd aged twenty years instead of three. He'd become more like an uncle than a brother. Wiser but distant, too. Harder. Not hostile but inflexible. Hard as stone.

He wasn't the only one who changed.

❦

By 1902, the public's opinion of the Philippine war had shifted. What had once been hailed as the liberation of an oppressed people was soon reviled as a brutal misadventure, unworthy of a republic and surely not at such a fearsome cost to the country's reputation. Daily, President Roosevelt's rivals—military, civilian, and political—called for inquiries into the military's conduct across the Pacific. Hearings were called in every state capitol and protests broke out in New York, Chicago, and Philadelphia, sure, but also in places as isolated and conservative as Caldwell, Idaho, and Hawthorne, Nevada. Yellow newspapers were filled with lurid accounts of soldiers' crimes, some of which were true.

Herbert Welsh, a dogged muckraker, dispatched agents to find ex-soldiers to testify before Massachusetts Senator Lodge's Congressional Committee about abuses against the Filipinos. One from Sacramento came all the way to our ranch. After ten minutes at our kitchen table, mostly complaining about the miles he'd ridden to reach Sweetwater, he finally got to the point.

"We want you to come to Washington later this month, Mr. Sunday. Your train fare, hotels, and meals will be covered, of course. In exchange for immunity from prosecution, you'll tell the committeemen what you know. You see, the Senate wishes to consider whether Governor Taft withheld evidence of abuse in his reports to Congress. You've heard, I presume, that Senator Lodge and Secretary Root called accounts to the contrary either the work of rogues within the army or outright fabrications. American soldiers are good men, Mr. Sunday—"

"Most are, sure."

Wade looked at me over the rim of his coffee cup but said nothing.

The agent continued as though he hadn't heard, "—but politicians and ambitious officers are slandering them to serve their own selfish aims. To cover their own misdeeds. Your comrade, James Heflin, agreed to testify this May and suggested we contact you—"

"Jimmy Heflin would say anything for attention."

The agent shook his head. "Nothing in his account contradicts others we've obtained. Mr. Welsh has copies of Major Gardener's confidential reports to Taft describing, for example, how entire villages were ordered burnt in pursuit of a few rebels. Livestock confiscated or slaughtered. Forced relocations, indiscriminate water tortures—"

My throat tightened. "Where?"

"The Phil…" The agent faltered, unsure what to say. "What do you mean?"

"Thousands of islands over there. Dozens of languages, religions, political systems…"

"The major's report describes the area around Tayabas," he said.

"And how would Jimmy know what happened there? We were nowhere near—"

"We're confident the major's report is an indication of conditions generally—"

"Well, it isn't. Jimmy talking about events in southern Luzon is like me talking about the weather in Missoula: what the hell would either of us know?"

Glancing between Wade and me, the agent leafed through a thick notebook. "Mr. Sunday, you served on Samar, did you not? Garrisoned at Balangiga before the unfortunate incident and afterward as volunteer scout for Major Waller's punitive force? Are you saying you witnessed no misconduct there? No reprisals of any kind? Nothing contrary to General Orders 100?"

This time, I was the one who faltered. My eyes watered. A calendar on the wall, provided free with our subscription to the recently-shuttered *Lyon County Monitor*, said it was April 1, but that year it felt like winter meant to stay forever. Huge snowdrifts lay behind the cabins and cowsheds and it was wretchedly cold, too. Fellow came a long way to find me, I remember thinking. This, and I'd no interest whatsoever in helping him.

"Don't know what Heflin told you," I said, "but I never saw anyone go to work without cause."

"'Work?'"

"We were good at it, too."

Across the table, Wade folded his arms across his chest and nodded almost imperceptibly.

The agent took another sip of coffee, clearly unsure which of us he should watch more carefully. "Governor Taft…" he said but stopped to clear his throat. "On February fourth this year, Governor Taft appeared before the Senate and conceded that summary executions and inhumane tortures were inflicted throughout the islands. That same month, General Hughes admitted that whole families—women and children—were killed in order to punish insurgents. As to who issued these commands, no one at the War Department will say and the American public deserve answers."

"'Thoughts that breathe and words that burn.'"

"Nothing poetic about it," the agent snapped, recoiling visibly. "Does your conscience bother you, Mr. Sunday? Unburden yourself; help set things aright."

"Congress' mess; they can fix it."

"They won't."

"They *can't*. Reno paper printed a transcript of Hughes' testimony; they never laid a finger on him."

"That's exactly the problem, Mr. Sunday."

"Not *my* problem."

"No? So like General Hughes, do you believe the Filipinos are a restless and savage people, deserving mistreatment?"

I shrugged, though I didn't feel that way at all. "Can't say what any man deserves."

"The American people deserve better, Mr. Sunday. Our civilizing principles, our belief that mankind everywhere has the right to be free: this is what sets the United States above all other nations. Or should men like Jake Smith, Tony Waller, and Edwin Glenn be allowed to subvert these ideals? To conduct war however they wish, like savages?"

"War *is* savagery."

"There are *laws*, Mr. Sunday. These actions took place under the flag of the United States. Wherever Americans go, our laws still apply."

"In commerce and diplomacy, maybe. Not in war."

"Well, some of us disagree."

"And I think you don't know what you're talking about. Rules and regulations sound right to you—even to me, now that I'm back—but mister, *they don't exist* over there. No civilizing principles; nothing but ambush and murder."

"What I mean—"

"Near Tarlac, six of us are in single-file on an elevated footpath. Carabao are being driven across this dike from one paddy to another so our lead halts. Group of natives walking the opposite way when one pulls a bolo from it's sheath and not ten feet behind me hacks a fellow from Oregon. Like that, we turn the Filipino in—"

"Oh? To what authority?"

"To the Devil, I hope; I meant we killed him. Then it happens again: while we're turned, another Filipino slashes one of my companions across his back—"

"Mr. Sunday," the agent started but damned if I was gonna let him derail me.

"Like sheep in a pen: can't go forward, can't turn back, so we jump off the dike and shoot every native there, maybe nine, ten in total. No commands, no orders given; we just do it, except it turns out, apart from those two bolomen, the others were only farmers. Civilians. Men and boys going to work their fields, carrying nothing more than wooden farm tools. Now, did they know those insurrectos were there among 'em? Can't say. Were they in on the ambush, or were they caught off guard, too? Again, I don't know but in that moment, no matter what you think, we did the only thing possible."

"Mr. Sunday, please—" the agent tried again but Wade shook his head and he stopped.

"What do you want me to say?" Reaching back to set my coffee cup in the wash basin, I saw Wade looking at me.

"You don't owe this one anything," he said, sounding so much like Dad I had to blink a couple times to make sure I hadn't lost my mind. Then he turned and shook his head and I swear the agent jumped a little in his seat.

By then, my head was pounding and my heart raced. I wanted to drink something but my glass was empty; wanted to hit something but what would be the point? "I still see those farmers," I said. "Every night, them and dozens more. Maybe you and Sam Clemens want blood but goddamn it, mister, I've seen too much and I *cannot* help you." Pushing back from the table, I knocked over my chair and didn't even stop to set it right. Out the door without a coat, up into the bare volcanic hills behind our house.

Beautiful day; not a cloud in the sky. To the east, Mount Grant was covered in snow. Down south, Big Indian, too. To the west, Grass Creek burbled under ice—a white thread stitching together red and yellow lands. All the landmarks of my childhood were there but I still couldn't fix my location. Everything had changed; I was lost in the place I knew best.

Before long, I watched the agent climb into his buggy and start down the canyon, back toward Sweetwater. He never looked up to see where I'd gone; I think he knew I wasn't coming back. Not long after, Wade rode his horse, Bear, into the hills to look for me, with Klondike trailing on a halter. Brought my coat, too, which I appreciated, and didn't say anything, which I appreciated even more.

∾

Later that night, once we got Mom settled, Wade and I sat by the fire and talked. For the first time in our lives, we talked until dawn. Heard things I'd never known: how Mom and Dad were cheated out of their store at Pine Grove; about a cousin I'd understood to have died of complications from a childhood disease, but who'd actually shot himself; and about Dad's oldest brother, one among William Ormsby's militia, wiped out by Paiutes during the Pyramid Lake War.

"Think I have the family's luck," I said.

"Survived, didn't you?"

I took a big, stinging gulp of whiskey. "Sure."

I told him stories from the service; about China and the massacre at Balangiga and the cruel months after. Not every last detail, but more than I'd told anyone else.

Once I finished, he let out a low whistle. "No wonder that spindly son of a bitch wanted you to testify."

"More in here, still," I said tapping my head.

For a long time we sat in silence, watching the fire bank. Then a knot exploded, startling us from our trance.

"Whole time you were gone," Wade said, "Mother was sure something terrible would happen."

"Good instincts."

Then I asked him what happened at Silver Peak and he ran his hand over his face.

"Hell, that was all my fault. Me and another fellow both liked the same girl. His girl, honestly. Baited him into a fight, let him hit me first, and then let him have it. Fractured his skull and he died the next day."

"Damn. You get the girl?"

"No." Wade let out a rueful laugh. "No, I didn't. She hadn't liked me much in the first place."

"How'd you stay out of jail?"

Wade shrugged. "Hired a lawyer from Candelaria. Figured I'd confess everything but he told me to shut up; called it self-defense and got me acquitted on the first ballot. Kept my mouth shut ever since. Honestly, Shep, I don't talk about it because I'm ashamed. Folks want an explanation, though, so they make up their own stories. I've heard said he pulled a gun on me, or that he was beating her, but neither of those things is true."

I took a drink and winced. "My friends always shook whenever you came around."

Wade shrugged. "I knew people were afraid of me and I guess I kind of liked it. Even Dad left me alone and I *surely* liked that." He took a drink—water for the teetotaler. "Lonely, though. Didn't realize the wall was so high."

Another slug of whiskey. "Sorry, Wade; wish I'd known."

"Wish I'd said something. Look, why don't you take a couple months and clear your head? I can handle things here. Should have plenty of runoff and grass in the pastures. Improvements are in good repair and Melvin Jim and the Higgins brothers all signed on for two more seasons. Heifers drop as many calves as I think they will, I'll hire another man. You can help with haying when you return."

In the other room, Mom coughed and groaned but didn't call out.

"What about her?" I said.

"Don't figure much will change anytime soon. She's tough as rocks."

"Stubborn," I said.

"Same thing. Weather improves, I'll wheel her onto the porch to smell the sagebrush. Maybe take her down to the springs at Hot Creek."

"Long trip for an invalid."

Wade shrugged. "Tough as rocks."

I rose, walked into Mom's room, and kissed her on the forehead. Atomizers, aspirators, and bottles of pills on her bedside table. Her breathing was slow and steady; no rattling sounds. That was good. She was still there but it was hard to know if it was what she wanted. Seemed callous to me, keeping her around just so we wouldn't have to live without her. Far as I could tell, Mom had already pierced the veil. Holding onto her like this was unkindness itself, but here Wade and I disagreed so under his diligent care, she lingered. As it happens, Mom died about three weeks later and Wade's letter didn't find me for two months after that. Seeing as she was already underground, I saw no point in returning from Colorado, certainly not in light of my situation at the time.

I backed into the main room. We'd let the lamps burn out and the room was dark. Rico, our big collie, was asleep by the woodstove, snuffling and pawing his way through jackrabbit dreams.

"I could stand some peace and quiet," I said. "Sure you don't need me here?"

"I'm sure. Watch the drinking, though. Don't give it the upper hand."

I set my unfinished glass on a side-table. "Habit I picked up in Manila," I said.

"Should've left it there." Wade reached out with his foot to rub Rico's belly. The dog hardly stirred. "Run into trouble, you get back here fast, understand?"

"Of course," I said.

⁋

I doubt Wade was anticipating this kind of trouble when last we spoke. Or maybe he was. I'm about to try the front door when I spy a man in a chair at the porch's dark end, a double-barreled shotgun across his knees and brass spittoon at his feet.

Even once I recognize Wade, my heart still races. "Bastard."

"If you're here for Christmas dinner, you're late." He chuckles to himself. "You look well, though—better than I expected."

"Which is what?"

He looks me over again and shrugs. "Worse."

A new dog stands beside him: a big, ugly, block-headed thing that growls at me.

"The hell's that?"

"Hatchet, this is Shepard—he's one of ours." Wade nudges the creature forward with his knee. "Go on, boy."

"Where's Rico?"

"Got old; coyotes jumped him over on Salt Creek."

The new dog trots warily forward, sniffs my hand, and wags his tail once before circling back.

"Guess you're okay," Wade says but it's hard to tell if he's joking.

"Hate to make him mad." I point at the shotgun. "You, too."

"Can't be too careful these days."

My brother opens the breech and removes both cartridges. He looks about the way I remember him, except now he has a beard to go with his mustache, both heavily streaked with gray. The house looks different, too. Wade's extended the porch so it wraps all the way around the front. Hard to tell in the dark but it looks like new outbuildings are set into the slope above the barn. The wind gusts hard, bending the tops of the poplars along the drive.

"Any poachers lately?"

"Not anymore," he says but that's it. Typical Wade: no explanation, no details.

I set my nearly-empty water-tin on the porch and the wind promptly tips it over. "Won't stay long; I'm in some trouble."

"So I heard," he says but without any meanness. "Woman from Delamar sent a letter."

"Helen Molloy?" I press a hand against the house's redbrick wall, still warm from the sun.

"That's her."

Suppose I should take this as proof Helen's looking out for me. Or maybe I should read it first.

"She explain my situation?"

"She did." He tucks the cartridges into a shirt pocket and inspects the gun's breech. "What happened, Shep? You were the good son."

"Save your sermon, reverend." Turning, I see the crescent moon setting over South Sister.

"Don't get sore." Wade yawns and stretches. "Hooligan."

In the pens beyond the barn, a noisy heifer catches the dog's attention. A braying mule catches mine and I shudder.

"You understand why I can't stay, right? Are those papers Luke forwarded in the safe?"

"Arrived last week. Supper first, then decide." Wade unloads the tobacco he's been chewing into the spittoon. "Either way, we're ready."

"Ready for what?"

"Trouble." He stands and spits one last thread of tobacco over the porch's edge. "Come meet Jess."

"Crackers, more dogs?"

The ghost of a smile crosses my brother's face. "Last time I'll let you speak like that about my wife."

"Hold up." I retrieve my chin from the porch. "You're joking, right?"

"Married last July." This time he smiles broadly. "The old bachelor had one last trick up his sleeve. And it isn't as if you'd have come around sooner."

"Would've if you'd told me! Congratulations to you both."

"Thanks. You can tell the missus, herself."

Leaning over the rail, he shouts toward the new cabins. One of the Higgins boys—whether Augie or Garrett, I can't tell—leans through a doorway, listens a moment, and goes to fetch the others. Seeing no one on the road behind me, Wade turns and starts indoors.

"Jess made chicken and dumplings. Come tell me what we're up against."

◌

Almost midnight and I'm lying atop a flat rock. The weather is clear and cold and the air is like glass. Can't recall another sky this brilliant. Not even in the Philippines, where some nights I'd steal away after roll call and lie on the beach, wishing I could fall upward and swim among the stars; nor among those I viewed as a child from this very same place. The stars tonight are incredible: innumerable, unknowable, turning in silent mystery above the pines. I draw the cold wind into my lungs and it settles my restless soul. With each breath, I sense infinity and the inherent goodness in the rocks' repose and in the rustling sage. Even what low spark of goodness still gutters in me.

But something has to change. I've protected a machine borne by many for the benefit a few. So many lives—men, women, and children—used up, cut loose, and then punished for the sin of fragility. Of innocence. Swallowed whole while a privileged few wallow in grotesque splendor, indifferent to the wreckage in their wake. Ravenous, insatiable: everyone and everything devoured for the sake of higher returns, and from within its bloody jaws every shred of our humanity, our innate divinity, is forgotten. I should've protected the weak from the strong, not the other way around. Should've stood watch instead of shooting into the pen.

Beneath this starlit dome, I am diminished, painfully aware of my mortal repugnance, yet lifted above myself and reminded of things I knew but had forgotten. Every breath is a sacrament—one strand in an eternal cord—and I resolve to never waste another fighting for something in which I do not believe. I want to get better. To be better. These shadows surrounding me, they're figments. Come daylight, all their malice will disappear and so I resolve to burn away my own shadows. Burn away darkness and fear. I've spent these years all wrong, in thrall to the shadow of death, but no longer. Tonight, I've glimpsed eternity. Taken the light in through my eyes and through my lungs, received this cold wind's blessing.

Only four hours until daybreak, so I'd better get down to the house and make sure everything is ready. I know the way now. I have always known the way. I could walk this path with my eyes closed.

FORTY-TWO

We hadn't planned to stand, hadn't planned to fight. Figured we'd all leave the house with Wade, Garrett, and Augie riding down to reinforce the Brunettis, and Melvin and I driving Jess and Amy—Garrett's wife—to relative safety in Sweetwater. From there, I'd have ridden west to Bridgeport, California. Figured the worst that could happen would be a ransacking of the house, or even its destruction, but that everything that truly mattered would be safe. Plan might've worked. Might've averted more bloodshed, but we ran out of time.

The wind is up this morning and dead twigs from the poplars litter the grass. The stars are all gone and any minute now the Sun will rise, and as I make my way toward the house, Hatchet starts barking. Walking a few steps ahead of me, Wade doesn't bother to shush him. Isn't as though anyone's asleep, anyway.

In the parlor, I set a pair of binoculars atop a stack of Mother's books. Augie Higgins comes in from the corrals and follows us in the ritual of scraping mud from his boots—for nine months out of the year, this is our principal religion. Amy and Jess are seated at the kitchen table, their travel bags beside them on the floor. Not sure where Garrett and Melvin Jim—Warren Jim's distant cousin—have gone but they aren't in the main house.

Wade steps over to the sink, watches his dog through the window. "Keeps sniffing the wind." He taps on the glass with his coffee cup and the dog stops barking.

Jessie studies Wade's profile. "What is it?"

"One problem after another." Turning to Jessie, his expression is grave. "You, Amy, Melvin, and Shep will have to stay here. Mack's fetlock is still hot and swollen so he can't be ridden, and Melvin discovered that the rig's bearing buckles are cracked so you couldn't take the buckboard into Sweetwater even if Mack was healthy."

"We'll be alright," I lie.

"He's right," Wade says. "They won't get this far."

"Can't Shep ride up into the woods so we can honestly say he isn't here?" There's an edge to her voice and I know she meant this as unkindly as it sounded. Can't say that I blame her.

"Doubt it'd slow 'em down any, and if they catch Shep out on his own—"

"Well, I don't think you should go," Jessie says to Wade. "Don't they need some kind or writ or something?"

I glance at Wade before answering, "Yes, but these aren't the sort of men who will wait for it—this is personal."

Jessie looks me over and I can tell she wishes I'd never come here—hell, *I* wish I'd gone somewhere else—but now it's too late and everything she has and everything she loves is at risk because her normally-levelheaded husband wouldn't tell his wayward brother to keep moving.

Distorted by distance, a gunshot echoes up the canyon. Two more follow in rapid succession and then a dinner bell peals. The dog resumes barking.

"Damn." Wade sets his cup in the sink. "August, go tell your brother. Tell him and Melvin to bring Doc, Cutter, and Red Boy out of the barn—we need to go."

Jessie gives Wade a quick kiss before she and Amy head deeper into the house.

My brother turns to me. "Three quick shots if you have trouble, right?"

"Yep. Any fewer, you'll know I handled it, myself."

"Any more and I'll know you're in over your head. Take care of her, Shep," he says, gesturing after Jessie. "She's everything to me."

I say I will and we shake hands. This is what passes for deep emotion between the Sundays. A few minutes later, Wade and the others spur their horses down the canyon and I'm left to listen and wait.

～

Sunday Ranch's headquarters rests in a saddle at the head of two canyons: short, shallow Wiregrass to the north, and bigger, deeper Cottonwood to the east. The road up Cottonwood is five miles shorter than the way from Sweetwater so we've figured it's the route they'd take. Those gunshots down at the Brunettis, a quarter mile east, seem to confirm this hunch. Hopefully, they can be turned there but if not, we'll need a second line of defense, so Melvin and I push the wagon across the road where it passes between outcrops. From the house and barn, we should be able to defend this approach from now until the sun sets.

～

Glancing through the kitchen window, Melvin turns to wave before he disappears inside the barn. I wave back. That's one angle covered. A long rifle stands beside a window upstairs, loaded shotguns near both doors, and the Colt is in my jacket on a chair in the parlor. Should have it on me but it's steps away and I figure I'll have time to retrieve it before anything happens.

More gunshots down in Cottonwood. Two, three, and then a barrage like I haven't heard since the Philippines. Like a slow drumroll, muffled as it passes through the cedars. Jesus, it's pitched down there. I waver between sticking to our plan and riding down to the Brunetti's, myself.

As the noise dies away, the only sounds are of wind and the women's muted voices on the other side of the wall. I stare through the big parlor window at the Three Sisters, their summits just visible above the trees. Should've hidden up there at the old Silverado ditch-camp, right on the Von Schmidt Line. That's where I used to go when Dad was especially crocked. Should've taken fishing gear and a bedroll and stayed lost for a while.

The dog barks, wrenching me from this ill-timed daydream. Glancing through the kitchen window, I see Hatchet's facing west, into the wind. From just inside the barn, Melvin gestures toward the wind-bent poplars lining the road out of Wiregrass Canyon: seven men in heavy coats and carrying shotguns are descending the hill. Running stooped, three clamber through the corrals, scattering the frightened animals, and break toward the main house. Led by Curt Broe, the other four move single-file toward the forge.

Christ, I've misjudged everything. Underestimated our foe, overestimated our odds. Brought murderers here and endangered my family. Should've gone the other way; should've gone east and lured these animals away from here, away from the people I love. Now it's too late.

I open and close the shutters once to signal Melvin. He ducks out of sight before opening fire from inside the barn. One man atop a cross-fence clutches his arm and falls to the ground; his companions grab him and drag him screaming behind a rock wall. In seconds, they're hidden from view.

I run into the parlor for my Colt. With my hand on the grip, I hear the kitchen door swing open. Whoever's there must be struggling to control his adrenaline because the door hits the wall so hard it rattles china in the cupboards.

"Goddamn," he whispers, straining against the wind to close it.

No point in waiting—armed men don't break in to deliver good news—so I kneel as I round the corner and squeeze off three quick shots. Don't even aim. Don't need to: the door is dead center and so's my target. No one I recognize, the intruder crashes backward against the door, shattering its center pane, and collapses on the back steps. Gunshots erupt near the barn, inbound and out, and Hatchet won't stop barking. He snaps and snarls and someone screams for help. I *love* that dog.

I pull the door closed and throw the bolt, although anyone could reach through the empty windowpane to unlock it. Sprinting across the kitchen, I'm reaching for my coat and more cartridges when a shotgun blast shatters the parlor window. Glass sprays the room, knocking over a lamp and cutting my hands. The Colt spins away from me, landing under the couch. I lunge for the shotgun in the corner but Jerry Rosen bursts through the door and fires. Buckshot rips through my left calf, knocking me down. On the wall's other side, one of the women lets out a yelp.

Scrambling for the corner on my three good limbs, Rosen clubs me with the buttstock of his shotgun. Close behind, another man kicks my ribs and sends me sprawling. Jerry lunges forward, stomps on my left hand, and the second fellow kneels to grab my right. More footsteps at the door.

"Stay down!" Rosen shouts.

"Jerry, you bastard!" Pulling free, I yank my arm from beneath his boot and manage to kick the other fellow's knee. His leg buckles and he falls backward but that's all the damage I inflict.

Two gunshots in quick succession. First bullet enters above my shoulder blade and exits through my collarbone, leaving my left arm dangling and useless. The pain is staggering. Second bullet punches me in the back, slamming my chest and face against the floor. That's all I know.

∽

When I come to, Jerry and the other fellow are back on their feet, standing by the door. I'm lying on my right side, curled up like a question mark. Can't move, can hardly breathe. Stupefying pain. Can't think.

Through the broken window, I hear Melvin shout but can't tell what he says. Hatchet's barking like mad. Shots follow and the men standing above me turn their heads, listening intently, scanning the big cedars above the forge.

Can hardly see, vision's so blurry.

Boots stop in front of my face. One rolls me over on my back.

"Jerry, go help the others," he says and I recognize Curt Broe's voice. He coughs.

Haven't felt this helpless since the Philippines. Lying still is pure agony and moving's even worse. No matter what I want, there's nothing I can do.

Jerry turns, pushes the door open with the shotgun's muzzle, and exits.

Standing over me, Big Curt coughs again and spits on the floor beside my head. He grins. "Son of a bitch, how's this suit you?"

My breath comes in short, shallow gasps, and everyone in the room—me, included—is sure I'm dying. Freezing cold. Burning pain. Blood seeps from the corner of my mouth and beneath my back, I feel a bigger pool spreading across the floorboards. Nauseous. Weightless. Shattered.

Outside, a shotgun barks, rattling panes of glass in their frames. Someone screams in agony. Scowling, Curt glances through the window.

I cough, spattering Curt's boot tips with bright red blood.

Still rubbing his knee, the other man gestures with his shotgun. "Hit him again?"

Turning away from the window, Curt squats on his heels to study my face. As best I can, I focus my eyes on a chair leg several feet past his heels. Only thing I can control is my breathing. I try to relax every muscle in my body, and while settling this way makes the pain flare, the longer he stares at me, the more relaxed I become. Unaccountably calm, given that I'm defenseless, full of holes, and leaking blood.

A moment later, Curt exhales and stands. "Nah, he's bleeding out. Want him to feel it before he goes."

"Should I look for the papers?"

Outside, a shotgun booms.

"Not yet. First, go settle with whoever's in the barn. Burn 'em out if you have to."

The other fellow pulls his hat down low and limps outside.

Unaccountably, Curt lingers, glancing around the room. Stifles a cough. Steps over to the bookcase, pulls out volumes, and drops them on the floor. Tolstoy. Flaubert. Wade's books on medicinal plants. Dickens. Shakespeare. Doesn't appear to be looking for anything specific. Coughs into his hand and wipes it on his trousers. Takes a Piute reed basket from one shelf and turns it over in his hands before dropping it on the floor. It's as if he doesn't want to leave. He coughs, shakes his head, and coughs some more. His face is red and I can see he's in pain, but I'm in no condition to gloat. So light-headed now, don't think I could move if I wanted to.

More gunfire draws Curt's attention toward the door. He glances at me once and then he's gone.

I fade again; don't know for how long. Don't know.

෴

Hatchet's barking brings me around again. A bullet breaks another window and wind rushes through the room, rustling the curtains and scattering sheet music from my sister-in-law's upright. Blood—my blood—everywhere. Slaughterhouse in here, Jesus. Need to survive this. Long as I'm able, I have to fight. With my right arm, I pull myself upright.

Vision's blurry. Can't control my left arm, either. Left arm, left leg, hell, that whole side of my body feels like it's on fire. Right side still functions but it's weak. Pitifully weak.

Fleeting thoughts of Helen Molloy and Joe McCuskey.

Of survival.

I pull myself along the sofa, half-crawling, half-falling toward the shotgun in the corner. Almost there when I hear noises behind me and figure all is lost.

"Shepard?" Jessie gasps. "Oh, my God, what have they done?"

Having known her for all of twelve hours, I'm inclined to pity her for the trouble I've caused but she won't have it. She sends Amy into the kitchen for towels and water before crossing the room to kneel beside me.

"Listen to me, Shep. Focus on my voice, understand? No, don't move!"

More gunshots from the barn.

"Sorry about your sofa." Don't know why I say this; it just pops into my head.

"Be quiet." She tears open my shirt, wincing at the exit wounds in my chest and shoulder. "I don't care about that."

Amy returns, arms full. "Press hard," Jessie tells her, "here and here."

"Made a mess," I say.

Jessie shakes her head. "Quiet, Shepard. You Sunday boys don't know when to quit, do you?"

No argument there.

She and Amy keep glancing through the shattered front window. Working quickly, they tear the towels into strips and pack my wounds. Hurts like hell but as they're working, my vision returns.

"Water?" I say, and Jessie sends Amy back to the kitchen, seeing as the basinful beside us is bright red.

Jessie wraps a towel tightly around my arm and ties it over my right shoulder. Hurts something awful. I cough and blood dribbles from my chin onto my chest. The sound of gunfire echoes off the hillside. Wish I hadn't come home; wish I'd shot Curt Broe there above Reveille.

Amy returns with a tin cup of water and news that the barn is on fire. I rinse my mouth, spit into the basin, and drink the rest, wondering if any will leak out elsewhere.

"Help me onto the chair near the window?"

"You have to lie down," Jessie says. "You can't do anything now."

"No." I point out the window. "The others. Help me lift the shotgun."

The recoil's gonna knock me over but I'll have less accuracy with the Colt. Jessie nods to Amy and the girl starts toward the hall. She's barely set her hand on the weapon when we hear footsteps on the porch.

"Quickly!" I whisper but there's no way she can hand it to me in time.

Amy sets the weapon to her shoulder and turns to face the door just as it creaks on its hinges.

"Jessie? Amy?" a man says and Jessie reaches out and presses the shotgun's barrels toward the floor.

"Nico, thank God." Jessie steps forward to pull a tall, dark-haired man through the door. He's holding a long rifle. Vaguely familiar but despite Jessie's prompt, I can't remember his name. "What's happening out there?"

This fellow looks me over and grits his teeth. "Jesus, Shep, you look awful."

"Feel awful."

At once, I recognize our neighbor, Nicolas Brunetti. The Brunettis run Riverbend, the spread east of ours, down to the Walker's eastern fork. Nico is closer to Wade's age than mine and I haven't seen him in nine, ten years, so maybe it's no surprise I didn't recognize him.

"Wade okay?"

"Yes. He and Len Snyder sprung Melvin from the barn and now they're up behind the forge. How are you?"

"Not good. How many still?"

"Four or five." He helps Jessie tighten my bandages, which makes me groan. "Wade and Melvin have two pinned between the barn and the cabins, and two are at-large. Augie says there may be another one still, but doesn't know where. One's dead in the yard and another's below the back steps."

I fight the urge to vomit.

Nico takes four twelve-gauge cartridges from his pockets and hands them to Amy. The smell of smoke grows stronger.

"Thanks for sticking with us, Nico."

"More help's on the way."

"Who, Nico?" Jessie says, helping me settle into a spindleback chair. "Who's coming?"

"Both of my brothers, the Keegans, and all our hands. The Hogues and Pavias, too. Others coming up from Sweetwater. An hour ago, the Keegans stopped another gang on the road below their place. They shot one of the Keegan's hired men, but the rest were driven off."

Jessie keeps one ear toward the empty window. "Why hasn't the deputy come?"

"Don't know. Sheriff's riding in from Hawthorne, but he's hours away."

"Mr. Brunetti," Amy's high voice catches in her throat, "where's Garrett?"

Amy looks like Alice Roosevelt, the president's daughter—another thought that just pops into my aching head.

Nico winces at Jessie before turning to face the girl. "Garrett took a bullet in his leg. Wade pulled him into the forge and he's okay. Lost some blood but he should be okay."

"Oh, my God," she whispers, covering her mouth with trembling fingers. Her eyes brim with tears.

Jessie stands behind her and wraps her arms around the girl.

Outside, someone runs past the broken window, too quickly to identify.

"Who was that?" Amy gasps. She raises the shotgun and points it at the door.

"Couldn't see," says Nico. "Which direction?"

Jessie points south, away from the burning barn. Outside, a rifle cracks. A shotgun answers, spraying the upper story. Glass tumbles from the window over the stair landing.

"I'm going out. Stay inside; stay away from the windows."

He chambers a round in the rifle and leans outside, glancing right and left. As the door closes behind him, I slump in the chair, nearly toppling forward. Jessie grips my good shoulder and hauls me upright.

"Jessie," I groan, "under the sofa, my revolver."

"Amy, watch him," she says, moving across the room, but the younger woman won't take her eyes off the door. Figure if I collapse now, Amy won't do anything to arrest my fall.

Jessie hands me the Colt. Right hand, solamente; only thing my bound left arm is good for is pinning the revolver against my thigh. Checking the cylinder, I have three cartridges left. With double-action, all I need to do is pull the trigger. Still, I'm so afraid I'll drop it that I ask Jessie to lash my hand to the grip. She tears another strip from a towel, wraps it tightly around my fist, and ties it off.

Two gunshots from the house's other side. Shouting, too, but I can't tell who's there. Leaning forward for a better view, I nearly fall. Pain surges from my shoulder to my leg. I gasp for air and Emma clutches my good arm.

"Can't hold myself upright," I whisper.

Jessie knots two towels together and runs them over my chest, under my right arm, and weaves these through the chair's spindles before tying them in the back. Can't lean forward now but it beats falling. Too weak to move the chair, though, and not being able to see much outside is maddening.

"Take the shotgun, hide in the library," Jessie tells Amy and the girl backs slowly into the hall, her eyes still fixed on the front door. "What else can I do?"

"Water," I whisper, staring out the window.

She returns with another cupful, I take a sip and ask her to pour the rest over my head. The cold is electrifying: clears my head but also makes me jump. Another squall of pain wracks my body.

"O-o-kay," I sputter, "Good, Jessie, thanks. Thank you."

Nothing more she can do so she goes to find Amy.

Gunshots erupts in the yard. Through the empty window, I see the man who burst in with Jerry Rosen. He's facing the barn, firing and reloading as he retreats. Bullets strike the ground around him, raising little gouts of dirt.

"Watch out for the dog!" he shouts, "Over this way!"

He raises the shotgun, taking aim at the forge. Feet braced beneath the chair, I rest my right arm on the windowsill and pull the trigger. No more than twenty feet away, the round smashes through his right side and drops him. Kicks and groans for a moment but that's all. I fight another urge to vomit.

"Jerry!" Curt roars, "They got Hitchens—Hitchens is down!"

From the porch's far side, heavy footsteps upon the planks. Someone moves just outside the door, edges up to the window frame, and fires uphill, blowing off bits of the wooden latticework beneath the gutters.

Can't see around the corner, can't see who's there. Even belted to the chair, I'm still wobbly enough I don't dare lean forward; topple now, I'll be as helpless as a tortoise on its back. Nothing to do but wait. Another blast, inbound this time; another shower of broken wood. Jerry Rosen steps forward, fires uphill, and retreats from view. He doesn't look my way, doesn't see me through the empty window frame and tattered curtains.

"They're on both sides of those cabins now," he shouts. "One got Hitchens."

From out of sight, I hear Curt coughing his lungs out. He rages and sputters and I imagine how red his face must be. Can't see him, though. Can't tell if he's against the door or protected by the wall. I can't shoot through bricks.

"Where are the others?" Curt rages. "They abandoned us!"

"Keep shooting," Jerry urges but Curt's too spun up.

"They're just *farmers*. No way they knew we were coming!"

Footsteps across the porch. I raise the Colt in case Jerry presents but he doesn't.

Curt shouts again, sounding like he's standing on the porch's far side, "South toward the trees. Circle back to the—"

Gunshots from the house's eastern side, followed by footsteps as Curt races up the steps onto the porch.

"We're cut off!" he shouts. He coughs so hard he can't catch his breath.

I lift the Colt and train it on the door. Dizzy now; getting harder to do. Despite Jessie's first aid, I haven't stopped leaking and the wind feels colder despite the brightening day.

Jerry Rosen darts forward, fires uphill, and retreats faster than I can follow.

My head bobs, sending another jolt of pain thrumming down my spine. This snaps me awake but underscores how weak I am.

"Back inside," Jerry shouts. "I heard women's voices earlier. Take hostages and ride for Bridgeport."

The door bursts open. Cold air, dust, and sweat as they stumble back inside the house, Jerry leading and Curt close behind.

I try to hold the revolver steady but my arm won't cooperate. Even if I pulled the trigger, wouldn't hit anything but the floorboards. I exhale heavily. Tried. Wasn't enough.

Jerry glances my way. Sees me in the chair, spots the gun, tries to turn. Still rushing forward, Curt runs squarely into his back and nearly knocks him down.

"No, *wait–*" Jerry shouts, struggling to right himself.

From deeper inside the house, a shotgun blast catches him and Curt both, though Jerry takes the worst of it. He crumples to the ground, nearly in halves, while Curt drops his shotgun, staggers backward, and collapses with his back to the wall.

Glancing left, Amy stands fifteen feet away, eyes wide, tears on her cheeks. One foot in the library and her other in the hall; both barrels are smoking, the shotgun's buttstock still tight against her shoulder. Thank you, Amy, thank you. Like I said, from time to time, we all need a little help.

Curt looks at her and blinks. "My, my," he says but that's all.

He coughs and spits up a gout of blood, slicking his coat and shirt-front. He tries reaching for his shotgun but his right side is shredded: arm, shoulder, and ribs. His hand spasms uselessly over the breech.

First few weeks in Delamar, I was Curt's right hand.

"Huh." He turns to look at me. "What are you gonna do now, Shep?" He flashes that nasty grin of his—narrowed eyes, raised upper lip, barred teeth— before tipping his head back against the wall.

I try to raise the Colt but again, the barrel wavers back and forth, up and down. Too weak. The weapon falls heavily upon my knee.

"No need, amigo." Curt slowly opens and closes his eyes. "She hit me good."

"We didn't…" I wheeze but can't finish the sentence.

He groans and coughs again, slumping lower against the wall. "Course we did. Only way this was gonna end." He glances along the hallway but since Jessie and Amy are no longer there, he turns back to stare at me.

Want to say something but my strength's gone. Mouth feels like it's been gummed shut.

"How 'bout that?" Curt whispers. "She saved me."

Voices outside: Wade's, Nico's, and others'. Louder by the second. The wind gusts hard, rustling the tattered curtains in the empty window. Glittering dust. Big Curt's chin tips slowly forward, and as boots thud across the porch, he coughs once and settles.

I'm fading, too, but the chair and the towel keep me from pitching forward. The door bursts open, sunlight floods the room, and that's the last thing I remember for a long, long time.

FORTY-THREE

∞

One commandment in storytelling is "show, don't tell," but most of what happens over the succeeding two weeks is recounted for me after the fact.

For one, I'm told that by the time the sheriff's party reached Sweetwater, even after Wade and Jessie bandaged us and applied their homemade medicines, my brother and I plus Amy and Garrett Higgins were already en route to the rail station at Wabuska, some fifty miles north. For protection, the Keegans rode with us as far as the old Reese River Road, and the Brunetti brothers, all conspicuously armed, accompanied us the entire way (it was Nico who loaned us the wagon, after all). Even Warren Jim and his cousin, Russell, fell in between Yerington and the railroad and volunteered to drive the empty wagon all the way back to Riverbend. Despite crowds lining the roads at various points along the way, at no time did anyone interfere or try to delay us.

Jessie, Augie Higgins, and Melvin Jim stayed behind to explain to the sheriff what happened and make sure the fire that consumed the barn didn't spread. Big Curt Broe, Jerry Rosen, and the others killed there—plus the fellow the Keegans killed—were transported over the mountain to Hawthorne and buried in the cemetery. Six men captured on the road up Cottonwood Canyon, including Isaac Reed, were taken to the lockup in Yerington, bonded out, and disappeared. Thus, in one afternoon, the Thiel Detective Agency ate $24,000 and state and local papers had a field day with the whole affair.

For another, once aboard the train, we continued past Carson City to Reno and its general hospital. Garrett Higgins spent three days there following an operation to remove six triple-aught pellets from his right hip and thigh, and for months afterward, wore a protective brace. Other than a slight limp, I'm happy to report he's fully recovered. I had two operations, myself, mainly to patch up arterial damage in my calf, upper chest and left leg, and repair my shattered left collar bone. Based on an estimate of five and a half pints of blood in my body normally, a surgeon told Wade he estimated I'd lost four. My heart-rate at admission was one-hundred and sixty beats per minute. Acute kidney failure, too, as a result of lost blood, and for a week after I was in something like a coma. One day of relative lucidity among others where I was completely unresponsive.

Wade tells me I had visitors almost every day, most of whom either he or the doctors shooed away, but evidently a few were important enough they were allowed more time. This latter group included "my" attorney, Porter Nielsen; a man representing Black Tiger Mines; and another standing for Governor Sparks. All three carried papers for my signature.

Room was so white, so bright, that until Wade spoke, I figured I was dead.

"Shep? This fellow here says Governor Sparks and his attorney general will grant you immunity from prosecution for everything that happened in Lincoln and Mineral counties so long as you hand over some documents he says you have. Are those the papers you asked me to keep safe?"

"For God's sake, are they back at your ranch?" the aide said. "Then why are we—"

"Hey, mister." Wade straightened his back and furrowed his brow. "Let me talk to my brother, will you?"

The aide stepped quickly around the foot of the bed.

Nielsen put a hand on the aide's shoulder. "Let's give the Sundays some privacy. Fred, Tom, we'll talk outside."

The door closed behind them. I stared at Wade, aware he was speaking to me, but the pain throughout my body was such that all I could do was sip air and blink.

Wade pulled up a chair and sat beside my elbow. "Fair deal's on the table, Shep," he said, scratching his beard.

I nodded and closed my eyes.

"You know better than I what it all means but I think it's a good one. Turning over those papers will go a long way toward lifting the cloud over your name. Give you a chance to start fresh."

"Yes," I whispered.

"You agree, then? I have the envelope here and I'll hand it over if you say so. Otherwise I can—"

"Give it to them."

Wade sat back in the chair and folded his hands in his lap. "Give it to them, okay."

A nurse came in with a tray of syringes.

"What are those for?" Wade said, suspicious of any medicine not swimming with leaves and berries.

"Pain and infection."

"Wait," I whispered, knowing how these injections affected me. "Sign first."

Wade looked at the nurse and nodded. "I'll go get the others."

Nielsen returned with the governor's document, summarized it again, and set it on a tray.

I couldn't manage more than a shaky "S" but with Wade's endorsement, the aide deemed this sufficient and departed with Delamar-Highland's union-busting records and letters from Senator Christy. The other fellow from Black Tiger Mines stepped inside and waited until Wade produced the envelope containing the Standard Trust survey plus Jack Lipford's correspondence with his various girlfriends. After leafing through these, he slipped them inside a locking satchel, nodded at Nielsen, and left.

The attorney approached my bed and gripped my right forearm. "Knowing how you must feel," he said, "I won't make you shake hands."

"Thanks."

"Thank *you*." He smiled. "Delamar's workingmen thank you, too."

"Won't do for the dust," I whispered. A jolt of pain made me wince. The nurse stepped forward but again, I raised my right hand.

"Black Tiger is committed to bringing in more water for wet-drilling and processing. They'll do all they can to make Delamar's mines safer."

Nice words, but who knows whether they're true? Another searing jolt of pain and that time I waved the nurse forward. "You'll tell me the plan? How you'll make Lipford pay?"

While she readied her trayful, Nielsen backed toward the door.

"Certainly, Mr. Sunday, and soon. I look forward to our next conversation."

The first needle went in and after the pinch, the relief was nearly instantaneous. Not one-hundred percent but a damn sight better than before. My whole body relaxed.

"Helen Molloy?" I said, already feeling drowsy.

His hand on the doorknob, Nielsen paused. "I'm sorry, Mr. Sunday, but I don't know her whereabouts. I imagine she'll want to get in touch with you soon but couldn't say when. Thanks again and so long for now."

He stepped outside and shut the door behind him. Despite his promises, I wouldn't see Porter Nielsen again for a long, long time.

The second needle went in and my eyes closed. Nothing to do then but rest. Nothing at all.

◐

Eleven days later and I'm sitting up, still in a hospital bed with my left arm in a sling but feeling better. Still hurts to breathe deeply, still hurts to move, but these are aches now rather than pains. Wade's gone back to Sweetwater but Amy checks in on me a few times each day. Across the street from the hospital, she and Garrett have rented a room above a Chinese laundry, planning to stay until he can walk without crutches before returning to Esmerelda County. Otherwise, the tide of visitors has ebbed and I spend most of my time alone.

I've read more these past few days than I normally manage in a month: pretty much anything the staff will bring me. Montaigne's *Essays,* all of Jack London's *White Fang,* and three-quarters of E.M. Forster's *The Longest Journey.* Newspapers, too. I'm flipping through the Reno *Evening Gazette* when an item catches my eye:

◐

DELAMAR-HIGHLAND CONSOLIDATED GOLD MINING & MILLING CO.

SOLD TO ENGLISH INTERESTS

Pioche, Lincoln County, Nev. — Confirming speculation long-held, papers were filed today formalizing the sale of Delamar-Highland Consolidated to Black Tiger, Ltd., headquartered in London, England, for $1.5 million in cash and stock. Mr. John M. Lipford, Delamar-Highland's principal shareholder, will receive some ninety percent of proceeds. As part of this deal, Black Tiger will redeem D-H notes for some $2 million. Speaking for the new ownership, Sir David Satterley, Esq., says that Black Tiger plans to modernize the company's mill, as well as augment the water supply currently available for both industrial and domestic consumption in Delamar. This paper believes the contract's price is a tacit admission that Delamar may not be what it once was. While we have no doubt Black Tiger, a force in its own right with annual earnings of around $2.5 million and significant proven reserves, will long benefit southeastern Nevada, its conservatism contradicts assertions by D-H's former management that the mine was worth upwards of $12 million. Either Black Tiger drove a bargain for the ages or Delamar-Highland got ahead of itself, so to speak. As always, the market renders a fair verdict. We are confident this new enterprise and the camp of Delamar are in excellent hands.

Well, goddamn.

I let the paper fall across my knees and stare out the window. Bastard's getting away. Prince Jack is walking away from Delamar with more than a million dollars. No doubt he's furious but as far as I'm concerned, he's getting away clean. Too clean. My right hand curls into a fist and I grind it into my thigh.

Amy Higgins enters the room carrying a bag. "Hello, Shep," she says. "Didn't know if you'd be awake yet." She hands me the sack. "A little bit of sunshine from Riverside, California."

"Oranges, thank you." I force a smile and take the bag. Garrett's a lucky man—Amy's good people. In a very real sense, I owe her my life and I hate that she crossed the road on my account. Hope she bears her burden lightly.

"Garrett says hello."

"Hello, Garrett. Is he doing better?"

"He is—I'll bring him over later this afternoon." She hands me a San Francisco paper. "You have more color in your cheeks today."

"Feeling stronger. Say, would you mind finding a nurse? Think I'm ready to take a few steps."

"Oh, Shepard, that's wonderful!" Amy brightens, although I'm glad once she leaves. Isn't her fault but at this moment, I don't much care for sunshine. Through the window, I see it's snowing again and I smile, an ugly one like Curt Broe always wore.

My mind starts turning.

༄

The sun is out and the Three Sisters look dazzling. Pure white mantles against a clean blue sky. Spring is still a long way off but today, I spotted a patch of snow crocus blooming between some rocks so there's proof it's on its way.

I'm halfway through my daily walk to High Pasture—my first without a cane. Leg still hurts but not so much I'm willing to forego my rehabilitation. This has been my routine since returning to the ranch: progressively longer walks and target practice, typically thirty rounds with a long rifle and twenty with the Colt. Need to get back into a physical state where I'm capable of action and reaction. Need to sharpen my mind. First few days, my aim was consistently left of center. No longer. Sharpening tools in the forge and helping to rebuild the barn, I can feel the muscles in my back and shoulder re-forming and growing stronger. Won't be long now.

Jessie says she worries about me going out alone but I tell her that while I appreciate her concern, my strength has improved and there's no cause for alarm. She says it isn't my physical state that worries her. Wade tells her I'm fine but as she watches me disassemble and clean the Colt, I can tell she isn't convinced.

∽

Sunset on the last day of March and down below, the lights of Minden, Nevada, are glowing brightly. I'm on foot now, having just completed a four-hour stage ride from Wellington.

My revolver is back where it belongs, properly holstered in a rig under my left arm. My left arm, itself, isn't quite as it should be: still weaker and prone to ache whenever the weather turns. Don't need it tonight, though. Not yet. My right hand, my shooting hand, feels as strong and quick as ever.

My boots crunch two inches of fresh snow, in and out of a single set of tire tracks going up the long driveway. Tall poplars on both sides, and a peach orchard on the hillside to my left. This is Jack Lipford's game ranch, a place he spoke of reverentially and I can see why. Two-thousand acres at the head of Long Valley, with mixed pine forests and grassland, and views north along the Sierra Nevada all the way to Carson City and the Flowery Range.

The stars shine brightly. As I walk, hands in my pockets, I think back to that hour on the hilltop above Sunday Ranch, lost in starlight, and how I swore to God and myself that I would do better with whatever time I had left. Not sure my current errand meets that standard but for everything he's done, I believe Prince Jack ought to pay a steeper penalty than retiring to the country with a million dollars.

Rounding a bend, his house comes into view. Vitrified brick with white trim: a larger version of the house he built in Delamar's High Side. To me, this speaks to Lipford's constancy: same house in two towns, same conniving bastard wherever he goes. Not for much longer though.

The tire tracks veer toward a garage some thirty yards to the left but I continue straight toward the house. One light burning in an upstairs window. I pause and lean against a large boulder beside a footpath up to the main door. Take out a flask and pour half its contents into my head.

Do I really want to do this? Set in motion another chain of events that could end in deaths by the score, possibly including mine? Can't imagine bargaining with Governor Sparks for a second reprieve. Hell, if I make him look bad, he'll be the one who throws a noose around my neck.

Seems everyone's getting away with something. Last month, Frank Croft sent me clippings from the Delamar *Lode* and it just so happens that Porter Nielsen, "my" attorney, is the Cromwell behind Black Tiger's throne. Not only was he secretly managing its run against Highland Con but all throughout the setup, he also bought enough D-H stock that he walked away with $80,000 from the sale and landed a position on Black Tiger's board. And given Helen's connection to Nielsen, did Black Tiger reward her as well? Was that her plan all along: using me to get at Lipford? Damn.

A herd of mule deer wander cautiously across a meadow below the driveway, sniffing in my direction and grazing as they go. Wonder if Lipford ever shot any of their kin. Four or five mounted heads hang on the walls in his Delamar offices and it's reasonable to assume he took them here. Prince Jack's taken quite a lot over the years.

I stand, unbutton my coat, and unsnap the holster's retention strap. My heart accelerates as I walk toward the front door but my blood runs cold. I pull the cord on a little bell hanging to the doorframe's right. For several minutes, nothing. Then an electric light over the door comes on. I hear footsteps on the other side, fumbling with a latch, and the door swings open. Right hand ready, I take a deep breath and step away from the door.

A truly ancient man answers, "Yes?"

I exhale and take another step backward, the heel of my boot connecting with the base of a post.

"Yes, hello, is Mr. Lipford in? It's late and I'm unexpected—I apologize for that—but he and I are old associates from over in Delamar and he said if I was ever in the neighborhood—"

"Mister…"

"Mr. O'Boyle."

"Mr. O'Boyle, I'm sorry to say—"

More footsteps from deeper within the house, followed by a woman's voice, "Roger, who's there?"

"An associate of Mr. Lipford's, ma'am," he says. "A Mr. O'Boyle, come to pay his regards."

A petite, gray-haired woman steps into view, pulling a patterned-silk dressing gown tightly around her waist. Thin hands; a large diamond on her ring-finger. Elegant but haggard, as though she's been carrying a heavy load for far too long. In the poor light, it takes a moment to recognize Jack Lipford's wife, Evelyn.

I remove my hat. "Good evening, Mrs. Lipford. My name's Allan O'Boyle and I worked briefly with your husband in Delamar and later in Ely. I apologize for my unexpected appearance but I was hoping I might speak with him briefly."

"Late for a social call," she scolds. Standing behind Roger's shoulder, she studies me closely, her soft brown eyes searching my face, and—although this might only be nerves on my part—reading the misshapen lump beneath my left shoulder. "Delamar, you say?"

I can't imagine she recognizes me, given that we met only once and in a crowded, noisy room, to boot.

"Yes, ma'am." I force myself to breathe slowly and evenly.

"Several people from Delamar have been through lately. So many that Jackson went back last week to settle affairs. Selling the house there, too. He won't return until mid-next week, at the earliest."

"I see." I listen for other noises from inside the house but there aren't any. I'm careful not to let my shoulders slump.

She steps around old Roger's elbow and leans with folded arms against the doorframe. "Does he owe you money, Mr. O'Boyle? So long as it isn't a great sum, I may be able to pay you now."

Hell, how do you like that? Wonder how many checks she's written lately. I've heard she comes from old California money—old by Western standards, anyway—and maybe she's as troubled as anyone by her husband's conduct. Probably not.

"No, ma'am, he doesn't owe me money." I curse myself for not clipping something from the Prince's windfall but it wouldn't feel right coming from his wife.

"Very well." The tight set of her mouth relaxes. "Is there any message you'd like me to relay? I expect he'll telephone here sometime within the next few days."

I smile again and back down the steps. "No message. Merely an old acquaintance passing through. Sorry I disturbed you."

She steps backward, too, allowing the screen door to close between us. Now she's a silhouette.

"I'll let him know you were here, Mr. O'Boyle. Good night."

"Good night, ma'am."

As my boots touch the path, the door closes and the light goes out. Just me alone in the darkness, with no plan now except for another long walk. A few hundred yards beyond the poplar lane, I stop and chew my lip. Drain the flask completely. With my boot, I nudge the snow off a tuft of grass.

Absolutely. Go.

I head straight for the railroad station in Minden, sleep for an hour in the waiting area, and catch the first train out the following morning. With five-hundred miles over five different rail systems, I figure I have only a few days to reach Delamar before my chance is gone.

FORTY-FOUR

I've never traveled this full route before. Due north from Minden to Carson City and then a U-turn south along the state's western side: Thorne, Adams, and a third change of trains in Goldfield. Luckily, it's snowing like mad there and no one in the terminal is looking at anyone else, never mind a fellow in a nondescript brown duster with his hat pulled low. The 22nd Infantry is long gone and with the union broken and every important mine under Goldfield Consolidated's thumb, the place feels deflated. Bad weather or no, the fire that burned here once is now dead.

I consider stepping away to see if anyone knows what became of Jordan Barley but I wouldn't know where to start. Union Hall? No, thank you. Who knows whether the poor kid ever even left the hospital? Hope he did, and perhaps we'll cross paths again. Or not.

The Las Vegas & Tonopah second-class coach is nearly empty and I have three hours to stare out into the swirling darkness. I overnight in Rhyolite at a mid-range hotel about a block south of the station and sometime during the night, the storm lifts. The following day, from Beatty all the way to Las Vegas, the tracks are clear and dry. Big desert down here. In Las Vegas, one last transfer onto the San Pedro, Los Angeles & Salt Lake northbound, a three-hour run up to Caliente, and for the first time since Christmas Eve, I'm back in Lincoln County.

Inquiring at the stationmaster's office, I'm told my friend, Frank Croft, is working the sidings up around Panaca tonight. Now there's nothing to do except wait for the evening stage to Delamar. Problem is, that service is running late. Real late. A ticketing agent steps out from behind the counter and announces to the room at-large that the Delamar Auto Stage is having mechanical difficulties and will arrive sometime after 9 o'clock that night.

I look up at a large clock suspended from the rafters: 6:05. Son of a bitch. Four of us—three men and one woman—glance around the waiting area and two fellows head straightaway to the bar at the station's far end. I debate walking to Delamar but that'd be a seven-hour enterprise on account of the dark. Nothing to do but wait.

I'd like to tell you that I use this time to reflect on my choices, to consider the wisdom of my plan, but I don't. All I do is sleep. On a hard seat with my back pressed against a pillar, I sleep like the dead. So soundly that the next thing I know, someone's saying my name.

༄

"Shep? Shepard, wake up. What are you doing here?"

My eyes flutter open and I reach inside my coat.

Helen Molloy.

Where the hell am I? My heart jumps, though whether from pleasure or suspicion, I don't know. Probably a bit of both.

This room: the benches, the ticket counter, the door to the bar at the far end. Caliente Station. Holy mackerel, Helen's here and I'm here. Are we going somewhere? Traveling together? Have I been dreaming all this time? I feel the holster's weight below my shoulder, the cinch of its straps—these things are real—so I slide my fingers inside the neck of my shirt and feel along my collar bone. Wicked scars, still tender to the touch. Feeling with my tongue, I find the new tooth a dentist made me to replace the one Curt Broe knocked out. Not dreaming. None of it, yet here she stands, still a dream.

"Hello, Helen. Oh, man, it's good to see you."

I stand. She leans in and wraps her arms around my waist.

"I heard happened in Esmerelda County. Are you still hurting?" she whispers.

"Getting better," I say.

For a long time after, neither of us says a word. The rise and fall of her breath. Her heartbeat. Nothing in the world could sound better.

"What are you doing here?"

"Going back to Delamar. You?"

She glances at the clock. "Home. Colorado. I sold the Belle; sold everything. My family…my brother and his wife need my help."

"For how long?"

"As long as I'm needed." She presses her head against my chest. "I don't know."

"I should come with you."

"Not this time."

I think she's crying but it's hard to tell. We stand motionless in the nearly empty room with no sounds except our breathing and, for a moment, the clack of the stationmaster's shoes across the stone floor.

I give her my handkerchief. "Thank you for the check," I say.

"What check? What do you mean?"

"Black Tiger sent me a check. You didn't have anything to do with it?"

"No."

A month after I checked out of the Reno hospital, an envelope arrived from San Francisco. Inside was a check from Black Tiger Mines for $4,500, signed by no one I know, and without explanation of any kind. After sending $500 to A.L. Hart's Goldfield office to perfect that Basin Creek option, I bought a new wardrobe. Wade gave me no end of trouble for this, at least until I gave him $290 to cover my medical bills. The rest is still in the bank. I was certain Helen was behind this windfall but here she seems as surprised as I was in the Sweetwater post office.

"I'm glad, though." She wipes her eyes with the back of one hand. "Whatever they gave you, you deserve it."

"Hardly," I say. I don't want what I deserve.

Helen glances at the clock before tilting her head back and looking into my eyes. "Why go back, Shep?"

I exhale slowly. "You know why."

"He might not even be there anymore."

"His wife said he was."

Helen releases her grip and takes a step back. She looks me up and down. "What if he isn't? Will you set off again? Chase him all over the world?"

"Might."

She takes another step away from me. From somewhere out near town limits, the faint sounds of an approaching train filter into the station. From opposite sides of the building, the stationmaster announces that the 8:40 to

Milford, Black Rock, Tintic Junction, and Salt Lake City is approaching, and an agent for the Delamar Auto Stage announces that it'll depart fifteen minutes after the train.

"Then what?" Helen says. "What will you do? You could do so much good, Shepard, why waste your life this way?"

I don't have an answer.

The train rumbles into the station, hissing and shrieking. I follow Helen outside to the platform. A porter separates her bags from the others, stacks them on the platform, and points her way to the first-class carriage.

"Helen, I'm sorry." Steam swirls around my knees. "I may go back just for a look and then leave. I don't have a plan." This is a lie but I say it anyway.

"Whatever he got away with, he won't live much longer. He's terribly sick—"

"Silicosis, I know."

She says something more but the train's whistle sounds and then no one within a hundred feet can hear anything else.

"What?"

"If things change—if you change—you know where to find me."

For a split-second, I consider asking whether she took the cash from my jacket—whether anything we had was genuine—but just as quickly decide I don't want to know. Already there's so much I want to forget, I see no reason to add more. Helen's leaving and she may as well remain perfect. For however much longer I live, at least I'll have that.

I rest my hands on her shoulders. "Don't be surprised if I turn up on your door someday."

"I hope so." She wipes her eyes again. "We'll do better next time."

One long, last kiss before she turns and climbs aboard the Pullman.

I stand on leaden feet until the train pulls away. I don't see her again. Maybe she's seated on the opposite side, or maybe she didn't want me to see her. Don't know. Thought I knew who she was but maybe not. It's impossible to know another human completely.

Back inside, piano music spills from the bar over on the terminal's far end: Scott Joplin's *Searchlight Rag,* popular for almost a year now. My head's a mess and I'm more than a little tempted to go put on sauce, but seeing others start outside for the Delamar stage, I think better of it. One problem at a time.

༄

If Goldfield felt comparatively lifeless, Delamar feels downright pitiful. First time I came here, from five miles out the clouds glowed red from all the lights. This time, as the auto-stage rounds Ferguson Hill's western spur, not only is there no glow but we've nearly reached downtown before I see any lights at all. The camp's western fringe is almost deserted.

Where Helene Road strikes Main Street, a few people are out on the boards but maybe a tenth of what I'd expect. Even more shocking, it takes a full minute to locate the White House Hotel. The stage lets everyone off at the center of town, opposite City Hall, and I set off like a drunk, weaving back and forth, trying to dead-reckon my way there. Crossing the street for a better look at its façade, there can't be more than a few dozen working light bulbs along its roofline and pilasters. All the rest have either been removed or burned out and left in place. God, you should've seen it in its prime.

One fellow I rode with is a young engineer whom Black Tiger is lodging at the White House until he can find something permanent. Thinking how expensive this will be, I laugh to myself, at least until I see a hand-painted sign over the main entrance stating that rooms are available at a weekly rate of $12. That's only two dollars more than I was paying across the alley. Never imagined a place so vital could crumble so quickly. Feels like I've intruded on a funeral.

Rounding the corner, I see a gigantic pile of lumber where the boarding-house once stood. Must've been one of the big snows that blanketed the state back in late-January. Wonder if any of my fellow renters were killed when it collapsed? Whereas seeing the White House diminished makes me wistful, seeing the boardinghouse in ruins has no such effect. Not at all. Can't tell you how many nights I shivered in my drafty room, determined to go look for someplace better, yet I never did. Not voluntarily, anyway.

I stumble around town in a daze. The Comstock Club, closed; the Palladium, shuttered. Down on Malapai, lights are on at the old High-Con offices but a sign over the door indicates the building is for sale. Walking past a fellow, I ask him where Black Tiger is headquartered and he says they keep a small office at the mine but nothing more. No ostentation of any kind; its new owners intend to exploit the big, low-grade reserves inside Ferguson with an eye toward absolute economy. I thank him and continue uphill toward Mazuma. According to a poorly painted sheet draped over its old sign, the Colorado Belle has been renamed the Gem. I can't even go inside. Charlie Witherill's old place is empty, too, all the glass in its windows broken.

I don't know what to do.

Thought I'd step down from the stage, walk to Prince Jack's house in High Side, and knock on his door. Blast my way in and take my revenge. Ever since I left his ranch outside Minden, anyway.

But now that I'm here, that spark is gone. Just gone. Feeling the Colt under my jacket, I snap the retention strap tight across its grip. I walk along High Street toward the Prince's castle, wondering what I'll do if I happen to see him. Protect myself, certainly: he may not be as ambivalent about me as I am about him. But I won't make a run now. Don't care anymore. In fact, where High meets Douglas, rather than making a right turn to look toward Lipford's place, rather than see if he's even there, I turn left and start back downtown.

However I'm feeling tonight, however I've felt these past several months, I know Lipford well enough to be sure he views Delamar as a catastrophic loss and for now, that's good enough. Has to be. Don't know what made me think he'd be the first rich man since Midas to pay for his greed. Scratch that: the man has silicosis. Won't be long before that bill comes due, with interest.

A hundred yards down the road, I feel the ground shake beneath my feet. A pair of stunted junipers growing in the ditch sway and release a flight of sparrows into the starry night. Deep inside Ferguson Hill, miners are still shooting rounds and pulling ore. Still inhaling dust. Still dying. New owners and new precautions, sure, but the rocks inside that mountain haven't changed. The Widowmaker hasn't finished killing.

I have, though. I've had about all I can stand.

⁓

Seated at the bar in the White House, I nurse a tall whiskey and think about everything that's happened these past few years. Everyone I hurt. Everyone who hurt me. It's an awful list. Seated by myself—not hard to do, since the place is nearly empty—I raise my glass and silently toast them all. Can't say I'm better for the experience but I'm still alive and I still have my wits about me. What's left of them, anyway.

The saloon's doors and windows are all open and a warm night breeze blows through the room. Outside, tiny moths flutter in and out of the façade's few remaining lights.

A short stranger approaches the bar from my left and orders a drink. White shirt, brown vest; a stockbroker, maybe. Can't be much of a market here now.

Attorney, then: they're always part of any salvage effort. I catch his eye in the mirror and he nods.

"Say, pal," he says, "hear the latest wag?"

After midnight now so I can't imagine it's anything important. "Don't think so."

"Jack Lipford's dead. Shot himself at his dinner table this evening. One of his servants said he had a coughing fit that wouldn't stop and next thing you know…They're bringing down the body now."

My eyebrows rise. "Jesus, no kidding?"

"End of an era," the stranger says. "Hell, six months back, he had this place under lock and key."

"Certainly did," I say, still in shock. "He certainly did."

While the stranger turns to speak with the bartender, I stare at my own reflection.

Holy shit, I won. This means I won. Yeah, that's as ugly a notion as you'll her, perverse in every way, but the fact remains that between him and me, I'm the only one leaving Delamar under my own power. And at this point, I'll take a win however it comes.

The stranger turns my direction and raises his glass. "Whaddya say, a toast to ol' Jack Lipford?"

"To the end of an era," I answer. "I'll drink to that."

◌∾

An hour later, I'm still at the bar, still nursing that same glass. I'm feeling pretty good, although now I'm even less certain what I should do. Tomorrow, catch another stage back to Caliente and buy a ticket to…somewhere. Can't stay here. Ghosts stalk this town: too many of 'em for me to make peace with so I think I'd better head out on the desert again. Not forever but for a good, long stretch. Ride out the rest of spring down in the Arizona Territory before going to see what's doing up in Nevada's western counties. Seems that's what I was made to do: chase boomtowns and push my luck as far as it'll go. Might as well see where it takes me.

Maybe Rhyolite, Gold Circle, or Wonder. No, not Wonder. Too close to Fairview, where I ran into trouble back in '06. And I keep reading about a young camp called National, up near the Oregon border. Don't know much about it except reports say that the ore there is unbelievably rich, and wherever there's gold, there's work for someone like me. Legitimate work, I hope, but who knows? Depends on what my shoulder will tolerate and whether my nightmares will leave me alone. Been a decent couple weeks and I feel like I might've turned a corner. We'll see.

Walking back across the lobby—across that ten-thousand-dollar carpet, now stained and frayed in the center—I nod to the desk clerk and start upstairs. No one else looks my way. Halfway to the second floor, my mind's made up; come June, I'm going up to National.

∾

THE END